The Complete
RICHARD ALLEN
Volume One

Skinhead
Suedehead
Skinhead Escapes

Publisher's dedication: To Drummy, a good friend who has fallen off the 23rd floor of a block of flats and been knocked half way down Great Western Road by a taxi, and lived to tell those and countless other stories. Partick Thistle ya bas!

The Complete Richard Allen Volume One: Skinhead, Suedehead, Skinhead Escapes.

© Copyright 1992. Richard Allen.

ISBN No. 0 9518497 1 9

First editions of the three books in this omnibus edition were published by New English Library in 1970, 1971 and 1972 respectively.

Printed by Loader Jackson, England.

S.T. PUBLISHING
P.O. BOX 12, DUNOON, ARGYLL. PA23 7BQ. SCOTLAND.

Putting The Boot Back Into Literature.

PUBLISHER'S NOTE

As I said in a recent issue of *Skinhead Times*, skinhead literature virtually begins and ends with the series of novels written by Richard Allen back in the 1970s. There were 18 in all if you include *Demo*, and they have sadly been out of print for well over a decade.

All that's about to change with the publication of *The Complete Richard Allen*, kicking off with this volume containing two million copy sellers in *Skinhead* and *Suedehead*, and the third book featuring skinhead Joe Hawkins, *Skinhead Escapes*.

We're really proud to have Richard Allen on board and would like to thank him for his faith and confidence in both the skinhead cult and ourselves.

George Marshall.
S.T. Publishing.

Once again, we would like to thank the readers of **Skinhead Times** for their loyalty and support. The first 100 copies of this book were bought by Stewart Ross for his fiancée Melissa, B. Thorpe, Anthony Atkins, Dave Epton, Gavin fae Edinburgh, Nick Hewitson, Chris Davidson, Chris Munday, Mike Johnson, Alan Sinclair, A. Crowther, Martin Wells, Nicola Taylor, Tom Thorn, Anders Halvardsson, Brian Adelgaard, Lee Thwaites, Steve Harrington, Udo Vogt, Mrs. K. Holmes, K. Barnard, Graham Hook, Graham Brown, C. Potter, Peter Verbeke, Laurene Cleminson, Lisa Chappell, Miss H. Rumsey, Geoffroy Violot, Franck Etchegaray, Jean-Francois Allard, Perry of **Boot Party** skinzine, C. Sutcliffe, K. Leech, Dave Inglis, S.G. Tait, Paul Simpson, Stefan Kestler, Alan Collins, Chris Price, Allan Williams, Jan Lund, Francois of Molodoi, Sarah Pickard, Bianchi Folco, Gianluigi Lenoci, Goran Johansson, Brian Pollihan, Tim Finch, D. Small, F. St. John, Elena Marini, H.J. White, Einar Vadstein, Brian Arnold, Mark Ellis, Marcus Brown, Sean Bulldog, Geir Brurok, Giles Henderson, Kevin Johansen, M.D. Murphy, Chris Formagin, Toast of **Tighten Up** skinzine, Tony Bates, Pieter Neefs, Trent Reeve, Andrea Rideout, Marco Rodriguez, Patrice Boisseau, Scott Robertson, Kevin from New Zealand, Richard James, R.A. Lucas, Pete Westley, Brian Babineau, Jon Verrill, Sid Skin, Anne Marie Harte, Herve Etchegaray, Heinrich Ariss, Simon Davidson, Tim McConaghie, Ramon Martin, Elizabeth Bellevou, Lorraine Munday, Davin Deans, Stephen Dalton, Gary Flood, Steve Elson, Nathalie Woulters, Jodi Bobak, Fats MacLochlainn, Andi Springer, Derek Perumean, Dave Whitelock, Brendan Hodges, Omar Brancorsini, Seth Price and Andy Purnell.

Fiction From S.T. Publishing

S.T. Publishing was started in 1991 to put some reality back into the cosy world of book publishing. We specialise in books from the dead-end of the street and are proud to offer you the complete range of Richard Allen novels, together with debut novels by up and at 'em authors.

•THE COMPLETE RICHARD ALLEN VOLUMES ONE TO SIX
Available again at long last, the classic Richard Allen novels that charted the changing faces of British youth cults during the 1970s. Each volume contains three complete novels. In Volume Two, there's Skinhead Girls, Sorts and Knuckle Girls. And in Volume Three there's Trouble For Skinhead, Skinhead Farewell and Top-Gear Skin. In Volume Four you'll find Boot Boys, Smoothies and Terrace Terrors. Volume Five will be available in the summer of 1995 and will contain Dragon Skins, Punk Rock and Mod Rule. Volume Six, the last in the series, will be published towards the end of 1995 and will contain Demo, Glam and Teeny Bopper Idol.

•SATURDAY'S HEROES by Joe Mitchell
An excellent debut novel, this time set in the brutal world of football hooliganism. Entertaining pulp literature in the tradition of Richard Allen.

•ENGLAND BELONGS TO ME by Steve Goodman
Another superb debut novel set in the London punk world of 1977. The safety pin might have been a fashion accessory, but the swastika was something far more dangerous. The finest street novel of them all.

All of the above books are available direct from the publisher. We also publish a range of non-fiction titles dedicated to youth cults and their music. For ordering details and a copy of our current catalogue please write to S.T. Publishing, P.O. Box 12, Dunoon, Argyll. PA23 7BQ. Scotland. We send books all over the world and welcome letters from our readers.

AUTHOR'S APPRECIATION

As a paperback writer whose sole aim was always to give his readers entertainment for their money, it did come as something of a surprise when *Skinhead* suddenly burst into the best-selling lists. More so considering the media's unfavourable coverage of this youth cult.

According to the doomsday brigade, skinheads generally were unintelligent, uncouth, sadistic hell-raisers who only ever visited a book store to thumb through the girlie magazines on the top shelves. How wrong these bigots were!

The majority of fan letters I received would have pleased senders' English teachers. And even more remarkable was the fact that very few expressed strong desires to engage in aggro for the sake of violence itself.

If these moralisers of old had the guts to admit that their columns of abuse were ill-founded speculations based on upper class life styles that the original skinheads could not <u>then</u> hope to achieve, I would be the first to forgive their former derogatory remarks.

But they never relent. Never accept the heights attained - even within their own profession - by many determined "old" skins. It is my honour to correspond on a regular basis with old mates who have, on their own initiative, succeeded against all the odds stacked against them.

The doubts and problems which confronted yesteryear's skinheads have multiplied at an alarming rate in today's world. Joe Hawkins and his ilk were, essentially, patriots fighting for a heritage. The battle was lost though, when many in high places yielded to pressures from beyond our shores. And these wishy-washy types celebrated what they believed was the end of a bothersome cult.

As in every war, when the overpowering might of an enemy appeared to have crushed the opposing force, underground armies regrouped and prepared to regain their rightful place in a homeland they had never relinquished. It has happened. Is still happening. Skinheads are everywhere. And if anyone doubts this fact all they have to do is try and obtain an old copy of a Joe Hawkins book. It is almost impossible to find one and if a fan does happen across a treasured paperback, the price alone is convincing proof of the skinhead revival.

During the early days of the skinhead series I was fortunate enough to be in contact with thousands of fans. Some may even have my replies to this very day. When possible I dedicated other books to those whose letters genuinely touched me. If I ever had to list the names of those skinheads, suedeheads, boot boys, smoothies, punk rockers and - never forgetting - sorts who put pen to paper, the resulting effort would read like an encyclopedia devoted entirely to presenting potted biographies of the cults stalwarts.

Recently, there has been a deluge of articles about me and Joe Hawkins. Not all mind you have been complimentary. But the majority, written by former skinheads, proved to me that the time was right to sanction reprints of all my books and - letting a very special cat out of the bag - write a new epic.

My sincere thanks to Mark Sargeant for his excellent *The Richard Allen Legacy* feature in *Tonight* magazine. to Stewart Home for *Some Reflections* on my work published in *Vague 20*; and, especially, to George Marshall for his terrific interview in *Skinhead Times*. With genuine former readers of my books like these three mates I'll save the expense of a publicity agent.

And as my Scottish ancestors would have said to the swirl of pipes, welcome to the skinhead clan all ye of faithful embracement in America, Australia, Canada, France, Germany, Sweden and other bonnie lands. Londoner Joe is proud of you, and your patriotic ideals.

Hoping all fans - new as well as old - enjoy *Skinhead, Suedehead* and *Skinhead Escapes* within one cover. Your comments will be much appreciated.

Richard Allen
Gloucestershire, 1992

SKINHEAD

By Richard Allen

CHAPTER ONE

OUTSIDE the shed, a freighter blasted the lunch-hour silence with her whistle. The churn-churn of props frothed the Thames as a Liberian registered vessel slipped from her berth, holds battened down on the vital exports bound for South Africa.

Inside the shed, surrounded by an untidy clutter of unloaded merchandise, the dockers relaxed - sandwiches eaten, tea brewed and being sipped, the flick-flip of cards the only sound they wanted to hear.

Jack Boyle grinned across the upturned crate at his mate Roy. "Whatcha doin', Roy?"

Roy Hawkins studied his cards for the fourth time. He wasn't much of a poker player. Solo was more his game. "Blowed if I know, Jack."

Ed Black leant across Roy's shoulder and snorted disgustedly. "Pack 'er in, Roy," he offered. "Let me take your seat an' I'll show you 'ow the game should be played!"

Roy glanced at Jack and got a nodded agreement in return. Slowly, he replaced his coins inside his dirty overalls, carefully stacked his hand on the discard pile and relinquished his seat. He didn't mind. He had only taken a hand because Ed had to see a union representative at the gates. "What happened about the meeting?" Roy asked as Ed slumped into his place.

Ed set twenty quid on the table with a flourish. He fancied himself as *the* poker player of all time. His claim to fame was his ten hour visit to Las Vegas when sailing the P. & O. line to Vancouver and Japan. He never let his mates forget how he managed to sit in on a game with Red Skelton and come out showing a profit of six hundred dollars. What he forgot to mention was his subsequent call at a Gardena, California club and the loss of that six hundred plus every British penny he had in his pocket.

"Jack's got 'em by the short and curlies," he said loudly. "They got until Monday to meet our demands . . ."

"And then?" Roy asked, stuffing tobacco into his old briar.

Jack gathered the cards and started to shuffle the pack. His attention was focused on Ed but it didn't stop him doing an expert job and dealing five cards to each member of the school.

"Then we go out," Ed announced.

Roy scowled. He didn't like strikes. He believed in Jack Dash; believed in a working man's right to withdraw his labour for better pay. He didn't believe in frivolous disruptions of work - and, in his opinion, this latest episode was decidedly petty. "I'm against it Ed," he said.

Black spread his cards tight against his chest. He was a canny man; a distrusting individual. He studied the cards pointedly then, having proved his superiority, glanced leeringly at Roy. "You'll do exactly as Jack says!"

Roy nodded. *Yes*, he thought, *I'll follow the bloody band. I dare not go against it.* He believed that Jack Dash was the man closest to God; believed fervently in the right of the docker - and every working man - to take measures to combat the capitalistic employer. He was completely disenchanted with this Labour government - but he wouldn't abstain nor vote Tory. He would vote Labour as he always had; as his dad and his grandad had. It didn't matter what he said between elections - that the long period of Tory rule had been the best in living memory - providing that when the day came, he could make his "X" against the local Labour party candidate. In his constituency, Plaistow, the ineffectual hands on the helm of England counted for less than a man's worth to an employer. 1926 and the "cloth-cap" image had to be preserved. Forgotten were the affluent days of Tory rule. Forgotten were the massive debts piled on a staggering nation by yet another Labour administration. It didn't count that Britain was being dictated to by the International Monetary Fund.

"Are we playin' cards or discussin' the political situation?" Jack Boyle asked.

Ed Black glanced at his fellow-docker.

Roy smiled, puffing contentedly on his briar.

Solly Goldbluff smacked a fist into his palm and demanded, "Fuck the politicians and Jack Dash. I've got a hand - when are we goin' to play cards?"

Ed glared at Solly now, relinquished his platform to the determination showing on that Jewish face. He had never understood Solly; just as he had failed to appreciate Roy's hostility to the Labour movement as specified by extreme adherents like Dash. He knew that Roy would follow along in the main-stream of opinion; knew that Labour had an unswerving vote from Hawkins; knew too that the disenchantment Roy felt was common to the majority of trade unionists. Yet, he was assured by "cell" leaders, Roy and his mates would vote as usual when the crunch came.

Studying his cards, Ed shouted, "I'll open . . ."

Roy watched the game with lessened interest. He saw his mate win the pot; saw four other hefty hands go to Jack. Then, suddenly, it was time to return to work.

"It's a bleedin' shame," Jack Boyle said as they stepped outside the shed, "that Ed has it in for you, mate."

Hawkins shrugged and puffed on his pipe. "Oh, he isn't so bad."

"Like hell! He's a rotten bastard . . ." Jack's antagonism boiled over as Ed stepped from the shed with four of his special cronies trailing behind like bodyguards, ready to prevent physical harm to their adored leader. "Why don't you let Joe do him?"

Roy ignored Jack's suggestion. It was enough that he claimed fathership to the lad. He didn't have to be reminded what a rotten little bastard his son was nor to inflict him on one such as Ed Black. Basically, Roy was decent; law-abiding within the limits set by dockland. He did not consider pilfering a crime; it was a docker's perks to purloin Scotch and foodstuffs and the occasional costly items from "broken" packing cases. In the old days, Christmas would have been a barren table if it hadn't been for the goods stolen from the docks. Mostly, the employers and the police turned a blind-eye to the petty stealing. Only the capitalistic insurance concerns made a hue and cry about the extent of dockland thievery. Like so many of his mates, Roy didn't stop to consider that £10 a month taken from somebody else's pocket could multiply into a fantastic sum when set against the total number of dockers in the nation.

"'Ow about it, Roy?" Jack insisted.

"Forget Joe," Roy growled. "I have . . ." He tapped the tobacco from his pipe and prepared to mount the gangway of a Norwegian freighter.

Boyle frowned. He couldn't understand Roy's attitude toward his own son. In his opinion, Joe Hawkins was only doing what all of them should do - have a go at authority. Jack was a rebel out and out. Only his hatred for Ed Black saved him from being classified as a militant - plus, of course, his friendship for Roy. He needed somebody like Hawkins to temper his viciousness; his addiction to causing trouble.

An hour later, Jack found himself forced to work with Ed. In a far corner of the hold, Roy slaved with a dedication Jack found sickening.

"Christ, doesn't 'e know when to stop?"

Ed Black welcomed the opportunity to take a break. He wasn't a man who enjoyed hard labour nor did he consider it necessary to kill oneself for the employing body. His creed was simple - "higher pay for less work." Productivity agreements were, to him, a means to an end. They sounded fine on an engineering contract but, in reality, they meant absolute zero in action. His brother in the *Mirror* had kept him informed of *their* productivity agreements and it was a family laugh when they discussed the way that union had buffaloed the government's prices and incomes policy.

"'E's a blackleg, Jack. I don't trust 'im."

Boyle moved away, wishing to hell he hadn't opened the door for another Black tirade. Roy and he may not always agree, see eye-to-eye but they were mates. Which was more than could be said for Ed Black. Ed was nobody's mate. "I wouldn't annoy Roy unless you want to meet up with his son, Joe."

Ed jabbed a finger into Jack's chest. "That little bastard isn't interested in the likes o' me. 'E ain't even worried about 'is old man."

"It isn't wot Roy said," Jack threw back, hopefully. "I wouldn't annoy Joe Hawkins. Not ever!" He shook his head thoughtfully.

Ed Black was thoughtful too. He was big, strong, had taken care of himself in some weird corners of the globe. As the union representative, he could count on certain heavies to protect him during a strike. His cronies would always rally round his particular flag, too. Yet - the mention of Joe Hawkins sent a shiver of fear down his spine. He couldn't understand this modern generation. Violence was a natural part of life as a docker saw it but the style of brutality these kids employed frightened him silly. Fists and the occasional kick happened; clubs with nails sticking through, and boots specifically meant for inflicting serious injury, were something else again. It wasn't just Joe Hawkins that worried him. One yellow-spined kid would never worry the likes of him. But Joe had a mob and even he was forced to admit that one man was no match for a bunch of savage little bastards ready to tear an individual apart just for fun.

"I'll talk to Roy," Ed said softly, moving away from Boyle.

Jack grinned. Slumping against grain sacks, he waited for Ed to return. When the union specified it took two men to lift what an old-time docker would have considered an easy weight, Jack believed in obeying rules. Two men it would be; and every lost minute meant a fatter pay-packet anyway!

Joe Hawkins hated his parents with all the violence in his young body. Especially, he loathed his father's attitude to life. What, he asked himself as he washed meticulously, had his dad gained from being a soft touch? The house they lived in was far removed from a palace. It was small, cramped, in an awful street. The neighbours were old, foul-mouthed and unintelligent. Not that Joe felt that he possessed a good measure of intelligence. He admitted, but only to himself, that his education had suffered badly. But he was foxy clever. He had a native intelligence that would carry him to heights his father had not inspired to reach. Plaistow and its dirt were not for Joe. One day, he would move away and never return. His sights were set on a plush flat somewhere near the West End. But that required money, and social position. And, as yet, he had neither, although his day was coming. Of that he was positive . . .

"Joe . . . you upstairs?"

He turned from his wardrobe mirror and scowled at the partially open door. His mother sounded in a vile temper - as usual!

"Yeah . . ."

"Come down 'ere."

His hand automatically reached inside his shirt for the comforting feel of the tool stuck in his trousers' waistband. He was proud of it. He had taken a week to make the weapon - thick rubber tubing filled with lead-shot and sand, and plugged securely until it was pliable without losing the necessary sting when used. Dropping his shirt over the cosh he slowly descended the narrow stairs.

"I arsked you to fetch me bread this mornin'," his mother snarled. She waved a loaf before his face. "'and over the money . . . this is stale!"

Joe grinned. "It was all they had."

"The money!" Mrs. Hawkins said again, hand outstretched. Joe didn't frighten her. She was one of those heavy women with massive forearms and a determination to match her girth. She had been born in Plaistow and fought for everything she had. All her life, Thelma Hawkins had known poverty and hardship. Unlike her husband Roy,

Thelma did not have cause to trust her neighbours nor believe in anything except herself. Even her son was an object of suspicion where it came to money.

"I ain't got it," Joe sulked.

Thelma's heavy hand swung, catching the lad across his cheek. "Joe," and she breathed heavily, "I'm not arskin' a second time."

The boy's hand dipped into his pocket and handed over a coin. Thelma sighed, fingered the coin as a priest would a statue of the infant Jesus. "Next time I arsk you . . ."

"I won't bleedin' go!"

Returning to his room, Joe contemplated his face in the mirror. Her hand-marks showed red. "The old cow" he muttered, fondling his cosh, wishing to hell he could get enough courage to use it on her. Pleasant dreams flooded his mind - and, he saw his hand streaking down, the cosh a blur as it slashed across her cheek, the sound of cracking a satisfactory end to a fleeting wish.

He fingered his face momentarily, then swung from the mirror with an exclamation of frustration.

Opening the wardrobe, he selected his gear from its shadowy recesses . . .

Union shirt - collarless and identical to thousands of others worn by his kind throughout the country; army trousers and braces; and boots! The boots were the most important item. Without his boots, he was part of the common-herd - like his dad, a working man devoid of identity. Joe was proud of *his* boots. Most of his mates wore new boots bought for a high price in a High Street shop. But not Joe's. His were genuine army-disposal boots; thick-soled, studded, heavy to wear and heavy to feel if slammed against a rib.

It was Saturday and West Ham were playing Chelsea at Stamford Bridge. He wished the match had been at Upton Park. A lot of his mates had stopped travelling across London to Chelsea's ground. Funny, he thought, how the balance of "power" had shifted from East to West in a few years. He remembered when the Krays had been king-pins of violence in London and the East End had ruled the roost. Not now! Every section of the sprawling city had its claim to fame. South of the Thames the niggers rode cock-a-hoop in Brixton; the Irish held Shepherd's Bush with an iron fist; and the Jews predominated around Hampstead and Golder's Green. The Cockney had lost control of his London. Even Soho had gone down the drain of provincial invasion. The pimps and touts there weren't old-established Londoner types. They came from Scouseland, Malta, Cyprus and Jamaica. Even the porno shops were having their difficulties with the parasitic influx of outside talent.

Like most of his generation, Joe *knew* about these things. At one time, East Enders enjoyed a visit to Soho and mingling with the "heavy boys" from Poplar and Plaistow and Barking. No longer. The word had circulated - stay away from Soho. Look for your heroes in Ilford, Forest Gate and Whitechapel. The old cockney thug was slowly being confined - to Bow, Mile End, Bethnal Green and their fringe areas. London was wide open now. To anyone with a gun, a cosh, an army of thugs.

Joe was brash enough to venture forth into enemy territory. He had seven mates - all tooled for trouble; all asking the same question: "Any aggro today?"

Slipping a light-weight cotton jacket over his gear, Joe studied himself in the mirror. The cosh didn't show under the jacket. He fingered his West Ham scarf, then threw it back into his wardrobe. *That* would be asking for police inspection . . . and the last thing he wanted was having his cosh found before he had an opportunity to use it.

He wasn't a bad-looking youth. At sixteen, he gave the impression of being at least nineteen. He was tall for his age - five-eleven. He had filled out and, at a fleeting glance, many a young girl's heart would flutter when he appeared on the scene. But his eyes could have deterred those females wary of sadistic companions. There was something in his gaze that spoke of brutality and nonconformity expressed in terms of physical rejection and explosive reaction.

At last, he was ready. Taking a final glance at his appearance, he nodded to his image, grinning approval. Then, with heavy boots making a resounding noise on the worn stair-carpet, he went to the front door, yelled: "I'm goin'," and left.

Outside, on the street, he paused.

God, how he hated this street! Next door, he could see that bitch Grace peeping from behind her curtains. What a bloody bitch she was! No matter how he acted, nor what he thought, he hated her for the way she had treated her husband. In a way, though, he was afraid of Grace. In his opinion, she was a black witch - and he didn't want to associate with her!

He hurried down the street, conscious of eyes following him. It was always the same. No matter how early he left the house, eyes always followed him. Sometimes he wondered if they ever slept in his dirty street.

He was whistling when he strolled down to the Barking Road. The cosh felt comfortable against his flesh. His boots felt solid, secure on his feet. In a few minutes he would meet his mates and, soon, they would be ready for aggro . . .

CHAPTER TWO

FRESH air in the pub was more valuable than gold dust. Smoke from countless pipes and smouldering cigarettes filled both bars, effectively helping to dull the clinging smell of cheap disinfectant. Nobody had ever asked the guvnor to list his establishment as a must on a tourist itinerary. It was unlikely anyone ever would.

If air was precious, a sentence spoken without four-letter emphasis was enough to bring sudden silence, raised eyebrows and get the speaker an award for bravery in the face of obscenity. Even the two barmaids spoke in anatomical descriptiveness and some of their suggestions were physical impossibilities except for a mechanical engineer.

His mates had the Saturday corner table and Joe shoved through the crowd, catching sight of Henry Downy at the bar. "Pint, mate," he yelled, getting a nod from the pimpled youth. Frankly, he couldn't stand the sight of Henry. The guy's pimples wanted to make him throw-up. Not just that, though - he had serious doubts about Henry's usefulness to the mob. He had always kept a close eye on Henry's activities and never ever gave advance information of an aggro when Henry was listening.

"You tooled?" Billy Endine asked nervously as he took his chair.

"Of course," Joe replied with an indignant sneer. "Think I'd go to fuckin' Chelsea without this?" His hand fondled the cosh under his shirt.

Billy shrugged and watched Henry struggle through the crowd with their beer. None of the boys tried to help the pimpled youth. It wasn't part of being mates to offer a helping hand. Not in their mob, anyway. "'enery ain't got 'is!"

Joe fixed Henry with a malicious eye. He watched how the beer slopped on the table as the other nervously set it before him. "Wot's this about you not 'aving a tool?"

Henry glanced over his shoulder then spoke in a whisper. "My old man found it. Jeeze, didn't 'e raise hell!"

"You're a bleedin' liar, mate," Joe said deliberately. "Go get a tool or forget the game." His hand closed possessively round the glass, his mocking smile destroying Henry's unspoken reply in advance. As the pimple-face youth walked dejectedly away, Joe laughed. "Serves the bastard right! Drink up lads . . . 'is beer is good!"

From behind the bar, Mary Sommers watched the group. She couldn't take her gaze off Billy and, she felt sure, he was returning her interest each time he glanced across the pub. She was nearly old enough to be his mother but it didn't stop her having physical yearnings for him. It hadn't made her say no two weeks previously when Billy accosted her after closing. Nor had she tried to get away when he seemed to tire of feeling her. In fact, she could admit to herself that it was her prompting that had seen their confrontation develop into a frantic mating behind the soaring Point flats.

She knew she was asking for trouble getting involved with one of them yet her knees shook when she thought about how wonderful it had been pressed against his hard young body. Looking at Joe and the others she even wished Billy would waylay her tonight and share her with his mates. The escapade with Billy had opened floodgates inside her; made her realise how tame the past ten years had been with a man who really never gave sex a thought. She could remember when she was eighteen. Her proud boast then had been "I've been screwed by every man in the district". Since her marriage, she'd had about six bits on the side - hardly enough for a healthy, passionate woman with her shape.

Bending to pour a pint, she became aware of eyes peering down her wide-fronted blouse. She looked up, and caught the old lecher leaning forward to see more of her breasts. He turned away, smiling secretly. He'd had his eyeful and that was his fair share. At seventy-three a man could look but not touch.

Mary shrugged, her breasts jiggling firmly. The motion did not go un-noted. Those closest to the bar grinned; those at tables tried to catch her act but she refused to co-operate, her attention still rivetted on Billy and his mates.

17

"You don't want little bastards like them, Mary-girl!"

She swung on the man. "Mind your own fuckin' business," she snapped.

The man frowned. "Christ, lads - she's really after Joe!"

Let them get it wrong, Mary thought, flouncing down the bar. They'll be trying to catch me with Roy's son and I'll be rubbing against Billy. *God*, she sighed. *I wish I was!*

"That old cow!" Billy snorted disgustedly. "I jumped her an' she raped *me*!

Joe twisted round, studying Mary with a lascivious eye. He had to admit she looked pretty good for a tart. Turning to Billy he grinned. "Was it good?"

"I've had worse."

"Arrange to meet her and we'll all be there . . ."

Billy frowned. "If she hollers, Joe . . ."

"Bloody hell, she's only a wet-knickered bitch! She won't holler. Go ahead - talk to her."

Billy got to his feet looking dubious. It was one thing trying to get a bit in the dark for yourself, he thought, but letting Joe and his other mates share - well, that was asking for big trouble. Since hanging had been abolished some magistrates were getting bleeding horrible with the amount of porridge they handed out. Especially when it involved tear-aways and girls! Bloody M.P.s, he thought. They got elected to do what their constituents wanted done and the bastards thought they were little tin-gods better than the voters! If he had his way every politician would be slung into prison and given a taste of what they deserved.

"Hey, Mary . . ." He leant against the bar between two huge coloured men. The stink of the blacks made him sick. He hated spades - wished they'd wash more often or get the hell back where they came from. This was *his* London - not somewhere for London Transport's African troops to live. He enjoyed the occasional aggro in Brixton. Smashing a few wog heads open always gave him greater satisfaction than bashing those bleeding Chelsea supporters.

Mary slopped beer into a glass and pushed it at her customer. She felt her knees go rubbery. Collecting the cash, she rang it up, then hurried along the bar to face Billy. Her eyes sparkled, her breasts heaved.

"Same again for the lads," Billy muttered, unable to tear his gaze from those beauties. It wasn't his round yet he couldn't come right out with the proposition. Joe's insistence on making Mary made him think about the other night and he suddenly realised how good it had been. Why should he share her with his mates?

"Billy wants to see you again, Mary . . ."

Billy glowered at Joe standing beside him now. Mary didn't flinch. She stared at Joe, asked softly, "Will you be there too?"

Joe nodded.

"When, Billy?"

The boy was lost. He couldn't understand a woman like her. He'd had his share of the little bits hanging around the fringes of their mob - the local girls trying to snare one of the better-known heroes. He'd even gone to bed with a Soho brass when they'd pulled a job off. But that had been a big disappointment. He'd felt sick, feeling around a professional tart.

"Tonight . . . when you finish here?" Joe asked.

Mary felt her throat constrict. She glanced up and down the bar. "Wait for me behind the Point?"

"We'll be there - won't we, Billy?"

Billy wanted to object. Knowing Joe, the woman would be subjected to extremes of intercourse before he - or any of the others - got their share. Yet, nobody denied Joe Hawkins his glory. "Yeah, Joe, that's fine."

Mary lowered her voice. "Forget this round - it's on me."

Joe laughed, returning to his seat. Mary would fiddle it. They were getting free beer on the guvnor for promising to give her what all concerned would thoroughly enjoy - especially Mary. The round was on her and everything else pleasurable would be on her, too.

The coloured man beside Billy laughed throatily, slapped Billy's shoulder. "Man, you'se got it made," he grinned.

Billy brushed the hand away and glared at the man. "Don't ever touch me, spade!" He backed away, ready to grab his tool.

Quickly, the two coloured men stiffened and moved to close in on their opponent. Then, suddenly - as the pub grew deathly silent - they glanced around and relaxed with foolish grins on their ebony faces. Even they had heard about Joe Hawkins, and his mob.

"Trouble, Billy?" Joe asked eagerly, watching the coloured men with what amounted to hungry appreciation. Like most East End skinheads - and, for that matter, population - Joe detested the influx of immigrants into what had always been a pure Cockney stronghold. It wasn't so much the colour of the skins that annoyed him. Any intruder would have been subject to the same treatment - be the man South African, Canadian, American. The East End was proud of its London-heritage; afraid to lose its ancient right to control what was, essentially, a Saxon bastion. 'Anglo-'had never been acceptable here. Loyalty to an established, accredited Cockney crown was taken for granted. In time of war, the East Ender had only to enter a recruiting office to be accepted as a fit example of a British fighting man. Nobody dare question that. Nor the right an East Ender had to voice his opinion regardless of Race Relations Board and governmental sympathies. Spades or wogs didn't count. They were impositions on the face of a London that should always be white, Cockney, true-British ... not so-called British because they claimed a passport and insisted on rights their independent nations did not grant to the inhabitants of the British Isles.

"No trouble, man," the first immigrant said.

"None," his fellow black murmured.

Joe grinned evilly. He wasn't satisfied to let it go at that. This was Saturday - a day for splitting skulls. What better warm-up than these two coons ...

"Apologize ..." he suggested antagonistically, moving forward with his mob stepping in tight like a gang of Nazi S.S. men about to interrogate a prisoner.

Billy grinned. He felt tall, more than equal to a couple of hefty niggers now he had the backing of Joe and the lads. "Tell me how sorry you fuckin' well are," he snarled.

The first negro blanched. He lived in Plaistow and knew how difficult it could be to oppose this gang of young thugs. He had heard of other immigrants whose homes had been terrorized. He had been warned by the pastor not to invite racial discontent with the 'ignorant' Londoner. Mentally, he rejected these white savages - and all Englishmen - as inferiors striving to prove their right to subjugate black peoples. He didn't stop to think about the poverty and superstition that made his homeland a place to avoid, or leave, nor the debt each of his people owed to the British administrators, the British tax-payer, the British sense of fair-play. He forgot these things because he wanted a job, a decent home - even if, after occupation, he turned it into a slum-dwelling - and a right to stand on his own feet without having a witch-doctor, a tribal chieftain, or an arrogant headman telling him what to do, when to do it, how to do it. He remembered his rights in England - the right to protest and call the British bastards and exploiters.

"I'se sorry, *boss*," he snarled.

Joe laughed. "Boss? Sambo - get stuffed!" He turned away in disgust. The Chelsea mob would offer more resistance.

Billy puffed out his skinny chest and pushed past the coloured men.

Conversation started again in the pub and Mary's eyes glittered frantically as she kept watching Joe, Billy and the mob. These were her type of men, she thought. She loathed serving blacks. She detested their lecherous looks, their arrogant attempts to strip her across the bar and the almost "don't dare refuse me" propositions they made. But the guvnor had warned her not to invite trouble by refusing to serve them.

CHAPTER THREE

WAITING for the District Line train to come in, Joe regarded his mob with a critical gaze. They were not an inseparable group. Billy and Don usually accompanied him on big bovver but Tony, Jack, Frank and Harry usually managed to avoid the more audacious escapades and shrank from physical contact with opposing forces of numerical superiority. As the leader, Joe felt his mob needed some backbone. It was disastrous to turn for support and find no-one there.

"We gave those spades something to think about, eh, Joe?" Billy laughed as they gathered outside the waiting room.

Joe shrugged. He wasn't interested in the niggers now. They were past tense; his mind was on present and future trouble. "Forget the bastards, Billy," he cautioned. His mind searched for something to vent his spite upon. His gaze lit upon the station sign: UPTON PARK. He grinned. That's what they needed - a sign to tease those Stamford Bridge yobs. "Tony, Jack, nick that sign!" he commanded.

Grinning, the two hurried off, tearing the metal sign from its moorings.

From his relatively safe position on the opposite platform, a stationman took a quick step forward, then slunk back to his post with studious concern for counting the small change people offered in lieu of correct fare. Six weeks previously he had been brave and tried to defeat the vandalism of these young thugs. Not any more. London Transport didn't pay him enough to wage single-handed war against savages. Nor did he consider contacting the police any solution, either. He didn't want them waiting for him after a night-shift. Occasionally, he glanced furtively across the track to see what they were up to next. He would have to make a report but that was going to be the extent of his involvement in the affair.

He would never know what his lack of involvement was going to cost his employer - nor the agony to one of his fellow-workers!

"WEST HAM ... WEST HAM ... WEST HAM ..." the mob chanted as they poured into a carriage when the train arrived.

Other supporters laughed, took seperate carriages - content in the thought that they were better off not riding with Joe Hawkins. Yet, they didn't find the mob's actions contrary to accepted behaviour for football supporters. None of them belonged to an official body attached to their club. That would be tantamount to accepting authority and civilized conduct - and these were anathema for the likes of Joe and other young tearaways.

Joe glared at the occupants of his carriage. Native cunning warned him that L.T. sometimes planted one of their trains likely to carry football supporters. He didn't give a damn about one man but he didn't wish to be trapped below ground when the dogs came. Boots and a tool meant nothing to a ferocious dog but flashing teeth meant a whole lot of pain for a skinhead.

Like frozen puppets, the other passengers sat in their seats, trying hard to forget Joe's presence. The fat woman with shopping bags glared right back at him then, conscious of the strained atmosphere as the train started, dropped her gaze and concentrated on the tips of her shoes. A small man wearing a scarf and hat examined the route map, reading and re-reading the names of stations listed. A young mother with two children suddenly discovered wonders outside the window to bring to their attention. A tall, portly gentleman in a window seat refused to be intimidated and stared at the mob until Joe's slow grin changed his mind. A newspaper opened and the man's face got lost in the spreading printed pages.

A man and woman sitting almost directly opposite Joe continued to discuss matters of intimate importance until Joe leered at the woman. She was tall, blonde, beautiful, and showed a neat pair of pins. She flushed and turned her head. The man, who was slightly shorter than his wife and looked as if he could take care of himself in a fight, turned and glowered at Joe. In a loud voice he asked his wife, "Is this layabout bothering you, hon?"

The woman muttered something too low for Joe to hear but he didn't give a damn. He had his target - the man. He didn't like people calling him a layabout nor did he like men to think they could put him in his place.

"Hey, Don - what about this piece?"

Don Taylor broke off his discussion about Bobby Moore's merits and stared at the woman. He smiled and gestured obscenely. "A bleedin' shame she's got 'im!"

"Shit on 'im!" Joe retorted. "She fancies you mate . . ."

Don moved down the carriage until he stood leaning on the seat the couple occupied. "That true, missus?"

The man got to his feet. There was no hurry in his movements and this lulled Don into false security. Anyway what did he have to fear? He had his mates . . .

"You bloody little swine," the man snarled and, without warning, his fist whipped upwards in a perfect uppercut to land under Don's jutting chin. Like a sack of grain, Don folded, slammed back across the carriage, and collapsed into Joe's lap. The train swayed, then slowed for the next station.

The woman gasped, hand reaching to touch her husband's sleeve but he shook it off angrily. "All right, you bastards!" he snarled. "Let's see how brave you are . . ."

Joe dumped the floundering Don on the floor, got to his feet, hand coming from inside his shirt with the deadly tool ready for its vicious work. Like clockwork soldiers, his mob filtered down the carriage, forming a semi-circle round the lone passenger. "You arsked for this, mister," Joe growled, whipping his tool against one palm, feeling the satisfying smack of it on flesh. "Pile in, lads . . ."

The man fought like a tiger. He caught several blows on extended forearms, landed his own counter-punches with devastating results but he was outnumbered and, slowly, he was forced back . . . back . . . almost into his wife's lap. Her screams didn't help him. Her struggles to avoid battering blows hindered him.

Joe grinned, feeling his cosh bounce off the man's temple, seeing blood spurt.

Frank landed a boot into the man's thigh hearing the agonized gasp.

The fat woman yelled, and leapt up to pull the communication cord.

The tall, portly man flung his newspaper aside, got to his feet, saw blood pouring from the man's face and slumped back into his seat - ashamed of himself but safe in the knowledge it wasn't his personal fight.

The man fought to get away from his hysterical wife . . . head down, charging into the slashing, kicking, maddened mob of attackers.

The train jerked to a halt, the doors sliding open.

The fat woman exploded onto the platform, screaming for help - her exit not adding to the excitement *inside* the carriage as the mob battered their enemy with relentless fury.

Running to the fat woman, a coloured guard felt himself pulled unwittingly to the scene of carnage. He had been warned by his union not to tackle rampaging fans on his own - but to call for police reinforcements and take a back seat regardless of what happened. Unfortunately, the fat woman decided otherwise and shoved him into the carriage, screaming for "somebody to do something to save that courageous man from those vicious thugs in there".

Joe saw the guard and stepped back. As though telepathically controlled, his mates retreated from the man, leaving him clawing for support as he folded over a seat, face streaming blood, body battered and bruised where heavy boots had taken their toll.

"A coon! A fuckin' coon!" Joe hissed, edging forward, suspicious yet sure the police had not been called this soon.

"Wha's wrong here?" the guard asked timorously.

Joe laughed, jabbing the guard's chest with a stiff finger, his cosh held in readiness down one thigh. "Beat it, coon! This ain't your business!"

The beaten man's wife stood huddled against a window, her face expressing the revulsion and fear welling inside her. She pointed, yelled: "Arrest them . . . can't you see what they've done to Jim?"

The guard felt a hard lump fill his throat. He could see what had happened - and he didn't want the same treatment for himself.

"Wot you goin' to do, mate?" Joe asked deliberately.

The guard swallowed. "Off the train, son . . . "

Joe's cosh lashed out, striking the hapless guard across the cheek. The crunch of breaking bone was a glorious sound for Joe's mob. Like a pack of wolves they swarmed forward, bent on the kill. Boots found their target, tools slashed viciously, fists landed with dull, sickening thuds. The guard wasn't a fighter. Not like the woman's husband. He melted away as the mob pushed forward, trampling him under foot.

"Leave the coon bastard," Joe yelled, surging through the open doors. "Let's get a bus!" He raced down the platform, scattering those passengers who had dared view the incident.

Billy - always one to take advantage of a beaten man - aimed a kick at the guard's groin, felt his boot sink in with devastating impact. He grinned, got ready to land a second blow . . . and then screamed as a hard fist slammed against his eye. Pain lanced through him and he stumbled from the carriage, yelling for his mates . . .

"Darling . . . oh, darling . . . don't!"

The woman grabbed her husband, clung to him, preventing him from following the fleeing mob. From the floor, the guard tried to gauge the situation, struggled to his feet and was immediately sick all over the place. His groin hurt terribly.

From the sanctuary of his newspaper, the tall portly man muttered: "It's about time the law did something to curb this violence. Young thugs . . . should be taught a lesson!" He didn't even glance down at the stricken guard nor the bloody face of the husband, still determined to protect his wife and fight on against impossible odds. He didn't realise it, but the tall, portly man was a statistic - just one of those who had allowed the likes of Joe Hawkins to rise to fame; one of the masses unwilling to share responsiblity for putting teenage hoodlums in their place and safe-guarding the nation from a wave of anti-social brutality. In a time of war, the man would have risen to meet the challenge yet he was unable to see that this conflict between the young and the State was, in fact, all-out war. A war threatening the authority that a country needed to keep it stable.

*

"Did you see how I booted 'im?" Billy asked.

"Yeah, mate," Don answered, eager for praise for his own efforts. "You saw me bust 'is head, didn'tcha?"

"You was terrific," Jack enthused. He glanced at Joe, anxious to please their leader. "Mate," he slapped Joe's back, "you got 'im good. God, 'ow he bleedin' well yelled when you caught him!"

Joe felt proud. His home-made tool had come through with honours. Blood flecked its length - that bastard's blood! He didn't enjoy thinking about how the man had withstood all their battering and still kept fighting back. He didn't like knowing that some men had more guts inside them than what his mob had in total.

Billy felt his eye. It would be black tomorrow. It hurt. "Fuckin' bastard!" he growled to himself. "I'd like to go back an' do 'im." He wasn't proud of himself when he touched the eye. He didn't pretend to be tough, nor brave, nor able to handle himself right inside where he lived. For show, though, he acted like he was Henry Cooper - fit fighting man, ready to take on all-comers. Especially, he acted hard when with Joe. That Joe, he thought - nothing scares him!

"What can we do, sir?" the policeman asked the bleeding man. "We don't know who they are . . ."

James Mowat dabbed at the blood trickling down his cheek, and felt the pain increase as his wife tried to stem the flow, too. "Isn't it about time you banned football supporters from using the Underground?"

"Ah, that would be difficult, sir," the constable replied. "Who can tell who is a supporter and who is a skinhead . . ."

"Skinhead?" Mowat asked.

"The ones who attacked you, sir," said the patient constable, "were skinheads. You've described how they were dressed. That's skinhead gear, sir."

Mowat shrugged. "I don't give a damn what you call them - why should innocent people be forced to share the same carriage with animals like that?"

"It's a problem of our times, sir . . ."

"The hell it is!" the man erupted.

Constable Monteeth was young, capable, dedicated. If he had been otherwise he would not be wearing his uniform. He readily sympathised with the battered man but he didn't believe in countering violence with more violence. He believed, as his superiors had taught him to believe, in the British policeman's duty to temper violence with understanding - and therein lay his problem. He could not reason that consideration for these thugs gave them a feeling of confidence, that it added to their determination to make fools of the law, society and their fellow men. He could not see that the teenage hoodlums needed strict measures and stricter punishment when caught in the act. He believed in justice without going further to see how the other side looked on justice as a blind, foppish old nanny administering a gentle slap when a cane should be used. He paid heed to the do-gooders who would treat all problems as the result of traumatic experiences in childhood and who would ban hanging for the most heinous crimes and institute psychotherapy instead of the birch.

"Yes, sir," the constable remarked with a lack of feeling. "Now, if you could come to the station . . ."

"To hell with that!" Mowat exclaimed. "What good will it do? You'll not lift a finger to apprehend the thugs and, even supposing you catch 'em - what'll they get? Ten pounds fine and the Social Security pays it from my taxes? Hell, man - can't you see what this bloody Welfare State is costing Britain?"

Joe stuck his feet on the front of the bus. From here he would be able to watch London jerking past; see the sights tourists paid a fortune to come see. None of the monuments nor architectural beauties made any impression on Joe. He was ignorant of historical heritage, believing in modern sterile skyscrapers as the ultimate in construction. The Bank of England only reached him as a source of ill-gotten loot; St. Paul's as a symbol of London and not a church dedicated to the advancement of Godliness within his City; Nelson's Column as a roosting place for dropping-birds and not the heroic valour that had made his homeland great; Admiralty Arch as a traffic hold-up and not the remaining splendour of a navy that had once ruled the waves. Joe, like his teenage hoodlums, had forgotten the greatness and the adventure that had given him and his ancestors that sense of pride which came from expansion, world domination, democratic rule.

For the most part, Joe and his mob loudly speculated about the sexual attributes of mini-skirted girls walking along The Strand, through Trafalgar Square, down Whitehall. When they were not doing this they concentrated on causing a disturbance with the other passengers on the top-deck - especially to the annoyance of a small, Dresden-doll girl with a perfect figure and a nice pair of thighs.

"Cor, doll," Joe drooled, arm over the back of his seat, eyes feasting on the girl's limbs, "won'tcha meet me tonight?" He leered where - just faintly - her panties could be seen. "I could make it luverly for you!"

The girl blushed, turned her head and tried to find interest in the

Houses of Parliament.

A military-type wearing an officer's coat grunted to the conductor and remarked, "I say, isn't it time you gave those young thugs a warning to behave?"

The conductor glanced at the first three seats, carefully avoiding a direct confrontation. "They're just high-spirited . . ." he mumbled, wishing that some people would mind their own bloody business.

"They haven't paid their fares," a stout woman snapped.

The conductor blanched. He *knew* that. He'd asked several times "any more fares" and they had done nothing to give him the idea that they intended paying. Normally, he didn't take any nonsense from layabouts and yobbos but he had been on the Brixton run two weeks previously and got a nasty punch for daring to request fares. Now, he knew better than to antagonize thugs. "They have, missus," he said, hurrying down the bus.

"Not so bleedin' fast," the stout woman shouted, grabbing the conductor's arm. "Make 'em show their tickets. Why should the likes of us pay if they don't?"

The conductor's jaw muscles tightened. He had prayed this moment wouldn't come . . .

"Fares, please," he said advancing on the mob.

Not one of them even glanced in his direction.

"Excuse me, sir . . ." the conductor murmured, standing over Frank Cooper.

"Fuck off," the boy snarled.

The conductor bristled. The beating was forgotten. He didn't like yobbos to start with and he didn't enjoy being spoken to in this manner in front of his passengers. "Tickets, please . . ." he snapped, instantly sorry as Frank turned around and laughed up at him.

Joe got from his seat, stood in the aisle facing the flustered conductor. "Wot's wrong?" he asked belligerently.

"Nothing - if you've got tickets," the other replied.

"We ain't - so wot?"

The conductor wanted to turn, run down the stairs and consult with his driver. He couldn't. The passengers behind him were glaring, waiting for him to assert his authority; consciously willing him to toss these young tearaways off the bus. "Where did you get on?"

Joe sneered. "Last stop, mate."

"That's a lie," the stout woman yelled.

Joe glared at the woman. It was his day for bumping into fat, old

28

cows determined to cause trouble for him.   "Fuck you, missus!" he shouted back.

The military-type got to his feet. "I say . . ." he began.

"Fares, please," the conductor interrupted, hands ready to issue tickets from his machine.

Joe shoved the man aside, shouted, "Our stop," and started walking down the aisle. Like automatons, the gang rose, followed their leader, each one making sure he pushed against the conductor, each pausing by the stout woman to laugh.

"Christ, Joe - we didn't have to get orf," Jack Holly complained as they stood watching the bus grow smaller in the distance.

"Look, mate," Joe replied firmly. "We want to see the match, don't we?"

Jack nodded.

"Then we don't want trouble with the fuzz until we get to Stamford Bridge, do we?"

Jack smiled. "Gee, Joe - you think of everything!"

*

Joe did think of everything. A bunch of skinheads entering the ground together would certainly attract the notice of coppers near the turnstiles. The group split - into pairs, Joe taking Billy Endine with him. Without West Ham scarves, acting innocent as new-born babes and trying to affect a nonchalance the police would overlook, Joe and Billy managed to slip past the scrutinizing eyes of the fuzz.

Don and Jack were unlucky. They got turned away, screaming protests, accusing the fuzz of being petty dictators and arousing the Chelsea fans to such a pitch that they got turned over before taking their hasty departure.

Tony and Frank, playing it safe, got in and joined with their mates.

Now they were four - all bent on mayhem; each wanting to vent his spite on the nearest Chelsea supporter.

"I don't like this place," Frank muttered, gazing around him.

Joe had reached the same conclusion but now that Frank had voiced his opinion it was imperative he - as their leader - should decide.   "It's okay," he grumbled, casting nervous glances at the fanatic Chelsea fans gathered about them. He could tell the others were equally bent on trouble - the standardized uniforms, the close-cropped heads, the boots, all spoke of opposition skinheads.

If Joe had but known!

For miles around the ground the word SHED was emblazoned on gables, walls, poster sites. It meant something in this area - a warning for those wishing to watch a match in quiet contemplation to stay clear of that area of Stamford Bridge commonly called The Shed. It was here that the fanatic supporters gathered, in their gear and with boots ready to inflict injury on opposing factions.

And it was there that Joe and his mates gathered! Unaware of the consequences they faced if, just once, they let their West Ham feelings erupt . . .

The man was alone, loud-mouthed and eager for crowd support when he glorified Chelsea's record in the league. He didn't mean to be offensive; he was an ordinary fan squeezed in with a bunch of savages. He tried to get crowd-sympathy for his tolerant club support - not honestly wishing more than a clean, well-fought game. He wanted his neighbours to yell for victory but was willing to go home relatively content if the match should end with Chelsea a goal down. Always providing, of course, the game was clean, hard-fought, played in the spirit of football.

In The Shed he was asking for a miracle if he wanted his support to be fair-minded and free from trouble!

Unaware that the boys behind him were avid West Ham supporters and boiling for a fight, he turned to Joe, grinned, and asked, "Ain't they the best?"

Joe laughed. His fingers closed round his tool, and eased it from under his union-shirt. "Yeah," he muttered, pointing with his free hand to the pitch. "There they come . . ."

The fan turned, and as he did, Joe whipped the cosh from his shirt and cracked it across the man's ear. He saw blood spurt - felt greatness descend upon him. *First blood to West Ham!*

The fan slumped.

Tony leered, slamming his boot squarely into the man's backside as he fell.

Billy - not to be outdone - kicked viciously, catching the man in the chest. His next blow broke the man's jaw - the crunch bringing a measure of satisfaction.

Like quicksilver, the message whipped around The Shed: "Tool up - the enemy's here!"

The kid next to Joe was no more than thirteen, and small. He had a close-cropped haircut and new boots. He had a sharp hunk of steel in his right hand, knuckledusters on his left hand. As the man slumped and fell under scuffling feet, the kid lunged at Joe, the sharpened steel finding its target in the ribs, the knucks flashing as they headed for Joe's chin. Joe ducked, pain lancing through his side. His cosh curved across the kid's tender cheek, smashing bone. Then it slammed down, busting the skull. Blood trickled down Joe's side, making him groggy.

"That's another of the fuckin' bastards!" screamed a Chelsea fan. His boot landed on Billy's hip, his tool finding the enemy's shoulder - the nails digging in with agonizing force.

Billy buckled, clawing at his shoulder. He could feel the rusted nails biting deep, screwed as the Chelsea skinhead tried to withdraw his weapon for another attack.

Billy screamed. He wanted to vomit as a boot landed right in his balls.

Joe yelled as a bottle exploded in his face - a jagged-broken bottle pushed at him with savage force. He felt his skin yield, crack, blood spurt. His cosh flicked . . . swung in a blind circle as the Chelsea fans swarmed in on him.

Tony and Frank battled gamely - clearing a path for the *hors de combat* duo struggling in their wake.

At the turnstile, Joe wavered. He didn't enjoy being victimized, nor sent packing without getting in a few licks of his own. The cosh in his hand itched to crack a few more skulls - yet the blood pouring down his face needed attention.

"Come on, mate," Frank coaxed. "Let's have a beer, eh?"

Joe accepted the out, pushed through the turnstile and hurried past an observant copper. The first cheers for the teams sounded from the ground.

"We won anyway, Joe," Billy grinned.

Joe glared at his companion, ready to argue the point but unwilling to make an issue right then. Once he stopped the flow of blood he would be in a better position to stress that opinion. He nodded, holding his handkerchief to his slashed face. "Yeah," he mouthed. "Yeah - we won!"

CHAPTER FOUR

THEY'D had an eventful journey back on the Underground. Fortunately, they were earlier than the police estimated trouble would begin. They'd terrorized a few passengers, slashed a dozen or so seats and broken the normal number of windows before reaching East Ham. There, they alighted and scared the hell out of the ticket-collector by stealing his small change from those who preferred to pay short instead of purchasing tickets at their boarding station.

Once outside the station, Joe decided to visit a bookie. He had heard one of his mates talking about a certain horse and he figured a few quid on it wouldn't go astray.

The bookie's office wasn't far from the station and it was packed. Joe scribbled his bet, handed it across the counter to a cute blonde and tried to date her for the night. When she refused he got mad - threatening to tear the place apart until a thick-set gent in loud tweed stepped forward and told him to "Get lost, sonny". He got lost - and when Frank returned with the news that his horse had lost by fifteen lengths he felt like a dictator who had been ousted from his seat of supreme power.

His one compensation was Mary, the barmaid. Everybody loved Saturday night, he reasoned - especially an old bag wanting a young lover.

"There wasn't much aggro, was there, Joe?" Billy remarked as they wandered down the High Street in search of adventure.

Joe touched his battered face. It had been enough for him. An inch closer and he could have been blind. His cheek hurt, his handkerchief in his pocket felt sodden with blood. His cosh had taken its deadly toll but he'd thirsted for more . . . much more than The Shed crowd had permitted. God how he hated those Chelsea bastards! If only he had a better mob to support his ambitions! Billy wasn't bad and Frank could use the boot if he got the upper-hand. Tony wasn't eager and Don wanted the odds always in his favour before resorting to violence. Jack and Henry were, in Joe's opinion, non-starters - they screamed before the first blow caught 'em.

"Not bad, mate," Joe said thoughtfully. "Did you see 'ow I got the cunt?"

Billy nodded enthusiastically, saying fast, "You got 'im, Joe. An' I didn't waste time puttin' the boot in, either . . . eh?"

Joe played the game - the Big Con. "You was terrific, Billy. We was both fantastic . . ."

"Yeah, Joe - fantastic!"

They searched the shops for signs of easy pickings and found none. The crowds were thick, the shops jammed with Saturday bargain-hunters. In East Ham it didn't pay to look for trouble where people gathered in bunches.

"Wot's the time?"

Billy looked at his watch. "Quarter past five, Joe."

"'Ow about Mary?"

Billy grinned. "She's easy, Joe."

"So?"

Frank rubbed his trousers and yelped, "I'm for her, mate. God, she gives me a hard on!"

Joe grinned. "See, Billy?"

Billy shrugged. He didn't give a damn either way. If Joe wanted Mary he got what was left. If he tried the old cow himself he got nothing that wasn't there after Joe finished. "Yeah . . . okay!"

"When's she start?" Joe asked.

Billy looked puzzled. "I dunno . . ."

"Shit! We'll go in soon's they open." Joe stalked down the street, reaching Barking Road. He paused, eyed the traffic coming from London, and wondered if - perhaps - some of the cars had been parked outside Stamford Bridge. He hated the bastards if they had seen the whole match; loathed those Chelsea cunts for getting them involved before the match started.

As he walked, Joe thought. He wasn't completely satisfied with his mob. For one thing, they weren't strong enough. He wanted command of a larger force. Say about forty guys all tooled up and ready to follow where he led. The other mobs had larger forces - he could name dozens like the Willesden Whites, the Hendon Mafia, the Kilburn Aggro Boys. Even in West Ham they had mobs numbering close on fifty qualified bovver boys. He knew what was wrong, though - he needed a helluva bigger reputation before he could see a drift away from established gangs into his own. He had a name but it was too local, too limited. He hadn't done porridge and he hadn't been written up in the papers as an outstanding example of skinhead terrorism. He'd have to do something drastic to make the grade. One big aggro with a reporter present and he'd have them all clamouring to get into his mob.

A Pakistani student appproached with an armful of library books under one crooked arm.

Joe grinned, whispering, "Crowd the bastard!"

With undisciplined compliance, his team formed a spearhead smashing through the scattered shoppers. Ten feet away, the Pakistani became aware of the advancing enemy, and hesitated. He didn't have to be reminded of the last exploit involving one of his fellow-students and a skinhead mob - it had made headline news in the Barking paper.

"Ain't he pretty . . ." Joe laughed.

A small man wearing a scarf and hurrying for his favourite pub abruptly veered into a side-street and took a detour that would not help his thirst for bitter.

A mother with laden shopping bags grabbed her two snotty-nosed kids and ventured across the road regardless of oncoming traffic.

A burly Irishman smiled inwardly, skirted Joe's mob and offered a silent prayer as he stared at the Pakistani and continued on his journey to the boozer.

"Lemme take your books," Joe said, knocking the volumes from the student's arm.

For an instant, the dark face angered then, abruptly, broke into a nervous smile. "Sorry . . ." he muttered, bending to retrieve his books.

"Bloody wog!" Joe snapped, kicking the Pakistani in the face, knocking him backwards across the pavement. His voice carried above the traffic growl to those watching the all too familiar scene. "You bleedin' wogs . . . you don't want us to . . ." A passing lorry swallowed his words and spat them out in a defiant roar of exhausts.

The Pakistani cowered against a shop window, watchfully aware that the books were being kicked into the road; seeing them flattened under merciless tyres.

"Look wot you done," Joe shouted, grabbing the frightened student. "That costs us money, mate . . . we pays for your books!" His right caught the Pakistani under the Adam's Apple, his left foot finding the soft underbelly of the other in a vicious kick. "You don't deserve to be 'ere . . ." He screamed, building to a fever pitch as his feet lashed out with frightening regularity . . . each blow finding its target.

Like ants swarming over a tasty morsel, the mob crowded the already beaten student, putting the boot in, helping Joe pulverize the Asian. All the hatreds for the newcomers blurred their ability to consider the battered man as a human being - not that they ever considered any target as anything other than a kicking bag for their perverted pleasures.

When it was over - less than three minutes from start to finish - Joe, tired of his kicks, walked away from the stricken Pakistani to get lost in a gathering crowd. One by one, his mob filtered from the scene ... vicious shadows flitting into the darkness of evil minds.

The pub was, as usual, jam-packed with Saturday night spenders. Joe felt inferior in the mass of hefty dockers and other assorted heavies. He was smart enough not to force his hand in the middle of such a gathering; he had discovered early in life that a stripling did not gain feathers fighting old cock-birds. These were men accustomed to fisticuffs, to putting the boot in, to brawling against odds. They didn't back down to anyone - not even with Joe Hawkins' reputation. Joe could heave sacks of coal around but the weight he could lift was nothing compared to what the average docker thought infantile ...

"Your turn, mate," Joe growled to Billy, shoving his empty glass across the table.

Billy got to his feet, feeling for spare change in his pocket.

"An' don't forget to chat-up the old cow," Joe admonished.

Billy fought his way to the bar. He didn't relish the thought of getting Mary outside. He'd had too many beers and all he wanted to do was sleep it off. Beer and sex didn't mix with him - certainly not in the quantities he'd drunk that night. Frankly, he regretted ever mentioning his escapade with Mary. The more alcoholic thought he gave to Mary the more he was convinced that she was a bloody good stand-by when he felt in the mood for cunt. He hated the idea of Joe shoving it into her and him getting seconds. After all, hadn't he been the one who discovered her liking for shafting?

"Billy..."

He leant against the bar with a drunken who-cares stance, affecting those movies with Sinatra playing the short-statured he-man-I-can-handle-'em-all attitude. His bleary eyes beamed on the woman, leering his sexual inclinations like a lightship warning off ships in the night that pass dangerously close to perilous sands. "Same again," he said.

"Will you be there?" she asked.

35

He straightened, and tried standing without the bar to support him. "Of course . . ."

"Don't drink any more, Billy," she said softly. "I wouldn't want it without you!" She gave him the all-promising eye.

"Joe's first," he said sternly.

"So?"

"He likes it different . . ."

"So do I, Billy. Won't you do it how *you* like it?"

He sobered fast. "You're big, Mary . . ."

"I'm smaller other places . . ." she countered neatly.

Billy wanted to scream. Suddenly, he felt that Joe was unimportant; that he alone was the big man in their mob.

"When Joe's finished I'll make sure you're pleased, Billy," she said, depositing the first pint before him.   Alec Jamison didn't like skinheads. He had good reason for his hatred; his daughter Alice had been raped by one of the bovver boys and the abortion she'd had resulted in an inflammation of the womb which had proved fatal. Now, a gaunt, lonely man with wife and daughter buried in the East London cemetery, Alec listened to the whispered conversation between Billy and Mary.

Alec liked Mary. He knew she was a tramp; available for any man with enough money to double her weekly take from the pub - and that included all her fiddles, too! He didn't care about fiddles . . . he got enough on the side from his milk round. He didn't give a shit whether she got into bed with her old man or some kid. His women on the round often paid with a bit and he didn't think any less of them for opening their legs.

But, somehow, he couldn't associate Mary with those little bastards in Joe Hawkins' mob. God, how he detested them!

He felt his glass almost creak as his grip tightened . . .

Then suddenly . . .

Mary gasped, hand fluttering to her open mouth as blood spurted from Alec's hand. The bitter spilled over the floor, glass shards flying willy-nilly, some sticking from the cut and bleeding palm.

It wasn't so much the shock of seeing Alec smash the glass in his fist; it was his expression - the wild-glaring eyes, the contorted features as he fixed Billy with his demented gaze.

She felt her knees turn rubbery. Alec wasn't the type of man anyone annoyed. Tall, heavy, with the face of an ex-boxer, he looked every inch the determined fighter he certainly was. She'd seen him in action; seen him beat a man to pulp before he recovered his temper. And she feared for Billy . . .

Glass stabbed into his flesh but he refused to be put off. The bastard had it coming to him and he clenched his fist into a hard-knuckled ball. All the pent-up loathing surged to the surface.

Before he could strike a blow, he felt the sickening weight of a hard object descend on his head . . . saw dim, flying lights circle the bar and heard the savage cry of one of the young thugs . . .

Semi-conscious, he felt boots seek his secret places . . . find them with excruciating thuds . . . and, as the boots kept going in, the pain lessened . . . lessened . . . grew more distant, less brutal!

CHAPTER FIVE

JOE flung the bedclothes aside with disgust. His body ached - especially where that rotten bastard had planted three darts in his arse. He could still hear the burly man's yell: "I got 'im . . . treble arse!"

He staggered to his small mirror and looked at his naked image. Christ, he thought, that thing should have been giving Mary a good go last night. If only Billy hadn't been stupid enough to get into bovver with Crazy Alec!

He grinned at his reflection. If he looked terrible Billy must be one awful mess. He'd clobbered Alec before his bloody fist could flatten Billy but that hadn't saved his mate from the ire of those others kindly disposed to Alec. He'd been bleedin' lucky to skip out with but a few fists shoved down his throat. Not Billy! The last he saw, Billy was sprawled on the pub floor getting the dockers' boots rammed home where it would do his sex life most harm. Mary must have gone without from all of them, he mused happily. If he was sure her old man wasn't home he'd go round there and give her what she wanted most!

In his chest of drawers he had some of those Swedish magazines - the type showing pubic hair and highly erotic positional poses between men and women. He got two out, turned to well-thumbed pages and studied a luscious blonde doing a wonderful thing for an unseen male with a tremendous urge for her; to a brunette climbing all over a dark-haired youth whose intentions could not be more obvious.

"Christ . . ." He flung the magazines back in the draw and covered them with dirty underwear. Sweat filmed his forehead. He dressed quickly, wearing his skin-tight Levi's so that his boots could be seen in all their savage glory, a skimpy grandad short-sleeved vest and draped a cheap sheepskin around him. Then he gave his boots a fast polish, slipped his feet into them and immediately felt two feet taller. Funny, he thought, lacing the boots, how they gave a guy a boost!

He didn't bother saying good-morning to his parents. They would rave about last night and the blood-stained towel hanging in the bathroom . . . Jeeze, that was a laugh! Bathroom . . . a pokey room with a built-in tin bath and a cracked basin. Even the bloody loo was ready to fall apart. When he got recognized . . .

One thing Joe really detested was a hippie. For a start, they didn't wash. Then there was the matter of their hair . . . so bleedin' long and matted with lice and dirt. And their clothes - well, he couldn't bear to rub against one of them anywhere! He always got the shivers thinking of fleas and filth and the sickening stench of unclean material.

Mostly, though, he hated them for not working. He had to work; if he didn't there'd be no cash in pocket. His father was hard when it came to earning money; like most men who had to slave since their early teens to make ends meet. But not the hippies! Not those bastards! The bleedin' Welfare State took care of them - grants if they were students (and that was a big laugh!), handouts from Social Security to pay fines for demonstrating and pot-taking, additional cash to buy more pot and, if they were really lucky to get a sympathetic guy at the Assistance Board, they'd have enough to take a holiday in Cornwall. Christ, what a rotten way to treat tax-payers he thought!

Well, today, they'd do a few hippies for the hell of it. After last night he wanted some easy aggro. No hefty dockers, no bleedin' crazy fools . . . just soft, dirty hippies to bash around.

Don Taylor tightened his clip-on braces and gazed in admiration at his brand-new Dr. Martens' boots. At ninety-five shillings they were a bargain in his estimation. Like Joe, he felt taller, more important when he wore boots. "It'llbe bleedin' cold in Brighton, Joe," he said.

"We'llfind a few hairies and get warm doin' them," came the reply.

"I dunno," Don muttered, looking away as Joe's hard eyes fastened on him. "Those Brighton fuzz are hard, man."

Billy nodded agreement. He ached awful and his face looked as though it had gone through a sausage-mixer. He certainly wasn't in the mood to risk another beating so shortly after last night.

"You gettin' yellow?" Joe asked menacingly.

Don shook his head fast. Billy took longer but again agreed.

"Okay then," Joe said firmly. "That's settled. We're goin' to Brighton. Let's get the others . . ." He strutted off, sure of his men now - a commander about to prepare an attack on an undefended town; a brutal Napoleon ready to strike with all the viciousness of his power-mad soul.

Once they reached Victoria Station, the mob were unanimous about what they intended doing in the seaside town. The proceeds of a small robbery they had pulled the week before would provide their fares, meals and booze. And, when they ran out of amusements, they would seek out a few scared hippies and do them.

The first train was The Pullman and Joe gave his orders: "No bleedin' trouble on this train, mates. We wanna get to Brighton - not arrested."

As they strolled along the platform, the guard eyed them suspiciously. He didn't enjoy having yobbos on his train; no more than the nervous passengers watching from carriage windows wanted them in their compartments. But Joe wasn't interested in annoying innocent travellers today. He was thinking about what would happen once they cornered their hippie enemies and enjoyed the prospect of putting his boot in.

"'ere'sone . . ." Billy pointed at a carriage where several teenage girls sat watching their progress along the cold-swept platform.

"Christ, can't you think of sumfin' besides girls?"

Billy shrugged, and waved to the stern-faced females. Joe wasn't usually so slow at taking opportunities. If he stayed in this mood they'd have a lousy day by the sea.

It wasn't often Joe felt compelled to explain his edicts, but he did, loudly: "We get in there an' there'll be bovver for sure. I don't want anyfing to stop us doin' them hippies." He smiled, shaking himself like some huge bear about to itch against a benevolent tree-trunk.

39

"After yesterday we're not goin' to have our sport spoilt."

Billy grinned happily. He, too, wanted to gain a measure of sweat revenge for the beating he'd taken trying to make Mary. But he also wanted a bird. The long hours contemplating how it would be with Mary had given him the urge. And all the boots, fists and broken bottles that had found their target in his flesh hadn't dulled his massive desire. If only Joe would let them combine pleasures . . .

"Ain't we gonna chat-up any birds, Joe?"

Joe shrugged, throwing open a carriage door. "Mebbe *after* the aggro, Don. Get in . . ." He stalked down the carriage, taking a window seat. One elderly man at the far end of the carriage glanced fearfully over his Sunday newspaper and hurriedly buried his nose in the latest scandal. Like so many people he figured that what he couldn't see wouldn't come to lay grief on his doorstep.

"'ow much we got, Joe?"

Billy rubbed his hands together, waiting for Joe's reply to Tony's pertinent question. He hoped it would be enough for them to make steak and chips - not the old standard fish with.

"Thirty knicker."

"Cor, we bleedin' well nicked over sixty-five!"

"Yeah," Joe said softly. "An' I divvied out some."

Tony dropped his gaze and sulked in his corner. He didn't dare query Joe further. He knew - as did the others - that Joe had taken a larger slice than any of them. He always did. As their leader he apportioned the spoils and, with deference to his superior position, allotted himself the general's ration.

Slowly at first, then gathering speed, the train moved out of the station, the crumbling warehouses and dilapidated homes along the track like sickness on the face of London. Joe didn't see the horror of railway surroundings. Nothing here was worse than his own neighbourhood; nothing dirtier than Plaistow or Poplar. Although he had ambitions to rise above the filth of working class districts, he had accepted conditions with the fatalism of those born to squalor. It was one thing to believe in a West End flat, a Mayfair bird, a gleaming car and new gear every day of the week, but the brainwashed mind could not see further than personal betterment. It couldn't realise that all of this slumland must be cleared and kept free from decay. It couldn't accept that people had to be educated to have pride in their surroundings, to make their district forever clean and fresh and on a par with other high-class areas.

40

As the train sped past a huge new office building near the Thames with its huge red sign announcing space to let, Joe felt a tremor of annoyance. From the top floor of that block, one would see across the river to the Houses of Parliament, down river, up river, see all the landmarks of the city. He had a fair idea what a flat there would cost always providing the landlords would rent to a private individual instead of a large company.

That was the closest Joe came to speculating on his future residential ambitions that day. For the most of the fast journey he allowed himself the luxury of imagining how they - the mob - would deal with his hated hippies.

Basically, Joe had a feeling for violence. It was an integral part of his make-up. Some do-gooders trying to explain his attachment to the skinhead cult would, no doubt, stress his environmental background, his childhood fighting for every scrap of education and clothing. They would point with undisguised delight to his father's tough profession, to the East End as a breeding-ground of crime and the conditions under which its inhabitants grew up. They would gleefully assign all manner of reasons for Joe being what he was without ever touching on the most important factor of all - his character weakness for brutality. It wasn't something that had grown inside him because of surrounding blights. It was him; he was one of the incurables - one of those born to be hard, mean, savage. Nothing had made Joe this. He had been born to accept crime and the ravaging of that which he found objectionable. Joe Hawkins was one of nature's misfits; one of her habitual criminals. And all the soft-soap and kindness would not alter him. Not one iota.

CHAPTER SIX

"JESUS, Don - you're a stupid bastard!"

Don laughed, dug his hands deeper into his pockets. It was freezing cold along the front and the wind-whipped waves formed salting white-caps as far into the Channel as the eye could see. "Relax, Joe-mate . . . they didn't get us, did they?"

Joe growled into his sheepskin coat, feeling his face getting numb as the wind continued to assault them. "They bleedin' nearly did, you bastard! If it hadn't been for Billy . . ."

Billy turned his back on the spray blowing over the sea-wall, hearing the incessant rattle of pebbles under the smashing waves. It had been bloody close, he thought walking backwards. They'd slashed the seats and bust a carriage window just as the train was entering Brighton Station but Don had to act the fool and throw light-bulbs onto the platform. If he hadn't run to the copper and made a complaint about a mythical member of the Hell's Angel's mob going for him, Don would be freezing his arse inside a Brighton cell now. "Fuckin' fool!" Billy said as the wind tore his words away and rushed them down to the marina.

"Let's eat, Joe," Tony voiced, glaring at the angry sea. "I'm starvin'."

Joe nodded. He was hungry too. And he didn't much fancy being blown to bits any longer. They'd seen the bleedin' sea and, for his money, Brighton could keep it. He didn't go much on sand and sea and sky. He preferred the city with its layers of smoke blotting out the sun, with its teeming millions struggling for a mere existence, for the aggro and for the clash of wills.

The caff catered to early holiday-makers but on a cold, lonely Sunday it was practically empty. The menu didn't offer much in the way of good eating but Joe wasn't one to know the intricacies of *Cordon Bleu* cuisine. His idea of a slap-up meal consisted of chips with everything and a steak could be raw, medium or burnt to a crisp for all the difference it made to his cast-iron stomach. He had no real sense of taste - a result of years spent eating his mother's cooking. In the Hawkins' household a chop tasted like fish and fish tasted like rubberized shoe leather. Nobody would ever honour Mrs. Hawkins for her cooking. Nobody!

"Listen sonny . . . I don't want any trouble, hear me?"

Joe grinned at the swarthy, heavy-set man behind the counter. He had a feeling the out-of-sight right hand was lovingly caressing a truncheon. He didn't want trouble then either. Especially not with a typical East Ender operating a profitable Brighton caff.

"Isn't it the shits!" Joe said in a low voice. "'ere we are in dear old Brighton an' he slaps a law on us already!" He laughed, motioned for the mob to take their seats, bending forward and telling the owner in a confidential whisper: "Mate we're famished - we wanna eat . . . okay?"

"Just remember," the other growled, "no trouble. You pays when

I bring the nosh!"

"Suit yourself, chief," Joe replied in his most casual manner. "Wot's your tip for the day?"

"Ham san'ich."

"Christ, I said we're bleedin' famished . . ."

"You got money?" the owner asked suspiciously remembering other skinheads and other non-payment of bills.

Joe deliberately withdrew his cash, flicked the fivers to prove his intention to pay. Inside, he boiled. It would serve the bastard right if they done his place and didn't pay. But he controlled his emotions and forced a smile. "'ow'sthat?"

"Right . . . What's the order?"

As Joe took his seat, Billy leant forward and snarled, "Let's do the bastard when he brings the nosh."

Joe considered the request, but brushed it aside. His plans were swiftly formulating. First, they'd find a few hippies and kick the shit out of them. Secondly they'd run riot in whatever amusement arcades were open. Thirdly, they'd come back here and bust the caff's windows and, if they could, break every stick of furniture in the rotten place. Maybe they'd even have the satisfaction of doing the owner. That would make the current backing down worthwhile.

"No, Billy," he said finally. "Save 'im for later." He winked, letting them all know he - their supreme commander - had a definite scheme afoot.

"Let's have the most expensive nosh, eh?" Don said with a sly grin. "We can always get our money back . . . *later!*"

Joe nodded, wondering if his plan would let them rob the geezer. He doubted if an East Ender would leave his spare cash lying around where yobbos could find it. He wouldn't . . . and he placed the owner in this category.

Without exception, the mob followed Joe's selection from the hand-scrawled menu: soup, minute steak with boiled potatoes and peas, cheese and biscuits, tea.

None of them complained when the soup arrived lukewarm. Nobody noticed that the minute steak was tough, sinewy, an unfrozen offering to nauseate a gourmet, and that the potatoes were a day old and reheated. None of them paid any attention to the tinned peas and the way they came up in solid balls. And even the cheese passed their non-inspection although it smelt to high heaven and had mould on the edges. As for the biscuits the least said about them the better.

Only one item on the menu passed for what it said - the tea. It was hot, fresh, sweet.

"Like it?" the owner asked with a secret smile as Joe again withdrew his cash.

"Not bad!"

Money exchanged hands - an exhorbitant amount duly paid without a query.

As the mob trooped from the caff, the owner laughed and muttered to himself, "Bleedin' fools!" Then leaving just enough change in the till, he folded his notes, placed them in a paper bag, put that inside an open packet of Tate & Lyle sugar and left it in plain sight on a shelf. Ringing up NO SALE he removed five shillings, put in a seven-sided atrocity which decimalisation had decided to thrust upon an unwilling public and helped himself to a packet of Everest cigarettes. As he lit one he watched the mob stagger down the front, the wind in their faces. "Bleedin' fools!" he said aloud and blew a smoke ring with expert ease . . .

"I feel full up," Don bucked the steadily rising gale, the remains of his meal resting like lead balls in his stomach.

"Let's have a few beers, Joe," Tony suggested.

"Yeah, thats an idea," Billy agreed.

Joe cut around the bus depot and past the dolphin statue. He knew a large pub where they could get served without the fuzz noticing they were in town. It made him feel good to exhibit himself in a conspicuous place like the pub he had in mind. Almost like those Western movies he avidly watched on the goggle-box. He pictured himself as the villain going into a strange town, ready to meet any challenge, prepared to face up to the marshall.

"Christ!" Billy examined the pub's interior with awe. He was used to East End establishments with their smaller bars, their dinginess. He hadn't expected Joe to select such an opulent tavern. He had never before seen such grandeur - unless one counted the time his school paid a visit to Hampton Court Palace. He had been seven then and his memory could still conjure up images of the vastness of those rooms, the armorial bearings an the instruments of torment with which the ancient men attacked their foes.

Joe stalked to the bar giving the snooty barmaid a wink and getting a haughty look in return. He knew the score - his kind were unwelcome in these hallowed precincts. But he didn't flinch. He ordered beer, flashed a fiver, and waited for the slow service which said more than any retort could have.

A log fire burned in a huge hearth, expensively dressed people chatted quietly and, across the room two young birds got their heads together and their legs further apart as Joe's mob swilled their beer.

"I can see 'er knickers," Don enthused.

"Bloody hell . . . 'er mate ain't wearin' any." Billy almost jumped from his seat, only to have Joe restrain him.

"Not in 'ere," Joe snarled.

"But, Joe . . . she's . . ."

"I said . . ."

"Okay, Joe!" Billy controlled himself, refusing to take his eyes from the delightful view of the girl with her thighs spread wide apart.

"I'd like to start a fight in 'ere," Don remarked with relish.

"Me too," Tony chipped in.

"I'd like to fuck that bird!" Billy said eagerly.

Joe scowled, finished his brew. "Let's find the hippies."

"Naw, let's have another . . ."

Joe turned on Billy. "I said - let's go!"

Billy drank his beer, wiped his lips, leered at the girls and followed Joe from the pub. On the street he glanced around. "There ain't goin' to be hippies out in this."

"If we walk towards Roedean we'll find 'em," Joe said with authority.

Don laughed to himself and finally said, "My old man used to tell us about the time he was stationed down 'ere durin' the war. They was in Roedean an' they 'ad a notice on the gates sayin' RING FOR A MISTRESS . . ." His laughter erupted anew; a lonely laugh the others failed to appreciate. Perhaps it was the way he told it.

"I'd like a bleedin' mistress now," Billy said hopefully.

"Me too", Tony quipped. He glanced at Joe. "'owabout it, mate. Can't we find a coupla birds an' . . ."

"After we find a few hippies!" Joe remarked adamantly.

He was consumed with hatred and anxiety. What if, he found himself thinking, they didn't locate any hippies? What would they do then? His leadership depended on getting the boot in.

They walked along the spray-swept front, past the marina, the motor museum, the rows of cold, unfriendly houses perched high on the hill. Hotel signs glowed faintly in the greying sky, offering some warmth and companionship behind their bland façades.

Out to sea, tossed as a cork in a violently disturbed bathtub, a small coastal vessel battled the frothed waves. When the breakers swooshed up the shore, row-boats rattled and shifted at anchor. And, always, there was the restless sound of stone under water as the sea rearranged the composition of the beach once again.

"It's bloody cold!" Billy wasn't thinking of birds now. The biting wind had long since whipped away desire, leaving him wishing for the warmth of a log fire and the sanctuary of a pub.

Up ahead, where their paths rose to meet the road to Hastings, a small group of figures detached themselves from a shelter and started walking down to the beach. Joe stiffened. Even at that distance he could see long hair caught in the freezing wind and could make out gear that wasn't worn by ordinary people.

He grunted, rubbing his hands together in anticipation. "Hairies!" he snarled.

Billy yelled and felt for his tool. The coldness of metal did not shock him; his senses were attuned to violence and the thought of laying into a bleedin' hippie made him feel suddenly hot.

Don and Tony too, had withdrawn their crude clubs - Don's had once been an axe handle while Tony believed in using a tyre iron cut down to right size in Ford's workshops.

Joe didn't have a weapon. He'd come to Brighton for the pleasure of kicking hippies - not bustin' their skulls with a tool. His boots were weaponry enough and, anyway, he wanted the satisfaction of feeling his toe sink in deep.

"Don't let 'em see we're looking for aggro," Joe warned. "Let it be a surprise, eh?"

From their vantage point, the five hippies saw the others approaching. They were cold, hungry, unafraid. They didn't consider an attack on a day like this as even a remote possibility. That they had roughed it for the last week didn't mean their natural enemies - skinheads and Hell's Angels - would brave the bitter weather and venture to Brighton's storm-tossed icebox.

It was afternoon and the last meal they'd been able to cadge had been in Eastbourne the previous night. They had some pot left, some cigarettes and tomorrow, Monday, the Social Security office would give them enough to take care of immediate problems.

"Turn back, Roger . . ."

Roger was a tall man with flowing dark hair and a small beard. His mandarin moustache had never quite succeeded in becoming Chinese and formed a wispy coating above firm lips. "What's wrong, Cherry?" he asked, unable to comprehend her.

"I don't like the look of those boys," the girl replied, fear suddenly tugging at her heart. She was only eighteen but she had had enough experience fighting off those who wished to destroy them. She had taken part in practically every demonstration in Grosvenor Square, been arrested sixteen times for obstruction or disturbing the peace and, always without exception, had the Welfare State pay her fine. She had had two abortions on the State, been in receipt of a student grant until she tired of her fellow students using her as a physical oil-change. Since meeting Roger she had wandered from one end of the country to another, sleeping rough, eating when they could, stealing a little here and there to pay for pot and, when they found a sympathetic Civil Servant, begging a pitiful sum from the tax payers to let them continue the anti-social life they insisted was right.

She was a pretty girl beneath the grime of their outdoor existence; a girl with a high I.Q. gone to "pot". She liked calling herself that. It amused her to watch intelligent faces light up and acknowledge her witticism.

"Cherry's right, Rog," Joel Standish said calmly. His American accent bit into the wind. "They're coming after us!" For himself, he didn't give a goddam what happened. He was sick and needed hospitalization anyway. His ulcers were reaching danger point. In a way, he'd welcome a beating and deportation. He could think of better places to go hippie than England. He thought about California and the communes; about the searing head of Death Valley and the wild life the likes of a Manson could have there. He thought about orgies where the girls were all naked and the pot was freshly imported from Mexico and the desert sun beat down to provide a love nest of shifting hot sand.

Then, suddenly, he thought about his draft dodging and how they'd grab him and toss him into a hoosegow once he set foot in Uncle Sam's land. Fear clogged his nostrils. "Let's get the hell away from here, Rog," he yelled, turning to run.

"No . . ."

Roger was too late. The moment Joel turned tail, Joe and his mob broke into a run.

47

Cherry screamed, threw herself over a low fence and rolled down the incline, her sleeping bag denting her soft side as she rolled over and over.

He couldn't tell it was a girl trying to escape. He jumped the fence, slithered down the steep incline and landed on top of her as she sprawled on the pebble beach. His tool rose ready to smash down on the unprotected head until he saw her face.

Slowly, he lowered his hand, ripped her duffle coat open and felt for her breasts.

"You bastard!" she screamed up at him.

Billy felt the old urge return as he squeezed soft yielding flesh. His hand worked inside her jeans down . . . down, until he felt her pubic hair. "Christ, I'm goin' to rape you," he mouthed.

Cherry fought. She didn't mind the act itself but she objected to being used in plain sight of these animals. His hand was hurting her, his fingers exploring without regard for the tenderness of her body. Her fist smashed into his face . . . into the damage of last night. He yelled, his tool catching her a hard blow above the eye. She slumped dazed, shocked, unable to resist his frantic attempts to rip her jeans off.

Joe felt his boot sink deep into the tall one's groin. He lashed out again, catching the other under the chin as he sank to the ground, hands clutching the injured parts. Like an automaton, Joe kept kicking . . . each blow bringing him greatest satisfaction as the moans of hurt rose above the screaming wind. He didn't care if he killed the hippie or not. He wanted to hurt . . . to rid himself of the feeling within his chest; a feeling bordering on murderous rage.

Don laughed, slammed his shortened axe handle almost down the hippie's throat as the man valiantly tried to resist. It was easy, Don thought, kicking his opponent in the balls, listening to the rapturous sigh, the explosive groan. He hit the falling hippie on the head, hearing the crunch of bone against axe handle, and kicked into the ribs.

Tony watched blood flow from the ripped head of his target. That made two for him. The other wasn't moving now. A few fast belts with his tool and several well aimed kicks had taken care of him. He glanced down the incline, saw Billy mounting the girl, and yelled joyously. He kicked his second opponent in the face, slammed the tyre iron down on the bloody head again and vaulted the fence.

"Me next, mate," he yelled, waatching Billy penetrate the half-stupified girl hippie. Her jeans lay on the beach, her thighs pimpled with cold, her buttocks bruised by the relentless rocks that formed this section of the shoreline.

Joe wanted to keep kicking the hippie but, somehow the pleasure had ebbed since the other ceased to fight back; since the unresisting body had stopped moving. He turned away in disgust to seek another fresh target for his rage.

"Bloody fools," he yelled, catching sight of Billy and Tony. He glanced down the road, saw a familiar car starting to enter it from the direction of the marina. He jumped the fence and raced downhill. "Get out of the bitch!" he hollered at Billy, tearing his mate from the girl's nakedness. "Fuzz . . ."

"I ain't finished it yet," Billy wailed, eyes wild and staring at her nudity. God how he loved thick pubic hair! She had the thickest covering of any bird he'd ever stripped.

"You'll be finished if the fuzz get you," Joe snapped. "Come on - run!" He started running along the beach, seeing Don slither and fall as he followed in their wake. He didn't care if Billy had to run with it out - that was his fault for trying to do two things at once!

*

The train took it's time leaving the station. Joe felt on edge, seated at the window, straining to see if the fuzz were coming down the platform. At last, as the wheels began to catch, he breathed a sigh of relief.

"Bleedin' lucky, mate," he told Billy. He saw Preston Park flash past as the train gathered speed. "Christ, can't you ever go on an aggro without trying to find a bird to fuck?"

Billy sulked. He felt worse than he had earlier. He had a bad case of "lover's balls". If only Joe had let him have just another couple of plunges . . .

"Did you see it, Joe?" Tony asked.

"Yeah, so wot . . . she's no different from other birds."

"Jeeze, she had . . ."

"Shuddup," Billy growled. "I know wot she 'ad."

Joe grinned. He'd expended his hatred. Now, he could afford to vent a little spite on Billy. "Tell me about 'er, Tony," he said deliberately. "Was she hairy . . ?"

Billy tried to close his ears as Tony delighted in describing the girl in intimate detail. He couldn't help overhearing how Tony had viewed his hasty mating nor how he had looked when Joe dragged him off the bitch. He wished the fuzz had caught the others and let him finish. He'd have to find a bird when they got back to Plaistow or else he'd have an awful night of it again . . .

CHAPTER SEVEN

FOR four days of every week Joe worked for a coal delivery merchant. He never worked a Tuesday, but that was tomorrow and his reasons did not bear thinking about until . . .

He hated Monday almost as much as he hates hippies. He had read The *Mirror*'s account of the young thugs who had viciously attacked five hippies in Brighton and tried to mass-rape the girl with them. He had read, with a high degree of pleasure, how the four male hippies were in serious condition in Brighton hospital and that the girl had been released after getting stitches in a head wound. Fortunately, the description issued by the police would fit any skinhead in London so he didn't think they'd ever trace the mob from Brighton.

His mate on the delivery lorry was a man of about forty - an illiterate Cockney with a fantastic sense of humour but nothing else to qualify him as Joe's mate. Joe worked his fiddles with a recklessness that increased the thrill of robbing old age pensioners and old women too timid to object to his overcharging. He had a standard method of getting a few bob from every customer - he simply altered their half of the delivery slip to read a higher amount. If they argued, which was seldom, he argued back - and usually won. If they threatened to telephone the company he'd back down with a grin and explain that some stupid bastard of a clerk had made a mistake.

There were a few calls where fiddles were strictly *verbotten* - like when they had a delivery to Mrs. Marrinor. He always let his mate heave the coal into her basement. And, naturally enough, he never appeared again until he had satisfied the middle-aged nympho's craving for a "dirty coalman to jump on top of my lily-white flesh".

Oh, there were perks galore for delivering coal!

Another non-fiddle place of call was on the estate. Mrs. "bleedin' heart" Bassault, the French bird whose husband always seemed to be away on some ship or another. Joe knew all about her. She was the Point professional fuck. Any man with enough ready cash left after a night in the local boozer could stop off at her flat to avail himself of her excellent services regardless of whether or not he could, or could not, perform with a skinful on. Mrs. Bassault had never been known to fail when she was paid for relieving frustrations. One way - or another - she guaranteed results.

This Monday they had six bags for Mrs. Bassault.

"Look, mate," Joe told his driver, "she's due for it. Let me 'ave it today?"

The older man screwed his piggish eyes into slits and considered Joe's request. He had been thinking how nice it would be for himself. He hadn't been getting his share off the old woman for weeks and he was overdue to make a personal delivery to Mrs. Bassault's bedroom. "I dunno . . ." he said.

"A quid if you let me . . ."

"Shit! I'd pay twice that to call at night."

"Okay, two quid!" Joe felt generous. He'd made forty-seven shillings that morning already. And, he had what was left of the robbery in his wallet, too.

"Done! Ram her for me, eh?" the driver chuckled as he eased his lorry into the Point driveway and parked directly behind the Bassault block.

Mrs. Bassault didn't question Joe's urgent knocks. She looked at him and said, "Coal today?" She stood back and added, "I'm short of cash but. . ." Her robe fell open displaying knickers and brassiere and expanses of creamy flesh.

Joe crudely pulled the front of her knickers down and studied the pubic region. "Sorry, Mrs. Bassault - we're short on cash this week. I'm afraid I can only deduct a quid . . ."

"You're a *big* boy," she replied. "I suppose . . ." She moved away as the coal-dust on his hand left a black mark down her gently-rounded stomach. Where his fingers had gripped her pink knickers the individual black prints showed too. She glared at these, and said testily, "I hate washing them, Joe."

"Take everything off," he said, starting to unzip his flies. "I won't dirty your bed today, either. The floor's great."

She spread newspaper on the carpet, stripped and lay back with her thights wide apart. Her hands came up, and out. "Don't keep me waiting, Joe . . ."

*

"Was it good?"

Joe inclined his head. "Like it always is . . . in, out, up, down and thanks for bringing the coal, Joe."

"We'vegot Sally Vincent today," the man said slowly, watching Joe's face.

Joe cursed. He should have studied the delivery sheet. If he'd known Sally was one of their customers he'd have let this bastard fuck the French whore.

"I get 'er, eh Joe?"

"Yeah, you get Sally!"

After he heaved the coal down Sally'schute he returned to the lorry and sweated out the half-hour before his mate returned. His imagination ran riot thinking of Sally. He knew exactly what would happen inside her house . . . he'd been through the procedure often enough to visualize her performance. She didn't believe in intercourse in the ordinary way. She didn't want a bastard, she always said. She had her own pleasurable method for making her delivery men pay for her creature-comforts. The milkman for one, got his treatment every Monday. The laundryman got his on Friday. The gas and electricity blokes always came away swearing she had been a frugal customer. And, whenever she wanted coal, she got a delivery and a forty-five minute thrill. Not to mention what the coalman got.

"Hey, Joe . . . she let me into 'er . . ."

Joe felt sick. Ever since he took this flamin' job he'd wanted into Sally. Now, this old bastard had done the bit.

"She was pissed," his mate kept saying. "Pissed! Seems she discovered her old man put one in her oven and she don't give a cunt anymore!" The driver chuckled, got behind the steering-wheel. "Cor, she did give me one! I tell you - there ain't no woman with a better set or a more active . . ."

"For chrissakes, dry up!" Joe shouted.

He felt so rotten he didn't even attempt to argue when an old age pensioner contested his charges. He changed her figures back to normal, stamped off to the lorry and growled for his mate to hurry. For once, the Cockney humour was lacking. His mate didn't wish to rile Joe. He'd have ample opportunity to sleep in a cold bed that night and cogitate over his earlier success.

*

The church basement was crowded with clean, respectable teenagers. They were enjoying their weekly social and the vicar kept changing the discs and serving the coffee without one single word of discouragement.

They were an exuberant crowd, perfectly content in the knowledge that St. James's was a church young people could be proud of, and assured of a weekly welcome from the with-it vicar.

Every Sunday, the church was able to boast of superlative attendances - mostly consisting of teenager adherents to the open policies that had initiated their decorous youth club.

Peter Bloomfield studied the group dancing and inwardly congratulated himself for the success he had had with what had always been classified an unruly element in his district. In his opinion, God was not a harsh God, nor an authoritarian. God was love and love should be that emotion shared with one's fellow man or woman (always depending, naturally, on the holy state of matrimony; he did not condone the permissiveness that certain elements of society tried to force churchmen into accepting).

"How are things at home, Albert?" he asked as a tall, thin youngster came to stand beside him.

Albert Newton shrugged casually. He wasn't one of those who accepted Bloomfield as the "teenager's saviour". He had his reservations and, mostly, they revolved around the vicar's pet theory that sex before marriage was illicit, immoral, bad for a "God-blessed" union. Albert was virile and could always get any girl he went after. He enjoyed feeling around and exercising his manhood. For that reason he was the blackest sheep in the vicar's little fold.

"Not bad, Mr. Bloomfield," he replied, conscious of the need to treat the man with a certain respect. He didn't realise that it was this deference that made him Bloomfield's special target. In the vicar's mind, any teenager willing to show respect was worth saving.

"Has your father found a job yet?"

Albert grunted. "How could he?"

There was no answer to that, Bloomfield thought. Mr. Newton was one of nature's favourite layabouts. He had feigned illness so long he would not know how to find the strength to go for an interview.

"I see Betty Rowe is here tonight . . ."

Albert tightened up inside.

"She asked if you were coming . . ."

Albert lit a cigarette.

"Have you thought about what I suggested the last time we met?"

The boy grinned. "Yeah. No!"

Peter Bloomfield felt the immediate urge to rant at the youth. He calmed himself and said: "There's nothing wrong with being a police constable, Albert."

"No?" Albert savagely stubbed his cigarette into the palm of one hand - a feat he had perfected since seeing it done on television by a so-called hard man. "They're underpaid, nobody likes 'em and I don't want my head kicked in at demos . . ."

"Ah,"the vicar smiled, placing a hand on the boy's shoulder. "I see." He didn't really! "You think all policemen spend their time getting maltreated?"

"Don't they?" Albert wanted to hurt. Ever since the vicar had suggested he join the force he had seriously tried to get his inner-self to agree. He liked the idea of walking round his district in a nice blue uniform. He enjoyed the prospect - imaginary, of course - of apprehending villains. Yet, he couldn't go against public opinion and his mates.

"What I had in mind," the vicar continued with his infectious enthusiasm, "was a course at a police college. None of the beat pounding trivia for you, Albert. I have funds at my disposal. The Church would provide a grant to see you through the course . . ." His face broke into a benevolent smile and his eyes searched through Albert - almost to the closed soul-door.

Albert hesitated. He wanted to accept - on the spot. He wanted to tell this man that he was the best person he had ever met . . . and couldn't. His upbringing forbade any emotional response. His father's constant claims that the State owed its citizens a living, that nobody got anywhere offering their services stuck in his mind; and in his heart.

"I tell you, Joe - they've got birds in there would turn your head," Billy remarked as they lounged outside the church hall.

"Wot's keepin' us from getting a few?" Don asked.

Joe scowled. He'd had his bit for the day and tomorrow was Tuesday. He had to keep reasonably virile for Tuesday! "Christ - you wanna go in?" he asked sulkily.

"Yeah!"

"Okay . . ." Joe shoved the door open and faced a frightened goody-goody boy. "Move aside, pansy," Joe shouted, shoving the boy over amid a collection of flying tickets.

For a moment, nobody noticed their arrival. Then, when Billy grabbed one of the girls, a scream split the hall into factions and Joe's mob found themselves confronted by hostile glares. Just glares. Nothing else.

"Keep dancin'," Joe announced. "We ain't goin' to rape you bleedin' virgins." He grinned and added in a stage-whisper to Billy, "Are we?"

"I bloody-well am," Billy said in a loud voice. "That one over there!" He indicated a girl of about fifteen wearing a mini and a tight blouse. Billy took a step towards the girl . . .

"Just a moment!" Peter Bloomfield tried to control his seething anger. First, he turned the record player off, then he walked through the parting crowd of his flock and stood facing Joe Hawkins. He recognised Joe; knew that this was the most serious crisis ever to be thrust upon his small gathering. Joe represented evil; Lucifer in clip-on braces and wearing devilish boots.

Joe laughed and touched Don's arm. "Get a load of 'im," he clowned, affecting the vicar's mode of walk.

"You bastard!"

Joe glanced round the hall, trying to catch sight of the speaker. It certainly didn't *sound* like one of the flock - not using *that* language here.

Albert stepped forward, joining the vicar as a team pitted against a superior side.

Joe felt apprehension race down his spine. He and Albert had attended the same school and the only boy he had never been able to lick was Albert Newton. He recalled several bloody noses and black eyes when he antagonized the same Albert.

"You don't belong here, Joe," Albert said evenly. "Get lost! Go bovver some other function but forget this one!"

Joe forced a scowl intended to frighten his opponent. He *couldn't* back down. Not in front of the mob.

"Please . . ." Peter Bloomfield smiled at Albert, placing a restraining arm before the youth, and took a tentative step to Joe.

Billy growled, aiming a solid kick at the vicar's groin . . .

Don whooped, tearing into three timid youngsters near him; his tool flashing, hitting; his boots finding their soft targets without much satisfaction gained.

Before he knew what was happening, Albert lunged forward, slamming a right, left, right into Joe's face. Joe staggered back. Albert closed in, not letting those deadly boots get freedom of movement, his bunched fists pounding into Joe's unprotected middle.

From his undistinguished position on the dusty floor, Peter Bloomfield watched the battle with prayers on his lips. His groin hurt, his hopes pinned on Albert's initiative. If only the others would back Albert . . .

Albert didn't require backing at this stage. He was hammering Joe into insensibility, driving rights and lefts at the skinhead leader . . . forcing him back . . . back . . . back against a solid wall from which there was no escape.

"That's enough m'lad!" A heavy hand pulled Albert off his enemy.

Joe shook his head, desperately trying to clear the fog that threatened to make him a sitting-bird. He heard the strange voice, saw Albert half-turn away from him and . . .

"*God*!" Albert sank to his knees as Joe's boot found his stomach. He wanted to be sick . . . couldn't.

"Little swine!" The stranger slashed a stiff-hand across Joe's throat, sending the skinhead reeling. Then, swinging into action, he vaulted the prostrate Albert, rabbit-punching Billy to his knees before making a flying tackle that brought Don down with a *whump*!

Joe struggled to his feet, his throat raw. Through the mist hanging over the hall he saw Don struggling with the stranger. It wasn't his fight, he reasoned and, sensing the nausea in his guts, he stumbled out of the hall into the fresh air. He was sick in the street, thankful for the fact that none of his mates could see him.

Inside the hall, bedlam reigned . . .

Don fought back with all the ferocity of his mind. His tool knocked the attacker flat, then, using his boots, he slammed kick after kick into unprotected ribs until the sickening sound of cracking bone told him he'd done enough damage.

Backing away, he helped Billy to his feet, but found his way blocked

56

by Albert.

"I'll kill you, you bastard!" Don snarled, brandishing his tool.

Albert shrugged and moved aside.

Don backed to the door and lumbered by the semi-unconscious Billy. As he pushed the door open, Albert leapt forward, his foot a blur in the subdued lighting of the hall. He felt the toe dig into Don's side and steadied himself for a second kick where it would count.

"Albert . . . NO!!!"

Albert hesitated, watching Don heave himself through the swinging door with Billy still clutched under one arm.

"Don't let them make *you* into what they are!"

Albert turned slowly. Peter Bloomfield swayed unsteadily before him. The vicar's face was a study of ecstasy and agony.

"Don't, Albert . . ."

Albert relaxed. The fury was spent. He went to the vicar, supporting him now.

"We'll need men of your calibre," the vicar said through his pain. "Think about what I suggested, Albert . . ."

"Excuse me, sir . . ."

Peter Bloomfield turned his attention on the stranger in their midst. Albert eyed the man with outright suspicion. He didn't trust sudden appearances nor did he like what was formulating in his mind. The man smelt like a copper. "I'm a police officer . . ." the stranger said.

Albert stiffened automatically.

"Do any of you know the men who attacked you?"

Peter Bloomfield smiled wearily. He glanced at Albert, feeling that this was the youth's moment of truth. He said: "Personally, I don't want to press charges, officer."

Albert smiled with his own weariness, too. He was being pressured. He knew it, as sure as he could feel the strength surging back into the vicar. He released the other, taking a few steps away to stand aloof from the interrogation.

"We're trying to encourage teenagers to accept us," the vicar continued. "It wouldn't help our cause to lay a complaint on one specific boy, or girl."

The police officer grunted. "That's where you're wrong, sir. It would help a great deal. These young thugs need to be taught a lesson. A six-month sentence would serve 'em right!"

Albert mentally agreed. Joe Hawkins and his mob needed a dose of prison.

"I disagree, officer," Bloomfield remarked. "They need charity and tolerance ..." His gaze swung to encompass Albert now.

The plainclothes man shrugged and turned to leave. "If you happen to remember who they were, sir - get in touch with your local police station ... before they commit murder, sir!" He opened the door and departed with a thought-wish expression.

"Mr. Bloomfield ..."

The vicar smiled at Albert.

"I'll take that grant you spoke about!"

Peter Bloomfield held out his hand. Perhaps, he thought, the agony searing his insides was worthwhile after all. "I'll make the arrangements, Albert. You'll make a wonderful policeman."

Albert grinned. "That's debatable, sir - but I won't let Joe and his mob get away with what they've done when I'm in uniform ..."

CHAPTER EIGHT

EVERY Tuesday, Joe left the house as though he was going to work. In actuality, he didn't. Never on Tuesday! Tuesday was his day for a piece ... a very special piece.

At Swete Street he almost got clobbered by a taxi-cab and he spent five minutes recovering, blasting passers-by with a violence that frightened off several old biddies going to the Co-op for their shopping. By the time he had passed the station where cabbies gathered looking for fares, he had cooled somewhat. But not enough. He stalked to one cab, thrust his head inside the open side-window, and cursed the driver until the man called for help.

Joe didn't wait for reinforcements to arrive. He knew better. Cabbies in this district could handle themselves - especially when they outnumbered the opposition!

He was feeling big when he arrived at *her* house.

Every Tuesday, her mother went shopping - not locally as most women hereabouts did, but to Ilford where bargains could be found and the larger stores offered a greater variety of goods for the housewife.

"Joe . . ." she hissed as she opened the front door.

"Christ, Sally . . ." He stepped inside, feeling her hot tongue probing his mouth, her hands feverishly unzipping his flies.

"Oh, Joe . . ."

"Can't you bleedin' wait?"

"No, Joe . . . feel me!"

He felt her breasts with their hard-tipped response arousing him immediately. He felt lower, between her thighs getting the same urgent reaction.

"Joe . . . Hurry . . ."

He rushed her along the short, narrow hall, feeling the almost impossible *hurry* she insisted upon. They were practically naked when they reached her cramped room - her abject surrender evident when she flung herself on the unmade bed and opened her legs wide.

He flung his clothes across the room, unable to tear his gaze from where her hand rested . . . agitating herself into acceptance of what was about to happen.

"Joe . . ." She held her arms out, shuddering as she saw his nudity. He fell on her, fumbling for contact . . .

"Joe . . ." she wailed as he inserted his penis. Then as he continued to plunge up and down on her, she gave herself totally to his frantic pleasure . . . gyrating; moaning; begging him to go faster . . .

"Okay?" he asked, rolling from her.

"Joe . . ." Tears stung her eyes. It had been beautiful. What she wanted from him every night of the week; what she couldn't have because her father forbade her to associate with a bastard like Joe.

"Let's have a kip."

She snuggled against his naked chest. Her hand fondled him, loving the slickness of what had recently been her passion. "Marry me, Joe."

He stiffened. "You're crazy, Sally. We ain't old enough."

"I'd run away with you, Joe . . ."

"Christ," he exploded. "You're fourteen, Sally!"

"And I take the Pill so you can . . ."

"Jeeze, I know, doll."

"Don't that mean somethin'?"

"Yeah, crawl over me. I'm getting the urge again . . ."

Her body flowed through his greedy hands, her thighs straddling him.

"Cor . . ." He kissed a breast, hands actively working between her thighs.

She bent over him, positioning herself . . . all fourteen years of experience doing what came naturally on their Tuesday.

"I'm ready," Joe whispered . . .

She sank onto him, loving the feeling of his penis buried in her body.

CHAPTER NINE

"IT was lovely, Joe." She lay by his side, her hand toying with his genitals.

He felt sleepy. Funny, he thought, how he wanted to sleep after a good screw. "That's terrific," he growled, twisting on one side.

"Joe . . .?"

"Yeah!"

"Can't we run away an' get married?"

"No!"

"Why not? Others do . . ."

"You're only fourteen."

"So what? I can take everything you've got, can't I?"

"When I'm ready to give, doll," he rasped.

She giggled playing with him. "It won't take long, Joe 'awkins."

"Crissakes, you've 'ad it twice already."

"So what?" She sulked, taking her hands from his flesh, rolling on her back and brushing his groping hand away with a certain amount of petulance.

"Shit!" He sat up in the bed and stared at the small window with its thin curtains doing nothing to hide a view of brick wall beyond.

"Joe . . ."

"Wot?"

"Don't you love me?"

"Yeah!"

"You're a rotten bastard. All you want is what I let you have every Tuesday."

"You enjoy it, too!"

"Sure I do - 'cause you're shovin' it into me!"

Joe felt a sudden flow of energy. "Want it now?"

She took his hand and placed it on him. "No! If you're feeling horny, work it off yourself!"

"S'truth," he panted, feeling over her nakedness. "This ain't my week . . ."

"Joe . . . don't do that unless you want to . . ."

"Wot?"

She whimpered. "That . . ."

He crawled down the bed, down . . . kissing her sides, her hip, her stomach.

"Oh, God - Joe . . . Joe . . ."

His hands lifted her buttocks. His mouth wandered over each thigh, down to the knee, back to the inner tenderness of the thighs and his hands kept opening the thighs, wider . . . wider . . .

So intent were they on their lovemaking, they couldn't hear the slam of the front door, the heavy footfalls of Sally's mother as she approached her daughters bedroom.

At forty-seven, Mrs. Morris looked, and acted, like a woman ten years older. The harsh war years had taken a deadly toll; and the constant battle to provide for a growing family had sapped all ambition. She existed now, for her infrequent shopping trips to Ilford and Romford; for the tea with gossip when she visited her sister in Barking; for the once monthly night at the pictures. She no longer fought her husband for her rights nor did she care what Sally did. She had tried with the girl - tried desperately hard to make her have respect for herself and stay away from that awful Joe Hawkins.

Today, she didn't feel good. The migraine had begun almost the second she entered Ilford and increased steadily until she had been forced to abandon her shopping and return home. She didn't like the frequency with which these blinding headaches struck; yet she did not want to see her doctor. She had a fear of medical men - a carry over from the war when she witnessed an on-the-spot amputation in a shelter.

As she slowly climbed the narrow stairs to her bedroom she paused, frowning. The sounds coming from Sally's room were suspiciously like those associated with passionate lovemaking. She listened, forcing herself to ignore the migraine for those vital moments . . .

"Oh, God . . ." She hurried now, moaning softly, hands shaking as she turned the bedroom door knob.

She closed her eyes tightly against the sight confronting her. "Sally!

God, no!" A black sheet of pain covered her head. She clung to the swinging door for support, unable to watch their cavortings.

Sally couldn't stop herself. She was at the peak of her orgasm. Her eyes rolled open, and fixed on her mother's face . . .

She wanted to yell; to draw away from her lover and hide beneath the rumpled covers.

For the first time in her young life, Sally Morris felt sorrow for her mother . . .

"Yes . . . yes . . . yes . . ." Joe's panted exhortation beat on her ears, his body a pistoning battering ram pressing her down in the creaking bed.

The physical sensations blew away her shame.

And then, it was over; and the dregs of passion ebbed into an ocean of remorse as she struggled free of Joe's weight and covered her nakedness.

"Wot's the big idea?" Joe asked testily.

She pointed, silently accusing.

Joe glanced over his shoulder and felt a flush of hatred. *How dare the old bitch come in on them!* he thought. *Tuesday was his day in this house!*

"Mum . . ." Sally grabbed a blanket, hid her nudity and ran to her mother. Tears rolled down her cheeks, matching those staining Mrs. Morris's face.

The woman brushed aside the hand on her wrist.

"Please, Mum . . . let me explain . . ."

"You little tramp! You slut!" The woman's eyes opened, staring wildly. "Get that bastard out of this room . . ."

Joe leapt to his feet. "You old cow . . ."

"Joe!" Sally swung round. "Don't call Mum names."

He paraded his naked, sweating flesh round the room, deliberately taunting both of them.

"Your father wasn't wrong about 'im . . ." Mrs. Morris groaned, pain lancing through her head. She leant against the wall as her legs turned to rubber.

"Make 'im leave, Sal . . ." she sobbed.

"Joe . . ." The girl pleaded with tearful eyes.

With an ugly grin, Joe began dressing, taking a perverted delight in their eyes watching him. He'd been satisfied with Sally's performance and now there was the bonus of knowing that her mother could not quite prevent herself peeping to see what he had to offer. Only when he had gratified himself did he leave them alone and walk downstairs to the front door. Before opening it, he paused and shouted: "When you want what Sally likes be sure an' let me know, Mrs. Morris . . ." Smiling, he slammed the door behind him, and walked to the nearest pub without one regret, without the slightest thought for Sally's predicament.

CHAPTER TEN

WHENEVER Sergeant Jack Piper came home, his parents dipped deep into their meagre savings for a special meal. Nothing was too good for their soldier son, the Pipers always told neighbours - and they meant it too.

Jack knew the circumstances and felt a bastard when he sat down to a perfectly-cooked meal with all the trimmings. But, he never complained, never spoke to his mother and requested a smaller tribute. He just fitted in with her plans and then, the day he returned to base, he slipped his father whatever he could afford to replenish the family coffers. Usually, it worked out well for the old couple. Jack was a decent son. Having a jar with the boys was always secondary to seeing that mum and dad had enough to exist upon. No matter what part of the world he was serving in, Jack always managed to send a parcel home.

Jack Piper loathed the district his parents insisted on making their home. He had been glad to join the Army just to get away from the rows of houses, the smoke-belching factories, the dirt-littered streets and the old-before-their-time people with their sad faces. He had never been able to understand why his dad wanted to stay put in the old, semi-slum home. His dad had been somebody in the Queen's Army in Africa and India - a colour-sergeant possessing medals and ribbons galore.

"Do you still follow the Hammers?" his dad asked.

Jack laughed. "When I can. They ain't doing too good lately."

"Give 'em time, son," the old soldier suggested placidly. "They're a young team. One of these days we'll be on top of the First Division."

Jack lit a cigarette and held his lighter out for his dad to place his worn pipe against the flame. He didn't want to discuss West Ham's chances of ever again topping the Division. He frankly had grown away from the local team, preferring to lend his support to an Army match down in Aldershot. "Found many winners over the sticks?" he asked, tactfully switching subjects.

Charles Piper glanced in the direction of the kitchen before answering. He knew that Madge knew he had the occasional flutter on the nags but he didn't like voicing the information in her hearing. They had long ago reached an understanding on his betting, and his visit to the local. What she didn't know didn't cause friction in the house. Each of them went along without ever mentioning the small win, the quick nip, the Saturday night dart game where stout and companionship compensated for all that was vastly different from the old days.

Jack grinned. He was a good-looking man in his late thirties. When his wife said he looked like a youthful Cary Grant when he grinned she was not far wrong. Of course, he wished he had the star's money. He would be able to afford a decent home for his parents, a plush flat for his wife and a private-school education for his two kids. For himself, he would buy a Rover car, a small cabin-cruiser, a retreat far away from the London filth and his freedom from the Army. Not that he found much wrong with an Army career. The forces had treated him generously and he had no valid complaints - except one . . . he didn't enjoy the unnecessary bull when some big shot decided to visit the camp.

The ancient features cracked into a smile. "I've had my wins, son. A tanner each way treble is good enough for me."

God, Jack thought, *they still take tanner bets down here!* "Anything worth betting on today?"

Charles Piper puffed contendedly on his briar, gazing into the fire. "Could be Mister Piercer will give them all a shock," he said with accumulated wisdom. "He's been running in low-class company. I say he's been held back for today's big race."

Jack grinned at a dancing devil in the fire. "Ten bob each way, eh?"

His father looked up, startled. "That's a lot of money to wager, son."

"I can afford it, Dad. Fact is, I'd like to split the proceeds - call it a father and son bet, eh?"

The old man shrugged. He loved his son, and the respect that a

64

man his age expected from an offspring. He wondered how many men his age in this area could get the feeling of parental love that they shared. Not many, he guessed. Not many!

"I'm not certain about the horse, son . . ."

"I am, Dad! Agreed it's a fifty-fifty proposition?"

"Agreed, lad," Charles Piper said, hiding the tears which threatened to spoil the gesture.

"Which bookie do you normally use?"

"Dick Hedley."

"What time is the race?"

"Three o'clock."

"Right - soon's Mum has dinner served we'll shoot down and make the bet."

"Jack . . ." Watery eyes surveyed the son.

"Forget it, Dad! Values have changed, that's all. Tanners are fine for old age pensioners but we're paid pretty good money in the Army today."

His mother stepped into the room. She had heard the conversation and decided it was time to rescue her husband from an overly-emotional experience. "If you gentlemen will excuse the cook," she laughed, "dinner is ready. I'm afraid it's only bangers and mash but can guarantee the sausages are the best in London."

"Just what the doctor ordered," Jack said with a smile. Embracing his mother he added, "You remember how I love bangers . . ."

She shook her head. "No, tell me, son."

Entering the kitchen, Jack wanted to cry on his mother's shoulder. Grandma's best china was on the table and heaped mash on his plate was probably what they both took during any given week of his absence. The six sizzling sausages for him and the three for each of them had broken the Post Office account. "It's fantastic, Mum," he said with a gulp. "I feel like a general . . ."

His mother laughed. "Get away with you, Jack Piper. Your generals eat caviar and smoked salmon and sirloin steaks. I remember once when Dad and I were in India and Sir John Clacksley came to the mess for dinner. He had a dozen oysters, a pheasant, soup, a Bombay duck and sweet with black coffee. And do you know what he said about the dinner afterwards?"

Jack shrugged. "What?"

"He said, 'Why is it always a sparse meal when one is entertained in India?'."

Jack gazed at the table before him. "I think Sir John was a bloody bore! This meal is fit for a Prince of Wales and I don't give a damn if Wales like sausages or not."

Jack Piper didn't pay much attention to the coal delivery men when they interrupted the meal. His father went to attend to the necessary arrangements for removing the wooden slat they had across the coal bunker and came back to finish his meal. Then, when the knock sounded, Jack leant back and waited until his father settled the bill, unconsciously adding this amount to what he would give the old man when he finally went back to his unit.

He half-heard his father's quavering voice contest the cost of coal, and figured it for another increase the old man hadn't heard about until . . .

"Pay up or else, you old bastard . . ."

Jack stiffened. In this district people addressed one another with what amounted to blasphemy, he knew. But this . . . He jumped to his feet, marched stiffly to the back door and stared at the cocky kid with a coal sack over one shoulder.

"Or else what?" he asked.

Joe Hawkins glared at the stranger. He hadn't expected the old couple to have visitors - certainly not one wearing the uniform of an army sergeant. "'e's refusin' to pay up," he said defiantly.

"Jack - look at this . . ." Charles Piper held out the altered bill to his son.

Jack took one fast look and laughed. "Sonny - your arithmetic is haywire. This says five times sixteen bob is five quid. That isn't right."

"Look, mister," Joe snarled, refusing to back-peddle. "I collect wot it says on the bill. I want five knicker or else."

"Or else what?" Jack said softly.

"I takes the coal back, is wot," Joe snarled, again.

"You'll leave it where it is," Jack said. "I'll 'phone the office . . ."

"You'll fuck off!" Joe shouted.

Jack studied the bill closely now. He sighed. "Seems this has been altered."

Joe tensed. He could handle old age pensioners but a soldier . . . those boots matched his for effect! "Do you want bovver?"

"Yeah, sonny," Jack said, smiling coldly.

Joe didn't hesitate. His right foot lashed out seeking a vulnerable

66

spot.

Jack Piper grinned, catching the foot, flipping the rest of Joe on his back. It was so simple when one took into account all those experienced instructors who trained men in the art of self-defence.

Joe came to his feet, caution forgotten. He had always made an extra quid at this house and he didn't want any clever soldier to spoil his untaxed income. He shot forward, hands slashing air, feet trying to find a solid groin to dig into ... finding only a hard fist to the jaw, a knife-edged hand to the Adam's Apple and a boot in the bollocks to send him gasping amongst the newly-delivered coal.

"Tell the office to send the bill by post," the soldier growled. "If it's right we'll pay. If it isn't we'll take it up with the accountant."

As Joe struggled to climb off the shifting coals, Jack Piper guided his father back into the house, and locked the door in Joe's face.

All the fury of his encounter burst like a bomb inside Joe's mind. He had been relegated to an inferior position and this riled him; more - it positively went against his grain. He wanted to make the bastard pay for the indignity of being sent on his arse in the coal; for being shown to fabricate delivery slips.

Shaking his fist at the Piper house, Joe swore: "You'll pay for this, you bastard!" He glowered at Jack's grinning face in the kitchen window and stomped off to berate his mate for not coming to his side in a time of extreme peril ...

CHAPTER ELEVEN

"'IM an' is mates," Joe concluded as he fondled his latest weapon - an ancient, rusted iron bar with sharp teeth serrating one edge. No doubt it had once been a gear-activator, a sliding set of teeth to regulate an obsolete device.

"It don't pay to bash-up sol'iers," Don remarked more to himself than Joe.

"'ere," Billy interrupted with sudden enthusiasm, "did you read the 'paper tonight?"

Joe studied his closest confederate, wondering what bright-eyed inspiration was forthcoming. One could never tell about Billy. He read every edition of *The Standard* - practically devoured each word a dozen times over - and although most of the articles and news went way over his head, he did have a knack for recounting specific items by heart.

"They arrested Ronnie Goodman larst night!"

Joe was aware of a tightening in his chest, a butter-flying sensation deep in his stomach. "And?" he asked eagerly.

"Six months!" Billy said proudly.

The tightness developed into a steel band round Joe's chest. He could hardly breathe.

"'ismob . . ."

Joe snapped, "'ismob needs a new leader!"

Billy grinned. "Yeah!"

"I know Hymie Goldschmidt," Don offered.

"Ronnie's lieutenant," Billy cut in.

"Christ,"Joe barked, "don't I know it, too!" He waved aside Don's open mouth and allowed wonderful thoughts to trickle through his mind. If Goodman had been put away for six months he might just be able to swing the command of his mob. It would take diplomacy; no single group of skinheads ever willingly joined forces with another yet . . . they were both West Ham supporters and both lots came from Plaistow. It may not be so difficult . . .

"Don, find Hymie an' arsk if he'll talk to me."

Billy rubbed his hands gleefully. "Cor, mate - won't it be sumfin' if'n we can get 'em in with us?"

Joe stared at his pal. How the hell *he* ever read so much and spoke so badly was a mystery. Even Joe felt he had a better command of the Queen's English than Billy. "You're a cunt . . ."he flung at Billy.

The youth grinned. "That means I'm useful, eh Joe?"

Ignoring the standard remark, Joe swung on Don. "Find Hymie. Tell 'im I want a meeting."

"Wot about the sol'ier?"

Joe smiled evily. "If Hymie an' Ronnie's mob join us we can beat the 'ell out of that bastard!"

*

Hymie Goldschmidt was a Jew. His father owned an empire of rag-trade outlets near Aldgate and they lived as his grandfather had lived in Prussia - in squalor conditions. He refused to belong to his native nation - preferring, always, to sponsor the Israeli cause and plough his gains into bonds for a foreign country. He did not sympathize with his English relatives nor would he ever bend a knee to accept the dogma that England, as a Christian land, could have anything he wanted . . . unless, of course, one took into account the plentiful supply of cash in this God-forbidden island. In all his business dealings, Solly Goldschmidt acted on the belief that an Englishman was a sucker and that the Jew-boy was supreme when it came to making money. He spent very little on family luxuries, accepting Council charity in the form of a home subsidised by the non-Kosher ratepayers, and devalued the worth of the security he had by possessing a British passport.

Where Solly was Orthodox, Hymie said "to hell with all that crap" and - when his father was working - helped himself to large ham sandwiches, bacon and eggs and anything else he figured would drive his mother insane. Many a time his grandmother scrubbed out their refrigerator to cleanse it after Hymie had deliberately insinuated ham into its Kosher depths.

As for Israel - well, Hymie must surely have been on the "most wanted" lists of their Secret Service. He hated Israel with Arabian loathing; he cursed the day Palestine had been handed over to "those European misfits" and offered proof that "no evidence existed to back the Jewish claims to the occupied territories they now controlled."

Hymie was, to all his friends, a non-Jew; a dis-believer; a semi-Christian. He even went to the extent of attending Mass with some of his mates or looking in on a service in St. Paul's Cathedral whenever arguments at home drove him to emphasise his Anglicized nationality. Occasionally, when the Rabbi forced him, Hymie would attend his Synagogue - but always under protest and always dragged by his father.

In a household dedicated to the accumulation of money and subjected to the belief that the Jews were God's "chosen children" - which he denied fervently - Hymie was, without any doubt, the greatest throwback in history. He was intelligent - knew every aspect of British history; could place spots on a global blank map with the accuracy of a Marco Polo; quote from Burns, Shelley, Wilde and Keats; argue politics and religion with great authority; bedazzle accountants with a natural Jewish flair for profits-versus-overheads.

Yet, notwithstanding, Hymie was also a skinhead - a violent little thug devoting his energies to the dismemberment of those who professed to love, adore and understand.

When Ronnie Goodman was sentenced to six months Hymie believed he could assume command of the mob. Believed . . .

His ego was shattered when the mob refused to obey his leadership edicts. He felt betrayed.

When Don came to see him, Hymie was more than willing to throw-in his lot with yet another Gentile commander and reassess his situation. He didn't make his feelings evident; he always hid his thoughts.

"Alright,"he told Don, "Joe Hawkins has a name - but is he capable of leading a big mob?"

Don glared at the Jew. Personally, he could have chopped the hook-nosed bastard to bits but he remembered how Joe would have acted. He forced a smile, and said, "Sure he can! Arsk anyone in Plaistow."

Hymie mentally agreed that Joe Hawkins had a name. There were enough people running scared to make him a suitable stand-in for Ronnie. Anyway, he wanted to set up a situation that would be resolved when Ronnie came out of prison. He wanted to watch the two leaders fight it out for supremacy. If either, or hopefully both, flopped then - maybe - he stood a chance of assuming ultimate command.

"We have twenty-five in our mob - how many are in yours?"

Don hesitated. Hymie knew, like everyone, the exact count. He tried to get around the issue. "That's not the point . . ."

"How many?" Hymie insisted sadistically. He had already decided to enlist the support of as many adherents as possible but he still had to place Don, and through him that bastard Joe Hawkins, on a spot.

"Seven . . ."

"Just seven?"

Don tried to make sense of his mental fingers. His worst subject at school had always arithmetic.

"Fifteen . . ."

Hymie ignored the difference. He liked Don athough he knew the other hated his guts. That, he told himself, came from the East Ender's inherent belief that all Jews were bloodsucking moneylenders and slave-employers . . . a fact he could not deny without bringing in statistics to show that there were others - Gentiles - equally guilty of the same charge.

"Where is Joe?"

70

Don beamed success. "I'll take you to 'im . . ."

Hymie laughed inwardly. Dropped Hs spoke of servility and inferiority in his book. He went with Don . . .

*

"Alright,"Hymie said. "We join mobs!"

Joe smiled. He didn't particularly like the Jew-boy but he did respect Hymie's abilities and his promise to bring Ronnie's mob in with his.

He thought of that bastard Piper.

"Look, mate," he told Hymie, "we're goin' to visit a house near 'ere tonight. I want a soldier done . . ."

"That's fine with us, Joe," the Jew replied nonchalantly.

"Bring your boys to the . . ." he thought, then said, "Greengage at seven-thirty eh?"

"Right!" Hymie shook hands, sealing the bargain. It was official now - Joe's mob had grown into a force worthy of his leadership.

*

Jack Piper got from his comfortable chair and glanced at his mother. She was snoozing, head propped on hands to make it appear she was interested in the television programme. Jack smiled, shook her, and said, "Mum - go to bed. It's an awful show."

The old woman shook herself awake, trying to smile. "I'm sorry, son . . ."

"Don't be, mum - go to bed. Dad's asleep too." He motioned to his father who was curled in his end of the sofa with eyes tight shut and snores gently issuing from compressed lips.

"He's a silly old B,"Mrs. Piper said lovingly. "Can't stand these late shows, he can't."

Jack grinned. It was not quite nine-thirty and he knew their need for sleep. "Mum, I'm going to the boozer. I've got a key so why don't you and dad go to bed?"

"What about your supper when you come in, son?"

"Mum . . ." He placed an arm round her shoulder, helping her to her feet. "Forget that! I'm not a child now. I can make something to eat when I come home . . ."

"You're sure?" she asked with a true mother's feeling every son was

71

absolutely helpless.

"I'm sure, mum. The army taught me to fend for myself."

She laughed, throwing her arms around him. "Jack . . ."she sighed. "Jack . . . you're a wonderful boy!" She kissed his cheek, then eyed her husband. "Isn't he a soppy date?"

They shook the old man awake and helped him upstairs. Jack knew that the Scotch - *Teacher's* from the off-licence - had taken its toll. His father wasn't used to a treat and, especially, for six glasses neat. Jack had wondered about the amount consumed. He believed in the *Teacher's* edict: Moderation has its rewards . . . or words to that effect. He didn't knock *Teacher's* Scotch whisky. He firmly held it as a friend of mankind. Providing one always held to the code of moderation, nothing gave such a feeling of well-being and relaxation as a good old *Teacher's* did. For himself, he never drank Scotch unless the label had the distinctive name on it.

When his father was safely in bed and his mother preparing to climb in beside him, Jack slipped from the house. Walking down the street, Jack felt that familiar desire to set fire to the slum properties. In his estimation - after seeing some of the places the army had to offer in far-flung regions of the globe - this district was sadly in need of an arsonist's expertise. He couldn't stand the run-down factories, the shops with their cheap goods, the overall impression of poverty and low income buying.

He was feeling in a bitter mood as he reached the local. He didn't honestly wish to enter. It was always the same these days when he came home on leave. He felt so bloody sorry for the old men sitting around the lonely bar. It wasn't too bad for the dockers and the Ford workers. They got a bloody good screw. But the pensioners - shit! he thought savagely, they've been robbed of decency begging to a Welfare system that demands they queue in sterile, unfriendly offices and go down on bended knee to some supercilious Civil Servant who only knows the rule-book method of handling people. Men like his dad who fought for their country didn't deserve to be treated as names in a book, rubber stamps on triplicate forms. They were men, and women. Solid people. The honest backbone of Britain. They deserved much better than a socialist free-for-all and begging for supplementary benefits.

"God help us all," he said aloud as he went in.

"Wotcher, mate," a hefty labourer laughed as he entered. "Christ, you get talkin' to yourself an' they carts you orf!"

72

Jack grinned, slapping the man on the shoulder. "Sorry, chum - I was thinking about me dad."

"S'alright, me son," the other cried. "'ave a beer on me."

"Ta," Jack nodded, shoving through the normal door-jam crowd.

"Beer fer me mate, Rosy," the man shouted to the Irish barmaid.

"Make that *Teacher's* and soda . . . I'll pay the difference," Jack said hurriedly.

The Irishwoman shrugged, causing her monstrous breasts to do a jig inside her sweater. She didn't mind his eyes feasting on them. In fact, she repeated the gesture to give him a second eyeful before smiling her way to the bottles. Jack hid his amusement. It never paid to take the mickey out of an Irish barmaid. The regulars didn't like it.

"Ain't you Jack Piper . . . Charlie Piper's lad?"

Jack turned slowly. The old man facing him presented a toothless smile and an outstretched hand. He nodded, accepting the friendly shake.

"Cor, I remembers you when you was a nipper," the man said. "An' look at you now . . ." He studied Jack with an admiring gaze. As the barmaid deposited Jack's drink the old man eyed it speculatively. "Lemme buy it, son," he said without an effort to reach for his pocket.

Jack grinned. "Have one on me, mister." He handed Rosey ten bob.

"Scotch?" the quavering voice asked.

"Scotch for the gent, Rosy."

"Bless you, son. T'ain't often we gets the chance . . ." He halted, conscious of his *faux pas*.

"Forget it," Jack smiled. His drink tasted perfect and he handed a cigarette to the old man.

"Where's Charlie?"

"In bed . . . where you should be!"

The man laughed, bending to light his cigarette from Jack's butane *Ronson*. "Son," he explained, "I sleep till noon so's I can spend every night in 'ere."

"It can't be much fun . . ."

"No," the old face grew serious. "These young yobbos make it hard on the likes of me. They don't 'ave respect no more."

"Do you play darts?"

"Me eyes ain't wot they was, son . . ." and when he saw Jack's sudden disinterest he quickly added, "but I could give you fifty up?"

73

"We'll start from scratch," Jack said. "Come on . . . let's have a game."

*

For an old man, the friend of Charlie Piper certainly threw a mean dart. He wasn't kidding when he offered Jack fifty-up. Playing for beers (and Jack was glad it wasn't Scotch) cost him a few bob. He didn't win a single game and when another couple of pensioners joined in for a foursome it still cost Jack his cash. After all, he reasoned, he was the worst player on the board and he didn't expect his mistakes to come out of a paltry allowance.

Walking home, he felt the evening had had its compensations. He had renewed his faith in a dying breed - the old soldiers of London.

He didn't have a chance. They came at him from every angle. With iron bars, broken bottles, steel-toed boots and chains. They swarmed over him, knocking him to the ground, kicking and gouging and slashing with all the ferocity of their ugly minds.

He couldn't recall much of what happened. He knew he'd been hit with something hard; something solid; something brutally unyielding. And, as blood spurted to blind him, he felt the waves of them pour over him . . .

CHAPTER TWELVE

"HIS condition is extremely serious, Sergeant."

From where he stood, Sgt. Snow could see the bandages, the ugly bruises. He was used to violence and broken bodies, just as Dr. MacConaghy was accustomed to making running repairs to them.

"Have you any idea who did this?"

The sergeant shook his head angrily. "Not by name, doctor. We know it was a bunch of skinheads and that's all."

"Skinheads! My God - can't our society control even them?"

Sgt. Snow stiffened. He didn't want to listen to a tirade about the ineffectualness of the police; nor did he have the inclination to have his role in the investigation questioned.

"Sorry, Sergeant," the doctor smiled wistfully. "I'm not condemning you and the force . . ."

Snow smiled easily now. ·

"I'd just like to know where it's all going to end," MacConaghy finished.

Snow didn't reply. One didn't make an issue of problems when one wore a uniform; regulations formed a tight noose round a man's tongue and political solutions were left to those chasing votes. Stricter controls over demonstrators, over students who forgot that the public paid for their right to education, over skinheads at football matches and on special trains were definately required. Stiffer penalties would help too.

The doctor made notations on Piper's chart, swung away with distant eyes surveying the stained, grime-coated exterior of the hospital as seen from a small window. "Same outlook for a man trying to recover body and soul, eh, Sergeant?" he murmured.

Snow studied the view. He found it repulsive, sickening, and was forced to agree with the doctor this was, indeed, the worst possible sight for a recuperative patient to watch. "Even a high-rise block would look better," he said slowly.

"There's half the trouble," the doctor remarked. "Environment! Can one blame people living in that for wanting something different in their dreary lives? The youngsters see it and remember it. They think of areas where other people live - Belgrave Square, Richmond, Surrey stockbroker belts where the grass grows green and a man can look around him and see just merrye olde England's glorious land."

"You're saying then that crime is directly linked to the slums?"

"Sergeant, when it comes to crime I'm a rank amateur," the doctor grinned. "I couldn't steal a purse from a cripple." He scowled. "That was bad taste! Seriously, though, I'd like to see what a dictator could do in this country. Slums wiped out, harsh measures to curb the grab-all boys, savage sentences for injury to persons, hanging for child rapists and cop killers, the birch for young offenders like these skinheads."

"Pretty effective penalties," Snow laughed as they progressed down a dismal corridor.

"Since when does molly-coddling criminals pay dividends?"

Snow refused to be drawn. He accepted the doctor's remark; could have enlarged on it. But again regulations stopped him.

"Get yourself an iron bar, Sergeant," MacConaghy suggested as they reached reception. "The next time one of those young thugs starts making noises, break his head. I'll have the pleasure then of sewing him so it hurts." He held out a hand. "I'm supposed to cure ailments and heal people but, just once, I'd like to slice away the evil parts some of these kids have in their heads."

Snow shook hands solemnly. He understood the doctor's feelings. Patching up cracked skulls wasn't funny. No more than seeing a damned good soldier stretched out flat because some of the kids he constantly defended against totalitarianism had decided to make mince-meat of him.

"When you've had a go at the little bastards bring them here, Sergeant."

"I will, sir," Snow smiled thinly.

Both of them knew it would never happen. The British policeman was allowed the private thoughts of his fellow-countrymen only in the seclusion of his home. Outside those walls he was a machine - ordained into an order totally against counter-violence. And for that reason alone, he should have been protected against those he tried to apprehend ...

His Thursday showed a profit of £2-15-0. His body ached but that twenty five minutes with Mrs. Scalatti had softened the pain. There was something about Maltese women that made him feel the itch. At forty, the Scalatti woman was going to fat but he didn't care. He enjoyed meat on them; and, as he told Billy that evening - "I bounced on her like an aircushion!"

"The paper says that soldier is 'overing close to death," Billy remarked, ignoring Joe's daily tale of birds screwed on the job. Billy was worried. He didn't mind the occasional punch-up, the aggro with other skinheads, the sadistic beatings they gave to hippies and the hard battles against the Hell's Angels' crowd. That was part and parcel of his life - why he wore skinhead gear and fashioned tools from the workshop at Ford's. But he didn't like kicking a soldier until he was nearly dead. He had a respect for soldiers - his dad had been one as were his brothers Tom and Eddie.

"Serves 'im bleedin' right!" Joe snarled viciously. He wished to hell the bastard had kicked the bucket. He'd never forget the indignity of landing on his arse ...

"Christ, Joe - if 'e dies ..."

"So wot? They don't know we did it!"

"I don't like it," Billy voiced, hands deep in pockets, kicking a tin-can into the gutter with a savagery that belied his concern.

"Fuck the soldier," Joe snarled. "I'm thirsty. Let's 'ave a beer, mate."

The pub was almost empty. The pensioners had already taken their pitiful allotment home after a beer and chat. The dockers and their wives wouldn't be here for an other hour yet and those layabouts who drew Social Security to keep their booze intake at a steady level were probably at the dogtrack.

As Joe and Billy entered, the landlord hurriedly sent Mary in search of unwanted spirits. He didn't want his pub mentioned in *The News of the World* as the location of a scandalous affair.

"Two pints," Joe ordered, watching Mary vanish down-stairs. He still liked the idea of them all ganging her. When they got her he'd have first go . . . and last too.

"There's a dance in Ilford tonight," Billy said, equally enamoured with Mary's swinging cheeks as she disappeared from sight.

"So wot?"

"So there's birds an' Pakistanis galore . . ."

Joe tensed. Pakistanis! "Where?"

"Hymie knows . . ."

"An' where's Hymie?"

"Right here, Joe. Make that three pints, guv . . ." came a sudden voice.

Joe didn't turn. He forked out the extra, then asked, "You always creep up on a friend?"

Hymie laughed. "I was here before you came in."

"An' where's the dance?"

"Are we going to be there?"

"Bloody right!"

"Abraham - move over. Hymie is coming to fuck a little hot bitch of a Jewish bird!"

Joe grinned. He liked this Jew-boy. All the stories he had heard about Jews and their continual search for money and Gentile birds meant nothing when it came to Hymie.

"You know, Joe," Hymie declared enthusiastically, "I've been trying to get this cow to drop her knickers for months. Her old man is a friend of mine and she won't say yes in case I put a bun in her oven. Moses, how stupid can she be! I always carry five French-letters!"

He quickly opened his wallet, displaying the Durex. "Anyway the way she rabbits around with that bloody Catholic Mike Kallinan she should be pregnant!"

"The soldier is nearly dead," Billy said, still wrapped up in his private worry.

Hymie chuckled delightedly. "So what?"

"So the fuzz will be lookin' for us."

"Mate, we weren't there," Hymie said. "I've got friends in Notting Hill will swear we were attending a party there."

"Notting Hill?" Billy cried. "Christ - that's miles away."

"Exactly," Hymie smiled knowingly. "Relax, Billy - that bastard won't kick the bucket."

"I bleedin' well hope not!" Billy said seriously.

Eric Wilson often wondered what made him turn a successful gambling hall into a teenage dance hall. He knew one reason was the way the heavies had moved in and installed their croupiers and gaming machines; he remembered the day that a certain known boxer had calmly walked through the door and announced he and his mate were now partners in the club. Wilson had been unable to combat the mob and reluctantly agreed to sign papers to that effect. His choice had been simple - sign or have the club wrecked.

Until the new gaming laws had come into force he had been forced to sit back - a manager in name only - and watch the steady downfall of what had begun as an élite establishment. He had seen characters he hated become regulars; seen the standard of play vanish into a crooked table catering to an eighty percent profit for the house; seen old customers tail off until they no longer felt it wise to buck the odds.

And then, when the new laws were passed, he had been thrown on the scrap-heap of unprofitability. The boxer had moved into fresh ventures not subject to strict control, and he was left with a shambles of a club - unsupported by the locals, avoided by the criminal element, shunned by those who would drink in a friendly atmosphere.

It was at that stage he decided to interest the teenage element and started the dances. He hired local groups hoping to play enough reggae to appease the aggro boys.

But now, he operated a veritable powder-keg of teenage violence. Every night, as he opened the doors, he wondered what had been so marvellous about his original idea and why he risked neck and limb for the few pence he made each week. Damages alone cost him a fortune; even his huge Alsation refused to act as Gestapo regulator after having his beautiful hide burned by cigarettes. A dog is a dog and after being savaged by thirty or forty raging teenage lunatics the Alsation had decided that discretion was the better part of valour.

Thursday night was generally quiet. Most of the yobbos got paid on Friday. Most of the skinhead element came to gawk on Saturday. Most of the problems and the police visits were confined to Sunday when nobody else catered for a growing menace.

Seated at the bar with Bill Thompson, a reporter, Eric felt reasonably secure. A girl in a slash-fronted dress played a fruit-machine; a man with a permanent leer trying to date her sat nursing a large Scotch and offered suggestions as the female levered the machine's handle.

"You were a damned fool ever allowing the mob in," Thompson said.

Wilson recalled the fateful night when his club was invaded, taken over, and sent in a tailspin plunge to hell.

"And you're a worse fool letting these layabouts hold their tribal dances here."

Wilson shrugged. "Bill, you're so smart you tell me how I'm supposed to get my money back from the investment if I don't cater to the money crowd."

"Teenagers?"

"Yeah, teenagers. They've got the dough today."

"And what about Mr. and Mrs. wanting a night out? Don't they rate?"

"Shit!" Eric exploded vehemently. "They spend a few quid and expect Savoy service. This is Ilford, mate - not Mayfair!"

The two men sat silent, watching the girl on the fruit-machine go through the antics of a gambling maniac. She wasn't in the least bit interested in the leering spectator. She had one thought - the urge to hit the jackpot. That it was, legally, limited to pay-out didn't stop her insatiable desire for a win. It was the gamble that attracted.

"One of these days . . ." Thompson said softly.

"She's terrible," Wilson confided. "I've had it - all pull a handle and no push a coin in her slot."

A group of boys suddenly burst through the front door. From his stool, Eric Wilson surveyed their gear and moaned. "Skinheads!"

Thompson tensed. Even the girl on the fruit-machine hesitated as she sank another sixpence in the slot and held the handle with grim determination.

"Telephone the police," Thompson suggested.

"Why? They haven't done anything yet . . ."

Thompson shrugged. "Not yet."

"Bill . . ."

"Thank you and goodnight," the reporter said finishing his drink. Waving to the girl on the machine, waving to the lecherous man seated by her side, waving to Eric, his friend, he left hurriedly.

At the front door he paused, glancing into the dance hall. He could see the first signs of trouble - skinheads pushing to get the birds they desired onto the dancefloor. He felt sorry for Eric Wilson.

"Where's the Jewish bird?" Joe asked, conscious of a mounting desire to find something that somebody else wanted. From what he could see in the club, he didn't much fancy getting his trousers down.

Hymie said, "At the fruit-machine, Joe."

Let's have it off, then . . ."

Eric Wilson watched as he saw the trouble develop. He knew, instinctively, that Joe and Hymie were only interested in Ruth. And, also, he knew she was only interested in the machine.

"Hiya, doll," Hymie said in his best Brooklynese-American. He liked affecting the accent, especially around Jewish birds.

Ruth ignored him, dropping another tanner into the machine.

"Look, chick . . ."

She jacked the handle then glared at him. "Get lost, you creep!" she snarled.

"Skip the machine," he told her warningly. "We're going to dance."

She fixed him with a hot eye. "Like hell we are!"

The machine clicked through its series, and spat out five coins. Her hand reached for them, but halted as Hymie grabbed her wrist. "Baby doll, we're dancing and then . . ." he leered.

"I don't enjoy it when they've been circumcised," she said hurtfully.

"This one you will," Hymie threatened.

"I'm not circumcised," Joe said.

Ruth glanced at him. "So, wank . . ."

Joe lashed out, catching her across the face with an open palm.

"Just a bloody minute . . ." Eric yelled, coming off his stool.

Joe swung, hand streaking for his tool . . . coming out with a knife. Eric froze.

Afterwards, Eric swore nothing would have happened if the girl hadn't screamed. She pushed past Joe, darting for the door with Hymie in hot pursuit. The scene scared Joe and he lunged, ramming the knife into Eric's thigh, his face flushed, his eyes bulging.

In the club, the noise attracted attention. Like automatons, the mob erupted . . . slashing, kicking, hitting.

From his corner, Frank White watched the battle progress. He wasn't involved . . . not yet. The fix he'd had before coming here left him immune to all happenings - his was a joyous scene on its own.

A boy charged forward, knocked off-balance. His knife glinted evily, his face taut with emotion.

Frank rose swiftly - faster than normal. He zipped a gun from his shirt, fired without hesitation, seeing his victim collapse on the floor as if it was all a dream; a cinemascope technicolor extravaganza to equal that last epic he'd watched in Picadilly Circus . . .

*

Sgt. Snow studied the chart. Even he could see that the graph was down. The kid had a bullet in his chest, dangerously close to his heart. Only top-doctoring could save him and even then it was doubtful if he would live more than a few days.

"You can speak to him, Sergeant," MacConaghy said. "He's conscious."

Snow studied the pale features. "Are you sure?"

MacConaghy shrugged. "Might as well get information while you can. He'll live - or die, depending on how we perform."

Snow felt sick. He couldn't understand the doctor's callousness. "It might lower his chances," he said.

"Like hell it will!" came the sharp reply. "He's on borrowed time now. Go ahead."

*

Roy Hawkins relaxed with shoes off, feet up on a small coffee table. The programme was interesting; an interview with Jack Dash on his retirement. Roy thrilled to the man's statements - especially those connected with a hardcore reserve left behind to look after the docker's interests in Jack's absence. He enjoyed the reference to containerization. He didn't like it any more than his mates did. He could see the system vanishing as new container ports grew in prominence. Falmouth first, then maybe such places as Scotland and Northern Ireland and Wales. No self-respecting Londoner would want work going to those areas, when, by right, it should stay in London.

Roy was feeling pleased. Not only was his ideal man being allowed to prove his abilities, but the trade figures again gave Labour an edge.

He heard the urgent knocking, ignoring it until his wife said, "Answer that, Roy!"

He knew Sgt. Snow. He grinned, stood aside, and said, "Come in, Sargeant."

Snow couldn't get used to warm welcomes with their cold-cold farewells. He preferred the suspicious half-open door, the growling display of indifference when he produced a search warrant, the laughing goodbye when he found nothing.

"They've got Jack Dash on telly," Roy said eagerly, leaving the door open wide for Constable Cheeseman to follow him inside.

"Is Joe in?" Snow asked.

Roy hesitated, then closed the livingroom door. His face was tight, worried. "What 'as he done?"

"A boy was shot tonight," Snow replied. "We think Joe was the leader of the gang that caused the trouble."

Roy opened the door and shouted: Joe . . . come here!"

Sergeant Snow watched the boy saunter to meet them. *A right cocky bastard!* he thought.

"What?" Joe asked, deliberately avoiding Snow's gaze.

"Joe Hawkins," the sergeant said slowly, "I have reason to believe you took part in a shooting tonight . . ."

"That's a lie!" Joe snapped.

Snow smiled. "Perhaps you could account for your movements, son?"

"I was home all night. Arsk Dad . . ."

Roy felt guilty immediately. He stared at the floor, saw a spot the missus hadn't polished and murmured, "That's right, Sergeant."

Snow wanted to shout, "Mr. Hawkins . . . Roy . . . don't cover for him . . ."

Roy met the sergeant's gaze then. "Cover for Joe?"

Snow shrugged, told his constable, "There's nothing we can do here . . ." and marched down the short path to the pavement.

"Joe, I want the truth . . ."

Joe laughed. "You didn't take that cunt seriously, did you?"

Roy's hand flashed, knocking Joe to his bed. "I like Desmond Snow," he said.

"Then take 'im to bed!" his son screamed.

Roy smiled easily. He didn't believe in violence, nor sadism. But, tonight, he would teach Joe a late lesson. His hand lashed out again and again . . . each punch a telling blow . . . each a lesson in itself. More than once he hoped Joe's manhood would assert itself and force the boy to hit back. It never did - and the beating continued until Joe lolled around on the bed in a semi-conscious state. Only then did Roy Hawkins stop. He just hoped his wife had not heard the beating nor guessed that her son was as good as a murderer.

CHAPTER THIRTEEN

NOBODY could have called Joe's week a raving success. From the failure to see the match the previous Saturday until last night Joe had suffered more than he gave out. He didn't enjoy looking back down the days; it was just one of those best forgotten periods in his young life. Yet, he couldn't forget. Sergeant Snow especially had to be remembered. Joe did not take kindly to his father's punishment and blamed Snow for bringing trouble into an otherwise tolerable house. Until now, his antics had been overlooked but he felt positive they would no longer receive his father's indifference. Once aroused, Roy Hawkins could be an unrelenting, authoritarian foe.

All day, as he worked his fiddles, Joe schemed revenge on Snow. He wanted to have the mob batter him but he knew this was a delicate matter requiring no more than three trusted mates. Once the fuzz started asking questions Joe wanted to be absolutely certain that the weak links were already eliminated. Normally he allowed his desire for violence and publicity to overshadow any fear of legal restraint. But what he planned was not normal. One didn't do a copper every day of the week - even such a terrible week as this!

What he needed, Joe thought, was a solid alibi. If only there was somewhere the mob could attack . . .

He laughed aloud. His driver mate glanced at him suspiciously. "Wot's the joke, Joe?"

Joe waved away the query, concentrating on private laughs now. During the next four calls he didn't even try to fiddle. He wanted a perfectly clear head free from other distractions. He did the job with a speed that surprised the hell out of his mate. And, he did not speak to the flighty bird in 17 . . . an unheard of feat.

When he jumped from the lorry as it entered the coal-yard, Joe had his scheme worked out. He was whistling when he entered his own home and washed, changed and left without once speaking to his anxious mother. For all her many faults, Mrs. Hawkins worried about her son. She would not hesitate to belt him around the ears nor did she believe he was a plaster saint. Yet, she was his mother and the maternal instinct did beat faintly within her. She knew something terrible had happened and knew too that Roy had unleashed his fury on the lad. But no more. And it grieved her to be completely ignored just as she was on the verge of displaying some tenderness and understanding. It never struck her that the offer would be years too late. No more than it struck Roy at work that his thrashing had been delayed to the point of uselessness.

*

"Right, mates, 'ere's wot I want . . ."

Hymie, Billy and Don leant forward, conscious of Joe's low voice and the need for secrecy. Around them, disinterested men drank and argued about the next West Ham match. Behind the bar, Mary watched Billy - hoping for an opportunity to catch his eye and make arrangements for another meeting.

"Hymie - you get your lot an' 'ave 'em at Ilford station by eight o'clock."

"Right, Joe."

"Billy - chat up Mary. Tell 'er you'll meet 'er tonight when they close 'ere."

Billy grinned. "No bovver there, Joe." He began to rise.

"Sit down, you stupid bastard," Joe growled. As Billy sank into his chair with a frown, Joe explained, "We've got to 'ave everything worked out first."

"Wot about me?" Don asked rebelliously.

"You, mate, can find all the lads you can. 'Ave 'em at Ilford same time as Hymie."

Joe sipped his pint, settled back with the air of a general about to outline a highly dangerous mission behind enemy lines. Planning confidence showed on his face when he spoke again.

"Now 'ere's wot we do . . ."

Hymie listened avidly, feeling excitement course through him as Joe continued to elaborate. He liked the step-by-step daring of the plot; the underlying sensation of crowding in a week's bovver into one night. Tomorrow's Upton Park lark would seem tame after this, he thought fleetingly.

Billy did not have Hymie's imagination. He enjoyed some aspects of Joe's grand plan and especially where they would finish the night having a real old bang at Mary. But he did not like the most important part. He felt scared - and refused to voice his fear. His position as Joe's best mate was at stake and all the doubts in the world would not jeopardize that.

Don was neither excited nor frightened. He looked on the scheme as just another aggro - one with more risks attached but still an aggro. He nodded as each step was unfolded and when Joe ended his instructions he got to his feet, drank the remaining dregs of his beer and announced: "I'll round up the lads now."

From his chair, Joe watched Billy approach Mary, saw the woman's eyes fasten on the youth and smiled as she nodded a furtive agreement.

"That's that," Joe remarked. "Get lost, Hymie."

The Jewish boy slapped his thigh. "Mate, it'll be a fantastic aggro."

*

Arthur Mason wished he had refused the offer of help. At the time, it had seemed a wise course to count on a few dozen dedicated fighters but not now in light of recent developments. What should have been a refuge for homeless students was, in reality, an armed camp controlled by uncouth, sex-crazy Hell's Angels. And, what hurt most was the sad fact that squatters had no rights inside the building they had commandeered.

"Can't we get them out?" Tony Maxwell asked.

The bearded student shook his head as the frustration became an overpowering urge to smash things. "How the hell can we?" He flung his few belongings across the dirty floor. "Once they discovered

85

the pot they took over."

From downstairs the sound of an orgy filled their ears. Arthur knew exactly what was happening; he didn't require a guide book around this place. They would be naked or partially dressed and the toughs would be having their fun before departing for yet another night. The bitches! he thought angrily. "Cheap tramps! Doesn't it ever strike them as degrading to have those bastards crawl all over them?"

Toni shrugged. She was a pretty girl, an intelligent girl. At twenty-four she considered herself the den mother of the house; a position she had abruptly surrendered when the other girls started acting stupid. "Is there a difference between men when all one wants is intercourse?" she countered. She could remember her own experiences with pot. She had not cared how she was used, nor by whom, nor how often providing the pleasures were fast and furious and the activity continued until her senses could stand no more. She didn't blame the girls for begging the Hell's Angels boys to make love to them; in fact, she considered all their unwanted visitors as strapping, virile men capable of sustaining sexual delight far beyond the capabilities of the male students. The outsiders didn't have the intelligent inventiveness of the more sophisticated students but how did one compare positional gratification when one was seething in convulsive passion!

"Oh, shit!" Mason snarled, digging into his jeans. "I'm not going to worry about them!" He drew a thin cigarette from his pocket, looked at Toni. "Want to?"

She nodded eagerly. "If you think it's safe . . ."

"There are sixteen girls down there - almost two for each of the others. Even they aren't supermen. No, it's safe enough!" He lit the joint, drew deep of its relaxing qualities.

"I don't want this bra torn," Toni said with a grin, remembering the last session and how impatient Arthur had been to fondle her breasts. She reached under, behind her sloppy sweater and unhooked the brassiere.

Toni accepted the joint and smoked it reflectively. As far back as she could recall she had delved in the mysteries of the occult. It was this addiction that had opened doors for other mysteries - sex and revolutionary movements and, then, pot. She wished, at times, she could slam the door just as that man had closed out interference a few seconds ago. Since becoming more involved with her demonstrator friends, she had not been given the opportunity to think things out for herself. She was caught up in a world of anti-everythings in the going-nowhere merry-go-round of pseudo-politics and, worse, the ecstatic mayhem that was surely destroying her body. Knowing this did not limit her writhing attendance on the physical side of "intellectual" companionship. Sex was, for her, an outlet; a means to prove she was above society and the dogma of the Church. It was a justifiable excuse for parading and defying authority; for committing herself completely to ideals which had already ruined her family link.

Inarticulate mouthings seeped through the wall, followed by frenetic bangings.

"Man, I hate those crummy bastards!"

She forced herself to return to the room, the lonely emptiness of sleeping bags and scattered clothing and the scrawled notations some of their companions had considered as decoration . . .

SEX - NOT GOD!

DOWN WITH AMERICAN PIGS!

LOVE THY NEIGHBOUR'S WIFE!

CASTR(O)ATE IMPERIALIST SWINE!

"What did you say, Arthur?"

He turned to her, leaning against her pliable softness.

His beard tickled, rubbing on her face, his tongue probing hotly into her willing mouth. His hand pushed aside the brassiere and cupped her breasts.

Over his shoulder, as he pressed her back down on the hard floorboards, she saw the scribbled red letters accusing her . . .

IT'S ONLY GOOD IF IT'S HARD!

She reached for him, hoping it would be good . . .

Constable Greenwood consulted his watch. Another fifty minutes and he'd be off-duty. He was sorry for the squatters but he didn't consider it a policeman's lot to mount guard over those breaking the law. Frankly, in his opinion, the force would be better off letting all the warring factions fight it out and then swoop on the weakened remains. His wife had a more profound suggestion . . . "Give them guns and maybe we can all sleep in our beds after they wipe one another out" was her idea.

As he walked back and forth, Greenwood studied the nice houses

87

along York Road. He had lived in Ilford all his life and this area - outside of the Cranbrook Road where the properties were élite - had seemed to him the perfect area for retirement. SInce the war, though, there had been a steady movement away from private ownership.

The road had changed drastically of late. What had been residential and tranquil was becoming a hive of transient parasites swarming in, moving out, doing nothing for the community except create problems galore for the authorities. He did not blame landlords for making a profit where they could; he did blame them for excessive rents, and an uncritical examination of those they accepted as tenants. A little more time spent asking questions, checking references and some thought to the district as an integral whole could save the police hours of wasted manpower chasing those who skipped out with rented television sets, unpaid bills and stolen furnishings.

From outside, he could see people moving back and forth in the house. *Damned shame!* he thought. *I can imagine how they'll leave it . . .*

His heart hammered. Coming down the road - like a small army knowing it has superior firepower and unafraid of the opposing force - a bunch of skinheads leaped and pranced as they studied the houses.

This is what the sergeant warned us about! were Greenwood's first thoughts. Then . . . *Christ, I can't be expected to make this lot behave!*

He moved to block the entrance, face set tight, hand hovering over his truncheon. He would have to use it. There was no mistaking the mood of the invaders - nor the target.

Joe wanted to do a war-dance when he saw the lone constable stationed outside the squatters' abode. He had reckoned on at least four fuzz guarding the hippies. This would be a walk-over!

"Never mind the fuzz," he yelled to his minions. "Charge!"

Swarming as wasps goaded into anger, the skinhead brigade surged forward, brushing aside Greenwood's lonely resistance. In an instant, weight of numbers battered down the front door, smashed windows, and raced round to the back in an effort to prevent the enemy from retreating.

Joe was in the vanguard as the skinheads ploughed aside the lightweight barricades the squatters had erected; still heading his men when they entered a reception room.

"Christ . . ." A huge, hulking brute wearing a leather jacket emblazoned with the Hell's Angel motif leapt to his feet, confronting Joe.

For the first time, Joe felt his intelligence had been faulty. Nobody had warned him to expect trouble from Hell's Angels. He knew, of course, that 144 Piccadilly had been swarming with the skinhead foes but this wasn't Piccadilly; nor even a place a thinking Angel would expect a skinhead attack. What had gone wrong?

Joe lashed out instinctively. His tool caught the Angel across the face - slicing through to the bone. As blood spurted, Joe kicked - finding the groin with a devastating boot. The Angel slumped to the floor, battered into unconsciousness by angry skinheads.

From a corner, the girl watched the mayhem without seeming to care. Her nudity attracted one of Joe's mob and before she could realise her partner had changed, she was thrashing under a new lover.

Joe was distantly aware of the rape; very conscious of the Hell's Angels coming at them from every part of the house. He did not know how many of them were inside; he only cared about the rest of his plan.

"Find Hymie and let's get out of 'ere!" he snarled at Don as they battled back to the front door.

For minutes, neither could move - they were trapped by the mob trying to enter the house and by the Angels attacking with their chains and lead pipes. Even the students had joined their protectors and were driving the mob back . . . back . . . always back.

Constable Greenwood had a broken left arm. The agony of it sent blinding flashes across his eyes yet he mustered his strength to reach for his walkie-talkie. Another thirty-five minutes remained before his relief showed. Too long! They'd be killing one another in there if the battle lasted just five more minutes. He had to summon help - had to!

*

Sgt. Snow came from the hospital feeling like hell. He had seldom seen such seething pools of accusation as he had when he gazed into Piper's eyes. The soldier would be fine - after a month's treatment. That helped give Snow hope but he would not easily forget how Piper

89

had silently blamed him, and the Force, for his injuries.

From what Piper had said, Snow knew Joe Hawkins was mixed up in the brutal beating. But could he prove it? He wanted to, very much!

Walking home, Snow reviewed the situation. Joe had tried to cheat Piper's father and the soldier had shamed the lad by knocking him down. That alone justified revenge in Joe's language. Then, the attack. It was all too pat for mere coincidence. It had to be Joe. Maybe if . . .

At the next corner he changed direction. He entered the local police station just as the news broke - a skinhead assault on Ilford squatters had resulted in a constable being injured and in several combatants going to hospital. One of the skinheads - a lad of fifteen - was in critical condition. He had been stabbed in the stomach. And, he lived in East Ham . . .

Sgt. Snow chewed his lower lip. Could this be the break he wanted to crack Joe Hawkins? he wondered. If the skinhead came from this area and Joe was a leader of the mob then perhaps . . .

"Cobb . . . get me a car. I'm going to interview that kid . . . " he roared. Quickly, he arranged to co-operate with the Ilford station. He couldn't just rush in when it was outside his jurisdiction. He had to have permission and, considering the circumstances, this was quickly forthcoming. In less than fifteen minutes Sgt. Snow was being driven to Ilford district hospital . . .

CHAPTER FOURTEEN

"That stupid bastard Hymie . . . " Joe thought as Don, Billy and he waited in the shadows outside the hospital. All his carefully prepared plans down the drain of Hymie's rotten luck.

"Look, Joe!"

Joe followed Don's finger. He tensed. Even at this distance he could see the sergeant step from the police car and enter the lighted area of the hospital casualty department's door.

"Is he . . . ?" Don started to ask.

"That, mate," Joe said harshly, forgetting that Don's concern was for their companion, "is the bastard I want done!"

Billy shivered. "Not tonight, Joe. Christ - Hymie's . . ."

"Hymie's a fuckin' Jew an' can take care of 'imself." Joe edged an inch closer to the huge gates guarding the hospital precincts. "'Ey,'is car's leavin' . . ." He wanted to shout so great was the joy inside him then.

"Ah, Joe - it's too dangerous," Don complained.

Joe swung on his mates. "It wasn't dangerous before Hymie got 'is, was it?"

"No - but . . ." Don spluttered into silence.

Billy wanted to run. Something was seriously wrong with Joe's mind if he imagined the three of them could take on a copper. Those bastards were *trained* to fight dirty!

"'owabout you, Billy mate?"

Billy bit his tongue and said nothing. His face showed the extent of his fear but he steadfastly refused to go against Joe.

"Right, it's settled. When 'e leaves we do 'im!"

*

From his vantage point across the busy street, David Sansome watched the furtive prowlings of the three boys. Half inclined to telephone the police he forced himself to wait. He did not like being a nuisance, nor did he truthfully know why he felt they were acting suspiciously. He had heard the news bulletin and could understand that even skinheads and hippies must feel a certain sympathy for a wounded comrade. He told himself it was his vivid imagination that made the shadows flitting back and forth near the hospital seem so wrong.

Just in case he was failing in his duty to notify the authorities, though, he kept his precious camera by his side. If anything did happen he would have a visual recording of the events.

Considering that he only worked as a maintenance man with Ford's he had an expensive array of photographic equipment in the house. He was, plainly, a camera-bug. Every penny he could afford went into new darkroom materials and his successes were many in the amateur field. It had always been his ambition to be a Press photographer although necessity had long ago relegated him to exhibition work and the occasional "London's Day" type of picture in a newspaper.

The camera by his side had cost him £350; the telephoto lens another £125. He was proud of camera and lens and, especially, his latest venture into the field of infra-red photography. Using this equipment, with a highly sensitive film loaded, he could practically guarantee results.

And, now, watching the boys across the street, he was sure he could snap them doing whatever it was he feared they may do . . .

Sgt. Snow was dissatisfied with his results of his hospital visit. Hymie was in bad shape; certainly too weak to talk to anyone. The doctors had expressed concern at the amount of blood the boy had lost and they rated his chances of recovery at a low ten percent. According to one doctor, Hymie had been stabbed several times with a bayonet.

As he approached the hospital gates, Snow was vaguely aware of the three youths coming towards him. He didn't associate them with danger; why should he? - youths came to visit sick people like any other human being!

It wasn't until his arms were suddenly seized and twisted behind his back that he realised something was terribly wrong - and then it was too late. Far too late . . .

He felt the savage kick catch his jaw, and sagged.

He felt a second boot crash against his temple and the night became inky-black, enveloping him in swirling mists of pain and horror . . .

CHAPTER FIFTEEN

JOE HAWKINS sounded cheerful at breakfast. His Friday had more than compensated for all the disasters of the week. He had his revenge and nobody would ever be able to point the finger of guilt at him. The vision of Sgt Snow returned, as it had all night, to please him. Looking at his mother's idea of bacon and eggs made him think anew of Snow - bleeding and battered, insensible and unable to identify his attackers. They had been careful; so bleedin' cautious.

Roy Hawkins entered the kitchen, face unshaved, hair uncombed. Rubbing sleep from his eyes he studied Joe's Cheshire face, and asked gruffly, "Wot's up with you?"

Joe stuffed bacon in his mouth, washed it down with insipid tea and got to his feet. "There's a pop concert in Hyde Park today."

"Wot about the football match?"

"Stuff that!" Joe replied lightly. Nothing could get him down today. Just nothing!

"You young 'uns." Roy shook his head sadly as if the world would end when a supporter would miss a West Ham game for any bloody concert. He swung to his wife. "The trouble is 'e thinks there won't be any bovver is wot 'e thinks!"

Joe shrugged and opened the door. "Jesus, dad - grow up! It's the first free concert of the year . . . I ain't goin' to miss that!"

As his son vanished, Roy stared at the unpalatable mess on his breakfast plate and shoved it aside. "I'm not hungry, dear," he offered as an excuse, wondering if Barney would have a decent meal at the corner caff. After years of his wife cooking Roy had reached a compromise stage - he feigned a weak stomach and ate out whenever possible.

In his room, Joe dressed with all the ritual of a soldier going on parade for a visiting brass. He couldn't tell the mob what a big man he was, not yet. Not until after the fuzz dropped their enquiries into Snow's beating. But he still felt tops. *It wasn't every skinhead done a sergeant, was it?* he asked his reflection in the mirror.

*

Outside the local, Billy darted from an alley and shoved the *Daily Express* at Joe. "Look at that!" he screamed, scared shitless as his trembling hands held the paper open.

Joe looked and felt instantly sick.

The picture carried the credit: *by David Sansome*. It showed Joe, Don and Billy in dramatic action as they attacked a beaten police sergeant.

"Christ, Joe - we've had it!" Billy wailed.

Joe couldn't hear Billy. He was struggling with the write-up:

LAST SECONDS IN BRUTAL ATTACK ON POLICEMAN
Hardly had the camera shutter clicked than Sgt. Desmond Snow fell

to the ground, yet another victim of skinhead thuggery.

Sgt. Snow was visiting a wounded victim of another skinhead encounter when he was suddenly seized and beaten into unconsciousness, a helpless victim of senseless viciousness. The frozen horror of this picture captures once again the problem of our times - The Youth Revolution. If we are to expect our policemen to give us protection we demand then surely it is our duty to stamp out this terrible evil that is threatening all of us. No father, or mother, can feel proud of her son when viewed in the light of this attack.

But it is up to you - the parents - to assist the police in their efforts to put a name to the vicious thugs who perpetrated such an obscene crime . . .

Where the hell had the photographer been and why hadn't they noticed the flash-gun? Joe thought immediately. Nobody could mistake his face. Nobody! He was a marked man; a criminal on the run now.

"Joe . . . Joe, for God's sake say something!" Billy wailed.

Joe started to push open the pub door. "Let's go to Marble Arch."

"No, Joe - I ain't goin', "Billy said.

"Why not?"

"Joe, they'll clobber us for this!"

"So?"

"So, I'm not going near Hyde Park tooled, is wot."

"Ditch it . . . I won't."

"Joe, for God's sake, can't you unnerstand - I'm scared! That was a copper we done . . ."

"An' so?"

"An' so I'm not goin' with you!" Billy retreated two yards, hands ready to fend off any blow.

"You're yellow, "Joe shouted.

"Bleedin' right I am, "his mate confirmed. "Coppers don't like their sort bein' done. If they catch us, Joe . . ."

"They remember the rule-book wot says they can't hit a prisoner."

"Shit! Joe . . ."

"Where's Don?" Joe asked suspiciously, feeling lonely.

"'E's gone to the match . . ."

"An' the others?" Now Joe felt really alone.

"They backed out. 'onest mate, I want to come with you but . . ."

Billy did a fine impression of a dummy being jerked off-stage. "I'm scared!"

"Wot a bloody mob," Joe snarled. "One picture in a fuckin' newspaper an' they turn yellow! To hell with you . . . I'm goin' to Hyde Park . . ." He swung away and stalked off.

*

On the Underground, Joe felt the loneliness of the Amazonian explorer; the feeling of departed civilisation; the glare of publicity that robs criminals of friends, neighbours, the sheltering crowds. At least, he reasoned, Hyde Park would shelter him from the spotlight. There would be so much going on nobody would want to concentrate on a single individual. After the show he would have a beer, a nosh, a chance to consider his future plans. He never considered the possibility of capture; the "he's not with us" ritual most of his type affected when confronted by law and order. He forgot the running scared streak down the back of every young thug - and old, for that matter - and the self-protective desire of underworld characters to save their own skins regardless. The code of honour that supposedly existed in criminal circles and was, again supposedly, relevant to skinheads, hippies, revolutionaries and Hell's Angels did not enter into his thinking. He placed his faith in his personal ability to avoid disaster; to apply the native fox-like cunning to any given situation.

By the time he reached Mile End the train was packed solid with teenagers going to the concert. He felt safer. His was a face that did not conflict with those around him. He had distinguishing characteristics and so did the others. Plus, of course, the fact that countless thousands would attend this special show. It wasn't every day that youth demanded its tribute to the revolution against society's strict codes on pot and LSD and free love. This was *the* protest to crush all opposed to youth's right to call the tune.

He was tooled but not in anticipation of bovver from hippies, Hell's Angels or any other youth cult. He was tooled because, naturally, this was a Saturday. No real skinhead ever ventured forth on a Saturday without his trusty weapon. None!

Today meant an extra few shillings for Constable Webster. He had no choice in whether or not he would give up a duty free Saturday.

If he had his way, Webster would have eliminated concerts such as the one taking place. He did not hold with policemen being forced to offer protective services to those ferociously dedicated to the total destruction of all that the policeman was forced to uphold. He did not take kindly to being shoved, pushed, called obscene names whilst smilingly upholding the peace of Her Majesty's lands.

"Move along, son," Webster said kindly.

"Fuck you, fuzz," came the short sharp reply.

Webster controlled his impulse to hit the young bastard. Instead, he laid a hand on the person's back and pushed. Gently, but firmly.

"'e's molestin' me," came the immediate retort as a scowling, antagonistic face was presented for the constable's provocation.

"I said - move along," the constable said again, minus the friendly tone.

The yobbo laughed, "'e's bein' nasty!"

A group of long-haired clipped-hair teenagers surrounded P.C. Webster. For a few ugly seconds he thought - *Lord, what have I done to deserve this?* - then, as a soulless sound burst from the microphones on-stage, he felt the mob melt away, surging towards their idols.

Like bad pennies rolling down a gutter, the mob rolled in a solid wave. Crowding, surging, flowing into an ever-packed mass. Closer, tighter, jammed into a mass that could not contain them . . .

Webster struggled to free himself of the crush - fighting to retain his official position on the *outside* of the gathering.

And then . . .

His jawline tightened, his hands itching to grab the young thug.

Joe felt the hand on his shoulder and figured it as another yobbo trying to get ahead of him. He wanted to be as near the platform as possible, wanting to hear the undistorted sound as it bathed him in ecstasy.

"Lemme go," he screamed above the raucous noise.

"Don't struggle, son . . . you're coming with me . . ."

The deep male voice stung Joe to action. He tried to whip his latest tool from its hiding place under his shirt . . . couldn't as the crowd grew tighter, less controlled. He glanced around, saw the helmet, the blue uniform.

"We wish to ask you certain questions, son . . ." the voice said in his ear.

Joe kicked . . . felt his boot strike a hapless shin, found himself in

In the lonely cell Joe felt the world was indeed a wonderful place. He had been questioned - without brutality. He had been identified by the photographer - although how he could see when he had been forced to use infra-red was a little beyond belief.

But it didn't matter, according to Joe's thinking processes. It didn't matter a bleedin' bit.

Once he paid his fine - which Social Security would fork over anyway once he pleaded "compassionate circumstances" - he would be free; free to continue as he always had; free to rule with an iron fist over *his* mob. None of them would dare question orders now. Not after he had made the big time by having his picture in the papers and being sentenced.

Oh, yes - Joe Hawkins had it made. He could go on to better things after this. He had been scared about how the fuzz would treat him but they'd been very correct - tea and sandwiches; questions without kicking him around; even a reporter allowed to get his viewpoint of the incident.

Somehow, he didn't mind missing the concert. Not when he was being given the full treatment. He didn't understand that a prisoner was innocent until proven guilty, of course. In Joe's book every one was guilty of crimes against him until he kicked the shit out of them and forced them to assume positions of subservience. That was the difference between society and Joe Hawkins - and he probably never knew it existed. His was a senseless world of violence for the sake of violence; his ideal devised by those wishing the end of civilised behaviour patterns; his the starstruck era of pop and pot and the belief that might is right even if might has to play games and call itself right.

From today, Joe Hawkins was made. His name would rank with those others in the crime underworld. He had done a police sergeant and he would face the consequences - a fine, a warning, a beration and the all-essential publicity.

Oh, the stupid bastards - didn't they ever learn! Didn't they know that his crime being publicized would make him a king of skinheads!

THE END

SUEDEHEAD

By Richard Allen

AUTHOR'S NOTE

IN the interests of sanity let no one be under the mistaken impression that the writer sympathises with anti-social behaviour, cultism or violence for the sake of violence. That Joe Hawkins - "hero" of *Skinhead* - should have aroused a national following and made the paperback a best seller is, indeed, gratifying to an author.

Any author worth his salt takes a fictional character and skilfully blends him into factual situations so that the reader is almost convinced the hero lives and what he is doing is in keeping with how it is logically assumed he would act under a given set of circumstances. *Skinhead* looked at the cult, took note of everything the average skinhead did in the course of his anti-social duties and faithfully represented Joe Hawkins as the epitome of society's menace. At no time did I attempt to glorify Joe Hawkins.

Suedehead, like *Skinhead*, is an attempt to show a specific section of the community in action. Both are maladies of our permissive society which has, rightly or wrongly, encouraged the growth of off-beat cults within a framework peopled by law-abiding, decent, sometimes dull citizens. Youth has always had its fling but never more blatantly, more unconcerned with adverse publicity than today. In fact, it is my opinion that leniency in courtrooms catering to fads by mercenary-minded rag-trade merchants, a soft-peddling attitude by politicians who look for teenage votes to save their seats and an overwhelming pandering by the news media are the real contributing factors of this instantaneous explosion which now places the nation as a whole in jeopardy. Britain cannot survive long in a climate of anarchy. Every man, woman and child must draw strength from a democratic, wholesome ideal - and those who attend to unfruitful, undemocratic, irrational pursuits only do so at the risk of losing those precious freedoms which this country has valued for countless centuries.

If this portrayal of a menace is used as an excuse to uphold deviousness then I surrender to the wiles of culpability. And having said that, I trust that the readers have enjoyed the story and will find some sane outlet for their various energies other than those Joe Hawkins enjoys.

Richard Allen,
Gloucestershire, 1972.

CHAPTER ONE

AS he stood in the dock, Joe Hawkins considered his situation with utter detachment. Legal procedures meant nothing to him. He had done a police sergeant and now he faced the consequences of that action. What *they* - those stupid bastards going through the motions of justice - did not know was how all this was making him an even greater figure in the eyes of his pals.

Joe listened to snatches of the case against him. He was not troubled about the outcome. It was always the same - a fine, a warning, publicity. He returned the magistrate's glare, he smiled cockily at the coppers in court. He refused to assume an innocent attitude. Nobody was going to say that Joe Hawkins ever knuckled down to authority. He was a law unto himself.

Suddenly, Joe felt tension mounting inside him. The message reached his shocked brain. This wasn't any common or garden fine. Not the way that old buzzard was talking. This wasn't a warning to behave like other decent citizens. This was the big walk - bird . . .

". . . *eighteen months* . . ."

Joe was stunned.

"*You may step down. Next case* . . ."

Stumbling from the box, Joe felt strong hands grab his arms. Realisation smashed into him like red-hot daggers probing for a vital spot. Eighteen days was a lifetime but months sounded like the total end of all his dreams. The gang would forget him in a few weeks. When he came out there would be nothing for him to command. Some rotten bastard would have taken control and he - the famous Joe Hawkins - would be a skinhead without mates.

"He can't . . ." Joe struggled. "He bloody can't do this!"

"That's where you're wrong," a harsh-voiced policeman said. "You've got off light. If I had my way . . ."

"Nobody arsked for your opinion," Joe snarled, striving desperately to keep his cool.

The policeman grinned and motioned for the others to remove this *object* from the courtroom. He had no sympathies for those who deliberately attacked coppers. The magistrate had surprised them all with his treatment of Joe and, the bobby thought, *about time too*. Practically every member of the force believed that stiffer sentences would eliminate eighty percent of the injuries they sustained doing their duty.

Joe's co-ordination vanished as his legs turned into elastic. He felt weak, ready to scream. Half-dragged, half-staggering, he made it downstairs into the cells. According to one of the fuzz he had a short wait - and then . . .

"Clobbered you, eh?" a thin-faced youth smirked as he picked at a sore on his ear. "I got three years."

Joe shuddered. "I expected a fine."

"That's the way it goes, mate. It all depends on how the beak's missus treated him the night before!"

"What did you do?" Joe asked unemotionally.

"Knifed my girl," came the easy reply. "The little bitch held out on me." Blood trickled down the ear and a dirty handkerchief was hurriedly used to stem the flow. "We had an agreement how much she would charge, then I discovered she was upping the anti and keeping the change." Narrowed eyes surveyed Joe's face. "You ever tried pimping?"

Joe's head shook a fast negative.

"Man, it's the life. They do all the work and you collect."

Something about the youth frightened Joe. Not a physical fear but a deeper menace which went against his grain. Not many things bothered Joe but pimps were scum and their treatment of girls they professed to care for left him cold.

"I once had a black chick . . ." The youth kept talking, evidently proud of his record. He was about Joe's age yet there was a worldly wisdom in those narrowed eyes which went with his thin, hungry, cunning face. Every so often he examined his blood soaked handkerchief and nodded.

Joe lost interest after the first few sentences. He had problems of his own and how this other prisoner had spent his freedom did not matter. Nothing mattered except those eighteen months inside. Could he take it? Could he emerge feeling like Joe Hawkins of old? Or would prison have a sapping effect on him? He knew several old lags near his home and hated to think he would ever look like them.

" . . . and you can have her address if you like."

Joe shook his mind awake. The youth had not noticed his preoccupation.

"Man, she's a terrific worker. Six, seven marks a night. That's money, man."

"I'll give it some thought," Joe said.

"Do that, mate. You'll be out long before me. I'm not going to get remission."

"Why not?"

The youth laughed. "I've done porridge before. I'm not worried about it. I like breaking every rule in their book."

The hell with that! I'm going to get full remission, Joe thought.

"Stick with me," the youth said softly, eyes wider and shimmering now. "I'll show you the ropes . . ."

*

Standing on the street with the Scrubs a gigantic horror behind him, Joe Hawkins took a gulp of air down into his starved lungs. It wasn't that this air tasted fresher, or had less pollution in it than the air breathed back there in Wormwood. It was just that here, on the outside looking in, there was a freedom quality he had been denied for far too long.

"You goin' my way Joe?" Nobby Clarke asked as he hefted his bundle under one ancient arm.

"Naw,"Joe replied thankfully. He did not want to be seen anywhere near the old lag. It had been great finding somebody he knew by sight in prison but once outside he was determined to avoid all ex-cons like a plague.

"Lemme give you a tip, Joe," Nobby said brightly. "Never get nicked for anything small. Next time make sure they gets you for a big job!" The old man shuffled a few feet, turned and grinned. "Go see that woman I mentioned. She'll help a kid like you!" He winked and hurried off.

Alone now, Joe thought back to the first day of his bird. That had been bad but not nearly anything like when he discovered he was a special target of every queer in the Scrubs. God how he loathed those bastards! He had always figured homosexuals to be small, dancing men with carefully manicured hands, lisps and a walk that signposted their aversion to women. He had found that they did not belong to any such tight limitation. Some of the ones who had tried to lure him into their cells were big, strong, typical heavy types. One especially had been sent up for murder - a vicious ex-boxer with a protection racket backing his penchant for desirable young men.

The queers had been bad but they had not been the worst of his problems. Even now, after all that porridge, he could not get used to regimentation and loss of identity. The soul destroying routine had shattered his self-confidence until Mr. Thompson had seen fit to take Joe under his wing. In a sense, Joe felt a debt of gratitude to Thompson. As a screw he was a pretty good egg. But he was a screw! And although he had gained permission for Joe to take a course in office procedure, and got him a job in the prison administration section, there was that barrier - prisoner and screw!

Some of the old lags had been kind, tolerant of youthful mistakes, eager to pass along knowledge gained from years spent doing prison sentences. Nobby had been most helpful. Thanks to him Joe had managed to evade the dirtiest jobs and make sure his lapses weren't reported.

"Never again, " Joe whispered to himself.

Far ahead, Nobby shuffled along - a lonely, beaten old man with but one thought gnawing on his saturated mind; back to Plaistow and the boozer. Joe didn't give Nobby more than a few weeks freedom. The man was beyond rehabilitation. He'd blow his bankroll, make a couple of visits to Social Security and then, when the boom was lowered, he'd do a sloppy job and get nicked again.

Now take me, Joe thought. *I'm young. I'm smart. I'm not going to commit a crime like Nobby. I've got an address and I can make out okay until I get a job. There'll be birds and booze, but not another visit to the Scrubs!*

Taking his time, Joe walked in Nobby's wake. He knew exactly where he was going. The magazine article had shown him the root. Skinheads were dead, man. Phased out. Home had never appealed. All his life he had dreamed about a plush flat somewhere in the West End. So now he would make the leap from poverty street into the affluent society. In one gigantic jump. The advice poured into his ears by all those old lags had taken root. If he was to succeed he had to plead, and beg, and make like a downtrodden slum-dweller whose environment had been the root cause of his imprisonment.

They must be stupid, he laughed silently as he began to whistle.

CHAPTER TWO

BERNICE HALE had known poverty as a child and this made her extremely susceptible to the pleas of those whose homes she could associate with her own background. When Joe Hawkins entered her pathetically small office she felt an immediate "relationship".

"Mrs. Hale?"

"Sit down, Joe. Relax. I'm here to help you - not scare the hell out of you!" She smiled and waved to a chair.

Joe sensed the desire to get on friendly terms. It was just as Nobby had said it would be. He sank into the chair and returned the woman's smile. After serving his porridge he needed to look at an attractive woman and think about some of the girls he had known before that old bastard of a magistrate handed him time.

"You've been a model prisoner," she said with blue eyes scanning the dossier.

He nodded, judging her to be around fifty. She was slender enough to be a movie queen and her vital statistics left nothing to be desired.

"I've a son your age," she said, fixing him with an expression that vaporised all his notions of an easy bit. "Being in prison sometimes makes a *man* . . ." and she stressed the man, "yearn for female company. I'd advise against hasty decisions, Joe. You're not in any position to spread kings yet."

"Nobby Clarke sent me to see you . . ."

"I have a dozen Nobby Clarkes on my books, Joe." She got to her feet and breathed in deeply. Her breasts thrust against a woollen acket. Her eyes caught his, and air whooshed from her lungs. "That was silly wasn't it?"

He continued to stare.

"Joe - get those ideas out of your mind." She came around her desk, hitched her skirt and sat half on, half off the edge of the desk. Her stockinged legs enticed, provoked, sounded clarion calls in his frustrated mind. "I'm being a tease, I know. But then . . ." and she laughed huskily, "I always am."

He could not make head nor tail of her tactics. She seemed to be begging for him to make a move. Yet, was she? He did not dare risk it. He sat hard on his chair, perspiration beginning to roll down from his armpits.

"You pass!" she said briskly and extended a slender hand. "If you had made one move to assault me that would have been the end!" She shook his hand, and hurried back behind the desk. "I've a thing about sex maniacs. I don't like them!"

"I only came here to ask for help, Mrs. Hale."

"I take it that means money?"

Joe nodded. He was confused by her tactics.

"For a room?"

"Yes. I don't want to live at home."

"Why not?"

He shrugged. "Reasons . . ."

"Name a few!"

"I've been inside. I don't want to go back. My parents would crucify me."

"I see . . ." She consulted her file. "You were a vicious monster, Joe. Skinheads are, unfortunately, a product of our ultra-permissive society. Have you changed enough for me to trust you?"

"I can go to Social Security," Joe growled, getting to his feet. So much for Nobby's bright idea!

"Sit down!"

Joe felt compelled to obey. There was hidden strength in this woman.

"We don't sponsor habitual criminals," Mrs. Hale told him. "Our aim is to give the first offender an opportunity to establish a working relationship with his fellow men. We have a strict rule - help once, no more."

"I'm not going back," Joe replied sourly.

"I should hope not. How much money do you have?"

He emptied his pockets, placing the meagre amount on her desk. Glancing at the pathetic result of his prison pay-out, she smiled scathingly. "Not much for what you've suffered, eh?"

"They haven't got unions in prison yet," he answered with a sneer.

"That's quite enough cheek," she snapped. Counting his cash she said; "That's grocery money, Joe. I have an arrangement with a landlady in Islington. She'll provide a room and breakfast. It's not a palace but you'll have a front door key and freedom to come and go as you please."

"Thanks!" He sounded bitter. Nobby had given him such glowing accounts of this outfit's cash reserves and how they treated their clients generously.

"Your attitude leaves much to be desired. I suppose your old lag friend spun you a yarn about how soft we were . . ." Her gorgeous breasts flattened on the desk as she leant forward. "Joe, pay attention to me."

His eyes fastened on her breasts. His pulse quickened. She was a magnificent woman and frustration seethed like super-charged electrons inside him. "I am," he said truthfully.

She ignored the obvious. "I'm going to tell you a story, Joe," she said evenly. "My son lives in Canada. He served five years in Kingston there and got a loan from this society. With it he met a girl, got married and found a job. Today, thank God, he's an honest citizen and owns his home, a business and has two beautiful children. That's why I work here, Joe. If my boy could do it - so can you."

Joe sat motionless. *Why did they have to pour on the soft soap*, he asked himself. He didn't believe her. This was a standard approach to someone fresh out of stir.

"You've got doubts?"

He shrugged. "That's not for me to say."

She opened her desk drawer and pushed three scraps of paper across to him. It took less than five seconds for his eyes to confirm the truth of her tale. The newspaper clipping had the name Hale in bold headlines. The society loan agreement photostat showed that Hale had been granted five hundred dollars repayable over a set period. The third item was a glowing account of John Hale opening a community centre which his prosperous company had seen fit to build for the town's youth.

"Satisfied, Joe?"

He pushed the material back to her. "Yes!"

"My son never had a decent thought in his head until he served time," she said. "I despaired of him but now . . ." and her eyes moistened in motherly pride. "He's justified the faith I've placed in him. I'm a sentimental fool, Joe. I know this will shock you - and the society. I'm going to give you a chit for twenty pounds. I advise spending it wisely. Take ten and get roaring drunk. Find a girl and take her home with you. Relieve yourself. But don't make a habit of it. Mrs. Malloy does not like her bathroom occupied by strange women every morning."

Joe felt strangely touched. This was against everything he had considered possible. He wanted the money. He wanted the society behind him. If his plans were ever to reach fruition stage he had to have the backing of a solid community agency. But Mrs. Hale was putting trust in him. Placing him in an invidious position. If he failed her . . .

He mentally rejected her wiles. What the hell! He was Joe Hawkins. Not a Hale. This stupid game was meant to soften him. He would not yield.

"Try to better yourself, Joe" the woman said, writing the chit for his cash advance. "I believe there is good in everybody. I hope you won't let me down."

He accepted the chit and smiled. "I won't, Mrs. Hale."

Outside her office he breathed deeply. So much for that! The woman was a sucker for a hard luck story. Once his twenty vanished he could come back and beg for more. He would have a story to tell - all sobs and under-the-skin frustration!

*

Mrs. Malloy was short, fat and ugly. She spoke with a thick Dublin accent, and smelt of wash-tub detergent. Rubbing clean, almost raw hands on her apron, she stood in the doorway studying Joe as he eyed his room with candid disgust.

"Bhoyo," the Irish woman said, "forget your grand notions. This is Islington and the Society are paying for your keep. Back in the Auld Sod there are fine fellas wishing they could afford such luxuries. Take my Uncle Sean . . ." She sighed as if trying to find someone to do just that! "He lives in me mother's auld house with its roof falling in and the rats climbing into bed at night just to get warmth."

"Where's the loo?" Joe asked.

"A fine thing . . ." She said "thing" like it had no "h". "You're everything Mrs. Hale said you'd be." Her ugly features showed contempt. "You'll be wanting a key, no doubt?" She walked to the window, fluffed curtains to hide the solid brick wall a mere three feet away. A thin shaft of light edged into the narrow confines of Joe's "home" and served to highlight the shabby furnishings. "I'm Catholic," the woman said stridently. "I'm agin mortal sinning but Mrs. Hale knows better than I . . ." She shrugged as if to state where Mrs. Hale stood in her estimation. "There's an awful lot of terrible diseases in London today."

Joe grinned. The old biddy was trying to warn him against bringing home an "unclean" girl! Looking at her he wondered if any man had ever managed to get close to her soft-centre. She was roly-poly in a most nauseous way. A man would have to be blind, drunk, desperate or very insensitive to take this one to bed.

"Patrick Kelly shares the toilet with you. He lives in the next room. You'll be wanting to meet the dear boy . . ."

Not me, Joe thought. *I'm not going to get tied-in with a bunch of booze artists from construction sites.*

He knew all about the Irish labouring types and how they roamed the streets before the pubs opened and how they sang their "rebel" songs with a skinful of booze making each and every one of them imagine they could wipe the floor with all English inhabitants after the pubs closed. More than once his gang had waylaid a lone Irishman and beat the hell out of him. Just for kicks. Just to even the score, as Benny had once said.

"If my husband was still alive - bless his soul - he'd tell you a few truths," Mrs. Malloy remarked, retreating to the corridor outside Joe's room. "He spent sixteen years in prison!" She got uglier as frowns creased her blubbery face. "What a rascal he was, Joe . . . broke heads like skittles in an alley, he did. There wasn't a copper could tame my Mick."

"Charming," Joe allowed.

The woman scowled which only served to heighten her bushy eyebrows and those hard lines near her mouth. A discerning individual would have understood the terrible hardships which had produced such an unattractive female. Not Joe, though. He was filled with self-pity, and other people's problems washed off his uncaring hide.

Taking a Yale key from her apron, Mrs. Malloy said: "Breakfast is at seven-fifteen sharp."

"Seven-fifteen?" Joe wailed. Looking frantically around the sparse room he asked, "Where do I cook?"

"Not in here! You can use the kitchen anytime after twelve noon if you have to eat in. My other bhoyos don't do that." She sounded anxious to put him off cooking.

"I was told . . ."

"Mrs. Hale doesn't live here," the woman said firmly. "She's a lady. I'm not. Nor are my guests gentlemen." The point was made and she relented briefly with a quick smile.

Joe kept his retort to himself. It pleased him to have one thin-edge to wedge in Mrs. Hale's door. He could always complain that his cash did not stress to restaurant or café meals. Any excuse was valid under the circumstances. He could not continue to live in this worse mousetrap which Mrs. Malloy called a room. It was ten times more horrible than his room at home in Plaistow - and that was bad enough.

"I'll be looking for a job," Joe said, changing subjects. "In the city," he stressed emphatically. "I'll want a key to the post box . . ." He could see that locked cage attached to the letterbox downstairs.

"You'll get your letters at breakfast," the woman said menacingly.

"Why can't I have a key?"

Hands on wide hips she snapped: "'Cos nobody but me is allowed to sort the post. I don't tru. . ." She stopped and swung abruptly.

"You don't trust jailbirds," Joe finished.

She hesitated momentarily, and then continued down the corridor as if afraid to pursue this line of questioning.

What a bloody mess, Joe thought angrily. *It's as bad as prison. I'm trapped with nowhere to go!*

Closing his door, Joe examined the dingy room in detail. That brick wall hemmed him in as effectively as bars on a window. The tatty covers on the sagging bed were below standard issue even for the Scrubs. As for the small chest of drawers, the wardrobe and one tilted chair, they had come from Noah's Ark and had been junk before an elephant sat on the chair or tigers sharpened their tearing claws on the other two items. A threadbare carpet from an Honest Ed's bargain basement did little to cover dry rot floors. Wallpaper that was so faded to have lost its distinctive floral design completed the picture of misery.

"Chrissakes, this is hell!" Joe yelled at that brick wall.

The touch of folding money in his pocket drained some of his hate. Then, he swore aloud again. What woman, or girl, or even club hostess would come back to this . . . this . . . this stink-hole of an abode? He hurried to the bed and pressed down on its wilted mattress. The rusting groan of battered springs sent their squeaking lullaby through the house.

"That's bloody it!" Joe shouted. Rage boiled up inside him and he kicked the chair. Splintering wood confirmed his fears. It had been an *impossible* seat anyway!

Thrusting arms into his jacket, he stormed from the room. His feet sounded like tanks rumbling down an incline formed of loose shell. He tore past a startled Mrs. Malloy and slammed the front door. Anger made him unaware of the pretty girl in hot pants brushing past him as she fumbled for a key in her Indian-style fringed handbag. He could only visualise Mrs. Hale and *hear* her remark: "It's not a palace . . ." *Bloody right it isn't,* he thought. *It's a tragedy - a free prison for ex-cons to discover how society gave to those who had repaid their debts!*

*

"Here's your bloody money back," Joe snarled as the twenty quid skittered across her desk. A fiver floated on an isolated air-current and drifted unheeled to the office floor.

Bernice Hale smiled grimly. In all her experience she had never encountered such an irate young man nor had money thrown at her. Usually they came in with their hats in hand and begging in their weak eyes. But not Joe Hawkins. He was strong stuff.

"When you make out a report be sure and mention this," Joe growled, beginning to turn away.

"There won't be any report, Joe."

He halted in mid-step, stared at the woman facing him across the paper-littered desk.

"What is wrong, Joe?"

He leant on her desk, face twisted into a contorted mask of frustration. "Mrs. Malloy is an Irish pig and expects everybody to act like she was giving them the world on a silver platter."

Bernice smiled generously. "That's not bad for you, Joe," she said softly. "Your kind don't normally stoop to poetic expression."

"You're making a bloody fool of me," Joe rasped.

"I am not! Perhaps you haven't stopped to examine what changes prison has worked inside your mind, Joe. Perhaps you always had a brain which could cope with the finer things your environment did not encourage. Perhaps not. Anyway, your choice of words strike me as being a notch above those skinheads I have the dubious pleasure of assisting."

"I'm not a skinhead now," Joe said, remembering his determination to disassociate with a former existence. He had to play his cards with masterly skill. He could not relax one single second in front of this woman. So much depended on getting accepted; established in an organised society to which she belonged.

"You were one of the best . . ." and she laughed lightly, adding, "or worst."

112

"I was,"Joe affirmed proudly.

"And?"

"I'm not going to stay at Mrs. Malloy's!"

"Why not?"

"God,"he exploded, "Have you seen that dump?"

"Is it that bad?" she brushed a paperclip which had attached itself from a blouse button. His gaze automatically fastened on her breasts. Self-consciously she covered her treasure chest with a file.

Joe got the message. *She's bashful after all*, he thought. *She's a tease who can't go beyond a certain set point. Once a guy gets the upper hand she's putty.*

Bernice Hale quivered inwardly. She hoped Joe Hawkins had not noticed her infantile attempt to turn his masculine frustrations away from those abundant charms which, she knew only too well, excited less deprived males. In a way she detested her wonderful bosom. It was a target for lasciviousness, for speculation, for passes she did not want made. She could not, however, deny herself the pleasure of mental seduction. She was all woman. All female as Eve would have it. And in the knowledge of the exquisite power her chest measurements gave her she basked in either glory or torment.

Joe calculated his chances. She was more than twice his age but he'd heard that the old ones were the best. Who was it who'd said: They don't yell, they don't tell and by jove they don't swell? Could he make the grade? Or would that ruin his ambitions?

He decided to play safe and ignored those hormones demanding he capitalise on the woman's confusion.

"I'd rather be in jail than stay in that room, Mrs. Hale," he said with a measure of truth which lent sincerity to his voice.

Thankful for small mercies, Bernice Hale breathed easier and placed the file back on her desk. The moment of indecision had departed on Adam-strength wings. Or the ones he wore before the apple was eaten! "I haven't personally visited Mrs. Malloy's establishment," she admitted. "One of my colleagues gave it a recommendation."

"He didn't look at *my* room."

"Nor have the experience of what happens to a man once those prison gates shut, eh?" She smiled to relax his tenseness. "Joe, tell me honestly - what did you dislike about Mrs. Malloy's place?"

He considered her question. The native cunning which had taken him to the top of a skinhead gang and brought him to that fragile pinnacle of success for those fleeting hours of glory came rushing to his rescue. He was totally incapable of matching intellectual fencing but he knew when to duck and weave once fists started to fly. And this was street warfare. He was the underdog, the underprivileged. She the power, the rich, the one able to take away or give freely.

"I'm trying to get a decent job, Mrs. Hale. I need an address managers will respect. I need some comforts if I am to work my way to the top - not broken chairs and a bed that belongs in a dump."

She nodded thoughtfully. "Can you find a place yourself?"

"Yes!" He shouted the word, anxious now.

"I'm going to go overboard for you, Joe," she said falteringly, not quite satisfied with her decision yet realising it was all she could do under the given circumstances. "I'll advance you a loan. You'll have to sign for it though," she added pointedly.

"That's okay, Mrs. Hale. I'll refund it when I get work." He would have promised the moon plus a shilling for cash.

"Mark my words, Joe - this is your lot. Blow the cash and you're out in the cold."

"I won't let you down, Mrs. Hale," Joe said with mental fingers crossed she wouldn't change her mind at this stage.

She drew a chit across the desk, glanced at his face before writing figures. She could not know that Joe Hawkins was an actor. That the face he presented for her approval was but a façade behind which woodworm worked its nefarious quest.

"Sign here, Joe."

Catching himself in the nick of time, Joe scrawled his brash signature. Fifty quid! No interest. No repayment date. Just a name and the money was his . . .

"Let me know where you are staying," she said softly. "I'll want to visit you there."

He killed a thrill. If she came to his room he'd try her, for sure. Mother-age or not, she was everything a virile hunk of manhood dreamed about. He had seen her in a dozen erotic nights as moonlight filtered through those prison bars. Her, or a thousand panting females of all ages, all colours, all sizes. His face withheld the untold pleasures his mind conjured up and he kept his voice level as he said: "Thanks Mrs. Hale. I won't let you down."

"You said that once before." She laughed, handing him the initialled chit. "Joe Hawkins, you're a challenge for me. You're so like my son . . ." Tears moistened her eyes. She forced herself to regain control. "Remember where he went once he discovered that people are not all bad. Good luck in your job, Joe . . ." Her hand reached out and she stood - an attractive woman in her prime - as the lusting young man standing on the threshold of life let her warmth briefly touch his hard, unyielding, unsympathetic palm.

CHAPTER THREE

JOHN MATSON had once been a chippie working the London stage but opportunity and an inborn greed which knew no morality had taken the ex-carpenter to heights which only those owning a Rolls could ever aspire to reach. Thanks to a steal-happy thinking process and a desire to become larger than life had ever intended him to be, Matson was now perched on the apex of an expanding pornographic empire effectively covered by an equally profitable florist chain.

The men Matson employed called him "God" - Joe Hawkins included. Matson could do no wrong, or so the tall, broad-shouldered golfer liked to believe. The castle in Spain, The residence in St. John's Wood, the estate down in Surrey were all tokens of Matson's income tax free rise to fame.

That the days of wine, women and illegal takes were fast approaching their end did not unduly worry the Matsons of Soho. They had made their killings. They had the wealth supplied by suckers seeking second-hand thrills from books, dirty pictures and available women. In his rise to the stratosphere Matson had used, abused, and thrown aside a string of excellent writers, photographers, models. He had made enemies but he was backed by heavies and a Vice Squad accepting his payola to such an extent that anyone daring to voice a protest found himself being turned over and in possession of damaging material. That was the way Matson operated and Joe felt himself unique when he suddenly quit.

He figured he got out just in the nick of time. Matson had not taken him on from sympathy. Matson had plans for Joe - another stretch inside, no doubt. In those three weeks working for Soho's undisputed kingpin, Joe had found himself being set up like a pin in a ten-pin alley. Ready to be bowled over at the first signs of trouble.

The second job proved less dangerous, more boring. It lasted exactly ten days - including a weekend off. Being a so-called accountant for a firm publishing sex manuals did not strike Joe as a route to the upper-bracket income levels. He quit, and appealed to Bernice Hale for help in securing a "decent" position with a City firm - without the necessity of explaining what he had done with eighteen months less remission.

The excuse offered by a believing Mrs. Hale appealed to Joe. Studies took full time occupation. One could not work as a coal-heaver and make the grade in accountancy. So, Joe applied for jobs armed with knowledge and a lie tailor-made to suit a discerning, inquisitive employer.

Stanman, Pierce & Solley had a reputation for integrity, a credit rating up to the moon orbit class, and a vacancy for a junior clerk which Joe landed. Mr. Pierce interviewed Joe and treated his prospective employee to a searching enquiry.

"Mr. Hawkins, let me say you have admirable qualifications," the dry starched City-man said as he examined the results of Joe's standard test. Rubbing his cold hands on a linen handkerchief, Pierce carefully replaced the folded emblem of his manicure clean life in a breast pocket and gazed at Joe through rimless spectacles. "You have managed to accumulate a remarkable total of points. Your chief ability appears to be speed - which is precisely what is required in this position.

Joe congratulated himself silently. Short cuts had always been his forte. The prison accountant had shown him several tricks and he had latched onto each with an alacrity which had astounded the once-top embezzler.

Long, lean, lonely Pierce continued: "Where did you learn to calculate percentages to such perfection, Mr. Hawkins?"

Joe smirked behind a hand ostensibly covering a nasty cough. Lonely Pierce! That suited the musty old bastard. No sane woman would let this parchment-crackling flesh into her bed. Removing his hand, Joe said: "I attended private lessons from a friend of the family. A chartered accountant, you know!"

Pierce was impressed. He positively beamed. "Excellent, young man. All too few of your generation bother to take instructions from the elders. Have you ever had a job before?"

Joe hesitated. "Yes, sir."

"With whom?" A pen poised ready to make notations.

He's after references, Joe thought quickly.

"Come, boy - with whom?" Pierce demanded slightly agitated.

"Er . . ." Joe swallowed, and confessed with Oscar-winning embarrassment, "I am not from a middle-class family, sir. I come from poor people. I worked with a coal merchant before I decided to better myself."

"Ahhhh!" Pierce bestowed a generous smile on his "find". "Rags to riches, eh? A modern progression, lad. Oh, well - we must accept your ability. How does eleven pounds a week sound?"

Rotten! Joe thought instantly. To Pierce he smiled and said: "Wonderful, sir."

"Settled!" The man rose to his creaking feet, began to extend a hand and withdrew it immediately. "Hawkins . . ." Joe noted the dropped Mr. or the familiar Joe. "We are short-handed. Can you start tomorrow?"

Tomorrow was Wednesday - middle of the pay week. Joe mulled over the problem of his next loan from the society. If he played his cards right he might just scrape home with an additional tenner.

"When do I get my first pay, sir?" He cursed himself at once when Pierce raised a scanty eyebrow and fixed him with an accusing stare. "I hate to appear anxious, sir but there are circumstances which I have not mentioned."

"Like what, Hawkins?"

"Well, sir . . ." Joe thought fast and found a solution. "I mentioned being from a poor family. My parents do not understand why I should want to better myself, sir. I have a small flat but I'm hard-pressed for the . . ." He had started to say "ready" but quickly changed this to, "money to pay my landlady. I'm alright until Saturday, sir . . ."

Pierce smiled until his dry lips started to crack. "I like your spirit, Hawkins. It isn't every day we come face to face with a lad willing to sacrifice home and family in an endeavour to rise above lower class graveyards. I'll personally make arrangements for you to draw a full week's pay this Friday. Is that enough?"

"Thank you, sir!" Joe sounded so convincing he began to wonder if, somewhere along the line, he had actually begun to *think* like these stupid creeps.

"Right, Hawkins. See you in the morning at nine-thirty." Pierce dismissed his "help" with an imperious gesture and sank back into his leather-cushioned chair. The sigh of relief spoke volumes as those long, skin-over-bones fingers began rifling through stock market tapes.

Leaving the musty office with its leather-bound tomes and its legalistic, money-making atmosphere, Joe felt the world had for once returned him a debt. He had been long overdue recognition. He might have preferred to be known as "king of skinheads" but by his reckoning, this set-up would return more authority and more eventual glory than all the commands ever granted to a skinhead leader.

Those silly bastards beating their heads against stone walls are trash compared to what I'll be once I'm established, he thought as he walked through the offices of his employers. *Look at those girls in their mini-skirts and hot pants. They're ripe for someone like me. And as for Pierce - crissakes, I could steal him blind and he'd never suspect.*

CHAPTER FOUR

IT was opening time and Joe hurried along the Bayswater Road. He felt thirsty - and randy. Maybe he could find a girl in the pub: one willing to come back to his flatlet and spend this Sunday afternoon in his company. He had no worries now about bringing anyone to where he called home. Although he lived on the third floor, the entire building was nicely decorated and modest carpets covered every flight of stairs so that passing feet did not disturb the tenants.

His own room reflected some of the large house's former glory - decorated ceilings with sunburst plaster-work round the hanging, shaded light, doors dating back to a period just after Regency. Joe did not know about such refinements. He knew that he liked the place and there his information ended. Abruptly. Sadly.

He shared a toilet and bath with two other flatlets but he had cooking facilities, a washbasin, a large closet which doubled as a kitchen-cum-storage room, and a spacious bedsitter containing twin comfortable beds, a dressing table, chest of drawers, armchair in fresh upholstery and three ordinary chairs for eating at the gate-leg table. The room was carpeted, clean and serviced once a week. He had purchased one of those plastic wardrobes for his coat and suit - singular since he had not bothered to visit his real home since walking free from the Scrubs. *To hell with the old man*, he kept thinking. *To hell with the old woman. Not even if I'm starving would I call on them for help.*

Artists were displaying their multi-hued wares across the Bayswater Road as he approached the pub. Dozens of gawking tourists strolled aimlessly past the over-priced paintings and miscellaneous artifacts. Behind the railings - seen through gaps left as an occasional painting was sold for a knockdown "bargain" - the green grass of the park looked slightly artifical in this concrete jungle that was seething, bustling, swinging London.

In his pin-stripe suit and clean white shirt with his conservative tie clipped in place by a Stratton gold pin, Joe felt quite the City gent. *Funny*, he mused, *how clothes change a guy's outlook.*

He could remember those far-off days when he felt ten foot tall dressed in bovver boots, union shirt and tight trousers with the loud braces boldly showing. He could touch his hair and recall the pride of a skinhead cut. *Recall!* His hair was growing now. In another month or two it would be suede ... in between being a skinhead and being what the Establishment liked to call normal styling. *Suede* - smooth, elite, expensive.

He smiled to himself as he entered the pub. That was his new image. Suedehead - a smoothie, one of the elite now, and with expensive tastes and ambitions.

Thumbs behind his lapels, he straightened his jacket and marched to the crowded bar. A huge roast beef stared back at him amid a variety of pickles, salads and other inviting snacks. He was hungry but he dared not spend on food. Mrs. Hale had paid for the suit (an extra loan once he got his City job) but the well was drying up. The society did not have inexhaustible funds for Joe Hawkins, apparently. Not that he minded. He made out okay. He was in for seventy-five quid. On his signature only. And unknown to the ever-smiling, ever-helpful Mrs. Hale he was working the dodge with Social Security too. Life was great. Terrific. Everybody paid for his pleasure. To a degree ...

Mentally he calculated what was left in his wallet. Certainly not more than fifteen nicker. Not less than twelve. He had to buy smokes - a decent brand now he was a *member* of Stanman, Pierce and Solley. He could still drink pints of wallop but he enjoyed putting on the dog and having shorts with soda. And they cost a packet! If he met a dolly-bird she would probably insist on some exotic concoction so . . . He fought back the desire to have a beef sandwich with a side salad and settled for a hot sausage on a cocktail stick with Seagram's *Hundred Pipers* splashed lightly with soda.

Squeezing into a seat between a man-wife duo and two hot-panted dolly-birds he eyed what the girls were drinking before unleashing a smile in their combined direction. He could afford to pay for a few rounds. After all, it wasn't every day a bloke got to grips with birds who preferred milds and bitter to shorts.

He munched the sausage like it was hors d'oeuvres, sipped his drink in leisurely fashion. He wanted to knock it back, order another, but discretion was the pocket dictate. He let the girls know he was interested without ever stepping on toes. The old methods did not work in this new atmosphere. Anyway the man-wife team were furtively watching him as if expecting a rapist to emerge from inside that pin-stripe suit at any second.

One girl - smallish, pretty, wearing her hair in a huge knot at the back - laughed as she finished her drink. "How about another Sandra?" she asked her companion.

Sandra was taller, leaner, less inclined to toss glances in Joe's direction. She was also in Joe's opinion, a spoilt brat and decidedly trying to put a wet blanket on her mate's fun. "Not for me," she pebble-mouthed. "I find this crowd disgustingly cheap."

Oh, la-la Joe thought. *What the hell would she think if she had to drink with his old crowd down in East Ham?*

"Sandra! That's awful . . . keep your voice low!"

Sandra giggled and sipped what remained of her pint. "Sorry if I embarrass you, Lois."

"You're deliberately trying to make me feel small."

"You are small," Sandra replied cattily.

The man and woman quickly finished their drinks and departed. Leaning across the table Joe said: "You're not that small, Lois."

The girl avoided a direct confrontation with Joe's hot eyes. Lowering her head she softly said: "Sandra believes every woman worth anything should be five-eight."

"Not true," Joe told her. "Would you like a drink - one on me?"

Lois nodded quickly.

"Sandra?"

The taller girl shook her head defiantly, then got to her feet leaving an inch of beer in her glass. "No thanks. I'm going. Are you staying, Lois?"

Joe tensed expectantly.

"I think I shall . . ."

Joe got to his feet with alacrity. "What'll it be, Lois?"

"Would you mind awfully if I switched to the same as you?"

He forced a brave smile. This wasn't what he had figured but . . . "It's Scotch and soda," he warned.

"Lovely. I often sneak a sample of daddy's scotch."

"Large?" Joe cursed his tongue immediately.

"Thanks - yes!"

As Sandra took a dignified exit Joe got the barmaid's attention and ordered large *Hundred's Pipers* for two. He did not think to bring the soda back to Lois so she could fix her own mixture. Instead, he liberally splashed both drinks and went back like an uncrowned monarch about to dispense favours to a loyal subject. He had a lot to learn though the lesson was not imminent.

Lois smiled, sipped her drink after a murmured, "cheers", and kept her gaze alerted.

"I haven't seen you here before," Joe said conversationally as if he was a regular. In fact, he had been inside this particular pub but only once before. The first night he took his flatlet.

"That wouldn't surprise me," the girl remarked. "I live on the other side of the park."

Joe stiffened. Her very word "other" made his side seem vile, vulgar, violent. He would have to be careful with this one. She came from a society family, he was sure. The "daddy" bit and Sandra's down-the-nose attitude spoke of slumming.

"I've only moved in myself," Joe said to lessen the antagonism between their classes.

She appeared interested. "Oh, where did you live previously?"

"Actually," he lied effectively, "I'm a roving bod." He was getting quite expert at inventing backgrounds and denying his past.

"That must be fun." She looked straight into his eyes and blushed a little.

"Fun is not being alone all the time," Joe said to open the conversation.

"I'm Lois, as you know. What's your name?"

"Joe . . ." He balked at the Hawkins. That sounded common!

A fat girl accompanied by a slender man slid into the unoccupied seats. "What'll you have, ducks?" The man asked.

"Pint of cider," fatso said eagerly.

Joe shuddered. Why did *they* have to invade his upper-class territory.

"I like this Scotch. What brand is it?" Lois asked as if the rest of the world did not exist at that precise moment.

"Seagram's *Hundred Piper's*. Quite new, I understand."

"Seagram's . . . are they the people who make Canadian rye?"

Joe wasn't sure but he tried to appear knowledgeable. Why yes, they are."

Lois glanced at the fat girl, smiled at Joe. "Crowded isn't it?"

You little viper Joe thought. "Sunday . . ." he explained.

"I'm hungry - are you?"

I'm bloody starving, his mind screamed.

"Finish your drink. We'll find a c. . ." He almost said "caff". "A cosy restaurant," he finished lamely. It was a bloody effort dealing with these snooty bitches. And trying to rise above his skinhead, East End background.

"There's a smashing one across the park."

There would be! He nodded thoughtfully. "Anything you want, Lois." *Within reason and my pocket-book.*

*

Immediately he saw the façade and the saw-dust floor he knew this was more than he had expected. And he had allowed for a costly interlude before bringing her back through the park and into his bed.

Once inside, however, he felt better. The menu did not read like the national debt. It was reasonable. He'd have to remember *Flanagan's*. Posh, a throw-back to Edwardian times and the right type of atmosphere to make any reluctant virgin say "yes" without hesitation. He felt better, more inclined to splurge. Soon, he'd have money to do those things he had always thought were his due. He'd be like the stars in a black void as gazed upon by astronauts - a millionaire. Hawkins would not be a surname to feel ashamed of then. It would be a title almost.

Thrusting aside his daydreams he concentrated on the menu.

"I'll have Royal Game Pie," Lois declared.

"Me, too." He dropped the menu.

"With Spotted Dick?"

"Naturally!" He feigned aloofness, not bothering to cast a second glance at the menu. The act went over excellently, he thought as her eyes shone enthusiastically.

"Shall we have something to drink?"

He swore inwardly. This was the test. He knew absolutely nothing about wines, about correct procedures. Beer was fine with chicken according to him, according to his old man.

"You must have a favourite," he suggested.

Lois smiled thanks. "I enjoy Sauterne."

The waitress nodded approval. Joe puffed out his chest. "A bottle of Sauterne, miss."

What the hell is Sauterne? he asked mentally. He had never tasted the drink. But never!

Waiting for their order, Joe studied Lois. She was more than pretty. She was beautiful. She had large, luminous blue eyes and the way her chestnut coloured hair was gathered into that back-knot made her face definitely exciting. Her figure left much to be praised, nothing to be desired. She had firm, high breasts; lovely legs admirably displayed in those velvety-green hotpants. Her skin was pure satin - smooth, blemishless, so naturally untouched.

"What do you do for a living?" she asked.

"I'm *with* Stanman, Pierce & Solley, stockbrokers."

Mrs. Hale had been adamant. She had insisted he refer to his position as being *with* the company. Not merely a junior clerk working *for* them.

Lois's blue eyes enlarged into liquid pools expressing her joy at finding "one of her own" on the Bayswater side of the park. "Fascinating, Joseph," she said.

The hell with you, bitch! Joe thought. *Joseph, indeed! Never!*

"The name is Joe," he said tightly.

She did not catch his tension. "I think that Joseph is a marvellous name. Much better than Joe."

"I'm Joe," he said viciously.

She began to worry. This wasn't a boy willing to please a girl's preference for a name. This was a stubborn man thrusting his opinionated self down a woman's throat. The arrival of the waitress saved her from an argument. She watched carefully as Joe quickly caught onto his duty and sampled the wine. He nodded, much too soon. *He isn't accustomed to this*, she thought.

Once - it had seemed like eons ago - Joe had read a book where the private eye had sampled wine and expressed his opinions on its merits. He saw those lines now and said: "A good year. Very palatable."

Lois frowned. Was she wrong? He sounded as if he knew . . .

*

"Shall we take a stroll around the park?"

Joe champed at the bit. The meal had been near disaster but by watching how she handled her knife and fork he had managed to avoid total disgrace. That time when a slice of pie had fallen from his fork had almost undone all he had hoped to achieve. Luckily, Lois had been lost in her flavour buds and listening to the conversation from the next table.

"Across the park," he said deliberately.

Her hand briefly touched his. "You're trying to compromise me, Joseph."

"Can't you do what I ask?" he requested pleadingly.

"What's that?"

"Call me plain Joe."

She laughed and concentrated on ducks floating lazily on placid waters. Their outrageously coloured feathers contrasted sharply with the brownishness of polluted, weed dank liquid.

"Do you have a job?" Joe asked finally. He was fast approaching tongue-tied frustration. If he did not have to keep being something he was not there were a dozen topics he could talk about. He'd have enjoyed discussing the merits of West Ham or Chelsea or Arsenal's chance of pulling off the "double". He could have spoken about the days when he ruled a gang with an iron hand and took those girls he liked with the simplicity of a stallion servicing a sprightly mare. But that was the past. His present image demanded less crudity, more gentility - and it was eating at his bone marrow at an alarming rate.

"A job?" She stared at him, trying hard not to show disgust. "Not a job, Jos. . .Joe! I am a partner in a boutique daddy bought for us."

"Us?" That gave him a new line.

"Sandra . . ."

She's not your type," he said firmly.

"She's a bloody good saleswoman."

Joe smiled. So she swore on occasion. That would make it easier

124

when he slipped back into the old mould.

They were now at the Bayswater Road with the pub to their right, crowds everywhere as the afternoon rush for bargain oils got under way. Artists no longer sat in their parked cars but mingled with the outspoken tourists and tried to cadge a quick sale once they heard a favourable comment on a specific work.

Joe had not experienced this seemingly positive urge to own an original oil but then, Joe Hawkins came from a home which had not been noted for its cultural belongings. The closest his family ever came to brushing against creative talent was the infrequent romance story borrowed from the public library and even that was usually a lesser work by a sausage-machine writer. Anything deep would have sailed above the heads of his parents. One head for two . . . Funny how he always thought of mother and father as a single unit! Perhaps it came from his own detachment from them both.

"I bought a landscape here once," Lois remarked acidly as he took her hand. She did not like having people guide her across busy streets. Without appearing to tear herself away she skillfully manoeuvred free and darted between moving vehicles until she stood waiting for her escort as he struggled with the traffic alone.

"You could get killed doing that," Joe panted as he joined her.

"If I do it shall be my fault, nobody elses," she replied with characteristic stubbornness.

Joe didn't quite know what to make of the girl. She had seemed docile, ready to be shaped for his passion. Now, he wasn't so certain. She had an iron will and a determination that society background and money in the bank made all the more frightening. He admitted that women like her scared the hell out of him. He preferred the little tarts utterly dependant on their menfolk. With them a man could get what he wanted without the bother of battling for mental supremacy.

"My place is along here," Joe pointed in the general direction of Devonshire Terrace.

Her face expressed concern. "A room?"

"A flatlet."

"Is there a difference?" she asked snootily.

God, I'd like to smack her ass, Joe thought.

"I'm not sure this is wise," Lois said, holding back at the corner.

"Look," Joe said in exasperation, "I'm not going to rape you."

"Bloody right you're not. I'm a virgin!"

"You mean . . ?" Joe asked in amazement.

125

"I've never been to bed with a chap!"

"S'truth!"

"Sorry you've spent money on me now?" the girl asked with a touch of sarcasm.

"Not at all." Joe attempted to put on a brave front. He cursed inwardly. Just his rotten luck. Of all the birds frequenting pubs he had to pick the only virgin left in the Bayswater district.

"You expected me to undress for you, though."

He nodded. The truth could not hurt. "Why not?"

"It's not being seen naked, Joe. It's what nudity arouses I worry about."

"Are you afraid to make love then?" He was getting lost in the quagmire of her purity.

"Yes - I suppose I am. One hears so much about venereal diseases these days."

"I haven't anything wrong with me," he said quickly.

"You may not have, Joe - but there's no medical certificate to say a doctor has examined you this morning."

"Damn! I'll wear . . ."

"Sorry. Not today, Joe."

"Don't you want to see my flatlet?"

"Can you promise not to start mucking around with me?"

"Yeah!"

"If you do I shall scream," she threatened.

Joe felt defeat heavy on his urges. He had gone too far to turn back. So what if she didn't let him. He'd scheme for the future. He badly wanted to bed her. A day, or two would still taste as sweet. If he played his cards right she would weaken until she begged him to strip off her garments and treat her as he had all those others.

"Lois, I promise there won't be any nonsense today. Okay?"

She took his arm, felt the hard muscles ripple. She liked Joe, wished there was some method for sharing a mental passion without the absolute necessity of physical contact between bodies.

"I'll bet lots of guys have tried to get you into bed," Joe said with a grin. He had decided on his campaign. Talk about love-making. Get her so excited at the prospect of being naked in his arms that she would be unable, unwilling to forego the ultimate pleasure when he made his big play.

He was still promoting verbal emotion as they climbed the stairs to his room . . .

CHAPTER FIVE

ENTERING the offices of Stanman, Pierce & Solley the following morning, Joe became immediately aware of a nervous silence. Three girls with heads together suddenly stopped chatting and gazed at him coldly. A young man carrying a tray full of letters already opened, briefly halted in mid-step before shrugging a casual welcome as he pushed into an inner office. In a far corner of the main reception area a balding, aged man rose to his feet and motioned for Joe to approach him.

"I'm Totter," the man said when Joe was a few feet away. "You'll be working directly under my supervision. Remove your coat, lad. We begin promptly at nine here."

Joe slowly took his coat off, wishing he could tell this grim faced old bastard where to stick his promptness. Inside the space of two minutes he was already sorry he had taken Pierce's job. He had an idea there would be no joy working for this firm.

"I understand from Mr. Pierce you've never been engaged in stockbroking before," Totter said, not bothering to show Joe where the cloakroom was. "We demand a high standard . . ."

"Do I drop it on the floor?" Joe asked sarcastically, gesturing with his coat.

Totter glared. "Your attitude is abominable, lad."

"Sorry, sir!" Joe compelled himself to make the apology and call this man sir.

"I should think so. Hang it on that peg." Totter pointed firmly at a row of pegs holding a variety of male and female coats, umbrellas and shopping bags. A nearby hat rack held a collection of spotless bowlers and one lonely fedora. Joe wondered which member of staff dared to go against the grain and come to work sporting a *normal* hat. He would make it his business to become acquainted with the rebel.

Carefully, Joe hung his Crombie, brushing a speck from the sheening velvet collar and returned to face the indignant Totter.

"You will, I presume, wear a hat tomorrow?"

Joe shook with silent laughter. This could be fun. He would make it his business to rile the old bastard at every opportunity. The man was a granny - one of those male wonders married to a position. Joe doubted if he had ever known the exquisite thrill of belonging to the

127

human race, of sharing passions with a woman.

"I asked you a question, lad," Trotter said.

"I suppose so, sir," Joe replied lightly. "Now where do I start?"

"Take this ledger into Mr. Solley's office and have him sign the last page."

"Which one is Solley's?"

"Mr. Solley to you, lad!"

"Which one, sir?" Joe ignored the correction.

Totter pointed again. Following the long, almost skinless finger, Joe entered a sumptious room containing a massive desk, a teleprinter machine, a well-stocked bar, several comfortable leather chairs and shelves lined with large bound books. Although it was relatively warm outdoors, a small fire burned in an Adam grate immediately behind the huge man seated at the desk. Lifting a shaggy head, the man stared at Joe quizzically; allowing a flicker of a smile to soften his lined features.

"Mr. Totter wants your signature, Mr. Solley." He set the ledger on the desk and stood back waiting.

"You're new," Solley said with a resonant voice.

"I started this morning."

"Having trouble with our Totter, eh?"

Joe liked the other. He grinned. "A bit."

"We all have problems with old Totter. Be kind to him, boy. He's a genius with figures and we couldn't afford to lose him." It was a gentle way of warning Joe whose services could be under the hammer should trouble arise.

Flourishing a pen, Solley made a hasty assessment of the figures prepared for his signature, and scribbled his name right across the page. That done, he closed the book and pushed it across the desk. "Are you a football fan?" he asked.

"Yes, sir!" Joe rose to the question happily.

"Like a couple of tickets for Saturday's match?"

"Which team?"

Solley grinned. "Tottenham. Is something wrong?"

"Those f..." Joe lapsed into silence, face tense. It had been a near thing. He did not imagine *Mister* Stockbroker Solley swore as expertly as he could.

"Those what?" Solley asked, bending over the desk with hands clasped.

"Fools," Joe replied lamely. "I'm..." he thought fast. He couldn't say West Ham and deny all knowledge of the East End. Chelsea went against the grain, just as Spurs did. "I'm an Arsenal supporter myself."

"One man's meat," the man laughed as he reached inside his immaculate jacket. "Here - have all the fun of watching next year's champs." Two tickets floated down on to the desk.

Joe picked them up. "Thanks Mr. Solley. Don't the other guys watch soccer?"

"I'm afraid they consider me a traitor to rugby. What's your name, son?"

"Joe Hawkins."

"Well, Joe - don't let me hear you refer to our staff as guys. They are chaps, or fellows, or if the mood merits, rotten bastards. Never guys."

"I'll remember, sir."

"Do you wear a hat, Joe?"

"I shall, sir."

"Make it a bowler. I alone break the rules." He chuckled. "I look damned silly in a hard hat. That's all, boy. Back to the grind."

As he took his departure, Joe dropped the notion of cultivating the fedora owner. He thought Solley a decent bloke but hardly one to call "mate" as they swilled pints together. It was a perk getting the football tickets but not one to make him a solid citizen in anybody's eyes yet. Given time, he'd qualify for a higher position. The burning ambition to succeed was in him. All he needed was a chance for some fast lolly, a few birds to make his evenings worthwhile and a gang to bolster his ego. Not a bunch of yobbos. That was out. He wanted some "chaps" willing to commit mayhem under cover of respectabilty.

*

He was eighteen, tall, not bad looking. In his City suit, the Crombie coat with velvet collar, his furled umbrella and the new bowler perched cockily on his head, he was enough to make silly little birds take a second glance and get their hormones working overtime. Every night as he travelled home from Bank on the Central Line he could feel those hot, passionate eyes seek to catch his attention. It was some strain to ignore each and every one of them but somehow he managed. Lois first - then the world of pearl-glistening oyster-

129

birds.

Even Totter had praised him that day which was a change. Usually the old bastard screamed and threatened when he made the slightest mistake. But today Joe had reaped rewards for spotting a glaring error in Totter's addition. Something was worrying the old man. Joe could tell. More than once he'd caught Totter peering out of the window with a vacant expression on his tight, parchment face. The fact that the firm's oldest, most trusted employee had faltered proved Joe's suspicions - Totter was having family troubles. Still, it was Friday and the office could go to hell until Monday.

Brushing a loose hair from his forehead, he caught sight of the man seated across from him. There was that pathetic desire of the homosexual about to smile in search of a mutually inclined soul about the man. Joe froze. If he made the slightest . . .

He unfroze quickly! Deliberately he yawned and smiled at nothing.

The man inched forward on his seat, returning what he thought was Joe's opening gambit.

The dirty old bastard, Joe thought. *He looks like he has a fat wallet. I wonder . . .*

At Holborn the train stopped and another seething mass of humanity shoved and kicked into the carriage. The man rose, giving his seat to a young girl. Joe wanted to laugh. He knew what came next was "standard procedure" and waited until the man sidled to a strap hanger directly in front of him. Their knees touched, pressure increased.

"Sorry . . . " the man said with an almost feminine voice.

Joe gestured expansively. "That's alright."

The knee assaulted anew.

God, it's too easy, Joe told himself.

By Lancaster Gate the man was mentally raping Joe. There was no pretence now. It was a plain case of "wait until we get to my place, young lad".

At Queensway the man smiled and said softly: "This is where I live, "and headed for the open door. Joe followed.

On the station platform the man took Joe's hand and squeezed.

"Do you . . .?"

"Anything,"Joe replied with a return squeeze.

Joe wanted to vomit. As a skinhead he would have kicked the bastard in the balls and hoped to ruin his love life forever. But that was not how the new Joe Hawkins operated. Not how a neophyte suedehead got the wherewithal to continue as a member of a decent community. The take home pay from Stanman, Pierce & Solley did not begin to pay for his clothes, flatlet, food or entertainment. It was a hand-out to keep him fed and sheltered so that he could slave his guts out preparing statements and tax returns. Only that.

"I'll follow you," Joe said in a whisper. "I wouldn't want my neighbours to know . . ."

The man trembled. "Yes . . . yes, of course. That will be better for both of us. I live with Auntie . . . she's a darling but so possessive. She's away in Bristol for the weekend, you know!"

Joe didn't know but he nodded sagely. "Lead on, McBent."

The queer giggled girlishly and hurried along the platform. He was delighted, intent on a weekend spent in this young man's company.

Poor Auntie, Joe thought. *She must be a right bitch. Stupid, to boot. Anyone could tell he's round the twist.*

Surprisingly, the man guided Joe into one of those sedate, family hotels catering for permanent guests along the Bayswater Road. Once inside the suite of rooms allocated to Auntie and her bent nephew, Joe found himself confronted by blowing curtains as a breeze wafted in from the park. One glance and Joe knew the bastard was well-heeled. Antiques galore dotted Victorian what-nots and Georgian sideboards, and the silverware displayed on a dresser had cost a bomb way back when men toiled for a pittance per year.

"Take your coat off and relax," the queer said. "Like a drink first?"

Joe kept his coat securely buttoned. "How much, pal?"

The man paled perceptively. "What?"

"How much?" Joe repeated.

"I . . . I thought . . ."

"Free love?"

"Er, yes."

"Sorry, luv - good times come expensive these days."

"Would five . . .?"

"I'm going!" Joe announced indignantly.

"Ten?"

"That depends on what you want, doesn't it?"

The man's fingers shook as he extracted a wallet from inside his jacket. He peeled off five fivers and offered them. Joe caught sight of tens and at least one twenty. Greed gnawed at his guts.

"I'll have a large Scotch first," Joe announced, ignoring the money in that trembling, eager hand.

"Certainly . . ." The twenty-five pounds lay on a sofa within reach as the man hurried to a cabinet and began pouring drinks.

Two drinks and then, Joe thought.

"You're sweet," the man said as he handed Joe the glass.

"You're dirty," Joe laughed.

"Ohhh," the man laughed, too.

"Don't you like it with women?"

A shudder raced through the man. "No! They're . . . they're . . ."

"Like Auntie?" Joe suggested.

The man's eyes narrowed. "Are you one of us?"

Joe finished his drink. He'd overplayed his hand. The next glass of Scotch would have to be taken, like this creep and his loot.

"You're not . . ." the man started to say.

Joe's toe caught him in the groin and, as the pathetic creature staggered back with hands flying to protect - and sympathise with - his injured manhood, Joe followed in with hard fist. All the fury, all the hatred went into those vicious fists. Slowly, steadily, Joe beat the man to a pulp until his whimpering ceased and he collapsed to the floor.

Working fast, Joe counted what was in the wallet. One hundred and seven pounds. Not bad! Leaving the man where he had fallen, Joe searched the entire suite. He discovered another thirty six quid and a small suitcase which he packed with silver objects he reckoned would bring the highest resale price.

As a final gesture of defiance he stole the man's Omega watch, his solid gold cuff links and tie clip and added insult to injury by appropriating a Sanyo global transistor radio which he liked.

A groan echoed from the depths of the man's chest.

"Tough luck, mate," Joe snarled and grinding his heel where the pain would be most acute, he bent over and belted the man again. "That'll keep you cold until I make my getaway . . ."

CHAPTER SIX

"THIS is The Voice Of America coming to you . . ."

Joe smiled indulgently and flipped through the pages of his

magazine. He adored *his* Sanyo transistor. With it he could catch up on world trends and dazzle his fellow workers with his global knowledge. He required very little sleep. After all, he was young, strong and healthy. Not one of those crusty old men the firm usually employed. If he got to sleep by three a.m. he could rise by seven-thirty and be at his desk promptly at nine - something Mr. Totter insisted upon each and every morning of the week.

Turning the page, an article caught his eye. The radio was forgotten now.

"Suedeheads," the article said, "are difficult to define. They belong to no known bands nor do they amalgamate into gangs as their skinhead predecessors did. They are an enigma. An anti-social anti-everything conglomerate affecting status as their protective cover whilst engaging in nefarious pursuits more savage, more brutal than other cultists we have seen rise - and fall in this past decade."

". . . and now, the Glen Miller sound. Little Brown Jug has been requested by Staff-Sergeant Harry Carr from Munich . . . "

Joe dropped the magazine to the floor and fiddled with the dial.

"Ici . . . "

He turned on. Foreign language programmes gave him a headache trying to cut through nasalness and unintelligible garble.

". . . Berlin: British troops staged a three day exercise to prove their readiness for any Soviet sneak attack . . . "

He whirled the dial viciously and then switched to another wavelength.

The suedehead article was a magnet he could not fight against. His fingers playfully shifted the selector to a music programme and dropped away. He picked up the magazine again and got involved in it to such an extent he did not hear the foreign disc-jockey's voice gutturally berate the latest offering from an established English pop group.

". . . and suedeheads have been known to use their umbrellas as weapons . . . "

Joe glanced across the room at his furled umbrella.

"Many adherents of this strange, loosely-joined cult have resorted to sharpening their umbrella tips . . . "

Immediately, Joe saw the possibilities. What a beautiful cover-up! Leaving the radio blaring on its alien station, he got his umbrella and examined the tip. By removing the metal end, he could easily have the staff fashioned into a lethal weapon. A dab of black paint would effectively camouflage his handiwork . . .

*

Being a suedehead with its loose links appealed to the new Joe Hawkins. He began to study those other young men on the Underground, trying to seperate the wolves from the ewes. He found it next to impossible to distinguish a sharpened umbrella point from a satisfied middle class stick-in-the-mud.

And, for a final try-out, he visited Mrs. Bernice Hale one evening by appointment. The killing he'd made from the queer's suite could be dented, but never fully given away.

"I've saved some money," Joe said as he reached ten quid across to her. "I promised to repay . . ."

"Oh, Joe!" Tears moistened the woman's eyes. She took the cash and hurriedly wrote a receipt. "I . . ." She wiped her eyes with a cheap cotton handkerchief. "My son would like to know you, Joe." She reached the slip across to her protégé. "It isn't often our judgement is justified, but you're the exception to the rule. It makes all our efforts worthwhile."

Joe felt like a louse until he gave due consideration to his own ambitions. It had been more than a good gesture making one simple repayment of his outstanding loans. It had got him in solid. Now; anything, any time . . .

"Are you sure you can afford this?"

"I'm sure."

"You must be living on a meagre budget."

"I'm existing."

"Well, Joe, if you should ever . . ." She hesitated. A brief flash in his eyes disturbed her.

"I think I'll be able to manage alone, Mrs. Hale."

Thrusting doubt into dark, forgetting recesses, she smiled. "Keep in touch, Joe. I'd like to know what you are doing and be able to quote you as an example for other unfortunates to follow."

Getting to the door, Joe dropped the hint he thought would bring her running. "You've got my address, Mrs. Hale. If you ever want to visit me I'll be home. I haven't found that girl yet . . ." He waved nonchalantly and made a hasty exit. But not before he caught a brief glimpse of her face. It gave him hope. He liked to imagine she was lonely - doing without. If only . . .

*

Soho at night was no place for a City type. Certainly not an affluent young man alone. Joe didn't give a damn. He could handle himself better than most of the long-haired touts flogging their wares. Almost as well as the heavy boys menacing frightened tourists into taking a walk down a back alley to watch a series of blue films performed by the most brazen of brass and defeated layabouts. Joe knew all the tricks or thought he did. After all, he had worked for "God" recently . . .

Lethargic crowds paraded the maze, seeking pleasures for a price. Hurrying inhabitants of the rabbit warren hawked their bulky packages of pornographic books in sight of strolling fuzz. Brass kept alert eyes peeled from bedroom windows as pimps worked their charms on possible targets in a variety of sleazy clubs and near-beer joints. The young didn't require pimping services. They got it free, for kicks, or for a pill or two. They got it better than the nervous, introvertish lecher afraid to ask for "special treatment". The youth cult had taken over old Soho. The coffee bars, the invasion of freelancing teenage nymphs and the vicious gangs roaming what had always been a stable belonging to older, wiser, shadowy figures had changed the area. Old-timers could no longer compete. Youth demanded, and refused to run scared of Manson "gods". Drugs gave courage and ill-advised bravado.

Joe considered the scene with a discriminating gaze. He was not interested in the flighty bits displaying their thighs nor the coaxing pleas of his generation trying to ensnare what they believed to be a provincial mark into a dark, over-priced den where even the ginger beer was watered.

Joe wanted companionship. Not womanship. He wanted to find his own . . .

Dean Street, Frith Street, Old Compton Street, Greek Street. He walked them all; leisurely, alert. He saw the sweating bald-headed ones dart from dirty bookshops with a wrapped parcel clutched feverishly in clammy hands. Saw tarted-up birds from Ilford, Battersea, Highbury and a score of other outlying districts scamper between clubs. They were easy to spot. Heavy eye shadow, hungry lean features, shimmering sweaters hoisting up fake breasts. Small make-up cases swinging to the beat of their tight, not-fleshed-enough bottoms. He saw the rolling drunks, the pop-eyed trippers, the swaggering thugs showing off a new horse-blanket made into a suit.

And there were the prowling cars with their look-everywhere-save-the-road drivers creeping from skirt to skirt hopefully affecting a it's-the-traffic-congestion-that-makes-me-drive-slow attitude.

There were cops and detectives. There were ordinary decent tourists or Londoners out for an exotic meal in one of the dozen or so famous restaurants. There were hard-working bartenders and waitresses going and coming as shifts started and ended. There were wide-boys studying passing faces for a good old-fashioned "steamer". There was Danny, Freddie, Bob, Fat John, Robin, Kenny, Harry, Angie, Mary, Molly and - always - Julie. Flies stuck in the ointment called Soho. Dying flies all. Too steeped in the terrible rat race, the daily routine to seek greener fields.

To think he had once considered this the acme of ambition! He wanted to belong to the West End - not Soho's grubby counterfeit acres. He wanted to be acceptable in that luxurious quarter adjoining this barbaric haven - the one across Regent Street. The one called Mayfair. That's where the money was - in every sense.

But he was inside Soho's hellhole. Looking for one sign. Searching for another who felt exactly as he did.

He had about given up hope when he entered Shaftesbury Avenue a third time. Traffic moved faster here. The people did not have those hard-bitten eyes now. These were theatre-goers and Soho proper advoidees.

The youth came out of the coffee bar and stood momentarily alone on the pavement. Joe tensed. A gaggle of chattering females descended on the youth and he quickly moved. Joe followed through fume-spluming taxis down into Rupert Street. Do-nothing teenagers hung around doorways leading upstairs to juke-box squalor. Music blasted into the drawing night like great blankets of sound enshrouding those not in sympathy with modern noise.

A queer minced into sight, blond(e) locks flying in a slight breeze, perfume wafting from his floral shirt in waves. *If he wasn't in such an exposed position I'd kick his sexy-ass*, Joe thought delightedly. Queer-bashing was not on the cards tonight, though. Some other time he could vent his hatred and capitalise from the pleasure.

The youth paused as he reached Leicester Square. Joe could feel his indecision - right, or left. To the Tube or back into Piccadilly Circus. Home or mixing with the drug-pushers forming their nightly queue as the desperate ones drifted into town.

Joe reached the youth's side. "I'm Joe Hawkins . . . mind if I join you?" He sounded too polite. That's what working under Totter's gimlet gaze did for him!

The youth stepped back a pace and deliberately studied Joe's mode of dress. "Do you read . . . ?" he started to ask with carefully modulated tones.

"Articles mentioning how suedeheads should dress?"

The youth smiled broadly. He nodded and tipped his bowler with an exaggerated welcoming gesture.

"You, too?" Joe asked tightly.

"Me, also!" came the easy reply. "I say, this is rather nice."

Joe shuddered inside where his East End skinhead longings still manifested some aversion to plum-in-the-mouthisms. He forced himself to remember his ambitions to rise above the common herd. He would have to accept an Oxford accent as he would have to refrain from instantaneous explosion whenever he heard those hoity-toity assumed sayings of the Mayfair fraternity. He was not to know then that the characteristics were as false as the strippers' bursting tits.

"We're a rare breed," the youth said over traffic roar. "Not many of us about, eh what?"

"I was beginning to wonder if I was the only one," Joe laughed.

"Not quite, old chap. There are others. I guarantee that."

Controlling an urge to turn tail and run for cover Joe asked: "How did you decide to join *us*?"

The youth flicked a speck of imaginary dust from his expensive Crombie coat. "What does that mean?" he asked suspiciously.

"I was a skinhead," Joe replied honestly.

"Oh!" There was a slight tinge of disappointment in the voice. "A skinhead!" That sounded like a curse.

"What were you?"

For a few seconds the youth stood frozen in deep dark thought. Then, suddenly, he relaxed. He was as tall as Joe, handsome without being attractive, and sported a huge solitaire diamond ring which flashed in the headlight passing of cars.

Joe shuffled his feet as the suspense mounted. What the hell was wrong with this guy? Couldn't he give a straight answer? Or was he pretending to be a suedehead and mocking me? In another second Joe's fists would have dented that smile.

"Mate . . ."and the vocal inflection changed drastically, "I'm like you

137

- an ex-skinhead. Chelsea Shed type."

Joe laughed softly, letting the tension within him then vaporise in a loud guffaw. "I thought you were from . . ."

"Some expensive college?"

"Yeah!"

"Shit on them! I was born in Shepherd's Bush."

"Up Plaistow and The Hammers!"

"A year ago I'd have done you for that!"

"A year ago me mates would have backed The Hammers."

"I've been inside," the youth said quietly next.

Joe hesitated. Confessions like this came hard after all those efforts to cover tracks.

"You've done bird, too!" the youth accused.

"The Scrubs," Joe admitted with reluctance.

"Derby, me." Their "old school tie bit" broadened conversation. "I met some big men there."

"I ignored 'em all," Joe said as if he had been the biggest man in The Scrubs.

"How did they nick you?"

Joe stood straight, proud still. "I done a sergeant in Hyde Park."

"I beat up on a Pakki and stole his savings."

"They gave you bird for that?" Joe sounded and felt amazed at such injustice.

"He was hospitalised for sixteen weeks," the youth explained. "And I got away with five thousand."

"They took it back," Joe said knowingly.

"Like hell they did! I hid it all."

Joe wanted to scream. The next question was so very important. "What did the magistrate give you for that?"

The youth's gloating rose above traffic, passers by, London's beating heart. Beating his mental breast for the world to witness his harsh sentence, he moaned: "I got a lousy eighteen months for doing a fuzz!"

"We all learn by our mistakes," the youth said, pouring on the misery.

"Have you got the cash?"

"Most every penny."

"And what next?"

The youth bent forward and whispered directly into Joe's receptive ear: "I'm going to make it work for me. I've got a plan . . ."

Joe didn't give a damn what plans the Shed bastard had. He had a few of his own. If only he could get his hands on that amount of money! God, what a haul! What a lovely set-up he'd landed himself in!

"I've a friend," the youth explained secretly. "He's got connections and I've promised to invest in his operation. I stand to double my loot in forty eight hours if all goes well."

"And if it doesn't?" Joe wanted to know.

"Shit, we all make mistakes as the telly commercial says."

That was poor policy according to Joe's current thoughts. A guy with five thousand in the sock should have more than a fifty-fifty chance. He should *command* a definite seven grand profit. No less. In this era money talked. More than in bygones. Especially illicit reserves. They spoke hardest, highest. What with inflation round the corner, bank loans tough to get and a semi-squeeze on, the guy with loot in hand had to be kingpin of all he surveyed.

"Have you handed him the money yet?" Joe asked.

The youth narrowed his eyes and pierced Joe with a menacing stare. "You're wanting an awful lot of information, mate. What if I have or haven't? Is it any concern of yours?"

Joe smiled to allay the other's naturally suspicious nature. "I don't give a damn. I was just being friendly."

"With friends who stick unwanted noses in who needs enemies!" came the retort.

"Okay . . . okay, forget I mentioned it."

"Forgotten, mate!" the youth held out his hand and they shook. "I'm Terry Walker. How about a drink?"

"Over there?" Joe nodded at the Green Dragon.

"No, thanks. There are too many ears in places like that. I know a small intimate club not far away. Care to become a member?"

"Not if it costs me."

"It won't. I guarantee that." The noise of a skidding car blocked his next sentence and when the taxi driver involved in a near miss got tired of the sound of his own voice Joe asked: "What was that you said?"

Terry grinned and tilted his bowler to a carefree angle. "I said we might find a couple of dollybirds, too."

"Nothing doing if they're Soho tarts."

"This club is in Mayfair, mate. Only the best for us suedeheads, eh?" He began walking down Shaftesbury Avenue with Joe matching

139

stride for stride. The youth walked fast and Joe was out of puff when they finally entered a narrow, twisting street partway up Regent Street. Opening a door, Terry paused at the bottom of steep stairs. "No name. No publicity. Members only and no cops allowed."

When Terry pushed him through a padded door which effectively deadened the sound coming from a L-shaped bar, Joe was instantly conscious of alert eyes watching his every move. There were about fifteen people in the bar - all with that quiet reserve associated with a better class Englishman. A brunette barmaid leant her small breasts on the counter and said: "Sorry - we only . . ." Her face broke into a large smile as Terry came into view. "Oh, you're with a member. That's fine. Come on, take a pew."

Joe let Terry settle his rump on a stool first and took stock of the barmaid. She was in her middle thirties, vivacious, darker skinned than the usual London girl, and she wore a mini-skirt which permitted the customers to see her very shapely thighs right to the flare of her buttocks.

"How about a membership card for my friend, Joe Hawkins?" Terry asked disinterestedly. His attention was focused on a slot machine standing idle in an end of the "L".

"Tokens, Terry?"

"A couple of quids' worth, Vera. I feel lucky tonight."

"Monica got the jackpot last Wednesday. I don't know if it's worth chasing."

"How much?" Terry asked.

"Sixteen pounds exactly."

"About ten of that belonged to me." The youth grinned, tossing his hat at a carved eagle. Apparently he made a habit of this feat. The bowler shook and firmly rested on the eagle's beak.

Vera slid a card across her counter in Joe's direction. "What'll it be gents?"

"Something strong and sexy,"Terry chided.

"Pink gin?"

"Hell, no. Rum and Coke."

"And you, sir?" Joe loved the "sir". Having to call old Trotter and the senior partners "sir"every day of his working week had made him yearn to get the same treatment elsewhere. "I'll have a large Scotch with soda."

"How about this?" Terry asked softly as Vera attended to their drinks. "Each of those blokes is worth a hundred thousand and more."

Joe glanced down the bar. The men in question stood in a small group engaged in almost whispered discussion. It was evident they were dealing with business queries from the number of times they referred to catalogues and printed broadsheets.

"Who are they?" Joe asked.

"Antique dealers. They're part of a ring."

Joe had heard about such things although he did not know how rings operated nor why they were supposed to be illegal. He did understand the amount of money to be made from antiques though. Providing one had knowledge, that was.

"What about them?" He gestured at another group.

Terry shrugged casually. "Society layabouts. They've got money but more credit than a bank account. I wouldn't waste time on them."

"Is your friend here?"

Terry placed a hand across Joe's blank application card. "We were going to forget that."

"Sorry." Deliberately now, Joe removed the youth's hand and asked: "Got a pen?"

"Before you fill it in - where do you live?"

"A flatlet in Bayswater."

"Not good enough. Use my address ..." A pen and business card were placed next to the application. "It's phoney but it gets results. Make it "care of" the office ..."

Joe was dicovering there was a lot to this Mayfair congame. The card Terry used said he was a director of William Blakison & Paartners, Property Management Consultants. The address was in the City and there was also a telephone number. "Is this real?" Joe asked, pointing at the number.

"Sure it is. That's where I work. I have a cubby-hole of an office with a private line."

"Your own office?"

"Use your noggin' mate. No! I'm not a director or anything like that. I'm a glorified message boy."

"Why work when you've got loot?" Joe was confused.

"'cause the bloody cops are still trying to find my cash, stupid." Vera came with the drinks and Terry's tokens. Taking his rum and the one-armed bandit's fodder the youth hurried to the machine.

"He certainly has gambling fever," Vera said confidentially.

"Yes," Joe murmured and began writing. He didn't enjoy being left

141

alone with the woman. If she questioned him too closely he might give Terry's game away. When he completed the application he pushed it back at Vera and quickly went to Terry's side.

"I thought you'd be raping Vera by now," the youth remarked.

"Is she . . . ?"

"Easy. We've all had her."

"I'm only here for the beer," Joe laughed to cover his inability to mingle freely with these people. If it had been the East End he could have handled any situation but there was a barrier somewhere inside him when it boiled down to leaping into the high income gathering. His was a fumbling in the darkest night effort to get to grips with a new way of life. The mistakes he would surely make could not be allowed to happen in this his first Mayfair jaunt. Later, once he solo-ed he would brush aside those little embarrassments and treat them as experience gained. Not tonight. Not alone. Vera could wait. The day would dawn soon enough for her brand of passion.

"Take your bloody hat off. Hang your umbrella on a hook. Relax. Nobody's going to debag you, Joe." Another token slid into the machine and the wheels whirred as Terry manipulated the lever to some secret pattern of pressure.

Coming back to Terry with his drink in one hand and a cigarette in the other, Joe asked: "How did you learn to talk their language?"

"I studied books. Novels about dollybirds and Mayfair rogues. I went into Bond Street shops and listened. It didn't take long to twig what they said and how they said it."

Joe admired the Chelsea skinhead's . . . ex-skinhead's . . . determination to break loose and establish his name in society. Frankly, Joe didn't read much. Headlines in the *Standard* or the sports news in the *Mirror*. A few times every year he bought a racy, sexy paperback but he seldom finished those. Once he devoured the violence and the sex he flung it away.

Three oranges came up for Terry and he scooped the coins into his hand. "Best way to get with it, Joe is to take one of their women to bed." Another token vanished into the machine's greedy jaw. "These birds talk all the while. They don't ever stop chatting about what is happening."

"Do you ever get into punch-ups?"

Terry scowled. "Not unless I have to."

"Don't you miss an aggro?"

"Bloody right, mate . . ." Terry glanced around. "Drop it, Joe."

"You going to play that thing all night?" The infernal whirr, clatter, tink of the machine was driving Joe nuts. He felt tight inside. The sensation was an old one. Back in the old days when his mates were with him he'd have found some bastard to kick or some bovver to relieve his tensions. Now, what was there to do? Bloody nothing! If it hadn't been for Terry's loot and a slim chance of getting his fingers on some of it he'd have taken off right then. Instead, he stayed - and suffered, and bought fresh drinks contrary to the rules of strictly membership clubs . . .

CHAPTER SEVEN

FOUR oily sardines stared up at him from the dark toast. An open tin containing a few broken bodies lay beside his teacup like a cramped communal graveyard recently violated. "What a bloody breakfast!" he swore at the Norwegian product. He'd been skimping on food lately. Getting a wardrobe of suitable clothes counted for more than filling his stomach with the kind of food would-be Mayfair clan considered barely adequate to sustain flesh.

He thumped a ketchup bottle, spilling sauce on sardines and naked thighs. Fingering the spilt ketchup back on to his plate he gazed across the small table to where a breezze blew his curtains aside from an open window. Directly across the street he could see the old biddy peeping from the shadowy interior of her room. He didn't give a damn if she got a kick out of watching his total nudity. He enjoyed eating breakfast in the buff. He felt like flashing it at her but decided to concentrate on the bloody sardines instead.

Attacking the insipid meal he thought about last night. That Terry was a cagey bastard. All he knew for sure was that the deal would be made today at Baker Street underground station. Nothing else. He was invited to be present for what he conjectured would be a highly crooked transaction. There was no inkling how many others would attend the great ceremony nor if he would ever get the slightest opportunity to grab off a few hundred for himself.

That was the horrible dilemma for Joe. He wanted in with Terry but he wanted to make a profit from their association. And he knew that any sleight of hand on his part would alienate the new friendship. He liked being a member of a posh club but if he double-crossed the youth he could not return there. Not unless he wanted to risk getting the hell kicked out of his hide. An ex-skinhead could revert to bovver boots if the occasion was provocative enough.

Spearing a defenceless sardine from its tin he told it: "I'd be worse off than you poor bastards. I'd be crippled - you're dead already!"

If only he could get his old mob back in action. They'd bleedin' take care of Terry's mates.

"Christ! Cut it out!"

The words exploded in the room, his head. Seizing the dirty dishes he dropped them into the sink and stared at his reflection in a stained mirror over it.

"The blokes you're meeting don't say bleedin'," he told the unshaved image. "They don't wish for mates, they don't give a damn about anything. Think posh, talk posh, act posh - and bloody do the screw-happy lot of 'em when you can."

He grinned and scratched his shoulder blade. Walking to the window he stood in full naked view of the woman over there. He made a gesture she could not fail to understand and saw a shape flit back into the dark interior away from the curtains. If only she would leave those curtains apart sometime he might get a peep and see if she was a worthwhile target for his frustrations.

Turning from the window, he considered what to wear. He wanted a change from the City suit and bowler. It may be a symbol of what he had become - in part. But a change did a guy good. He'd spent his ill-gotten gains extravagantly. He still had a nest-egg but he was nursing that. This room was getting on his wick. He wanted a bigger, better pad. One with private bath and decent kitchen, seperate bedroom and a fashionable lounge. He'd studied these things recently; listened to the office wallahs talking about their mews cottage, or the flat in St. John's Wood, or the *pater's* town house. Dissatisfaction burned at his guts like hell's fires. Going up in the world meant an abode to match one's opinion of oneself.

Carefully selecting a frilled shirt, he put that on then flung it aside when he felt his stubbled chin. Quickly, he washed, shaved, applied talc and deoderant. He didn't favour the smells but his in-crowd insisted they were vital. Now, he donned the shirt, and buttoned it. Next, he chose a dark blue suit and highly polished shoes to match;

a floral wide tie, brilliant white socks and lightweight cream-coloured gloves. He would not wear a hat but his umbrella belonged. It was, for Joe, a suedehead's "bovver boots" insignia. Anyway, if Terry got nasty the umbrella was his weapon of escape. He fondled the sharp tip. He'd done a marvelous job on it - just like a sword point and skilfully blackened so not to attract undue attention from the uptight mob.

He frowned. Perhaps he should apply a covering coat of brass-gold paint to make it appear more like an authentic metal tip. He wished he could afford to buy a sword-stick - always providing he could find a dealer stupid enough to flog him one. That was the trouble with items classified as dangerous by the police. Dealers seldom left themselves open to . . . *Hey, wait a mo!* he thought. Those blokes in Terry's club were antique merchants. If he could get the goods on one of 'em he might make a blackmailing switch. Sword-stick for dropping out of the picture.

"They're worse than any heavy mob," he told himself after a few minutes exciting contemplation. "They'd cut me into so many bloody pieces I'd be lucky to have a leg left for burial."

It had been a lovely thought though. One to forget in the light of cold, hard reasoning. He didn't want undue trouble. Terry was bovver enough for the moment.

*

Drugs - that's what they're bargaining for!

Joe stood frozen as the realisation struck home. Terry didn't need to tell him anything. He recognised those samples being secretively passed from hand to hand - all except his, naturally. He was the outsider looking in; the guy who wasn't there.

"A quick sale'll make you two cool grand, mate," a thick-necked man was saying to Terry. He got his samples back and dropped them into a jacket pocket. "I'll give you a few addresses for starters."

"How come you don't flog the stuff?" Terry asked with suspicion shadowing his features.

"You must be jokin'," the man snorted. "The fuzz know me by sight. I'd get within a mile of Soho and the bastards would nick the lot."

"Has it got to be right in Soho?"

Joe had the same idea. Something about the deal stank. He

couldn't see a middle man backing off from a handsome profit this close to payday.

The man shuffled, passing a handkerchief across a sweat-filmed forehead. "Sonny, lemme explain how we operate. I import it, have it mixed and packaged and up the anti to include my rake-off. You take the big - and I mean BIG - risk getting in touch with the street pushers. I'm not a mug. I want a return on my investment - not two, maybe three years."

"I still can't see why you . . ." Terry mumbled.

"Crissakes, it's bleedin' simple," the man said in exasperation. "I'm not goin' to push the stuff. I'm selling for a big price. You make yours and we all go home happy. Okay?"

Terry turned to his mate a small, fat guy with glasses and pimples on his neck. He dressed neat but no amount of new clothes would ever make him appear more than a cheap spiv.

"How about it, Fred?"

"It's up to you, Terry. I like the deal."

Terry's eyes flashed at Joe. "And you?" he asked.

Joe hesitated. There were a few questions he would have liked to ask but just putting himself that far into the picture would have given away his ultimate aims. "Do we have to cart loads of packages in plain sight of the law?"

The man chuckled. "Easy seen you kids are rank amateurs," he said sarcastically. "It's all in those lockers . . ." He pointed at a row of storage lockers nearby and produced six keys from a trouser pocket. "Each locker has enough stuff to make one delivery. There are three of you. If the fuzz gets wise then you don't lose too much profit."

"Hey," Joe said. "If they grab the stuff they also grab the bloke."

"S'truth . . ." Terry exclaimed.

"Jeeze," the man exhaled. "Don't tell me you haven't thought about getting nicked?"

Terry covered fast. "Of course we have, old chap."

The man laughed. "Old chap? God, you kids!"

"I'll take it," Terry said suddenly. "Pay the man, Fred."

As Fred handed over Terry's cash, the youth drew Joe aside. "Are you in with us?" he asked.

Joe hesitated dramatically. He was in - right up to getting a few of those locker keys. But he wanted Terry to believe he felt apprehensive. It wouldn't do to jump too fast. Not now. Not knowing how bloody suspicious his new mate could be. "Well . . ."

"Ahhh, come on, Joe. I need your help. I'll pay."

"How much?"

"Half of what we make on your deliveries. How's that?"

"Fair," Joe allowed. "I'm in, Terry."

The youth breathed relief. "God, this is not going to be a quick turn-over," he said softly. "We've got to find buyers."

"Your friend mentioned some addresses," Joe reminded.

Terry tore back to Fred. Speaking to the man he asked: "Where's the addresses?"

The man wadded the money into his small case which had been ready by his left leg all through the discussion. "Got a pencil and paper?"

Terry found an old envelope and used Fred's pen. The man reeled off five names and club addresses adding a few words of caution after each. One struck Joe as being a complete waste of time when the man said: "He always takes deliveries in the club as he makes his contacts. You may wait a few hours but he's not mean. You'll get top whack there."

"Like being a sitting duck for any cop doing an undercover job," Joe thought. *"That one is not for me!"*

An idea lit up Joe's brain. A brilliant notion for getting away with his haul and not having Terry on his back. One of those million-to-a-quid brainwaves. He felt immensely better for having had the solution to his problem landed right inside his mind.

At last, the locker keys changed hands and the man lost himself in the growing crowds fighting their way in and out of the station. Joe noticed another man join their late associate, and smiled. Trust that type to bring along protection in case the buyers decided to pull a fast one!

Terry rubbed his hands and chuckled. "We've got it made, mates," he announced. "Let's get started . . ."

*

By seven-thirty exactly, Joe had collected six hundred quid near enough. He had given Terry the bulk of it and kept his profit percentage - a mere eighty five pounds. Fred had departed for his third contact's pad and Terry was all set to send Joe into the lion's den when Joe suddenly said: "I got a tip from my last sucker."

Terry's face tensed. "Bad news?"

Joe laughed and slapped the youth on the back. "Great news, mate!" He eased two packets into his pocket, hating the way they spoilt the cut of his jacket. "I'll have an extra lot. This guy gave me a sure thing. Said he'd personally make a telephone call and describe me in advance."

Terry frowned at the envelope in his hand - the one with the address of their last contact. "I wanted you to handle this, Joe," he said slowly. "I could make your delivery and explain . . ."

"Too late for that, Terry," Joe said apologetically. "I can't get hold of this bloke again and he did say how . . ."

"Hell!" Terry exploded. "Okay, it's all loot. When you've got the money meet me here. Looks like I'll be there for a few hours."

Joe studied the address carefully and nodded. "Is Fred coming along too?"

"Yeah. We might as well finish the day having a few drinks. We can unload the last lockers tomorrow night."

"I won't be long, Terry. Let me have those five packages, eh? If my man doesn't take 'em I can bring it back to your bloke." Joe held his breath. This was the vital moment.

Without anticipating trouble, Terry handed the extra over. *Probably trusts me after all,* Joe thought. *A typical Shed idiot!*

Waving his farewell, Joe sauntered into the mainstream of traffic, moving down into the bowels of London's rabbit warren. When he reached the bottom he waited five minutes and hurried back to the lockers. One was empty and he emptied his pockets, placed a coin in the slot and removed the key. Whistling and twirling his umbrella, he walked out into Baker Street and across the road to a pub. Two large *Hundred Pipers'* and he went back to the underground station. There were telephones inside and his call was most important . . .

CHAPTER EIGHT

THE story had been buried inside the newspaper. Joe read it with unsuppressed excitement as his train slowed at Marble Arch. He had expected a front page banner headline, but he appreciated the eventual outcome of his tip-off regardless.

Police last night raided the premises of Soho's Oblique Club and confiscated a large quantity of narcotics. Two men are presently facing charges following an anonymous telephone call. The club management denied any connection with the men. A spokesman told our reporter: "We operate within the law. Any member suspected of using drugs is automatically out."
The Oblique Club is normally frequented by teenagers and has a good reputation although, as the owners point out, "Rotten apples are found in every barrel and I suppose we're no exception."
The men are due to appear this morning at magistrate's court.

The locker key felt very comfortable in Joe's pocket. He could afford to allow a few days to pass before capitalising on Terry's *misfortune*.

Smiling at a bird seated across the aisle, Joe calmly progressed to the sports pages. Nothing old Totter would say today could damp his high spirits. Tonight he had a date with Lois. In this mood she would lose her cherished - but hardly priceless - possession. He would buy a bottle and ask her to help him find a decent flat somewhere closer to Mayfair. Being a suedehead had more compensations than being crowned king of all skinheads. What did he need with gangs backing him! He had accomplished a masterful stroke without even resorting to violence. Not that he would ever outgrow the basic need to use force whenever the occasion demanded, or whenever he felt it necessary to relieve pent-up frustrations. The world was a savage place and only the strong and the brutal could ever rightfully claim a niche. That was his thinking!

Letting the paper slip on to his lap, Joe tried to calculate how much he was currently worth. He had his "commission money" kindly paid by Terry for "services about to be rendered". That was a bloody good laugh! Getting paid to doublecross a mate! The fool! He had a locker key and inside that locker a cool four hundred quid's worth of pot. At market prices, that was. He'd find a buyer, make the deal and drop out from the scene. He didn't like messing around with drugs. The profits were fantastic but he had an aversion. Nothing to do with morality. Just - it wasn't his pitch.

Almost five hundred sounded nice in his mind. With that kind of loot he could easily afford to splash out on decent food, more top notch gear, a snazzy flat and a couple of birds. Not just Lois, although making her was of paramount importance. He did not like admitting failure. She would be his. Tonight. After her, there would be others. Ones used to performing bloody wonders and not bothered about getting pregnant or betraying daddy's trust. God, that was a lark. Imagine a bird in this day and age keeping herself whole because she had promised daddy! It was unbelievable. Fantastically so.

The newspaper dropped to the floor and went unnoticed by Joe. He was way ahead of the present - this dreary day with its breathless waiting for events to mature. Everything he had read about suedeheads made him want to develop his talents to the exquisite point offering ambition's fulfilment.

If he had to appear above suspicion he would, of necessity be compelled to belong to some notable, worthy youth fraternity. That meant questions in the office. Some of his snooty-nosed workmates attended clubs specifically aimed at helping out less fortunates than themselves. Joe would get some names and make enquiries. When he found the one he reckoned would suit his purposes best he would join. Until then, he had more than sufficient to be getting along with . . . Lois, flogging the dope, finding new accommodation . . .

Lois's large, luminous blue eyes widened in surprise when she saw the liquor bottles arrayed on a table. She did not know that Joe had bought the reproduction sofa table on his way home especially for the occasion . . . well, not quite especially. He would need decent furniture when he got his close-to-Mayfair flat. This was a start and making an impression at the same time. He had also splurged on drink - a bottle of Hundred Pipers, Captain Morgan Rum, Noilly Prat and several types of mix.

"Joe, how much do you think you can drink?" she asked with a pleasant smile.

He placed his bowler on a peg and removed his coat and jacket. "Get comfortable, Lois and forget about putting a limit on booze. Let me have your sweater."

"That's all you're getting, Joe," she replied firmly as he helped remove the pearl-studded Austrian sweater. He could tell it was expensive from the way it felt.

Ignoring her remark which was too pointed to please, he poured a treble Scotch into each glass and added the minimum mix. Even with the window open the flatlet was hot - clammy hot. And he could see the old biddy across the street doing her peeping from behind those static curtains. God, he hoped she'd get an eyeful tonight! If she was that bloody frustrated she'd have an emotional kitten when he began stripping Lois.

Handing the glass to Lois he said: "Cheers,"and settled on the bed. "I'd like to ask a favour of you, Lois," he said finally as she prowled the room sipping her drink and pulling faces at its strength. "I'm not happy living here and I thought you'd like to help me find another place - nearer the West End; something better."

Her shoulders moved in a shrug which only served to emphasise her lovely breasts. She was wearing a frilly blouse, a - of all things - suede skirt down to mid-thigh, tights and flat-heeled shoes. Her hair was still tied in a knot at the nape of her slender neck - ready, Joe believed, to be untied and caressed as passions began to rise.

"Why me?"

"You've got taste. You're extra special in my estimation." He hid a grin. Terry had suggested reading books and he had. One. The line came directly from that! Admittedly the book lay under his bed open at page twenty three. He was a painfully slow reader but his memory for things which could progress his ambitions was excellent.

Lois preened self-consciously. She adored men payng her unsolicited compliments. Joe grew a foot in stature in *her* estimation! "Thanks for that, Joe. I'd be glad to assist you."

He had his campaign all mapped out. First the feint, then the lull to throw the enemy off balance until, finally, the main body was sent in to totally destroy opposition.

"I'm so tired," he lied. "My back aches something awful."

Lois came and sat on the bed beside him.

"Would you like to massage me?" he asked softly.

"I'm not much good at that."

"Every little counts."

She sipped her randy-making drink again, face slightly flushed already. "Where?" she asked politely.

He grinned, began removing his shirt. Her eyes blinked, staring unkindly. He quickly explained: "You can't massage weary muscles through a shirt."

She accepted his excuse and waited until he lay along the bed. He was muscular, with no unsightly fat on his young body. Her hands went unerringly to his shoulders and began to knead the flesh. He groaned in simulated ecstacy.

151

"Lovely, Lois. I could have this done to me all night."

"Not by me!" Her hands temporarily ceased their ministrations.

He sat upright and finished his drink. Gesturing for her to follow suit he poured fresh supplies - making the second one stronger still. Seated beside her he raised his glass, drank half in one go. He had, apparently, never heard of moderation. "Want to massage me again?"

She felt slightly woozy. "Only for a minute," she said.

Flat on his stomach with her tender hands sliding over his skin Joe sensed the moment right for that lull. He moaned. "Thanks, Lois. You're sweet ..." *Another line from the book.* He twisted around to face her. "Have you ever had a massage?"

She sampled her drink. "Once. After a Turkish bath."

"Did you like it?"

"Smashing!" She giggled. "I'm getting sloshed, Joe."

"On two drinks?" he asked.

"They're strong."

"Don't you drink much?" He knew she didn't.

"Not much," she confessed. "And I haven't eaten yet."

"We'll go out for dinner, eh?"

She nodded. "I think we should - and soon."

He avoided saying when they would eat. "A friend of mine taught me how to massage," he said nonchalantly. *The campaign was reaching a crucial stage.*

"Oh!" her eyes suggested interest.

"Would you like me to show you?"

"Do I have to take my blouse off?"

"But not your brassiere," he joked.

That seemed to satisfy her sense of decency. Without a word she removed the blouse to reveal breasts barely concealed in a half-cup bra. It was all he could do to refrain from taking those beautiful orbs from their exciting cups and showering them with lustful kisses.

"On your tummy," he commanded.

When his fingers began to knead her silken flesh he deliberately hooked himself into her brassiere straps several times before saying: "I can't get the right sweep to this with that on."

She rose on an elbow, took another drink. "Joe . . ."

"I promise no tricks, Lois," he said hurriedly.

"Oh, hell!" Her hands came back and unhooked the offending straps. She held the front cups tight against her breasts and sank back on the bed.

Slowly, he massaged her spine ... up, down, around. Like a spider spinning a web he covered her entire back, moving in the direction of her sides, on to the lovely surface of those exciting breasts, under her armpits.

"Like it?"

She moaned. "Lovely."

"If I could get to the base of your spine ...

Without thinking she writhed, unzipped her suede skirt and pushed that and her tights down to reveal the thrilling curves of her gorgeous buttocks. The top of her brief panties showed and in seconds his fingers worked them down ... down ... until all her bottom was uncovered.

The final attack was due!

His fingers curled round her exquisite curves ... probing regions not normally included in the masseurs' attentions. Her gentle undulations encouraged him; her gasping sent him into a tizzy of uncontrolled brashness.

"Lois . . ." he panted turning her onto her back, hands now demanding as they pushed the offending clothing down ... to reveal in entirety.

Her chestnut hair had loosened and spread to frame her face. Her eyes closed, her mouth pleading for his hot kisses.

Watch this! Joe mentally told the old biddy across the street. He tore his clothes from him, flung himself down on the bed with Lois surrendering to his adventurous gropings. His tongue darted into her open mouth, his fingers curled into her tights and panties as her legs came up to facilitate the completion of her abandonment.

In those precious seconds before he mounted her, Joe thought: *She's better than anything I've ever had* ... and then her flesh held him in a vice, her desire a seething, boiling mass which could not be denied ...

CHAPTER NINE

LIKE a king in residence in his castle Joe marched from room to room and luxuriated in the knowledge that his deflowering of Lois had not been without its compensations. She had been terrific. He understood now why some men *insisted* on having a virgin to bed when the experienced world of professional women was always available. But there was more to Lois than mere sex although that had been quite a thrilling lesson in the "unknown".

Lois had society tastes which he could not begin to understand. She had helped him select the average flat for an up-and-coming young executive without knowing that his income was strictly derived from illicit activities. The amount his office paid would furnish a bedsitter in Balham, nothing more.

It had been four weeks since he last bedded Lois. After the initial ritual she had grown less attractive, less interesting. Her notions of security, marriage and children scared the hell out of him. Anyway, he never had any intentions of sticking with her. Her virginity had been the prime target. Once that went, so did his desire to count her amongst his "friends".

He frowned at an Empire mirror with twin candlestick sconces. What friends did he have? Since going "inside" he had been alone. There had been Terry and, of course, Lois. But they had not been friends. They were people to be used. Mrs. Hale tried to befriend him, but unless she could offer something sexual she would remain a means to an unending source of quick loans.

He was friendless!

He was nature's castigated soul!

Laughing as he strolled from master bedroom to lounge he again marvelled at the compactness, the luxuriousness of this elite flat. Sixteen guineas per week for what should have cost twice as much. Lois had been invaluable. *An associate of daddy's had informed her of a place he wished to rent.* Naturally, as a close social acquaintance he would let it go for less than market value! Naturally! Half-price yet!

God, what bleedin' fools these upper-class people were! How the hell did they ever make the money they had when the old school tie governed their every move?

On the open market the flat would easily have fetched £40 per week inclusive. Joe knew. He had studied the ads in the *Evening Standard*. Places less than a street away went for sixty per week. Exclusive, too. And this one was tastefully and completely furnished.

Lois had demonstrated her "in" with snobland. No references. No guarantees. Just a simple lease and a fifty quid deposit against undue

154

wear-and-tear on the furnishings. One week's rent in advance and - hey, presto - he had arrive in style! What a place compared to his Plaistow home!

In every way he ruled supreme. Authentic antiques as against Co-op furnishings of the cheapest variety. Spacious rooms and wall-to-wall carpets when he had been used to cramped surroundings and threadbare rugs trying to cover ugly floorboards. A modern American-style kitchen with all the latest gimmicks. His mother still cooked on an ancient gas stove and used utensils so thin on the bottom they could almost be used as sieves.

He went to the front windows - plural. From one he could see Marble Arch. From the other an expanse of expensive flats above élite shops. The windows had lace curtains and heavy velvet drapes to match the decor of the lounge. The fireplace was large and suitable for burning yule logs fifty two weeks in the year. There was even an extractor fan in the room and fan heaters which blew cool air in summer or hot in winter if lighting a fire proved too much of a chore.

According to the owner, the porter collected the garbage every second day and a maid was available if one wished to shell out an additional £1.50 per week. Joe didn't bother with the service. He had a vacuum cleaner and could do that much for himself. Or would until Dame Fortune smiled more benevolently on him! His money would not last forever. With the coppers hot in Soho he had been lucky getting a quick one-shot sale for the drugs at a rock bottom price, bringing him £375. And stupid bastards like Terry did not grow on trees. Not in Brooklyn or in London!

He grinned at the leather-bound bookshelves. He had got *that* title from the owner's penchant for reading best-selling novels. The flat was a junior library. He reckoned there were more than six hundred books in it - every room had its private bookcase; its personalised reading. The kitchen contained volumes on cookery; the lounge *Encyclopedia Britannica*, Shakespeare and poetical works with a scattering of Tolstoy, Marx, Hitler, Browning, Byron, Pope, Milton, Macaulay, Burns, Scott and Hemingway; one bedroom devoted entirely to Chandler, Moffatt, Runyon, Fleming; the master bedroom exclusively reserved for erotica and witchcraft.

His "fortune" was disastrously low now. His salary barely covered current expenses. He had coaxed Totter to suggest he deserved a higher stipend than starting pay and been agreeably shocked at receiving an extra four pounds a week. On reflection, he agreed with their new assessment of his worth. He had managed to pick up quite a lot of know-how. Totter could take sick or fade away any time and he would be able to carry on for a short period without help.

"*I wish the old bastard would die,*" he thought. "*I could make a bomb from cooking those books!*"

He shrugged off the thought. Totter could last for another decade at least. He was one of those dried-up old prunes who show their wrinkles but don't get older. Not mentally where it counted in accountancy, anyway! The infrequent slip-up was minor - certainly not a capital mistake like Joe hoped to come across.

With what he had salted away and what he got each week he could manage. Just! It meant dipping into ill-gotten gains but he did have an exclusive pad, a decent wardrobe, a swish address. He was all set up and rarin' to go . . .

*

Marissa Stone was celebrating her forty fifth birthday alone. She knew the terrible frustrations of spinsterhood. At night, she lay in bed writhing in untold agony wishing a man - any man - would burst into her room and rape her. Her only sexual memory was the vicar near Oxford and even that had been discoloured by his wife's ghostly presence and the organ-loft trysting place which did not remotely resemble her pre-conceived idea of a nuptial bed. She had found the floor hard, unyielding. She had not been keen on baring her limbs to centuries old dirt nor to having her virginity taken in the midst of tolling bells and swelling organ music.

For all the enjoyment she felt there were a hundred displeasures to counteract the briefly concluded memories shared.

She had no comparison to judge her vicar by. She read startling modern novels and often attended the cinema where bare bosoms and panting cut-short scenes suggested more to sex than she and her vicar had ever experienced. She wished to know the full scope of emotional permissiveness yet lacked the gall to offer her flesh for just any young blood's lust.

In her search for fruition she had thrown herself body and soul into youth club activities. As a Sunday School teacher she felt she had accomplished enough to teach the youth of today where they had detoured from the "true path". Yet, she did not honestly understand where the same path took one. She was a lonely woman wandering in the tracks of a celibate Son when all she wanted was *the* hot-blooded encounter with a Devil's Apprecentice.

Marissa did not consider herself a hypocrite yet she was the acme of hypocritical disillusionment. She loved speaking of God's commandments but, in private, she absolved herself with nightmares voicing their disapproval of her chaste spinsterhood.

The club held nightly meetings in a former warehouse not far from Marylebone station. After two years operation, the trustees had managed to discourage certain Edgware Road types from venturing into their sanctum sanctorum. At first, brawls had been commonplace. More than one local alderman had demanded that the club be closed. But, with perseverence and a slow weeding-out process, they now enjoyed praise, support and approval.

In her capacity as a senior counsellor, Marissa Stone came into contact with every member. She formed friendships with those willing to take her advice yet not once had she dared to exploit those associations. Many a time she wished she could kick over the traces and have an affair with some of the athletic youths she dreamed of nightly. Always, though, decency forbade her the ultimate intimacies of man-woman relationships.

In a sense, she knew that some of the boys would have taken her to bed had it not been for her stern, uncompromising attitudes when more than a friend-in-need emotion began to raise its lovely-ugly head. Truthfully, she was scared stiff of getting involved. Those lonely hours spent writhing in bed could not make her waking self condescend to having physical contacts with any of the young, virile, panting men. Much as she wanted them, there was a conscience-created barrier denying her fulfilments so extraordinarily sought after in the dark privacy of night.

Undoubtedly, she was an attractive woman. Age had not been unkind. She could still favourably compare with women ten years her junior. She had a slender appeal most men found exciting. Her breasts were still firm, her thighs solid and softly cool to the touch. Her touch. Mankind had yet to sample those delights in a comfortable bed. She had a pleasant face with warm, green eyes, a slightly sensuous mouth and silken honey-blonde hair. She was neither tall nor short and her clothes *always* were bought to please the opposite sex.

She had definite likes and dislikes and her political leanings sometimes shocked those liberals she compelled to associate with as a youth club organiser. She did not believe the permissive society had to be encouraged. In fact, she did her utmost to foster old-time family pangs in the hearts of her converts.

Perhaps, she thought wearily, *that is why I am still a spinster; why those with whom I could gladly fornicate refuse to consider me an object of lustful dalliance* . . .

*

Joe heard about the club in a roundabout way. One evening, as he relaxed in Terry's old Mayfair hangout, he happened to get drawn into a conversation dealing with Terry's sentence.

"You were his pal," a brash loud mouth said as he downed a pink gin. "Didn't you know he was a drug addict?"

Joe contemplated Vera's hidden navel and wondered if he should make the grade with her that night. She gave every indication of being available, willing, excited by the prospect of being his "mate". Their Tarzan-Jane mental clashings had aroused in him a desire to find out if she performed as well as she suggested she would. And yet . . .

"Terry wasn't addicted," Joe informed the group. "He never took drugs. A friend of his coaxed him into a one-time deal and it went sour."

"Come off it," loudmouth exploded. "People don't get coaxed into sordid things like narcotics."

"Have it your way," Joe sighed and signalled Vera for a refill.

"Do you take drugs?" the man asked next.

Joe swung on his stool. "Mister, leave me alone!"

The man inched backwards, eyes suddenly alert to his danger. Joe looked positively menacing. "Kids," he said covering his inability to match Joe's ferociousness. "Man, I wouldn't have a job trying to sort them out these days. I know of a club of drop-outs in Marylebone. It's supposed to make saints out of sinners but that's debatable."

Joe suddenly found himself interested. He had been searching for a youth club, or some fraternity catering for the modern society. He asked: "Where is this club?"

Loudmouth scoffed: "Don't tell me you're a do-gooder, too?"

"I'm not against progress," Joe answered in his best "Totter" retort. Shrugging, the man dived into a pocket and withdrew a bunch of business cards. Sorting through them he singled out one. "That's it," he said nastily, reaching the card to Joe.

Committing the address to memory, Joe smilingly returned the card saying: "Thanks. I don't believe it's my scene . . ."

*

Marissa Stone studied the new arrival with a jaundiced gaze. She did not particularly like the mode of dress nor the supercilious air with which the newcomer considered her group. Getting to her feet, and making excuses she approached the youth and asked: "May I be of some assistance?"

Joe sensed her animosity towards him and smiled. He invariably enjoyed a clash of personalities. He didn't give a damn what she thought of him nor did he have to belong to this outfit. That's what made his attitude harden. "That's doubtful," he said. "I came expecting something more lively."

Marissa refused to let her feelings get the better of her. "What precisely did you expect, Mr . . . ?"

"Joe Hawkins." Leaning on his umbrella he affected an upper-class frostiness - or what he hoped was the icy blast he sometimes got in the Mayfair bar. "I had an idea this would be some sort of sports club with nightly dances."

"Oh," Marissa said coldly. "We do have sporting activities and dancing but not every night. We try to act like responsible adults. All play and no work makes for weak characters."

"Tell that to the House of Lords," Joe sneered.

"Are you a communist?"

Joe laughed. "Do I look like a *Morning Star* reader?"

"People who answer questions with questions are usually afraid of their own convictions," Marissa said primly. "Mr. Hawkins, just what are you doing here?"

"I heard about this place and came to look it over," Joe replied with honesty.

"Are you seriously interested in joining?"

"That depends." He did not particularly care for the young people seated across the huge barn-like room. They gave him the creeps. Each one looked like a goodie-goodie - especially the girls.

"You think we might be too tame for you, is that it?"

He nodded. The woman appealed but he did not reckon her as a

159

source of pleasure. Her type seldom indulged in extra-marital excursions. Anyway, she was old enough to be his mother. Belonging to an acceptable organisation had advantages but one had to weigh every aspect of a situation before being committed. There must be clubs where a preponderance of the members were full of fun and not a bunch of sour-faced mummies.

"I'd like you to try your strength against Brian over there," Marissa said softly. "I should inform you he boxed for this club against the best German competition last year."

Joe sneered. Who the hell did she think he was? Boxing didn't appeal any more than wrestling. If he got into a fight it would be on terms he dictated, not rules laid down by some moth-eaten old earl long since dead. Anyway, he wasn't a muscle boy. He had worked as a coal-heaver and developed hard, durable biceps. But being able to throw sacks of coal didn't necessarily make a man another version of Samson. He preferred to toss a bird around a bed and nurse his energies through a night filled with passion.

"I'm not a boxer," he said. "I can fight but not for fun."

"If you'd care to join us you might be agreeably surprised," Marissa said finally. Something about Joe attracted her. At first, she had felt nothing but detestation for his cocky perusal of their club. She didn't like his outlook but then, she very seldom found new members making a big hit with her. She was always willing to let a youth's personality grow on her. Surface values were not measurable guides to what lay inside. Many people presented a hardened exterior to shield themselves from the hurts a mercenary world invariably dished out.

"Alright, but don't expect me to like it," Joe said as he followed the slender woman acrosss the room.

*

Basically Joe Hawkins had a "feeling" for violence. Regardless of what the do-gooders and the socialists and psychiatrists claimed, some people had an instinct bent on creating havoc and resorting to jungle savagery. Joe was one of these. Being part of a club which tried to foster a live-and-let-live fellowship did not weaken his desire to unleash brutal assaults on innocent folk. The club was a front to cover his deep, dark nature. A requirement for his suedehead cultism.

160

Unknown to Marissa Stone and the other adult workers, the Marylebone premises housed a growing collection of addicted youths. Joe found himself invited to join in extra-curricular activities which would have meant immediate castigation had Marissa heard the slightest whisper of what went on. It was as if Joe had been *guided* to the barn-like old warehouse. As if he had been fated to meet those others sharing his unsocial feelings.

Jeremy French came from a middle-class family shattered by scandal. Divorce and a succession of parental mistresses had sent him down the wrong road until, as a skinhead, he had been brought before a court and given a suspended sentence.

Larry Miller had always been on the "wrong side of the tracks" according to his story. His mother had been a gypsy, his father a lazy loafer unable to hold down any job for more than a month. When they moved into London from their native Birmingham, Larry had taken up with a gang and been it's leader until the Uxbridge police had finally laid a trap and nicked them all with the sole exception of Larry. Since then, he had kept his nose clean but had not deviated from a life of minor crime.

Walter Spencer had never belonged to a gang and had never seen his home ruined by infidelity. He had always been treated fairly and had been given the best possible education. Nevertheless, he had graduated into cultism from a sense of loyalty to his fellow teenagers and had grown to hate those things for which his family had stood. Decency, democracy, dedication to ideals sponsored by community committees held no appeal to his fertile brain which was totally devoted to the destruction of all that the elder generation considered "dear".

John Moore neither cared for life nor brotherliness. He hated because he did not get along with others. Although he formed an association with Joe, Walter, Jeremy and Larry he did not have any loyalty to them. No more than he felt it necessary to treat Marissa Stone as a benefactor. His entire attitude was one of "screw you, Jack - I'm okay." And he was okay, too. He had a highly paid position with an advertising agency, shared a flat with a sexy bird who loved him and got knocked about for her trouble, and had seven hundred pounds in the bank - a result of following form in *The Jockey*. John was no mug punter. He studied his nags, studied what the experts had to say and made an assessment from this. When he bet he could be sure of at least third place.

One thing Joe's crowd had in common was football mania. They did not support the same teams but they did stick together. Saturday was brutality day for each of them - be it at Upton Park, Stamford Bridge, Highbury or White Hart Lane.

A memory of getting "done" tormented Joe as he eased into Stamford Bridge behind Larry. They had agreed - no "Shed" today. They did not fit in "The Shed". Their clean-cut clothes, their aloofness, their lack of colours flying in the breeze would have invited automatic jibes - and worse. Chelsea's skinhead supporters had not lessened in their desire for trouble-making although great efforts to curb their vicious effectiveness was beginning to have results. The old days of outright slaughter had vanished as surely as bovver boots were a dying symbol of a passing phase.

Joe was happy to mingle with a more elite crowd than had been his normal Saturday afternoon wont. An umbrella did not stick out like a sore thumb here. Nor did those greying skies and weather forecast mean police suspicions as they entered the ground.

"There's a bunch of Chelsea fans," John exclaimed, pointing.

Walter grinned and gripped his umbrella as a General would his sword preparing to engage the enemy. "I see space behind them."

Larry and Jeremy were already pushing their way through the chanting crowd, climbing the steps to get on a level with the unsuspecting fans they had spotted. Yard by yard they advanced making room for John, Walter and Joe to squeeze through in their wake. Once, a woman screamed abuse as Larry trod on her foot but a growled oath soon stopped her cold. There was something threatening in those cold, detached faces to make her suffer in utter silence.

"This'll do," Jeremy announced.

Joe studied the position. When he had his gang his word had been law. No longer. The group he now found himself with refused to follow a leader. Each member was an individual, each permitted to voice his oppinion without fear of contradiction by a "king". In the three weeks plus a few days they had been together they had agreed to remain loosely linked whilst keeping personal identity and personal choice. Their only concession to a union had been in a name for themselves. That had been Joe's suggestion although the name had come from Larry's mind.

"Marylebone Martyr's" sounded like an ancient rebellion in Joe's ears but the others agreed it was fitting. After all, as John had said:

"In ten years time there'll be dozens of gangs aping us. Maybe we won't make headlines but somebody will get to hear about us. They always do . . ."

"The nearest exit is in the next aisle," Joe said softly.

Larry grunted and glanced over his shoulder.

Walter grinned, brought his umbrella up and removed the false tip which effectively hid its lethalness. Now he *was* a General with sword in hand!

John unscrewed the handle of his umbrella and withdrew a wicked little blade from the body. "Six inches of joy," John called his hardened steel toothpick.

"Watch where you jab that bloody thing," Jeremy snarled. "I don't want to be accused of murder."

"I can handle it," John replied indignantly.

The Chelsea supporters were beginning to howl as their team took the field. A scattering of Newcastle United fans sent up a valiant roar as the Geordies came into sight.

A police helmet moved back and forth across Joe's range of vision and he wished he had the guts to pig-stick the copper. The glare of publicity he had once adored did not appeal, however, and he concentrated his blind fury on the nearest Chelsea fans.

"Two . . . four . . . six . . . eight, who do we appreciate," a supporter hollered.

"Chelsea!" came the answer from a thousand throats.

Tension mounted within the packed stands. Newcastle won the toss and elected to play with the breeze behind them. The season was young and the teams suspect. According to last year's form, Chelsea should have an easy game but Newcastle were never a team to roll over and play dead for London clubs. They could fight hard and more than once took full honours back North.

Joe's umbrella snaked out and found a target. The man's anguished yell rose above his chanting comrades. By the time he turned, hands clasped to back of thigh, Joe was leaning on his umbrella with an innocent expression ignoring the other's hate-directed gaze.

"What bleedin' bastard stabbed me?" the man asked. Two of his fellow Chelsea mates were also facing Joe, anger darkening their heavy jowled features.

Joe tried to control a twitch in his left eye. "I beg your pardon?"

"You'll beg for bloody mercy you little . . ."

"Hey, Harry - look!"

The injured man tore his gaze from Joe. John stood with umbrella body clutched in one hand, wicked blade plainly seen in the other.

"It was 'im!" the third man yelled, surging forward.

Like greased lightning Larry sent a foot into the Chelsea fan's belly, his umbrella slashing upwards . . . cutting across the grunting throat in a perfectly executed motion.

Joe, not to be outdone, stabbed at the already injured individual, catching him in the forearm, drawing blood.

By now, the entire section was alerted to trouble. A sea of angry faces looked away from the pitch - Chelsea colours prominent on each neck or lapel. Jeremy, John, Walter and Larry were each engaged in unsporting contest - their umbrellas taking terrible toll on the opposition. Joe found himself pushed back as his companions fought a retreating action. In harmony, his weapon slashed and jabbed as the Chelseaites showed confusion in their solid-packed ranks. Joe didn't blame them. He would not have wanted to thrust himself onto a lethal blade or a rapier pointed sword-stick.

"Exit fast," John howled.

Joe caught sight of the coppers. He took one final look, felt his umbrella bury itself in a soft buttock and pulled it free before hurrying after his fleeing Marylebone Martyrs . . .

CHAPTER TEN

BEFORE he rebelled against society, Jeremy French had studied art. He had an ability which could have taken him to the top of the commercial profession but since dropping out, he had forsaken his sketching for a less ambitious position in the City. One evening, as the gang sat watching television in Joe's flat, Jeremy idly selected a pencil and paper and began to create a true likeness of Larry. In minutes, the gang forgot the TV and posed - one by one - for Jeremy's talented pencil.

"Can you letter, too?" Larry asked as excitement flushed his already highly-coloured face.

"Of course," came the egotistical reply.

"Then let's get together and make a code of ethics for the

Marylebone Martyrs," Larry suggested. "You know the kind of thing ... We, the undersigned, believe."

"We, the undersigned, hate ..." John corrected.

Walter sighed: "You advertising bods give me a fat pain."

"My boss would love to caress your pained area," John quipped. "He's as bent as hell."

"Did he sample yours?" Walter asked viciously.

John got to his feet, eyes narrowing.

"No fighting among ourselves," Joe said. "I don't want my pad ruined."

"Another remark like that and something will be ruined - *his sex life*!" John growled. "I don't ..."

"Crissakes, shut up!" Joe screamed. "Let's concentrate on what we hate."

"Queers," John said pointedly.

Walter smiled, still provoking; "Advertising bods!"

"Skinheads," Larry voiced.

Joe glared at him. "That isn't ... oh, yeah, I see. I hate social workers."

Jeremy sucked his pencil for a few moments and then said: "Marriage."

In rapid succession they had second thoughts, then third, fourth until, finally, John scowled and set his pencil down. "That is all. To cover this lot I'll need a bleedin' great sheet of board."

"Five boards," Larry reminded. "One each."

"How about a crest for the Marylebone Martyrs?" John asked with a watchful eye on Walter.

"You're the ad man," Joe said quickly. "Why don't you design something?"

"Agreed," Walter said sleepily. He was bored with the game. He felt in the mood for excitement followed by a good dose of sex. He'd taken a lot of booze on board that day and only fresh air, a dark alley confrontation and a bird in that order would bring him back to near-normal. He did not give a damn about John or their efforts to avoid trouble between themselves. He would just have willingly slashed John's throat as some other unfortunate guy's. Drink made him particularly nasty and he realised this. Yet, it never stopped him from over-indulging his taste for liquor. "I'll see you blokes at the club tomorrow. I'm splitting."

"What about ...?" Joe began and hesitated when Jeremy gestured him to be silent.

Once Walter departed, Jeremy laughed softly. "You could have caused a stinkin' bovver, Joe. He's in a bloody-minded mood."

"Since when is he anything else?" John wanted to know.

Larry grinned. "Sore because he doesn't like advertising bods?"

"Watch it, mate."

"Shit! I'm not ..." Larry shrugged. "Okay. Okay. Let's all behave like good little girls." He winked at Joe. "Any more Scotch, fellow Martyr?"

"Where's your money?"

"Do we have to fork out for drinks?"

"Bloody right. I'm not a charity. Two bob ..."

"Ten New Pence," John corrected.

"Stuff those," Joe snapped.

"Right into my pocket," Jeremy joked. "I'll have one, too. A large one, Joe!"

"And that's three bob, mate."

"How long's it going to take you to finish those cards?" Larry asked Jeremy, as Joe attended to refilling their glasses.

"A week - once John lets me have a design for our M.M. crest."

"M.M.," Larry mused. "That gives me an idea. A pair of lovely tits and the initials M.M. ..."

"Monroe's dead," Joe called as he went heavy on his drink.

"She's still something in my mind," Larry said thoughfully.

"Can you do Old English lettering?" John asked their artist.

"Naturally!"

"Good. I'll give you a rough sketch tomorrow night." He took his drink, paid Joe and tossed it back. "I'm going home. I've got a hot woman waiting for me."

"When do we get to meet her?" Joe asked.

"Why do you want to?"

"Not to screw her, that's for sure," Joe replied fast. He didn't want John getting wild again.

"Why then?"

Joe thought he detected a trace of mischiefmaking in the repeated question. He shrugged and collected from the other two. With his back to John he said: "Only because we're all mates, John. If you ever wanted her to come along with us it'd be nice if she knew us by sight and name."

John scowled. He protected his bird jealously. He didn't trust any

166

of these bastards. Not with anything and least of all with a woman. Under no circumstances would he ever invite Doris to join them. She was over-sexed and liable to get the bright idea of taking them all just for kicks.

"Get home to your woman, John," Larry said. "Leave us pathetic do-withouts to our booze." He grinned and waved a farewell which John accepted sullenly.

"Now we are three," Jeremy announced as the door closed.

"I'm bleedin' randy," Larry sighed.

"Who isn't?" Joe asked.

"We could visit Marissa and rape her," Jeremy suggested.

"Would she nark?"

Jeremy smiled at Joe. "What do you think? She's getting older and hotter between those lovely legs of hers. No, I don't think she'd grass. Fact, I honestly believe she'd appreciate what each of us could do for her." He appeared in deep contemplation, his pencil darting across another sheet of paper as his imagination went into high gear. When he finished the sketch he held it out and breathed fast. "God, if she really looked like that . . ."

Larry and Joe got to their feet and went behind Jeremy's chair. Joe felt sweat burst out on his forehead. If this was the nude Marissa Stone then he would definitely be interested in taking her to bed. Jeremy's talent was positively pornographic. The face belonged to Marissa. The body, too - from what they knew of it clothed. But what she was doing did not fit . . . or did it?

*

As Joe dressed, he glanced at Jeremy's masterpiece. The artboard was a good twenty-four inches long by twelve wide. At the top was a self-portrait of the artist flanked by photographically accurate sketches of Larry, John, Walter and Joe. Under this came the Marylebone Martyrs' crest - an elaborate creation faithfully reproduced from John's design showing a shield, quartered, with crossed umbrellas in the upper left field; five sets of nipples in the bottom right field; five hands reaching for a bottle of Scotch in the upper right field and a refuse bin with five pairs of bovver boots showing in the last, lower left field. Rampant above the shield were a man and woman - naked and definitely about to copulate. Below, curled like a banner, were the words: IN UNITY - NOTHING.

167

Then came their creed . . .

WE THE MARYLEBONE MARTYRS DO SOLEMNLY
SWEAR THAT WE HATE, AND ABOMINATE . . .

QUEERS
CHILDREN
LESBIANS
LANDLORDS
SOCIAL WORKERS
COMMUNISTS
SKINHEADS
CONSERVATIVES
HELL'S ANGELS
LABOURITES
PRIESTS
LIBERALS
RABBIS
ANARCHISTS
FUZZ
RUSSIA
BLACKS
AMERICA
VIRGINS
CHINA
RUGBY
EMPLOYERS
HIPPIES
BLOOD SPORTS
SERVANTS
PROTESTERS
CRICKET
WINE
YIPPIES
MAGISTRATES
MARRIAGE
TRADE UNIONISM

It's not right, Joe thought. *It's stupid wasting time on something so infantile. It could have said: "We hate everything" and be done with it. That's what we do hate - everything, and everybody except ourselves.*

Taking ten quid from his hiding place under the carpet, Joe

wondered where he was going to get some extra loot. Totter had successfully blocked Joe's request for a salary increase. The profit from Terry's drug haul was fast evaporating. In a few weeks he would be back down to living on the pittance he earned which did not please nor even pay the rent. He had to find another source of income. An illicit one, too. He could not afford taxation on "capital gains" . . .

He laughed softly. He should be so fortunate in finding a woman like John had - one paying her share and giving her all every night. That's what he wanted. Not a wife - they were burdens. A girl who liked what they did together and had a steady income. A girl he could boot out of the flat when she began to bore him.

Maybe . . .

He sprinkled after-shave on his face and used the deodorant spray under his arms. He felt fresh after his bath - clean enough for the fastidious Marissa Stone!

Now there was a woman with money. Could he talk her into sharing a flat together?

His image in the mirror scowled. "You're a silly twit," he told the reflection mentally. "Marissa wouldn't dirty her belly for you!"

The hell with Marissa, and the Marylebone Martyrs. To hell with everything. He would visit the club, take a walk down Regent Street into Leicester Square and pick up a queer. They still hung out there, like they always had. If he went to the toilet - the public one in the Square - he was sure to be accosted. He'd play the game and nobble the bastard once they reached where the queer lived. No hotels for Joe Hawkins. That didn't let him see how much there was to steal. None of those fast masturbations in a locked toilet, either. He wanted money - not homosexual thrills.

God, what the hell kick do the bastards get out of men? he asked his conscience. *We like girls, don't we?*

His little man in the chest cavity did not answer.

Selecting his brown tie with the artistic squiggles on it, he finished dressing. The flat came complete with a cheval mirror and he studied his presentation with a critical eye. Not bad, he allowed generously. Terry will never know how much he has done for me!

His hair had grown and looked like pure suede which was hardly surprising since he'd been having a Mayfair barber treat it at an exorbitant cost. Even Vera had once remarked how caressable his hair looked. Not that it got her into his bed. He had refrained from pursuing cheap tarts since seeing a television programme dealing with V.D. The sight of a male organ ravaged by disease had scared the living daylights out of him. Now, he selected his bedmates with a fine toothcomb efficiency which left him frustrated more than relieved.

"Shit on girls," he exploded, and then, smiling into the cheval mirror, postured to get the full impact of his gear.

No umbrella tonight. No bowler, either. Just his suede hairstyle, brown shirt, brown tie, tweed jacket and cavalry trousers. He thought his orange socks did something for the outfit. Like the Oxfords did, too.

But the hidden glory was his underwear. God, if those sexy birds could see his mauve jockey shorts and specially dyed emerald green vest!

He felt naked without his umbrella and gloves, but Marissa had asked why he thought it necessary to carry his symbol of City gentlemanliness when he was supposed to be relaxing at the club.

I'm a gas, he thought as he went to the door. *I'm a real gas!* He had been listening to Mason Williams records and reading American private eye literature recently. He liked to affect Trans-Atlantic accents and dialogue. The East End words no longer jumped straight into mind when he was confronted by weird situations. He had matured and believed in his abilities to handle each and every problem in a sensible, unhurried way.

So many changes had worked their individual miracles on Joe since leaving prison, his old mates would have found it impossible to link the two personalities. Joe Hawkins, skinhead, had been an uncouth, uneducated lout drifting on a sickening tide of violence, drink and cheap tarts. Joe Hawkins, suedehead, was semi-educated and capable of affecting a partially-polished front whilst enjoying the charade of decent citizen even as he battered some innocent's skull to a pulp. Exterior-wise, the two did not match. The brash, cheaply clothed bovver boy certainly had no place in the City world of elegantly garbed, expensively clad *Mister* J. Hawkins.

Also, Joe Hawkins as a skinhead had been a member of a recognisable cult with strict limitations on what to think, what to do - and how to do it.

Joe Hawkins, the suedehead, did not belong to any classifiable fraternity, good or bad. His sort hated each and every amalgamation, belief and *modus operandi*. A genuine suedehead had neither creed nor association. He could form a loose friendship with those sharing his lonely existence and run riot in company for a brief space of time. He could not be a member of a gang, nor belong to a permanent process. The Marylebone Martyrs were, in fact, against what suedeheads held dearest - personal freedom to come, go and think as a hate-filled individual.

What had really altered Joe was his new-found penchant for books. He thirsted for knowledge and although profound novels and historical yarns went over his head, he did manage to broaden his mind - in a minor way - by devouring anything with a sex-violent theme coming from the States.

The mere fact he bothered to read was, in itself, a drastic change. A gigantic improvement.

Taking two large drinks he began to whistle. This was his night!

CHAPTER ELEVEN

MARISSA Stone lived in a suburban house with her own private entrance. She had resided there for three years and not once had she missed rent day by a second nor been accused of causing undue noise. She liked padding around in her stockinged feet immediately she got home. She kept her television or radio turned down to a whisper and although her bed creaked, she had taught herself to remain in one position all night.

When she allowed herself the luxury of playing the *1812* on her outdated record player she invariably got to thinking about her stereotyped existence. Having to care for those underneath her flat was not the way people were supposed to live. Always being considerate of others had never been returned. She could recall many parties down below to which she had not been invited and which had gone noisily into the small hours of a working morning.

Thoughtfulness should have been a two-way pleasure. It wasn't. And she knew she was considered a foolish *old* woman by her landlord. *If only I could alter my basic character*, she often told herself as she lay in her lonely bed and listened to a late film blaring its gunshots into the silence of her night.

As she opened the door of her upper flat, she wondered if Joe would take kindly to removing his shoes. Then, she smiled as her feet found each dark stair with Joe's progress behind her coming as a series of stumbles and muttered oaths in the lightless stairwell. She had intended asking the owner to have a light fixture in the upper hall - one she could switch on from the door. But her intentions usually melted into nothingness when it came time to make her request.

She reached the kitchen and switched on a light. She saw Joe's outstreched hand feeling for the side walls, his foot raised and poised in hesitation.

"I'm sorry about that, Joe," she said as he came steaming up the last five steps.

"It's dangerous," he told her. "Can't you get a tiny nightlight fixed down at the front door?"

She had not considered that possibilty and made a mental note to have an electrician fit one. It shouldn't be difficult. And it could operate from the bell's battery. That way, she would not be breaking her tenancy agreement. Nor place herself in a position of eviction.

"I hope you like my home," she said, hands extended for his jacket. She wanted him to feel relaxed, completely at ease.

There was an atmosphere of female occupation which did not grab Joe too kindly. He preferred a totally masculine brutality in his home. Frills, lace and pastel colours were not exactly his cup of tea. He had to admit what he saw in a few glances put his parents' abode to shame. His mother had never known how to mingle colours nor did she have an artistic sense. In fact, Joe could truthfully state that his mother had been utterly devoid of taste all her life. Her idea of something smashing in the house was a cheap, garish table bought in Brighton one Saturday afternoon. Or plastic horses purchased in the local Woolworth.

"Coffee or tea, Joe?"

Her voice brought him back with a mental jerk. "Er . . . I'd like something stronger - if you have it?"

She refused to look shocked. "I have sherry somewhere."

Joe witheld comment. Sherry suited her fine but left him colder than yesterday's leftovers. "That'll do."

She switched on the light in her lounge and ushered him in. The colour television caught his eye immediately. He had not expected that extravagance. The room had a lived-in warmth to match her friendliness. Those green eyes, her silken honey-blonde hair and slender - yet desirable - figure went perfectly with the subtle shades and soft furnishings she had. He sank into a low, large, embracing sofa and sighed.

"I'm not much on entertaining at home," Marissa said. She crossed the room, kicking off her shoes automatically. "Do you like good music?"

"Not really. I'd take The Stones any day."

God, how awful! she thought.

"Have you heard the latest . . . ?" Joe started to ask.

"I seldom get to hear pop, Joe," she interrupted. Her hands caressed the sherry bottle. It had been seven . . . or eight? . . . months since she last had a drink. Maybe she should not let it go so long in future. All the kids seemed to imbibe with a frequency rate that amazed her.

"You're missing terrific stuff," Joe said unabashed.

"We all miss something in life."

"I try not to," he grinned, studying her figure with every intention of enjoying yet another of life's pleasures shortly.

"I envy you and yet I don't," she replied mysteriously. She carefully poured two glasses, wondering if she was exceeding the limit or being miserly.

"That's a rotten answer."

She handed Joe his glass and noted his frown. *Too little*, she thought. *Too late now to add more. Oh well - he'll surely accept a refill!*

"Joe may I say something honestly?"

He gestured with a generosity he did not feel.

"Those socks . . ." She shuddered visibly. "Must you wear them so loud?"

"Loud?"

"Orange!" The word came spitting from her mouth.

"I like 'em. I've got others brighter than these."

"Lord . . ."

He sipped the sherry. It was a cheap brand bought from the keg. He could tell his palate did not appreciate it . . . his only criterion on things other than beer and Scotch.

"Do you have a job or do you have a lot of money in the bank?"

She laughed. Trust Joe Hawkins to ask questions like that and expect an honest reply. She hedged. "Do you think I'm wealthy, Joe?"

"You've got a pile set aside," he allowed.

"I've got precisely two thousand pounds and I *do* work."

Joe rubbed mental hands. Two grand. That was worth chasing. "Are you an executive?"

"Not exactly, Joe. I'm in charge of a typing pool. I'm classified as a supervising typist."

"Does it pay much?" He took another sip of his sherry and placed the glass on a nearby table. He didn't want much more of that. It tasted sweetly sick to his tongue.

"Why are you interested?"

"No reason," he lied. "Just conversation."

"I get twenty seven pounds a week after deductions."

He whistled aloud. "That's a lot."

"I've been with the firm many years, Joe."

"Is the boss a friend of yours?" he grinned slyly.

"That's unfair!"

"Sorry, I'm being jealous . . ." He let the remark sink in before adding: "I like you a lot, Marissa."

She tensed. *Marissa*, indeed. She got set to let go at him, but noticed his eyelids partially close as he stared pointedly at her bosom. *Oh, God - is this the one?* she asked in silent prayer.

"I'd like to kiss you, Marissa . . ."

She didn't speak. Instead, when he took her in his virile arms she let him drape her along the sofa so that he now assumed a masterful position above her. She watched his mouth come closer . . . touching . . . then . . .

He took her sherry glass and placed it next to his on the table. He placed a hand deliberately on one breast and, as she moaned very softly, his open mouth closing over hers.

All her nightmares, her erotic dreams came surging to the conscious surface when his tongue invaded her mouth. She could not restrain her desire to experiment with this brazen, unmitigated young lecher. The doors she had kept so tightly shut burst open.

What a tit, Joe thought as he felt the firm breast swell inside his cupped palm.

He won't stop at feeling me, she thought when he pressed her back into the sofa and lowered his body on to hers.

His mouth tore from her greedy one. "Marissa . . . let me take your clothes off!"

"Joe . . . no! Don't . . . oh, darling Joe . . ."

She lay supine as he undressed her. Every revealment excited him tremendously. She had the silky flesh of a screen heroine, the maturity of a godess. Touching her naked skin sent shivers coursing down his spine, arousing his manhood.

A kettle could not have boiled in the time it took Joe to whisper his lustful demands. Marissa writhed - eager as a teenage virgin for this marvellous youth's strident passion. His hands roamed her nudity everywhere; pleasing her, teaching her, bringing her womanhood to blossom-bursting beauty.

"Joe . . .the bed creaks," she moaned as he tried to pull her off the sofa.

"Let it!"

She pleaded. "Do it here, Joe . . . not in the bedroom."

"Beds are for what you're going to get," he panted.

"They'll hear us downstairs . . ."

"Let 'em . . . maybe he'll give his old woman what you're liking!"

CHAPTER TWELVE

"YOU'VE got to stop saying those terrible words, Joe," Marissa said as she cradled his head against her moistly warm breasts. "I can't stand them."

"What do you mean?" he muttered to a turgid teat.

"You know . . ." She refused to repeat his pleadings at the height of their mutual climax. It had almost ruined a delightful, exquisite moment for her when he began to four letter her into wild spasms of glory.

"You mean f . . ."

"Joe!" She pulled back and held his face in her soft hands. "Please don't say it again. Please?"

"You're crazy."

"I'm not. I'm a lady, Joe."

Suddenly, he knew the difference between his East End tarts with their lavatory-wall language and the genteel taking of a superior woman like Marissa Stone. But she must have words for what they had done, for urging her mate to reach that exotic plateau when all but the pulsating togetherness seemed remote and immaterial.

"Joe . . . Joe . . . Joe!" Her fingers curled into his hair. "Let your hair grow long. I like doing this." She caressed his head, massaging the scalp.

His hand rested on her stomach. "I like this, too." He massaged her with newly aroused inclinations.

"You're a naughty boy," she giggled, spreading herself for his pleasure.

"The bed creaked like hell!"

She pushed his hand away and sat upright. In the semi-light of the lounge he could see her marvellous breasts and her slender body until it dipped invitingly under the sheet. "It did?" She sounded nervous, almost frightened stiff.

"You said it creaked - and it did!"

"Joe . . . stop! Don't touch me there . . ." She brought his hand above the sheet. "Oh, this is terrible . . ."

"Are you worried about the downstair's people again?"

"Yes!" She kicked free of the sheets, stood naked and unashamed in her confusion.

"If you want me to do it again . . . ?"

She knelt on the bed, listening to the rusty creak. "I do, Joe - oh, God, I do!"

"Then find another pad!"

"It won't be easy getting a decent place for this rent."

"You could share my place . . ."

She blushed. "I could *not*!"

"Why?"

"It's out of the question. I just couldn't . . ."

"You'd like it every night, wouldn't you?"

She touched his cheek with fresh love tenderness. "Yes."

"Then move in with me."

"Joe, you're a darling but I can't. It wouldn't be right!"

"What the hell is right?" he asked savagely. "Listen, Marissa - we're good in bed together. I like the way you make it and you like getting me. Okay, so who cares if you're older and paying me rent . . ."

"Rent?"

"Sure - you didn't think I was wanting a wife, did you?"

She chuckled. "Joe, you're fantastic. All right, I'll think about your proposition."

He shoved the sheet back and got randy when he saw what she could offer. "Come here, Marissa . . ."

Willingly, she flung herself down on him, her hands as eager and as intimate as his. Pent up years surged to a forgetful surface and she wallowed in instantaneous thrills . . .

CHAPTER THIRTEEN

IT was surprising how little Marissa had to contribute. Her soul cried out for a kindred mate which it could never find in Joe. For the young man, Marissa was a frustrated old woman soiling her flesh in pursuit of youth's virility. They had nothing in common outside the bedroom athletics which both indulged in to demented extremes. Dishes did not get washed after the evening meal, so great was Marissa's desire to recapture those excrutiating cadences Joe's love-making produced inside her long without body.

Once, after a lengthy session striving to bring the woman to full fruition, Joe remarked: "Can't you make it quicker?"

"Joe, darling, don't be greedy and don't ever be too selfish. Let me have the same amount of pleasure you're getting."

"Okay - but don't drag it, eh?"

Marissa sighed. "Can't you feel things building to a wonderful climax? Can't you hold back a few minutes until I'm with you?"

"I haven't got time for fancy stuff."

"Fancy stuff? Joe, you're so wrong. A woman enjoys being a plaything for a man's slowly emerging passion. You're so quick I get frightened. You can't just think it and have it happen, you know. There are so many beautiful sensations we can share if only you remember it's not just for me . . . it's for us both. Slow and easy is best. Modern slap-dash isn't letting either of us find the *true* wonder of love."

"I want to go to the pub, Marissa," Joe said as if that finished the discussion, the excitement his hand was sending through her loins.

"And am I supposed to stay here and wait until you come home drunk?"

"You can come with me."

"I don't like pubs."

"So stay at home!" He got from the bed.

"You're like all those Jamaicans I've ever met. A woman is a receptacle for their lust - nothing more."

"You're letting your bias show."

She got off the bed and stood stark naked before his admiring gaze. She knew he adored her body - those sensual curves and her mature slenderness which could still perform sexual miracles his little trashy girlfriends could not begin to understand.

"Want it now?" he asked crudely.

"Not now - not tonight, Joe. You go to the pub and find a tart to satisfy your wham, bam techniques."

He put on his jockey shorts and his vest. She had already covered her essentials with a pair of cotton knickers and a bra. The need for getting-to-it talk had vanished. "You're a bitch," he said. "You profess to like everybody yet you single out Jamaicans for ridicule."

"I'm allowed to think the way I want, Joe."

He pulled his electric-green socks on. That she had not been able to stop. His socks were as important as the Crombie overcoat. Even in summer he felt it necessary to sport the coat. There were suedeheads who did not take kindly to bowlers and umbrellas, he knew. But none of the fraternity would ever be caught dead in "ordinary" socks. Regardless of all those statements to the contrary each suedehead had a large part of the skinhead left in his symbolic attitude towards recognition.

"Are you going to meet your friends, Joe?"

He glanced at her with mounting disgust. She was old enough to be his mother and every day saw her acting more and more like an instructing mother-hen. She had tried, unsuccessfully, to "beautify his thinking processes". She nagged when he went to football matches, when he got away from her demanding sexual possessiveness. It wasn't that he didn't enjoy screwing her - he did. But there were other woman equally qualified to relieve Joe Hawkins. Women who would not stop short because what he suggested was *morally* abhorrent. The vicar's ghost still haunted Marissa even if she denied it.

In the months they had shared his flat, Marissa had given him a new slant on life. She had taught him how to hate sections of the community without realising that she shared those aspects of the confirmed bigot. Joe had been unable to associate her work at the club with her very narrow views at first but the more she opened up the deeper insight he got. She was a frightened woman packed with vastly contradicting motivations. She liked to be seen as a neighbour, a "sister in need to the oppressed", a do-gooder without blemish, a social reformer. Yet, inside her fears manifested themselves in night's terror, she loathed coloured people, detested anything remotely connected with trades unionism, opposed blood sports, decried a widening of British involvement in Europe because "those foreigners will overrun us" and could not tolerate a different religious viewpoint.

All her pet hatreds brushed off on Joe. All her noble - but insincere - mouthings, left him untouched. The only really lasting impression Joe would ever have of her when they eventually parted would be the memory of her slender nudity writhing beneath him, of her almost insatiable desire for orgiastic completion.

"I asked if you were going to meet your friends, Joe?" she repeated with hands on firm hips, face drained of colour.

"What if I am?"

"You might be chasing after some little whore."

He laughed. "If I find one I'll do more than chase!"

"You couldn't . . . I won't allow this!"

"You won't allow it?" He moved across the untidy bedroom. "Listen, Marissa - you don't own me and you don't give me any bleedin' orders, either."

"You're mine," she said as tears suddenly trickled down her pale cheeks.

"I'm not, you know," he grinned deliberately provoking her. "Why don't you find an old man your age and screw him to death. That's what you want, Marissa - an old bastard willing to be hen-pecked."

"You're a rotten devil!" she screamed.

"Cool it, Marissa. I don't want *my* next door neighbours thinking what an old slut you are."

Her fists beat against his chest.

"I'll bet half of them don't believe you're my aunt."

She stepped back, stunned. *"Wh . . . at?"*

"I told everybody you were my aunt. You didn't imagine I'd have 'em believing I was getting off with some ancient biddy, did you?"

Her hands clawed wildly at her brassiere, yanked it off. Next she ripped her knickers and flung them into his face. Sharp fingernails raked down her magnificent breasts drawing trails of blood. "I'll have

179

you arrested for rape," she moaned, swaying from side to side in a hysterical fashion. "I'll accuse you of perversions . . ."

An explosion erupted in Joe's head. Blind, red rage took a hold of his muscles and his clenched fist bounced off Marissa's jaw. Her eyes glazed but he didn't notice. Like a prize-fighter gone berserk he attacked, slamming her back against the wall, hitting, bruising, battering as she slowly sank to her knees. Even then his viciousness could not be checked. His toe smashed into her stomach, caught her full in the face. Only when her pathetic groans subsided into unconscious silence did he relent and step back to examine his handywork.

There was nothing beautiful about Marissa now. She was what he had said - an old woman bleeding and discoloured and ready for the refuse heap.

Joe felt terrific. The unleashing of jungle emotions did something wonderful for his savagery-starved system. It was like the days when the gang had taken brutal delight in mauling anyone stupid enough to stand in their way.

Washing the blood from his knuckles he finished dressing. Taking a final look at Marissa he frowned. "When those heal she can get the hell out of here," he said aloud . . .

*

Two hours later, Marissa Stone pulled herself to rubbery feet and staggered into the bathroom. Great racking sobs shook her when she saw the terrible condition of her face and flesh. A bath did not take away the aches nor lower the swellings. Naked, she reeled into their bedroom.

I must have been mad to let the bastard talk me into living with him, her mind screamed. *I've got to get out before he comes back . . .*

Forcing her unco-operative body to act, she found her suitcases and threw clothes and belongings into them. Fortunately, her precious furniture had been stored in a warehouse. Joe had not been able to convince her she should bring everything to his flat. Maybe it had been a premonition that had saved her from having to stay in order to safeguard her life's belongings.

She did not care how she looked. She just wanted out. Fast. Dressing, she closed her cases, locked each securely and telephoned for a taxi. She would stay in a hotel until fit. She would inform the clubs she no longer cared to give of her time. She would report sick to work. She would hibernate until not one trace of Joe's handiwork remained. Then, and only then, would she re-enter a society for which she had nothing but contempt.

*

Joe slept like an innocent that night. Being alone did not bother him. When he first saw she had gone he had been crazy angry. But, slowly, her absence had assumed pleasant proportions. She had outgrown her welcome, her sexual hold over him.

"To blazes with her," he had muttered as his drifted off into that semi-sand heaviness when all things, all dreams can be seen with startling clarity.

CHAPTER FOURTEEN

PIERCE sat unyieldingly stiff in his ornate chair, fingers steepled pontifically before his nose. "Mr. Totter informs me you've been returning from lunch smelling of drink, Hawkins."

"God almighty," Joe retorted indignantly. "One lousy beer to wash down a dry sandwich."

"That is not what Mr. Totter says."

"Then he's a liar!" Joe suddenly got a cold, crawling sensation racing down his spine. He knew, instantly, he had committed the great *faux pas*.

"That will be enough of that," Pierce said quickly. "I have never known Mr. Totter to castigate an employee without justification. Personally, I agree with his assessment of your condition. I have seen you looking the worse for drink, Hawkins. And heard your language, too . . . in front of the ladies!"

"A few little oaths," Joe pleaded.

Ignoring Joe's attempted reconciliation, Pierce unsteepled his fingers, lifted a paper and held it menacingly in front of his face. "If that were all, Hawkins!" he said behind the official looking document. "I requested our bankers investigate you and they have turned up

181

rather a remarkable history . . ." His eyes darted to one side of the paper, fixed Joe with unflinching disgust. "You have been in prison, Hawkins."

"So what?" Joe felt no need now to hide his past. He was sick to death of Pierce's attitude. He was going to get the boot so why not enjoy himself.

"Your salary is being prepared. We shall not require your services any longer."

"I paid my debt," Joe growled. "But that wouldn't interest a snooty-nosed bastard like you or Totter. You think everybody has to be pure, eh? Like hell they are. You'd climb into bed with that sexy secretary of yours if she gave you the chance . . ."

"Leave this office at once, Hawkins," Pierce roared, the paper dropping from his hands. Coming to his feet, the stockbroker placed bunched knuckles on his desk and bent forward. "Young man, I could thrash the hide off you but I refuse to soil myself. However, a word of warning - if you are not outside these premises in five minutes, I shall forget my upbringing and give you what you most deserve."

"You and Santa Claus," Joe sneered.

Pierce straightened and moved round the desk. Something in his expression warned Joe he could do exactly as he said. Raising a hand in defence, Joe said: "Okay . . . okay . . . I'm going!"

"That's true," the man said grimly.

Watching Joe hurry from his office, Pierce breathed deeply. His age and health did not warrant such extravagant thoughts as he had nurtured then although he had meant every word. He was glad that Hawkins had not stood his ground. These young louts seldom cared for their elders. One blow could have sent him into hospital.

*

I've got two alternatives, Joe thought as he nursed his Skol lager in the remotest corner of the pub. Most of the regulars had dashed back to work leaving the unemployed, the problem drinkers and the expense-account layabouts to wait out the afternoon closing hour. *I can wait for Totter and follow him home and beat the bastard to a pulp for grassing on me. Or I can report to the Labour and draw dole. I'm entitled to do that. I got kicked out.*

A pair of young people took the table next to Joe's. The girl wore

182

beads, a long mauve dress without shape or attraction, a band around her uncombed, straggling hair and a minimum amount of lipstick. Her bare feet certainly showed how much dirt London's streets held. Her companion was likewise barefooted, had the same colourless straggling hair banded in Indian style and there the resemblance ended. He had a handsome face whereas hers was plain and pock-marked. He had a hairy chest peeping from under a loose, unbuttoned shirt and she was practically flat - with or without hair! He wore tight Levis and made no attempt to conceal an overly developed manhood.

Joe leant back and considered their way of life as against his. They could never get decent jobs in the City but then, maybe they thought he was uptight being chained to the Establishment. One had to admit they were "loose people". Not hippies, certainly. Listening to their muted conversation Joe could tell they were highly educated, completely extrovertish, distantly aware of his interest and uncaring for his opinion.

Bloody fools! Joe concluded. *Them and hippies, yippies, snobs, drop-outs, protesters, shop stewards, bus conductors, manual labourers, desk-jockeys, soldiers, shopkeepers, fuzz, skinheads, Hell's Angels . . . the bleedin' lot! All stupid. All bastards.*

Finishing his drink, Joe pushed past the girl. She exuded some exotic scent which assailed his nostrils like a joss-stick would an opium hater. He was glad to gulp London's polluted air and smell the fumes belching from passing lorries.

It was late when he made his decision about the future. He would sign on the Labour, apply for a Social Security hand-out and do a bit of queer bashing on the side. Totter could go boil in his senile juices. Much as he wanted revenge he did not see any way of getting even without the fuzz clanging doors on him again. And that he was determined to avoid. He liked his freedom to pursue his solitary campaign against all humanity too much to give the law another opportunity to remove him from society's playground.

He'd make out okay. He'd wangle another job once he got a duplicate set of insurance cards. That was easier than explaining away why he had been dismissed from such a prominent City firm. He knew some influential men now. Those antique dealers in his Mayfair club must have use of a bright boy. He could cook books given half a chance. Or run errands for about £20 a week. Or learn the racket and set up for himself when he got a few thousand together.

A few thousand! That bleedin' Marissa had that amount. Why hadn't he treated her right until after she had parted with her loot? he asked his agitated mind.

Navigating a steady course from City to Mayfair and, when he found Vera alone in the club, back to his fashionable flat with its now totally masculine atmosphere he let several ideas run their winding road to that most deadly "detour" sign. No matter how tantalising the notion seemed at first light there was some dark dread which prevented him from fullest acceptance. He was not afraid of getting into trouble - just of finding himself in the dock before that same magistrate. He'd done his wack of nick. Once of that was ample.

Pouring a stiff drink he whooshed in soda and sipped it as he bathed. Refreshed, helping himself to another triple pleasure he changed into casuals - cntent to regard his symbolic Crombie and bright, plaid socks uniform aplenty. Counting his dismissal pay he frowned. With the dwindled cash he had put aside his finances had a decidedly bleak appeal. He had to get another nest-egg, somewhere.

Entering the warehouse clubrooms he looked in vain for Marissa. He had believed she would return by now. A new face smiled at him. *"God, don't they ever get young birds to take these cushy jobs?"* This one was older than Marissa, more motherly, more syrupy voiced. She advanced on Joe, hand out ready to draw him into her all-embracing, responsible arms.

"I'm Jenny Price," she said. "Are you a member?"

Joe smiled, ignoring the hand as he looked around for Larry. He was reminded of Vera when he first entered *her* sacrosanct barland. "Yeah, I've been here before. Seen Larry Miller tonight?"

"That one!"

Joe quizzed her with his eyes. She had a smug, almost omnipotent chastisementic expression going.

"I told him his sort are not welcome here!"

"Who the hell are you to say who can, or cannot, come?" Joe asked in sudden anger.

"I have responsibilities . . ."

"You're supposed to keep an eye on the equipment, the premises and help us if we ask for help. That's all - and don't deny it. I know. Marissa told me."

The woman blanched. "You're that beast Joe Hawkins!"

184

"You've heard about Marissa's shack up?"

"I certainly have. You may leave immediately."

"Shit on you!" Joe strode away. Down in the far corner of the huge room a couple of youths were heading a soccer ball. In the centre, several birds wearing stage tights tried to keep in step as an ex-dancer went through the weary motions of terpsichorean dilemma. A larger group of mixed sexes sat on the bare floor listening to an unkempt liberal spouting poetry and general blasphemy.

"Hawkins - come back!"

Jesus wept, Joe thought and continued to seek someone who might know where he could locate Larry. It was important. And he did not intend to have that old biddy scream at him for long. Her brand of authority was what his hatred was all about.

John Moore looked up, caught sight of Joe and left the "education circle". "What the hell is she yelling at?" John asked as he joined his mate.

"Not what - me! I'm not an honoured guest . . ."

"No bloody wonder. Where is Marissa?"

"Gone. Left. Where is Larry?"

"In the nick doing six months."

Joe wanted to weep. There went another of his big ideas! "And Jeremy?"

"In the coffee bar down the street."

Jenny Price swept up, hand gripping Joe's sleeve. Savagely he tore the Crombie material from her arresting fingers. "Leave me alone, cow!" he snarled.

The woman seemed on the edge of hysterics. John nodded and said: "Better go, Joe."

"Not until . . ."

"I'll call the police!"

Joe froze. She would too. He decided against further antagonism. "Okay, I'm going." Turning, he walked defiantly to the door. He was burning up inside. Only the threat of police action prevented him from asserting himself and giving the bitch what she deserved.

It had been a rotten day. Fired from his job, tossed out of his Marylebone clubhouse. Larry in the nick. He felt uneasy. Maybe he should go home and sleep off the bad luck dogging his heels.

Jeremy was chatting up a fifteen year old nymphet. He did not greet Joe with any enthusiasm. Now Joe was sure he would call it a day! A lousy day!

"Can you meet me tomorrow, Jeremy?"

"What time and where?"

"My flat after seven?"

"Have Scotch and American ginger."

Joe shrugged. He had both already. "Alone?"

Jeremy narrowed his eyes suspiciously.

"I've got something I wanted Larry in on but he's . . . "

"Out of circulation," Jeremy laughed.

"Yeah. Okay?"

"I'll be there. Say," as Joe started to leave the packed coffee bar, "where is that Marissa bird?"

"How the hell should I know?" Joe shouted in reply and pushed a long-haired girl aside. He did not hear her expletive nor see the coffee she had just bought trickle down her faded blue sweater. He had other things on his mind - like a drink and sleep.

CHAPTER FIFTEEN

"YOU'RE stark, ruddy crazy," Jeremy remarked as he pushed his empty glass across the coffee table. "Make it larger." He deposited cash on the table with a show of disgust. If they were having a party or just shooting the breeze as the Yanks called it he did not object to paying his fair share for liquor. But when Joe had brought him to the flat and wanted to involve him in a highly off-beat, wild scheme it was etiquette to provide a guest with free drinks.

Joe scowled as he poured generous helpings of his best Scotch. He could not understand Jeremy's reluctance to jump at the opportunity to get some easy loot. Larry would not have hesitated. Of that he was certain. But Larry was not available and Joe was in a hurry to build his nest-egg into an aviary-sized deposit.

"I still say it will work," Joe said, handing his companion the extra-large drink. "Bloody Pakistani bastards don't fight back 'cause they're scared of us. Hell, we used to bash 'em for kicks!"

"Used to is the operative phrase, Joe."

"What do you mean?"

Jeremy shrugged nonchalantly, sipping his drink before adding to

Joe's consternation. He could not quite put a finger on the root cause of the retrogade step Joe seemed to be taking. He wondered if it had something to do with Marissa. Since she had shacked up with Joe, the youth had kicked over many traces.

Settling back in a comfortable sofa, Jeremy asked: "Mind if I discuss this fully?"

"No - what did you mean about "used to"?"

"You brought up bashing Paki bastards. That went out when you turned away from being a skinhead. Hate them, get the boot in sometimes but don't revert to bovver-boys aggros and expect me, or us . . . to back you, Joe. We're beyond that. Making a "hit" for hard cash sounds terrific but not when it's linked to the old methods."

"Bloody hell," Joe exploded, draining his glass and leaping across the room for a refill.

"What's happened to you recently, Joe?"

The question caught Joe unawares. He frowned, liquor spilling on to the cabinet top.

"Marissa wasn't all she was cracked up to be, was she?"

"She wasn't bad . . ."

"She made problems for you, Joe. She made you frustrated. And when she cleared out you fell off a cliff."

Joe mopped up the liquor pool. "What are you? A bleedin' head shrinker?"

Jeremy smiled tolerantly. Educationally, he left Joe miles behind. His ability to probe a problem and make a fairly accurate analysis came from an inherent knowledge of what made people tick. Joe had, in his opinion, created a sex-goddess and when that object of his worship failed to produce the vital pleasures in the abundance Joe had sought, something had snapped and thrown the youth into a tailspin. The result - backtracking and a desire to refashion a life form long since consumed by times forgetting fires. Joe as a skinhead now would be like a lamb amongst wolves.

"Are you going to help me?" Joe asked angrily.

"No, thanks. Count me out."

"Some mate you've proved to be."

"My advise to you is to drop the crazy idea, Joe. You'll get nicked. Things aren't what they once were. Pakistanis are acceptable members of every community . . ."

"You mean you like *them*?" Joe asked in amazement.

"Not me," the other replied hurriedly.

"Then let's do the job?"

"No - and that's final."

"I'll do it myself," Joe threatened.

"Fine. I'll send you a Christmas card to Pentonville." Jeremy climbed to his feet and finished his drink. "I'm shoving off, mate. Think over what I've said. You're muddled. Take a few days and get roarin' drunk."

"The hell with you and the Marylebone Martyrs . . . I'll get along on my tod."

"Bloody good luck, mate . . ." Jeremy snarled as he opened the door. Standing half in, half out he grinned evilly and added: "May all your troubles be fuzz!"

*

Sunday, and Joe's dilemma had multiplied instead of diminishing. The more he thought about Jeremy's visit to his flat the worse his mental confusion became. Word had circulated. The Martyrs no longer existed - not for him, anyway. He had been given the cold shoulder treatment by John and Walter. He had been "allowed" to overhear Walter say: "I hate skinhead punks and ex-skinheads trying to look like suedeheads." That had been the kiss of death.

Had Jeremy been right in tracing his failure to Marissa? Undoubtedly he had suffered at her hands. Those nights spent trying to make her react to his erotic suggestions had done more damage than he had thought possible. He could see it now - her mothering, her efforts to create in him something which was basically against his violent grain, her lack of compassion when he sought to get his hands on her money, her deep-rooted morality which refused to recognise things as they really were. She had been brazen about living with him. Her prejudices had been more volatile, more convincing than his shallow pretence to understand why everything should be classed as a suedehead hatred. He hated, true. He hated violently. Yet he did not hate with conviction as against Marissa's bigoted look at the world. Parts of her had gladly rubbed off on him. Other facets of her being had reacted with devastating results. He was caught between her good, her evil, and totally incapable of distinguishing a real Joe Hawkins path.

"I've got to do something or I'll go mad," he told his breakfast egg. He considered several Sunday possibles and brushed all but one aside. Hyde Park Corner . . . There would be blacks and Irish and commies galore there. He might be able to forment trouble. Maybe even a king-sized aggro . . .

He was thinking wrong again! He was *not* a skinhead. He belonged to the elite. All he required was a bit of *gentlemanly* bovver to rid his body of the ambition-eating cancer that daily grew larger.

*

"This is me - the real me," he mused as, flicking a speck of dirt from his velvet collar, he posed before a restaurant window outside Marble Arch Tube station. In his estimation he was a walking example of how the well-dressed socialite should appear in public. Crombie (with velvet collar), dark blue suit, brilliant yellow socks visible under his trousers, highly polished shoes, frill-fronted shirt, narrow floral tie and bowler perched jauntily on his head. The umbrella completed a picture of sartorial elegance.

Several tourists paused to chuckle as he passed them. A pair of hippy-types smiled behind his back. An elderly man blinked and muttered about fashion decline. A schoolgirl sighed and tried to catch his eye.

Joe was totally alone. He did not see the girl, nor the man, nor the hippies, nor the tourists. He walked with back ramrod straight, head high, umbrella swinging. His mind was already over there - in Hyde Park. Memories returned to torment him. Had he spat in the wind of fate? He felt a warm, satisfying glow permeate his being. Something was going to happen today. He sensed it . . .

The largest crowd was gathered around a rostrum flying a flag of a newly created African state. An ebony man wearing gaily coloured robes occupied the rostrum, gesturing as he spoke in a loud clear voice.

"The Great White Queen sent her royal message-boys into Africa with orders to rape, and loot, and steal," he roared. "She sent us justice in place of gold taken from our mines. She made us slaves - for that's what her justice was. White men didn't get brought before colonial administrators for crimes committed against Africans. Only blacks were sent to penal settlements . . ."

"Liar!"

The speaker gazed at the back of the crowd with a huge grin displaying pearly white teeth. He had been waiting for somebody to

189

object. He knew how to arouse a crowd and counted on his tirade getting a heckler going. Once a verbal battle began his audience would grow, and grow, and keep growing providing he could handle himself.

"Are you a student of history, friend?" the African asked.

"I'm English. We don't want your crowd here!"

"Oh, my," the speaker said, gesturing to his listening sympathisers. "I'm African, sir," he spoke directly to the hidden heckler. "Does that mean your people got out of my country and left me alone?"

Joe pushed through the thickening mass and placed himself defiantly before the rostrum. His umbrella waggled imperiously. "Your country was rotten before we took it," he shouted. "A bunch of savages who couldn't work or build towns . . ."

"Thank you, sir," the African interrupted. "Took it, you said. And that's what the British did. Took - by force, by underhanded deceit. We didn't ask you to come and occupy our lands. We didn't . . ."

"You hate our bloody guts yet you all flock here to get jobs," Joe roared.

"Why shouldn't we? You stole everything we ever had. We've a right to get it back."

"Not from me mate!" Joe screamed, his fury beginning to take command. "I don't want niggers in London."

"Niggers?" The African scowled, leaning over the rostrum. "Don't dare call me a nigger!"

Joe grinned sadistically and jumped forward. Like a spear his umbrella tip found a soft, fleshy target. The african's anguished bellow sounded like a cat call to arms in Joe's brain. The umbrella slashed out catching an innocent by-stander across the nose. Cracking bone increased Joe's desire to inflict pain. He lunged, aiming for the speaker's shoulder . . .

Blood spurted from the man's throat as the vicious tip pierced his windpipe.

Joe suddenly blanched. He didn't like the way the man instantly sagged, nor the free-flowing blood, splattering robe and rostrum. A self-protective instinct sent him spinning into the stunned crowd. Eel-like, he wriggled from grasping hands trying to halt his progress. Cries for help rang in his ears. A police whistle drove him wildly into the heavy traffic circling the park.

I've got to get into the tube, he told himself as he dodged cars and buses in headlong escape. *The bastard deserved it . . .*

190

Monday's *Evening Standard* carried an Identikit picture of Joe. Underneath the likeness, an article condemned the violent society and those who would inhibit free speech. The writer - a distinguished legal mind - made no bones about his personal feelings. "Thugs like the one who deliberately attacked this coloured orator deserve to be put away for a very long time."

The front page, too, carried a report on the disturbance. Eye-witness accounts proved conclusively that the assailant had not been physically provoked. A police statement said that "The attacker is expected to be apprehended shortly". The spokesman hinted that "He is known to us".

He studied the Identikit picture as it accused from the floor. How the bloody hell could they know him? A picture taken during his skinhead era would not even remotely look like one of him now!

He had to admit there was a superficial resemblance. But then, it could have been any one of a thousand other suedeheads.

Okay, he told his tortured mind, *let's reason this out. Can they trace me?* He shuddered. Damn his rush to sign on the dole. They had a name and address there. If the fuzz were really looking for Joe Hawkins they'd have him!

Flinging his bowler across the flat, he dressed in casuals. The law was searching for a suedehead. They'd never stop him when he looked like an ordinary, decent citizen. He felt better immediately. Packing his Sanyo and some underwear into a small suitcase, he collected what was left of his cash and had a final drink. It was farewell to the flat. He could go North. Manchester had a going scene. In a few months the fuzz would forget him.

His hand was on the doorknob when he heard the solid feet approaching outside. Fear tore at his guts . . . *No! They can't have worked that fast . . .*

". . . A menace to society which must be stamped out. Apparently you do not understand the meaning of leniency and so I shall safeguard the public for the maximum permissible by law. I sentence you, Joseph Hawkins, to four years . . ."

He was dead inside. The lengthy condemnation had stolen any

hope he had entertained when entering the courtroom. Now, he knew. Four years! And that bloody inspector had mentioned another charge just before he was brought to face his nemesis. It seemed the queer had made a complaint. And the Sanyo had given him away!

"You're lucky that African didn't cop out," a stern policeman remarked as he took Joe back to the cells.

"Lucky?" Joe screamed. "I got four years!"

"Not a day too short," the officer grunted. "Take my advice son - have psychiatric treatment when you're inside. The world'll have changed drastically before you get out . . ."

Joe frowned. It had altered enough the last time he did bird. What would be the vogue when he stepped from those gates again? Would there be a new fad to capture his imagination? Or would he simply drift into crime *à la mode*? One thing he knew for certain - no headshrinker would examine him. He didn't intend to become a sissy. They could say whatever they wanted but Joe Hawkins would always remain Joe Hawkins. If he was wrong then he could only blame himself. He didn't want other people putting loony ideas into his mind. Next time he would capitalise on his experience . . .

"Just like you did after eighteen months?" a small voice asked . . .

THE END

SKINHEAD ESCAPES

By Richard Allen

AUTHOR'S NOTE

Judging by the popularity of the paperbacks, SKINHEAD and SUEDEHEAD, the pundits are totally wrong when they state that teenage cultism is fading away. It would appear, from the response to SUEDEHEAD, that skinheads are like old soldiers - they are forever there in the wings.

After two books featuring Joe Hawkins, it was my intention to let the character rest for an indeterminate period of time. The readers, however, have decided otherwise. Letters from the book-buying public make it patently clear that Joe is an established favourite. Almost without exception, these letters request - no, *insist* - on another Joe book. Whilst it is exceedingly gratifying for an author to find his works included in the top ten paperbacks of the year, it poses certain problems to meet the demands.

Joe, we remember, found himself confronted with a four-year prison sentence in SUEDEHEAD. That seemed, to me, to put paid to his activities for quite a while. But Joe Hawkins is a resourceful character. An old adage mentions not being able to keep a good man down. The same holds true for the Joes of this world. Bad pennies, like good men, have a habit of turning up at an alarming speed.

In years to come, Joe Hawkins will probably be quoted as an example of this era we have named "the permissive age". If so, then the author can count on more than sales success. With that thought in mind, I wish to thank all those who have spread the gospel and taken the trouble to write. It is for you that SKINHEAD ESCAPES is specially written.

Richard Allen,
Gloucester, 1972.

CHAPTER ONE

FROM his cell window, Joe Hawkins could see the high wall forming one side of their rectangle exercise yard. Beyond it, he knew, were a few scattered cottages belonging to the prison staff with neat, cared-for gardens reaching down to a small stream and the woods that filled his horizon. This morning, he could not see past the wall. In fact, it was getting so bleeding misty he was having difficulty making out the worn, pocked bricks of the wall.

He smiled at the thoughts the all-embracing mist brought in its chilling, clammy wake. If only he was in a working party with permission to go outside the bloody prison! Man, he wouldn't waste a single precious second lingering with doubts in his mind. He'd make a break for the wide open spaces and freedom.

The sounds of pot-carriers brought him back to reality. It was an indignity forcing men to carry their covered pots through seemingly endless corridors and empty the rotten things in a communal latrine. There was no valid necessity for this outdated duty. None except the Victorian concept that prisoners should be treated like so many animals.

He was still mentally tearing the system apart when they went outside. He was glad he had a three-quarters length coat to wear. The weather had turned nasty. He saw other prisoners in their lightweight jackets slapping arms round their chests to keep out the insidious fog. All right for them, he thought viciously. When this lark is over they'll go indoors to semi-warmth. I've bleedin' got to clean up this rotten yard.

Angling across the tendril-deep yard he joined a group wearing coats like his. A grim-featured warder scowled at him, silently motioning at a stack of brooms. The others watched with expressions Joe found difficult to describe. Something was wrong. He sensed it. There was just a prison feeling in the air that "spoke" of conspiracy. He grabbed a broom and moved to one side. The last thing he wanted was to become involved in a kangaroo court punishment.

The mist swirled round them. A whistle blew and the great mass of prisoners began to form into lines. Exercise, for this day, had ended.

"Keep your nose out of what happens, Hawkins," a gruff voice said in Joe's ear.

The man looked straight ahead, broom making sweeping gestures without accomplishing much in the way of cleanliness. Joe recognised him, and a sudden tremor of anticipation raced through his body. He'd been wrong about this being some sort of convict court execution. He knew what was going to happen as surely as if he had been in on the plan from the beginning.

"I'm going with you, McVey!"

Cold snake-eyes bored into Joe. "Try it, kid. Try it an' you're dead!"

Joe forced a grin. He saw the warder sidestep a broom and lean against the moist running wall. "I won't hinder you - I promise."

"Damned right you won't," the heavy man snarled with mounting anger.

"Turn it up, Charlie." The speaker drifted between McVey and Joe, glaring at the unwanted intruder as he did. "Get lost, Hawkins!"

"I'm going with you," Joe whispered.

A broom handle slammed into Joe's gut, sending him reeling. A wave of nausea washed over him and it was all he could do to maintain his balance. Tears stung his eyes.

"I'm going," Joe said through tight lips.

McVey smiled, and told his companion, "He's got us, Len."

"Gutsy," the other allowed.

"Pity to kill the bastard," McVey remarked.

Joe felt terror crawl through every nerve-end. These men did not joke about such things. Killing him would be no more on their conscience than him killing a spider.

"Ten minutes from now," the man Len said. "Other side of the yard." He straightened and faced Joe. "You've been warned, kid." He started sweeping, crossing the damp yard without pause, deliberately coming between McVey and the frowning warder.

"Sorry, Hawkins. There's no room for an extra passenger." McVey actually appeared to feel something in that brief moment.

Joe leant on his broom, his stomach hurting. Whatever they said he fully intended to make the break with them. He loathed prison, the years that stretched ahead of him behind grey walls. He would have to take a chance and, once outside, evade their clutches. They wouldn't stop him during the actual break-out. That would be risking too much.

"You're not 'ere for your 'olidays, me lad," the warder bellowed. His large feet sounded ominous as he walked across the cobbled yard to stand over Joe. "Are you sick?" The face looked anxious as his eyes searched Joe's features.

"No, Mister Simpson."

"Then sweep!"

Joe worked furiously, conscious of the warder's gaze and the ache in the pit of his stomach. That bloody broom handle had hurt. He owed the bastard Len one.

Somewhere on the other side of the wall a car engine roared into life. A figure appeared on top of the wall - ghostly as mist clung to it. A rope ladder snaked down into the yard and smacked the cobblestones with a dull thud.

Simpson, huge feet sounding on the wet stone, slid to a halt, mouth hanging open as he stared upwards in amazement. Before he could raise an alarm, McVey brought his broom down on the man's head with a crashing sound of splintering wooden handle and cracking bone. Simpson toppled and lay still.

Joe wanted to drop to his knees to examine the felled warder. He had not counted on murder being part of the plan. Now he had a momentary doubt about joining the mass exodus - but only momentary.

Six men weaved as the rope ladder swung wildly, hands and feet fighting to retain their precious hold on the precarious escape hope. Joe jumped forward, unaware that he still clutched his broom.

"Not you, kid!"

Joe skidded to a stop. Len stood at the foot of the ladder, knife in one hand, eyes slitted. *If only I had my bovver boots*, Joe thought and automatically used the only weapon within range - his broom. Len wasn't prepared for this strange kid coming at him. If he had taken time to acquaint himself with Joe's record he might have been more inclined to treat the youth as an equal in viciousness. But he hadn't. And that was his downfall!

The broom reversed with a swiftness that caught Len totally immobile. Only as the rounded, unyielding butt end speared at his face did the crook try to duck. Too late. Joe felt the shock travel along his forearms, saw the man's lips split and blood spurt. He heard the telltale crunch of bone and teeth hung loose amid the destruction of Len's features. Nothing daunted, Joe brandished the broom again, bringing it crossways onto the man's nose. Len sagged, knife falling from hand. Dropping his broom, Joe slashed at the other's groin with his hard prison-issue boot, spat at the stricken

198

victim of another aggro, and vaulted onto the rope ladder.

He was agile, a monkey climbing a tree. He arrived breathing easily on the wall as McVey's head was disappearing down the outside. Their eyes clashed and, in that instant, Joe realised he could never reach the ground with his fellow-escapers and stay intact.

Down below, like some gigantic monster from Earth's dark past, a moving van waited in the mist. Judging the distance as best he could, Joe leaped into space . . .

CHAPTER TWO

CONDENSATION trickled down the inside panes of the tall window. On a coffee table beside an expensive, antique sofa a national newspaper lay neatly folded across the middle. With some difficulty, Joe managed to make out the splash headline.

4 ESCAPEES RECAPTURED

Shivering as rain beat a mysterious drumming on the foliage surrounding the house, Joe cursed his lousy luck. His ankle hurt something awful. It was swollen, throbbing like a bad toothache. He knew to remove his boot would be fatal. Yet, he wanted to rub the bruised bone, the puffed flesh.

God, he thought. *I've got to find some grub!*

He pondered the advisability of breaking into the house and kicked the idea out almost immediately. A man entered the enormous room, went directly to the newspaper and opened it. Where the condensation formed irregular patterns on the glass the man's face floated in absurd contortions - wavering, twisting, shapeless often, forming anew into a picture of country squire the next. Not a man to tackle in his condition, Joe allowed. Probably an ex-army officer with more than a little unarmed combat experience. The type to clear steer of right then.

Limping away from the house, Joe slunk through woods to the cottage he had skirted earlier. It seemed like months since the jail break. He was so bloody cold and hungry. So unsure of this green, spacious nowhere. Give him the concrete pavements, the belching exhaust fumes, the warren of streets with their hiding places and dolly birds willing to feed and shelter a man for a few quick feels.

The cottage looked empty. He approached a window cautiously. After what he had gone through he did not want his freedom to end right here. Peering inside, he saw dust sheets covering indistinct furniture. He went to another window. The same scene greeted his gaze. He tried the window. Locked, doubly secured with spikes driven through both frames. He swore mentally, then went to the rear door. Testing it, he felt a give. He rubbed rain and dirt from the upper glass. One Yale-type lock and a bolt. A bloody large bolt.

He wrapped a soiled, wet handkerchief round his fist and drove the glass pane in. Carefully removing jagged shards, he reached inside, undid bolt and lock and swung the door open.

A mouse squeaked as it ran for cover. He plodded across a large farmhouse style kitchen to cupboards filling one entire wall. He opened them eagerly. Tins lined the lower shelves, sacks of sugar and flour the upper ones, packets of biscuits and cake mixes a corner area.

His hand hesitated near the tinned foods. Beans? Cocktail sausages? Spaghetti rings? Pineapple chunks? Bully beef? Chilli con carne? (*What the hell was that?*) King crab? Shrimps? Chicken Gumbo soup? Lobster Bisque soup? Tuna?

Wolf-like, he tore at the key of the bully beef timn and opened it. As he swallowed hunks wholesale he found a wall-bracket can opener and removed the tops of shrimps and beans. With that inside him he felt better. But still ravenous. He needed tea and bread. The refrigerator was empty and disconnected. The gas stove had been turned off at the main. The bread bin was spotless; empty, too.

Rain slashed into the kitchen and he closed the door. No sense asking for some nosey bastard poking his head in where it wasn't wanted!

He searched the cottage from bottom to top. In one bedroom he discovered decent clothing. He changed from his wet prison gear and dried himself in the bathroom. He enjoyed the feel of clean underwear against his skin even although it was just a shade too large for him. It didn't matter about the bulk-knit sweater, though. Nor the faded slacks. Tucked inside the pair of gum-boots he had noticed he would be like many another local farming clod. There was an old hat, raincoat. He studied himself in a mirror. Nobody would ever take him for an East Ender. He felt satisfied, still hungry . . .

An hour had passed now since he broke into the cottage. A heap of opened, empty tins littered the kitchen table. His belly rumbled from being over-stuffed. His ankle hurt worse than ever although the torn sheet binding it helped considerably. At least, he mused, he hadn't broken the bloody thing!

He considered the telephone in the lounge. Dare he make a call to London? He gave up the notion. If this place was on a manual exchange his goose would really be cooked.

He smiled. His thinking machine was working in top gear. Native cunning had its good points. Those stupid bastards getting caught would curse him but he didn't care. He had outsmarted all of them.

The rain was easing off. He would have to move along. God knows how far he was from civilisation, from London. He did not relish the prospect of travelling in daylight yet he had no choice. Hanging around this cottage was an invitation for that army character to take a walk and find him. Whatever he did, distance had to be put between the cottage and Joe Hawkins before the police got a description of the missing clothing. As it was, he was too close to the prison yet for comfort. He could have covered a greater mileage if only he had managed to keep his footing on that moving van's roof.

He could still see those startled faces peering upwards as he careered off the greasy roof and landed in fall-breaking bushes. Luckily, surprise had been with him. Before the others could apprehend him he had limped off into the swallowing mist and vanished from their sight. It hadn't been easy getting away. But for the fact that the authorities had been chasing the van he could never had made good his lone escape.

What he needed most was money. And cigarettes. After that he would play it cool until the heat lifted . . .

*

Lottie Newman lived alone with her dreams. At twenty three she did not classify herself as one of those on-the-shelf women without hope of ever snaring a husband. She could, if she wished, have her pick from a dozen or more eligible males. Modesty, and a desire to be completely honest with herself prevented her from calling the mirrored image confronting her beautiful. She was pretty, and shapely. That sufficed for a personal examination. When she decided the time was right for picking a husband she would pick carefully, security being the uppermost consideration. She did not go for having a handsome man about the house, nor one addicted to giving her a good time on dates. She preferred to know that there was money in the bank and a roof over her head which neither loan company nor mortgage society could ever take away. These things were paramount.

She turned slightly, posturing. The green velvet dress held against her nudity did something for her blonde hair, her bright green eyes. It also did more than something for her pert, thrusting breasts when draped round her slender figure.

Smiling, she threw the dress aside and raced hands lightly down her smooth flanks. She was an unabashed sensualist. At night, when reality subtly changed into erotic dreamland, she forgot security and concentrated on the pleasures of her flesh. She was not a prude although there was never any suggestion she was a permissive slut, either. She had been to bed with men and enjoyed the ecstacy of mutually sponsored gratification. The Pill was a boom when the mood for intercourse filled her being with uncontrollable longing.

Like now!

Shaking out her long blonde hair she swung towards the window. What she wouldn't give at that moment for a man to come into view and see her nakedness. *God, I'm a perverted bitch!* she thought happily. Standing in a doorway kitty-corner from her window she saw the man. Or was it a boy? She bent forward, her breasts pressed against the cold glass.

A shiver approaching orgasm flooded her loins. She could see those narrowed eyes gazing upwards, devouring her body. Suddenly, she retreated - ashamed. What must he think of her? She was behaving like a common prostitute advertising her professional ability. She blushed and hurriedly slipped into the velvet dress. The mood had vaporised. She was back to semi-normality . . .

*

What a bird! Joe thought as he strained to catch another glimpse of that lush nudity. His situation was desperate yet the need for a woman's hands on him, the touch of silken thighs slowly widening, was every bit as strong within his mind as getting loot.

A green dress moved across the curtained window. She had covered herself! Bitch!

Cold, unrelenting rain fell, bouncing off the lonely street. The doorway wasn't deep enough to prevent some wetting his trousers. He bent, tucking them inside his gum-boots. To hell with what these hick townspeople thought of a country yokel. His comfort was more important than the opinions of a few thousand idiots.

He had never heard of Kidderminster before and never wanted to see it again. The town was dying on its feet. Empty shops and rubbish-littered pavements reminded him of Plaistow and the degree of poverty one found there. From the huge signs outside some of the factories he knew they made carpets here. All he could say to that was "people are covering their floors with newspapers these days". If the number of cars parked in the factories' parking lots was any criterion they were working at half capacity.

Congratulating himself on his perspicacity, Joe began to wonder about the girl. She had looked like a decent sort. Not the usual run of whore. Yet, what was she doing showing her natural beauty and living in a dump like this?

The house opposite was old, sadly in need of paint and new guttering. Rain splashed from the roof in cascades, racing down stained walls, flooding over a small canopy which barely managed to keep steps dry. He could see nameplates on the door. He grinned, trying to figure which room she occupied and darted across the street.

Why not? he asked himself. *Why not indeed?*

The names were written in a spidery scrawl. Mr & Mrs Vernon. Jonathan Selby. L. Newman. Mrs Brown, caretaker.

The girl did not strike him as a caretaking type. Nor did he feel she was a housewife. That left L. Newman. In flat 3.

The inside stairs were creaking like crazy as he ascended. There was an un-natural quiet which bothered him. What if she screamed when he pushed her into her room? He stifled a laugh. There had to be women like her, men on the run like him. The law of averages gave the desperate an advantage. He wouldn't wait for her to scream. He would place a hand over her mouth, whisper his intentions and see if she wanted what he could give.

He was feeling bloody randy when he reached the door with its figure 3 swinging on one nail. Maybe, if she pleased him, he would bang another nail in the number to keep it straight-up.

Placing his ear to the door, he listened. He heard softly muted music and the sound of light feet pacing back and forth. No voices.

Nothing to suggest she had a visitor.

He knocked, ready to spring.

CHAPTER THREE

THOSE suspense-laden seconds waiting for her to open the door gave Joe the shakes. His entire life flashed across the mental screen called memory. In his skinhead days, rape had been but one of the vicarious pleasures running around with a gang allowed. During his period of employment when he sported an Abercrombie and furled umbrella - getting a bird to put out for him had not always been a simple matter of dating, drinking, convincing. There had been the occasional physical taking a City "gentleman" would have balked at.

But a man on the run had to be extra careful. Rape, as such, was great. Sometimes Joe figured the thrill of illicit intercourse more pleasurable than getting it laid on the line. The "I love you and like doing this" brigade seldom *worked* hard enough to satisfy a man. They believed in self first and if he pants for a minute he's happy.

Should he wait? Or should he skip out before it was too late?

He was debating the pro's and con's when the door vibrated and swung inwards.

"Bloody hell!"

"Yes?"

Joe wanted to grab her and do it there, in the dirty hall. His involuntary exclamation had been one of admiration. He had known many girls - and women - in his time but this one surpassed the lot. At close range he sensed her undecided desire to get acquainted, to let her passions run riot in his arms. Her sensuality seared his brain, her perfume assailed his nostrils. Yet, too, there was an inbred reserve. A with-holding that somehow contradicted her appearance.

Lottie could not compel herself to slam the door in the youth's face and lock it securely against what was so obviously burning in his eyes. In her dreams she had been confronted by many situations of a similar nature. Men shattering her door, raping her. Men refusing to be put off by her spoken denial of the emotions rampaging through her loins.

But those had been erotic dreams. This was fact. Stark, brutal fact breeding fear and indecision. Leaving her incapable of reaction.

There was, in the way they stood with the thin wedge of door offering solid - if ineffectual - proof of their "in" "out" status, something comical, and deadly serious, about the tense situation. It was as though each wanted the other to make the first, tentative overture.

Suddenly, Joe struck. His hand shot out and clamped across her mouth. His other arm snaked round her body and pushed her into the room. His heel flicked the door shut. He was breathing laboriously. Their eyes clashed - hers wide with fear, his brightly intent.

"I'll hurt you if you scream," he warned.

A low, scared moan muffled against his sweating palm.

The heat of her drove him wild. She wore nothing under the bloody dress! He could feel the velvet slide over her silken skin.

"You stood naked at the window," he accused as if seeking justification for what was about to happen.

Lottie wanted to cry. She struggled.

Joe's fingers hurt as he squeezed her face into a puckered contortion. His breathing sounded ragged, his voice harsh. "Cut that out, you teasing bitch! You're going to get screwed . . ."

She fought like a madwoman. Her knee came up, missing its target. Her hands levered between them, striving to force his body away.

"You've asked for this!" Joe released her with unexpected suddenness. As she staggered back off-balance, his fist caught her jaw. She slammed back across the room, teetered when a divan buckled her legs and fell lengthwise along it. Her dress rode high to reveal what Joe had imagined down there on the rain-swept street.

Unable to control the lust coursing vigorously through his veins, Joe quickly divested himself of damp clothing. For an instant he gazed down at the girl then, grunting, he twisted her until the velvet green dress dropped to the floor.

"I don't want her like this," he said aloud. He slapped her face and shook her. An unconscious woman would be like making love to a plastic dummy. Slowly, her eyes opened.

"Oh, God - no!" Her hand waved weakly, warding off his nakedness rearing above her.

The very sight of her moving flesh sent Joe into action. His mouth brutalised hers, his tongue probing the resisting moist cavern. His hands sought, found and fondled her lovely breasts.

She would never dream about he-men again, Lottie thought. All her varied experiences had not conditioned her for what Joe was doing. She had only known gentleness, mutually respected caresses. Not this. Not this animalistic self-gratification that left her coldly unresponsive. Even when he forced her legs apart and mounted her, she did not associate their coupling with sex. There was no heightening of sensation. None of the glorious pleasures she had found so ecstatic, so geographically wonderful in past copulations. This was like being separated from her body, like watching a man take some other woman in one of those horrible blue films her first boyfriend had insisted she watch with him.

God, how she hated this beast using her. She could have killed him and considered herself doing a public service.

Joe knew she was totally rejecting him. Not a quiver excited her flesh. She lay corpse-like, letting him piston on her coldly warm body until he could contain himself no longer. And, at the supreme moment of conquest, he sensed her revulsion.

Rolling from her he laughed. "One day you'll regret not having enjoyed me."

"You've had your fun - now, get the hell out of my flat!" Her voice sounded so unemotional, distant.

"Yeah," Joe said, roaming round the room. There was one helluva contrast between inside and the scruffy building's exterior. The girl had her place decorated tastefully. The furnishings were modern but matched the pictures, carpet and colour scheme. He particularly liked the table-lamp with its nude supporting a tassled shade. It was the first time he had ever seen a nude statue on a fixture.

"I said get out," she repeated.

Joe studied her. She had not moved since he dismounted. Her thighs were still apart, their soft inner curves slightly red where his body had frictioned against the tender skin. Her breasts had that flattened supine look so highly provocative in the object of male passion.

"You're a bloody tease," he told her. "You deliberately showed yourself at the window . . ."

She sat upright, crossed her legs and folded her arms across her breasts. "I didn't see anyone," she lied.

"Have you got a kitchen?" His other hunger had to be satisfied next.

She narrowed her eyes. This question confused her.

"Shit!" Joe stalked bare-footed into a bedroom and swore again. The girl watched him calmly now as he entered the small, compact kitchen. She had always been told her I.Q. was above average. Certain things about this youth began to make sense. She could see her evening newspaper in the magazine stand near her television set. A tremor raced down her spine. Maybe rape was the least of her worries . . .

*

"That'll keep you from trying to sneak out on me," Joe said as he tied the last knot.

Lottie frowned. The idea of spending the whole night in bed with this escaped convict did not appeal. She had no illusions regarding his ability to rape her a third time. She blamed herself for bringing on the second. If only she had kept her knowledge to herself he might have taken the few pounds she had in her purse and left during the late evening. But she hadn't. She had been so cocky, so sure that he'd run like hell.

Testing the dressing gown sash that connected his uninjured ankle to hers, Joe lay back with both elbows behind his head. It was a treat having a comfortable bed to sleep in. Since the break-out he had roughed it.

"How did you guess?" he asked.

"Rapists aren't usually starving," came her reply.

"You've had so much experience?" He laughed at his wit.

"You have, I'm sure."

Memory returned with a bang. He remembered Brighton, and how the gang had raped that bloody hippie girl. Billy had nearly let the fuzz nick him he was so hot for the bitch.

"What happens tomorrow morning?" the girl asked.

"I'll screw you and leave."

"How can you get pleasure when I don't co-operate?"

He grinned, twisting to one side. His hand moved over her taut nipples, down the expanse of ivory silken flesh to her abdomen. He toyed with her, building her hatred into a fiery furnace. "With what you've got it's easy blowing my mind," he taunted.

"Filthy pig!"

He hit her hard. The imprint of his fingers left ugly red welts on her face. Tears sprung into her eyes and she turned her head to avoid letting him see her anguish.

"Maybe I'll beat you first," he mused to frighten her.

She whimpered. This was a nightmare.

"If you made love like you meant it . . ."

She glared at him. "I couldn't - wouldn't!"

It's your funeral," he said softly.

CHAPTER FOUR

CHARLIE MCVEY propped his morning newspaper against the ketchup bottle and poured a second cup of tea. He had expected a front page banner headline to announce the capture of Joe Hawkins for the last few days and still nothing. Not front page, not inside pages either. The little bastard was proving a slippery customer.

From the kitchen, the noise of dishes being washed intruded upon his concentration. He opened his mouth to yell, then closed it. *What the hell have I got to gripe about?* he asked himself. Not many crooks on the run have their wives keeping them company.

"Charlie, is it safe for me to go shopping?"

He glanced round and smiled generously. She looked a sight in those bloody curlers - but a wonderful sight for his prison-sore eyes. Six years makes a man wish for his wife regardless of how she looked in the early morning. Frankly, he'd taken her in preference to all those mini-skirted dolly birds the other blokes spoke about continuously in the stir.

"It's okay, Martha. They haven't circulated your picture yet."

"I'm worried, Charlie." She came into the dining room. "What if some bastard talks?"

"They wouldn't dare."

"Oh, I don't mean deliberately."

"Then what?" He was perplexed.

"That Joe Hawkins would . . ."

"Him?" McVey laughed loudly. "The little bastard doesn't know about this house."

"You're sure?"

"Sure!" He slapped her protuding rump playfully. He liked his women plump and Martha had ample flesh for what they jokingly

208

called their cavorting.

"I'm glad you're home, Charlie." She kissed his forehead. "I wish it wasn't this way, though."

"I couldn't stay inside any longer, girl," he said seriously. "The prospect of serving another seven years porridge nearly drove me insane."

"When would you have been eligible for parole?"

"Whenever they got around to drawing my name from a hat. Is that what you wanted to hear?"

She sat heavily opposite him, face strained, eyes clouded. "I've prayed for you to quit, Charlie."

"I have - once I . . ."

Fear contorted her matronly features. Once, she had been quite a beauty but the criminal years had taken a sad toll. "He's not worth the risk, Charlie."

"He is - to me!" The man's lips formed a tight, menacing line. "Len didn't even get to see over the bloody wall."

"Len wouldn't want you to be brought back for that."

"If it hadn't been for Len's contacts I would be rotting in there." He pushed his plate away in annoyance. On his feet, he towered over the furniture. Huge hands opened and closed like a circus strongman flexing sinews before tearing a telephone directory in half. "The word is out - get Joe Hawkins and bring him to me. Afterwards," and he relaxed abruptly to smile down at his wife, "we'll be in clover street . . ."

*

Unaware that the underworld was alerted for him, Joe felt that life offered compensations for men on the dodge. In his pocket he had the proceeds of Lottie's purse and what he had managed to get for her jewellery and flat contents. Sixteen quid in all. The old pawnbroker hadn't been generous but in an area of high unemployment he had done better than anticipated.

He walked past the police station and entered a narrow side street with billboards announcing the forthcoming visit of a famous international pop group. He would have liked to stay and hear them but discretion was the stuff freedom used for creative moulding.

He thought about the girl then. She would be hungry and sore before she got free. Serves her right for being such a bloody-minded bitch! If only she had made love to him the way he had suggested.

To blazes with her! It was no skin off his nose if she wasn't found for a week. By then he'd be in London with a few million people crowding round him as a protective shield. The fuzz would have difficulty tracing him in the Big Smoke.

*

Lottie Newman found the policewoman very considerate. More so than that officious sergeant who kept trying to have his stupid questions answered.

"Don't worry about Sergeant Hazleton, dear," the policewoman smiled. "He's really a sweet person when the villains let him alone. This young Hawkins is a real swine . . ."

Lottie nodded. She hoped they would catch Joe - maybe even castrate the bastard before sending him back to prison. If ever a man deserved to be without the wherewithall to interfere with another woman, it was that rotter.

"Did he mention the names of his friends?"

Lottie frowned in concentration. She just couldn't be positive. When she had accused him of being one of those escaped convicts he had laughed and made some reference to the other mugs. But had he named people?

The policewoman tried a new tack. She understood the girl's confusion yet, too, she had a duty to perform. Not to the victims of a criminally sadistic thug but to the general public. They had to be protected from this maniac. Nothing could be done for Lottie. Not unless the girl had been mentally disturbed by the rape. Then it was for the doctors to repair the damage. Not her. Not the force.

"Did he say where he was going then?"

Lottie nodded. "London, I think."

"Did he definitely say so?"

"He spoke about his pals in the East End of London."

"Anything else, dear?"

"A lot. He was crude. He kept telling me about other women he had raped." She dropped her face in her hands.

The policewoman signalled her sergeant and placed an arm round Lottie's shoulder.

"We'd best call in the medical department", the woman said quietly.

Hazleton turned away, face flushed as anger mounted inside him.

210

He hated this part of his job - having to see how broken a girl could look after some pervert had had his fun. He wished to hell the politicians had not removed the birch as a deterrent . . .

CHAPTER FIVE

GEOGRAPHICALLY, Joe Hawkins was riding a lorry to nowhere. The signposts did not have any mental connections. He knew, approximately, where The Wash was, where Wales was, where Cornwall was - and there his knowledge ended. Certain place names reminded him of blokes in prison. Nobby Clarke had come from Worcester. Little Ronnie Gray from Redditch. But where the hell those towns were was beyond him. They simply existed, and that was all.

A new name flashed past as the lorry swung onto a by-pass. Cheltenham!

Christ, he hoped this bleedin' driver wasn't going there! He knew that Cheltenham had one of the most vicious Hell's Angels chapters in the entire country. Every skinhead knew that! One of the Sunday newspapers had given the bastards enough publicity to make Cheltenham a No Man's Land area for his own fraternity.

He watched for other signs now. The driver was a sullen type not given to more than grunting replies. For miles, Joe had been wondering why the man had even bothered to give him a lift. It certainly was not for conversation. That had been quickly made evident.

Cheltenham eleven miles!

The races! That was it!

Screwing round in the tight confines of the cab he glared at the horse-box construction immediately behind the small rear window. Racehorses for the Cheltenham track.

"Let me out anywhere, mate," Joe said.

The driver grunted, keeping his foot hard down on the accelerator.

"You going to Cheltenham races?"

"Yeah!" The lorry slewed round a corner and Joe gave a fleeting thought to the pathetic horses inside the box. Bloody animals getting bashed like this won't be able to run worth a damn, he thought. No wonder the bookies make a bleedin' fortune!

"Is there anywhere here I can hitch a ride to London?"

"Best chance is in Cheltenham," came the *long* reply.

"Is it a large town?"

For an instant the driver's eyes came off the road and brushed across Joe's tense face. "Don't you know it?"

Joe swore mentally. He remembered what he'd told the other - he had been born in these parts.

"Something funny about you, mate," the driver said then.

Joe blustered. "I've been up North for years."

"Prison, I'll bet!"

Joe tightened up inside.

The driver laughed for the first time. "I did five years on the Moor once," he confided.

The countryside had a green colouring totally alien to Joe. The small villages all seemed so neat and cut-off from the modern world that demanded a high price of its adherents. There was a tranquility and a sense of relaxed sharing here that made Joe feel like he had entered another world. He was a stranger in paradise. A blight on this landscape. A not-belonging creature invading the peaceful haunts of a different England.

Joe shook himself and grinned as the lorry took a side-road between trimmed hedgerows. "I've been inside," he allowed.

"Thought so," the driver remarked.

"What did you do?" Joe asked.

"Manslaughter!"

Christ! A killer!

"The missus started playing around. I killed her!"

Joe wanted out of the lorry more than ever. He could visualise how the police would have this bloke's face on file, or in memory.

"Don't get the shits, kid," the driver said. Strong hands handled the heavy lorry like it was a mini. They were doing forty-five along narrow country lanes and it seemed like a ton on a motorway to Joe. "I don't like talk," the man said after some reflection. "I'm a lonely bird . . ." he laughed.

Joe got the message. Loud and clear.

"Were you in long enough to go the other way?"

He's queer! Bent! Homo! Joe inched away from the gear-stick.

"Were you?" came the insistent query.

"Naw, I like girls."

"Pity,"the driver sighed and lapsed into silence.

A sign read: Winchcombe. Joe was not familiar with his history. The long, narrow street curving through ancient buildings and picturesque houses did nothing for him. It was just another community en route to Cheltenham. That this had been the county town of a Saxon region which had slowly been swallowed up in Norman re-organisation did not hit home. Nor did the ancient squabble over tobacco growing ring a bell.

"An important village this,"the driver said as they made it through to the new housing estate.

"Well, it's not much now,"Joe replied with disinterest. He had too much on his mind to bother about trivia. The driver's bent, Cheltenham looming closer on his hilly horizon, his need to find a large, teeming community in which to hide. These were important. Not a bleedin' county village.

"You get out or skip?" the driver asked, suddenly curious.

"Got out!"

They were climbing a hill now.

"How far to Cheltenham?" Joe asked.

"Across Cleveland Hill only."

"Where's the nearest city?"

"Gloucester - about nine miles to the west."

"Is it big?"

The lorry growled as the driver slipped into a lower gear. "Not very. Why?"

"Is Birmingham far?"

The driver laughed, geared down again. "You'd last about a minute in Brummy."

That rankled Joe. "Lissen, mate . . ."

"Go on, tell me how you beat up on old ladies,"the driver teased.

Joe scowled and watched the scenery spread into a panoramic wonderland as houses and churches appeared in the valleyed distance. In the misty hinterland a range of hills started to rise, forming a sort of barrier to the view. Hotels and bed and breakfast residences formed a strip-development to the Cleeve Hill side as a few tenacious abodes clung to the steep falling-awayness on their right.

"You're on the run, aren't you?"

Joe blanched. The trouble with old lags was they knew all the signs, all the actions of that special breed of men who had spent time inside.

"Bloody trouble for me, you are," the driver moaned as they pushed in front of a bus which was about to depart its turning circle. The hill went down now . . . down, down, into the valley.

"Let me out then," Joe snarled.

"When we reach Prestbury!"

"Where's that?"

"Cheltenham racecourse."

Joe clung to his seat. The lorry careered down the incline like a run-away. Far behind, the bus formed a lessening blob against the road and the hillside. The needle was touching sixty now and Joe wanted to bale out while he was still in one piece. *The bastard wants to kill us both*, Joe thought.

Southam slipped past, a few more houses appeared and the lorry began to slow. Not fast enough. Joe knew, instinctively, that the driver was not going to make the sharp turn ahead. When a Triumph Herald swung wide as it took the L-shaped bend at speed, Joe was already opening the door . . .

*

The cab was a crumpled mess, the horses snorting furiously in the undamaged rear section. He could hear the frantic hoofs kicking hell out of the thin container walls.

People were coming and he slipped into a lane with the battered lorry forming a shield between him and the village beyond. It did not matter about the driver. He was getting what he deserved.

The stupid prick! Joe thought.

A couple of dolly-birds in mini-skirts wheeling prams came from the new estate and glanced at him. He avoided them, and hurried through the bungalow development. He liked the new constructions better than the mullioned-windowed, Cotswoldian stone facades of the older, larger residences he had caught a glimpse of before fleeing the doomed lorry. Thatched bakeries, bow-fronted windows on a chemist's shop, an old pub with ancient hanging sign and countless additions did not tempt him. He liked things modern, all glass and dull brick or, contrasting, dirt-stained and decrepit like they had in the East End.

He climbed a fence, cut across a field and came into a lane with olde worlde cottages and a main road not far away. He reached the main stem, and sighed relief. An A.A. sign with a pointing finger said: TO THE RACES. A bus ambled towards him and he spotted the stop. He ran, caught the bus and paid his fare to a small, fat, friendly-type driver. He felt strange amongst the passengers. They were too chatty, too neighbourly for his liking. None of the London frozen countenances, the dejection of living in squalid conditions existed here. Everybody seemed too happy, too pleased with life for him to comprehend their outlook.

In a way, he was glad when he reached Cheltenham's town centre. *At least*, he thought, *I'm just one of a bunch of strangers here.* Some of the types he spotted on arrival gave him a sense of security - long-hairs, mod-geared girls, leather-jacketed youths carrying helmets decorated with Nazi insignia. His types. Ones he could communicate with again. Not old lags, not county folk, definitely not up-tights.

CHAPTER SIX

HIS types were a minority, although outstanding in a sense. The majority were well-dressed, well-fed, well-heeled. They walked with gracious airs and spoke as if carrying mouthfuls of plums between upper and lower dentures. They wore tweeds, specially-created dresses and drove away in Jags or Rolls or Mercedes. They used walking sticks, carried swagger sticks to prod aside this insectuous creature from *their* pavement.

It was Joe's first confrontation with a "county set" and he got an eye-opener. He had never known such people existed. Even his dalliance in the City where affluence and arrogance walked hand-in-hand had not prepared him for the upper-limits of Shire snobbery. What he didn't realise was that these people were friendly, sociable, if just a trifle on the borders of being too good to go to bed with themselves. Under circumstances calling for an outward display of acceptance they were as all-embracing as the local gossip in, say, Greengage or Barking Road. They had their faults but so did the great mass of people in working class areas.

I'll bet they've got some spare cash at home, he thought.

The glimmer of an idea started festering in his skull.

Catching sight of a blue uniform he sidled into a street and cut back across the main shopping centre. He had read the markers and knew

215

now which road would take him to London. The need to get lost in East Ham or Poplar was assuming major proportions. He had to feel at home - at one with his society.

He watched a young girl leave the Co-Op store and cross the road to the bank almost directly opposite. She wasn't more than sixteen and the bag she carried suggested a snatch of some thousand or more pounds. He liked the way her ass moved inside her maxi, the way her liberated tits jiggled. *Christ, he wanted a woman again!*

A clock said 2:56. He paused, and waited. The idea was gaining impetus.

In those precious seconds prior to the bank doors closing he counted no less than five girls of tender age entering with swag-bags visibly displayed.

What a bleedin' set-up! he thought.

Instead of hitching a ride or taking a bus to the outlying districts, he walked the streets, not conscious of distance or how his feet ached. His mind was working out the details of a super-scheme to relieve the dolly-birds of their loot. And calculating the difficulties of getting out of Cheltenham in a fast get-away car . . .

*

Plaistow hadn't altered much in his absence. Taken in small doses it stank. In large, it became a cesspool from which only the dead escaped and the living fought to eke-out a somewhat stereotyped existence. Here was an in-betweenness which was composed of gossip, wife-beating, husband-cruelty and all that small-mindedness entailed. Life, as such, in Joe's old street had always been a struggle against the intolerance of a working class fervently voting against any kind of Tory infiltration whilst wishing like hell that the Labour man had the guts to combat an ever-growing union monster.

Joe stood at the Greengage and breathed in the polluted air. It was wonderful, if rotten for his lungs. An old biddy across the street reminded him of another woman - a so-called mother whose daughter had had seven illigitimate kids before her twenty-fourth birthday.

It hardly seemed possible that less than five hours seperated him from Cheltenham's completely opposite environment. The sensation of gracious living and Cotswoldian space within easy reach no longer touched him. Here there was only filth - in papers blowing along the pavements, in the grubby clothing of senior citizens, in the exterior walls of business houses.

At least, though, he felt as if he belonged here. This was his warren, his type of people.

Once he had been king of all he surveyed here. He had had a reputation, a following. Not many had dared challenge his authority in the good old days. When Joe Hawkins walked into a pub he got service with a capital S. And his word had been a law unto itself.

The need for a change of clothes, a decent meal, a place to kip and cash in his pocket, hit him hard as he watched a long-haired youth stroll from a bookie-joint counting fivers. Being on the run he couldn't ask Social Security or any of the ex-convict associations. Getting bread was up to him. But where? From whom?

In this rabbit-warren of streets and terrace houses there were guys he had known. Hymie, Billy, Don. No doubt the London press had carried the story of his fantastic escape. No doubt the local fuzz were watching his home, the hangouts frequented by his old mob. Going into any of the pubs was like asking for the beak to hand him an additional year for going over the wall. Very few of the pubs in the district were without their grass or police undercover merchants.

What the bleedin' hell did I come back here for? he asked himself as he moved from the corner into a less conspicious side street.

He knew the answer, as every criminal did - London's teeming millions gave more cover and more shelter than anywhere else in Britain. Nobody in the Big Smoke was a person. Each was simply a face in the crowd, a being to be ignored and pushed and thrust aside as the mass moved on its personal, selfish, all-embracing forward march.

"Christ, I've got to find somebody!" he said aloud and heard an old biddy mutter something about lay-abouts and little bleeders. He wanted to belt her, but held back. The last thing he wanted right then was to draw attention to himself.

*

Darkness was an envelope closed round him. Safe as a letter being carried by a nonentity postman he walked the streets, hands in pockets, eyes searching for just one familiar face in the boisterous throng. He noticed the increased numbers of Pakistanis occupying the pavements and found it more and more difficult to contain his urge to bash a few of the bastards. His old hatred had not been curtailed by events.

God, those were the days, for sure! he thought.

He let himself be taken and carried forward by the crowd as he recalled how the mob had followed his orders and gone on Paki-bashing sprees every so often. How they had made hippies and Hell's Angels bend a knee to their superiority. He remembered times when they had smashed a railway carriage or terrorised bus passengers on the way to a West Ham away match. Especially, he recalled the Chelsea games and those bastards at The Shed - the Chelsea skinheads!

Skinheads . . .

What was it they called themselves now? Boot Boys?

First there was skinhead.

Then came suedehead.

Now it was Boot Boys . . .

All the bleedin' same but with subtle differences creeping in to make older mobs less effective, less cemented to one leader. Many of the first brigade had married, changed their image. In their hearts they longed for the original way things had been. That he was sure of even if people denied the existence of skinheads as a force today.

The figure on the opposite side of the street looked like an apparition from some seance-directed recall-desire. He hesitated, almost losing his opportunity to shout as the shape started to enter a pub.

"Stan . . ."

The figure halted, then swung with East End curiosity and suspicion.

Dodging traffic, Joe raced across the road.

"Jesus! Joe Hawkins . . ."

"Come down here, Stan," Joe said fast.

Stan Clegge rubbed palms against his greasy overalls and darted glances up and down the street.

"For cryin' out loud - move your arse, Stan!"

Joe stood expectantly on the pavement, ready to grab the frozen youth.

"Bleedin' hell . . ." Stan murmured, moving quickly to join Joe.

"Don't say a word about my escape," Joe breathed as he drew Stan into a doorway. "Have you seen Hymie or Billy today?"

Stan shook his head vehemently. "Naw - they're both married!"

Joe felt some of the pace leave him. *Married!*

"Hey, Joe - ain't you askin' fer trouble . . . ?"

"I need bread, man," Joe replied. "How much you got?"

Stan hummed as he dug into his dirty overalls. "Not much, Joe. I'm a working slob now."

"How'd you like to split about five thousand?"

Stan stiffened and glanced out of the doorway. "Joe . . ." he wailed.

Grabbing a handful of Stan's overalls, Joe hissed: "Lissen mate - I've got a sweet set-up. We can knock of a bundle if I have the right blokes to back me!"

"The mob has broken up," Stan complained. "Anyway, I've got a job."

"Shit on that! The mob can do with some extra cash, can't they?"

Stan sheltered against a window with television sets flopping over as an example of reception in this area. He was not conscious of the programme being shown on ITV - one of those all-violent American shows which pretended to make the good guy come out on top but which never lessened the impact of crime always pays.

"How do I contact Hymie?"

Stan shuddered, then shrugged. "I'll get him, Joe! I swear - I'll get him!"

CHAPTER SEVEN

JOE HAWKINS looked at the faces before him and wanted to shout a triumphant, *"I've done it!"*

Hymie, Billy, Don, Stan, Alf, Dora and Flo all stood there looking distant, aloof, totally removed from his past.

The main thing was, of course, that they had come!

That meant something!

"I've got an idea," Joe began after cold reunions.

"Forget it, Joe," Hymie snapped. "We haven't got time for your sort!"

Joe trembled.

"That goes for Dora and me," Don said with more guts than he had ever displayed during Joe's leadership.

"Let's hear it," Flo shouted, glaring at the others.

Billy shifted his feet, edging closer to Hymie and Don. His eyes refused to meet Joe's. He had grown a small beard - one of those pointed little Jewish efforts which Joe had always loathed.

"I'm against getting into anythin' bad," Billy said.

Alf Page was the oldest member of the group. He wore a Crombie, Squires and Ben Sherman. His hair was neither long nor short and his demeanour was one of total disinterest except when he asked: "Is it bread man?" and glared at Joe.

Joe winked at Alf. "Bread galore," he said.

"You're crook," Hymie said and turned, with Dora's tugging on Don's hand making it a trio of exits.

The bastard! The bitch! The weak-kneed . . .

"Forget 'em, Joe," Alf said fast.

"Look," Joe yelled, his ire up. "I'm not trying to form a mob again. I've got a certainty and I want help. It'll take four, maybe five blokes to knock off the birds . . ."

Billy shrugged and tugged at his pathetic beard. "I'm legal, Joe," he mentioned, backing to the door.

"How's about it if I tell you there's birds to screw?"

Billy hesitated, and sniffed.

"Christ, if it makes it easier for you, take my knickers down," Flo yelped.

Billy bulged hard and moved back another foot. His face was red, his eyes piggish as he glared at Flo.

"Don't you want me?" the girl asked.

"Yeah . . . yeah . . ."

Joe understood Billy's dilemma as his old mate sought for the door handle with his free hand. Billy had always liked girls - especially if he could get 'em free and willing to try something fancy. But Billy has not been the most courageous of the mob. Billy had his fear - this inborn sense of survival.

"Let him go!" Joe said as Flo opened her mouth to berate Billy when he backed out of their gathering.

Stan, Alf and Flo waited patiently as the door shut.

"Who can drive fast?" Joe asked.

Flo grinned and jabbed a finger at Alf. "He's terrific!"

"You in, Stan?"

Stan nodded and moved a few inches closer to Flo who sniffed and screwed up her nose. "You've got B.O." she said.

"I've tried everything including Lifebuoy," Stan replied with sad eyes surveying the girl's mini-skirted frame. "It's no good . . ."

"I'll say it isn't!" Flo tossed her head, then looked at Joe. "How about it?"

"I can get two blokes," Alf said.

Joe winked at Flo, then asked Alf, "Are they good?"

"The best! They've done porridge and want bread."

."Get them!" Joe went to Flo and held her against him. His hands fondled her lush buttocks. "Do you have your own pad?"

"You bet!" She brought her right arm between them and toyed with him.

"Let me know when everything's lined up," Joe said over his shoulder, too busy concentrating on Flo to bother with trivialities now.

"I'll get 'em round to Flo's tonight," Alf said as he pulled at Stan. "Come on, voyeur - we've got other work to do . . ."

*

The flat was one of those cheap, so-called furnished two rooms with kitchen effort that landlords charged the sky for in a crowded city. It required painting, decent carpets on the floor and something better than homemade tables and chairs. At half its rent it was still over-priced.

When Joe first noticed Flo she had been thirteen, flat chested and had long, thin legs. She had wanted to join his mob but he had told her to get stuffed and come back when she filled out enough.

He had no complaints now. Flo had been stuffed, and the amount of padding she had acquired in three years more than satisfied his notions of how a woman should look.

"Like?" she asked, slipping a semi-transparent nightdress over her head. She still wore brassiere and panties. Her attempts to get the briefs off gave him an adequate chance of viewing the thatching covering her loins.

"Not bad," he allowed.

"Not bad!" she wailed. "It's bloody good!" She hoisted the nightdress and left her bottom parts exposed as she deliberately unhooked her bra and displayed her pert, hard-nippled breasts.

"Not bad!" Joe said again and dropped his pants.

She eyed his nakedness and grunted. "That's terrific," she exclaimed.

"It'll fit," he said with a nonchalance she loathed.

"I take the bloody Pill," she announced as she flung herself across a creaking, sagging bed. The nightdress did little to shield vital statistics from his rampant lust.

"Just as well," he grinned, advancing on her. "They don't issue French letters in jail!" He postured above her with an obscene handling of his privates. "You don't want me to feel you up, do you?"

"She touched herself and laughed. "No Joe - I'm ready!"

He came down on top of her, positioning himself as she fumbled him into place. Their eyes met for a split-second and then he speared deep into her warmth . . .

*

"God, that was the best I've ever had," she panted and rolled off the bed. He lay like a log, gasping a little, watching her hurried sweeps with Kleenex. The bitch in Kidderminster had been a beautiful woman; all a man could have asked for in looks and body shape. But Flo had been tops in the gymnastic department, in bringing him to that soaring height so often denied the male.

"You haven't gone without since you got out, Joe," she accused.

He grinned and held out his hand for a Kleenex.

"So what? I raped a dolly in the country."

"Cor, I like that!" She wiped him and kissed his chest. "Joe, I've always wanted to be your girl."

"Don't get your knickers in a twist," he warned. "I haven't lost the knack . . ."

"Knack?" She twisted and grabbed him, doing such sweet things he wanted to dash out for the nearest sex shop and purchase a virility tablet or six. "You've got everything it takes, Joe."

His fingers coiled in her hair and forced her to come up until her face was in close proximity to his.

"Can't you settle for just one special girl, Joe?"

He kissed her like a bull in heat, hands quickly roaming her tight buttocks, her thighs, her abdomen. As the feel of her penetrated to his emotional seat he got a mental glimpse of prison again - of randy queers trying to seduce him, of old lags saying how he was young and freshly-interesting, of cold nights doing without as the thud of a guard's feet made sleep impossible. The mood for her vanished. Pushing her away he pointed at her naked major attraction and growled: "Cover it, Flo - you won't be needin' that for a while."

"But, Joe . . ." she wailed, staring at his lean, hard body.

He dressed slowly, cogitating on the pressing problem of getting his hands on loot. Flo wasn't much even if her technique was super. What he wanted was one of those society bitch-daughters of some old Cheltenham colonel with expensive perfume clinging to her virgin flesh and a yen for it bigger than the leaning tower of Pisa. He knew the type. Had seen a few of them walking down the Promenade with their poodles and flat shoes and those cheeky bottoms wiggling like crazy. He believed all the dirty yarns told by toothy touts about the rich women who just couldn't get enough of what made them yell and swell. With bread in his kick he could call a few tunes for his brand of orgy.

By then, Flo had the message. She started dressing, sulking and darting the occasional glance at his body as he got into his clothes.

"What's been happening since I been away?" he asked.

She bent forward, let her knockers fall into her bra and jerked erect to hook the strap. "Nothing, Joe. That's the trouble."

"Don't they have an aggro?"

She pulled an old dress over her head, and palmed it down her hips and flanks. She couldn't stop trying to excite him. "Sometimes, Joe. Not like before, though. We like reggae and soul and going to discos and having a bash if some of the other kids don't fall into line, but it isn't the same. None of the old stuff."

He combed his hair, studying his face in the mirror. Time had brought its changes there, too. He was still tall - had topped the six foot mark now. His eyes, though, hadn't undergone any drastic alteration - they could blow a girl's mind if he was inclined to do so and the old coldness, the old savagery, burned in them yet. Only the prison-pallor was different - the slight greying of skin and a few extra lines round nose and mouth. That would drop away with freedom's air and being top dog again.

"Do they go to West Ham matches?"

"Every fortnight for the home games."

"What about aways?"

"Seldom." She splashed cheap scent on her dress and behind her ears. The smell of it almost made him sick.

"Can't you afford better than that?" he asked.

"Christ, Joe - I'm only a shopgirl!"

"What about your old woman?" He said it not because he was

223

interested but for a subject to keep her talking. He didn't want to indulge in petting now. That perfume would have softened his desire in seconds.

"She's dead! Stepped in front of a lorry with the weekend shopping."

He refused to sympathise. Flo's mother had been one of his worst enemies, a woman who had called him everything.

"And the old man?"

"Stays at the Sally Ann! He went on the meth kick!"

That amused Joe. Another docker's son would find a place. He could imagine his father, Roy Hawkins, making some humane gesture like having a whip-round for Flo's old man and Ed Black shoving the collection into his pocket to cover some mythical union expense. It was a bloody mess! Dog eat dog. And, as always, the shop stewards or the union representatives came out smelling of proverbial roses while bastards like Flo's father got a flea-bag bed in a lousy Sally Ann hostel where some other no-goods were making a bomb cheating the till. What a bleedin' circle!

"You ever visit him?"

Flo burped and covered her mouth with an apologetic hand. "Not me!" she stressed. "I went once - God, what an awful place! Full of layabouts and smellin' of piss! It's a shame they get away with it!"

"God's on their side," Joe grinned and dropped the topic. He went to her handbag and opened it.

"Hey . . ."

He stared at her and she melted. Completely. He took a fiver and a oncer.

"That's all I've got, Joe," she said softly.

"You'll get a share of what we get," he replied and put the cash in his pocket.

"A boy should pay for what I let you have," she complained without making the issue a crisis.

"I should charge you for what I let you have," Joe countered and raced his comb through his hair a second time . . .

CHAPTER EIGHT

ALF looked foolish when he entered Flo's flat. His eyes avoided a direct confrontation with Joe's and he stood in a servile position common to most privates being compelled to explain their failure to a stern, demanding general.

"No dice, Joe," Alf said. "The word is out - you're wanted!"

"Christ, I know that!" Joe exploded.

"Not just the fuzz . . ."

Joe tensed.

"McVey sent out orders . . ."

The memory of McVey's eyes peering at him as they made the escape came hurtling back. Joe wanted to vomit. McVey was a big man in the underworld. Bigger than a mere skinhead-cum-suedehead-cum-whatever he was now. A shiver slowly crawled down his spine and settled like an Arctic iceberg at his arse.

"Nobody wants to know, Joe!"

A prison cell, "Mad Monk" seated on a bunk cackling, with his crumpled face forming distortions against a window whose four iron bars made the sky seem as if it had been neatly partitioned, came shooting back into Joe's mind. It had been right after his second term of bird. He'd wished for a cell-mate around his own age. Instead he drew "Mad Monk" - all of fifty and as nutty as a fruitcake. But one thing he had learned from the old lag - the underworld did not end in the East End, nor in Acton, or Brighton. It reached up and down, across and beyond England's limits. It poked into Scotland, Wales, Ireland and France. It had connections and, for a price, a man could be found faster than Interpol could issue a wanted notice.

"What about you, Alf?" Joe asked.

"I dunno, Joe."

"And Stan?"

"He's chickened out!"

"Have you any connections for getting shooters?"

Alf paled. "God, no!"

"Flo?"

The girl sat down heavily and crossed her legs. She had lost all enthusiasm for Joe's grandiose scheme now. "Not me, Joe!"

"Does Wilson still own that club?" Joe asked Alf.

Alf nodded with alacrity. He hated Don Wilson as much as Joe.

Trying to visualise the club brought furrows to Joe's forehead. He had only visited the place twice and then to create havoc with Wilson's mob. There was, he remembered, a rear entrance along a corridor and the front door which looked like another of the old-fashioned houses in the street. No signs. No outward display of what went on behind the "private membership" entrance.

"Wilson keeps a collection of shooters upstairs, doesn't he?"

Alf laughed bitterly. "And all loaded too! He's a mean bastard!"

"So if we got in and got upstairs . . ."

Alf brightened up and, for the first time since coming into Flo's flat, met Joe's intense gaze. "Yeah! Yeah, Joe - what we need, eh?"

Speaking more to himself than his companions, Joe paced the cramped room and gave vent to his innermost desires. "If we had guns we could really clean up a fortune. Those dolly birds wouldn't say no to handin' over the loot. And if McVey wants a showdown he can have it - face to face! Christ, this is my big chance! I've got to get Wilson's shooters! Got to!!!"

Alf and Flo exchanged worries. The girl's body had grown taut, bowed ready to send a pleading arrow at Joe's head. It was very obvious she wanted nothing to do with guns or with violence outside her ken. Alf, too, expressed his disclination for warfare on this scale. Putting a boot in, bashing the occasional Paki or Shed fan was part of life. Not maiming somebody with a bullet.

"Are you with me?" Joe asked.

"I dunno, Joe . . ."

Flo laughed and raced hands down her thighs. "He's scared - like me, Joe. You're jumpin' the moon without a vaulting pole."

"You whore!" Joe spat. "Take her, Alf - she's randy as hell!" He strode across the room, hesitating with hand on door. "Fuck you both!" he yelled and slammed out.

*

Kenny Walker had followed trends all down the line. Very few girls had ever taken notice of him, no matter how much he spent on gear and after-shaves. He was skinny, small and had a wart on his nose which made most of his friends regard him as something just short of a freak.

He did not really belong to the East End. He had been born in

Ashford but his father had been booted off the farm for paying more attention to a bottle than pigs. Now, his father worked his arse off for a peanut concern whose gimmick was stuffing bags of supposedly top-quality nuts with second rate products from Israel.

Kenny had never been sure whether or not his Kentish background or his ugliness contributed more to his castigations. He was different. That everybody knew. He spoke with a distinguishable twang and thought like a farm-boy. No matter how he dressed, he was "that yokel" . . .

When Joe bumped into Kenny he felt an urge to belt the Kent youth. Then, as quickly as he had allowed the thought to enter his mind, he permitted another to invade his reason.

"Whatcher, mate . . ."

For all his faults, Kenny was not the slowest thinker in West Ham. "Joe Hawkins - you're wanted!"

"So what?"

"So nuthin', Joe - I mentioned it, that's all!"

"How's everything?"

"What do you want, Joe?"

It was Mutt and Jeff as Joe and little Kenny stood outside the television shop with its interference-blotched screens trying to entice a gullible public into buying.

"A few friends," Joe replied honestly, but deviously.

Kenny sighed and thrust his hands into his pockets. He felt the ten quid he had and promised himself that nobody - least of all Joe - was going to beg, borrow or steal his spending money.

Cars purchased on a hire-system blocked the High Street and a variety of drivers - some white, some coloured - fumed as the traffic lights continued to show red. People came and stayed as the local pubs got their usual crowds. Joe remembered the days when he could walk freely into those same pubs and was treated as a special character. He thought about Mary and how Billy had made it with her. How they'd all made it with her! Gang . . . bang! And bleedin' good, too!

"Want to make a lot of dough?" Joe asked, sounding like an actor in a BBC *Tough Guys* movie.

Kenny fondled his ten quid and wished it could multiply ten-fold. "Yes, Joe."

"Have you got a few blokes willin' to risk the nick for a bundle?"

Kenny was interested now. He knew several youths on the outskirts of East London acceptance. Blokes like Tom Randall and Billy Bird.

"I need a driver and two hard cases," Joe said.

Tom could drive like the bloody wind! Kenny thought.

"We'll be using shooters," Joe added.

Kenny trembled. He had always thought of himself as a dab fast-draw merchant. Westerns were his favourite films. He had even spent money on one of those Canadian made B.B. authentic sixgun models and gone down to the Old Kent Road where they made holsters to order. He figured he could twirl a Colt or draw a bead to beat the best in Britain - those jokers who frequently appeared on the telly as if they, and they alone, had the right to represent the country in an international challenge.

"Fab", Kenny chortled.

"What about the yobbos?"

Kenny frowned. He didn't like his friends being called common "yobbos".

"Sorry, Kenny ..." Joe laughed and draped an arm round the wart-nose kid's shoulder.

"That's alright, Joe - I'll get the *blokes*!" He made sure he emphasised "blokes".

"Meet you later at ..." Joe paused, trying to come up with one safe location.

"My place?" Kenny suggested.

"Great!"

Watching the small Kent youth hurry away, Joe thought - *What a bleedin' fool! He's so grateful for being accepted he doesn't know what time of night it is!*

He was whistling as he took a bus down to Aldgate and a pub where he wasn't known. A few beers, a couple of bangers and an hour listening to an old biddy chatting up an old soft bastard whose entire life revolved round beer and bed, and the idea he could still make it to Elysium fields if only his bedmate had his king-sized (hopeful thinking) urge. After that, he knew his lot wasn't so bloody bad!

He wasn't a regular and he got the boot at closing time. Some of the others dragged and he had the impression they could stay until their cash ran out. That was Aldgate, and Upton Park, and the Elephant, and most parts of the country unless the cops had been denied privileges.

The bus back to Plaistow had a majority of Paki cutters and tailors.

He fumed, wishing to hell he had his old mob along.

He reached Greengage and hopped off. The smell of Plaistow filled his nostrils and he was not aware that, subconsciously, he relegated it to an inferior position. All he realised was that this area had been home for too many years, that here were familiarities he could touch, sense, guess about. He lit a cigarette and blew a smoke-ring. *Shit on everybody living here*, he thought.

CHAPTER NINE

"THAT'S one," Joe said as he sat in the stolen car and watched the dolly carry her blue canvas bag across the street.

"Let's knock her off," Billy Bird said.

Joe twisted on his seat and glared at the over-anxious youth. "You stupid bastard - she's just the first! We've got to time them so we get the most at once!"

Billy shrugged and settled back against the Cortina's upholstery. At twenty one he was beyond reach of the do-gooder society's leniency. Beyond the screaming newspapers' cry for leniency. Beyond *all* leniency! A quick scan of his record would have convinced any magistrate or judge that he deserved a minimum of ten years bird. And Billy knew it!

But, he hoped - and not without reason - somebody would come to champion his "right" to go free and commit the same crime against humanity if only for a few column inches in the local, or national, press. That was the scene! The big giggle!

Tom Randall started the engine and released the handbrake. Signalling for a turn into traffic he inched the Cortina forward from the kerb.

"Where the hell are you going?" Joe asked.

Randall's head jerked once and the car smoothly slid between a lorry and a Bentley.

Joe whistled and relaxed. He had seen the copper bearing down on them at the last moment.

"If we're only marking down times we should do it on foot," Randall snarled. "I don't like to be caught with a stolen car under my arse."

Joe nodded agreement. It had been dangerously close to a *faux pas* parking on that bloody double-yellow line.

Billy started to make a two-finger gesture out the rear window at the copper who stood watching them depart. Joe's hand knife-edged across Billy's wrist. "Stupid bastard! What's the idea? Want us run-in before we make a hit?"

Billy's face showed his hatred for Joe's action. He, like the others, knew Joe's situation - that McVey had issued the word . . . *get Joe Hawkins!* It was not inconceivable that once they pulled off this job they would swipe Joe's share of the loot and make a bargain with McVey. Helping out a criminal of Charlie's standing could be more rewarding than simply settling for a few thousand. Once the fuzz caught up with him - as they would eventually for some job or another - prison could be a real home-from-home for a bloke who was known as Charlie McVey's pal.

Joe sat back and thought. Billy was worth keeping an eye on. He didn't trust the bastard nor did he believe for an instant that the youth could keep his bleedin' trap shut. But what the hell! He was already a wanted criminal and another mark against him wouldn't add too many months to his sentence. Not that he intended getting caught. He had plans. Big schemes brewing in his agile mind. The days of wine and cheese were ahead. What with Heath forcing an unwilling nation into the Common Market he could operate as easily in France as England. He enjoyed the prospect of lazing around in some Cote d'Azure hamlet with a stack of half-naked birds catering to his every sexual whim. Ambition burned strong in him. This hit would give him a start. The wherewithall so necessary to hire a gang and go for bigger and more profitable robberies.

The car entered a back street and came to a halt before a row of old houses now used as offices. He noted they were mostly real estate agents or removal firms. That fitted his mood - the desire to accumulate and become a man of property.

"Do we go back on foot?" Randall asked.

Joe considered the question. If that copper was still parading near the banks it was taking an awful chance. He grinned, letting a current thought bring him some slight amusement. "We stay - but Billy can go!"

Bird grunted, refusing to budge.

"I said you can go," Joe repeated.

"Shit on you, Joe Hawkins."

Joe's fist glanced off the other's cheek. The blow was not forceful,

230

nor was it intended to be more than a minor chastisement. "Go!" he spat.

Billy's eyes narrowed. "That's going to be repaid in spades!"

"When you feel you're man enough," Joe smiled.

As Billy walked away from the car, Randall shook his head with evident regret. "He can be a bad enemy, Joe."

"So can I . . ."

*

Martha McVey opened the parcel and felt a wave of nausea wash over her. Her hand trembled as she gingerly removed the shooter from its oil-skin wrapper. Trust Charlie to somehow manage to have his delivered by post.

"A little beaut!" Charlie said from behind her.

"God, you take awful chances."

He grinned and patted her bottom. "Make me a cuppa. Don't concern yourself with this." He lifted the revolver and hefted it expertly. The weight told him it was loaded without opening the chamber.

"Please, Charlie - he's not worth a life sentence."

"I'm not going to kill the bastard," he said with astonishment flooding his face. "You didn't actually believe I'd stoop to murder, did you?"

She let tears roll down her cheeks. "I hope not, dear!"

He placed the gun on the table and held her tight against his bear-like hardness. "Martha, don't . . . I can't stand to see you cry."

"Forget Joe Hawkins," she pleaded.

"I can't!" He tensed suddenly. "I can't, Martha."

She brushed her tears aside. "Any news of him?"

"He made it to the East End of London but he's gone again. There's a rumble he's planning a robbery in Gloucestershire but nothing definite yet."

"Couldn't you let the coppers deal with him?"

He sighed and sat heavily in a chair. "That's not our code, and you damned know it, too! We take care of our own. He's got to answer to us for Len. The fuzz can have him afterwards . . ."

Kenny Walker touched his wart and scowled. Trust Joe to relegate him to keeping their B&B joint inviolate. What did it matter if the bloody prying landlady did come into their rooms? She wouldn't find anything. They had nothing to hide - yet! Not until they got their hands on all that lovely money!

Christ, how he wished he'd been given a few more inches on his frame. He realised that his weakness came as a result of lack of height. Nobody ever paid any attention to a runt. And he was a bloody runt! All his efforts at keeping up with trends were to no avail when it boiled down to conquests over girls and being somebody in a mob. He was the complete nonentity. The has-been who never had-been.

He opened a magazine and stared at frontal nudity as if the hairs could come alive and tickle his nostrils as he got . . .

He slammed the mag down on a rickety table and heard legs groan. Two pounds a night for bed and breakfast and they had the fuckin' cheek to supply beat-up old furniture! Trust the landlords. Bloody profiteering bastards!

He wanted a woman. Any woman. A nice little fresh bit from a backwoods village. A fat old cow from some farm. A hairy-lipped bitch like their landlady. Anything. He had to have something soon. He was fit to blow his mind and all . . .

*

Lottie Newman came from the doctor's office, face pale. She couldn't believe the result of her test - positive! She knew that missing one day on the Pill could have disastrous results but it just wasn't possible that she had fallen for a bastard. And that's what it would be - a bastard! Belonging to a rapist!

Why the hell didn't I accept my fate and do as that Chink said: "Relax and enjoy it!" she thought.

If only she had been more inclined to let him have his fun and butter him she could have taken her Pill on time - not after she recovered from the shock of having it savagely forced into her.

A baby - who the blazes wanted a baby?

Certainly not her!

It would ruin her figure and spoil her chances of ever finding a monied man in Kidderminster willing to undertake the responsibility of fostering a bastard resulting from her ultimate shame.

She thought hard about her torment. Pregnancy resulted not from the man's ejaculation, but a mutually responsive female orgasm. Had she actually spasmed when he reached his climax? She didn't think so but . . .

If only I could even the odds, she thought. *I'd like to see him sentenced to life!*

CHAPTER TEN

CHELTENHAM on a Friday afternoon was a busy community. Housewives shopping for the week-end, traders busy re-stocking shelves. All the fun of the fair - and banks doing roaring business as shops sent their takings in for safekeeping.

Joe felt his shooter hard against his belly. Shoved into the waistband of his trousers, it gave him a security he had never before known. All his aggros and adventures pitted against other skinhead mobs or Hell's Angels had lacked this vital spark. Now, he was equipped to meet anybody on his terms - cordite-belching terms with death riding the explosive flame spitting from the end of a gun.

Billy Bird was down the street, loitering with intent. Kenny Walker peered into a Chelsea Girl shop for the fifth time - a poster showing nudity still the major attraction in a window display meant to appeal to girls, not blokes like a wart-nosed trendy. Randall sat behind the wheel of a Jaguar which he had nicked the previous evening in Oxford - far enough away to give them a fighting chance of its licence number not being fully circulated here yet.

They had timed it perfectly. Five girls were soon to converge on Lloyds and Barclays . . .

Five rake-offs worth . . . how much?

Joe tensed. The girl was about sixteen, wearing a mini and flaunting her tight little ass. She stood at the kerb, hand clutching the takings as she tried to decide if there was a space she could dart through.

The other girl dodged traffic and made it to the pavement within twenty yards of Lloyds.

A third girl sauntered in the crowd and swung her blue sack containing the day's takings. She had a coat which flopped around her ankles and a pair of hot-shorts under it which revealed long legs and lovely thighs.

The woman was not being open about her chore. She hugged the paper bag close to her monstrous tits and tried to look like a housewife as she went in a direct line for Barclays.

Number five sent Joe's temperature soaring. She wore a see-through blouse and her breasts were female perfection. Her shapely thighs stood out in the crowd as she strode along in hip-shaking glory with her mini-skirt almost matching the colour of her coppery hair.

Joe moved in and saw Billy and Kenny do the same.

He was outside Barclays when the woman approached. He grabbed and got his hands on the paper bag. She screamed, stumbling back into the throng. Joe jumped forward, bag held before him. The girl in the see-through blouse stood still, eyes daring him to molest her. Joe grinned, tore the sack from her hand and hissed, "Prick teaser!" before swinging away.

Billy had cornered the sixteen year old and the second one. He slashed at the sixteen year old's face with his shooter and grabbed her takings. Blood spurted freely as she slammed hard against the wall of the bank. In less than ten seconds, Billy had the second girl cowering and had her loot.

Kenny jumped at the maxi-coated girl, seized the money, shoved his hand into her coat and gave her a feel. Her hand automatically came round and caught him across the nose with an open slap. He dropped the money and grappled with her.

Joe was already within ten feet of the car, with Billy close on his heels. Randall's head stuck out of the driver's side-window. "Kenny . . . what about Kenny?"

Joe tumbled into the car. "Get going - quick!"

Billy tore at the rear door, found it sticking and shouted: "Open this fuckin' door!"

Kenny recovered, swooped and seized the money a second time. The girl lashed out, caught him in the rounded rear and yelled.

A familiar blue uniform forced through the startled shoppers and raced towards Kenny.

The car shot into the traffic, forcing a lorry to break hard. It slewed across the road, blocking pursuit. Tom Randall grinned and sent the car into a skid for the pavement and Kenny.

The copper was only inches away from Kenny now . . .

Joe leant from the car, his shooter level.

The explosion sent the women scattering. Blood spurted from the copper's back. Kenny paled, darted round the hands-out, staggering policeman and raced for the car.

Randall gunned the engine, waited just those few split-seconds for Kenny to fall into the car and then, rubber screaming as friction burned the tyres, he shot off . . .

*

Joe counted their loot. "Five thousand quid and some change," he announced triumphantly.

Kenny sat huddled in a chair, eyes closed, hands grasped tightly in his lap. He had the shakes.

Billy got to his feet and kicked at the bed. "You cunt!" he said tightly. "You stupid cunt!"

Joe smiled and fondled his shooter which lay on the table with the money.

"Let's have my share," Randall said and held his hand out. He alone seemed unaffected by the shooting.

Joe counted out five hundred pounds and shoved it across the table. "There . . ."

"I said share - not a fee," Randall told him.

"Five hundred is good pay for driving a car."

"Not for bloody murder it isn't," Randall proclaimed.

"I killed the pig - I take the lion's share," Joe announced.

"I don't want anything," Kenny muttered as his eyes popped open.

"Give yours to Tom then," Joe laughed.

Randall took two shares, then lit a smoke. "I'll wish you life if you ever get caught, Joe," he said quietly.

Ignoring the driver, Joe turned to Billy. "Any moans in advance?"

Billy shrugged, accepted his five hundred in silence and backed across the room.

"Leave your shooter, Billy," Joe told him.

The gun came out from a side-pocket and fell to the floor with a thud.

"If you're thinking of turning me in . . ."

"Not bloody likely," Billy replied. "I'm going to inform McVey . . ."

Joe went cold.

"That grabbed your balls, eh?"

Joe's gun came up, cocked.

"You wouldn't dare blow the hideout," Billy remarked and opened the door. In a second the door slammed behind him and the sound of running feet echoed through the room.

"Another hundred for transportation," Joe told Randall.

"Three hundred," the driver smiled.

"Okay!" It didn't matter how much he made a bargain for then, Joe thought. He had no intention of paying anyway.

"In advance," Tom said.

Joe counted out three hundred. He would take it back plus Randall's two shares once they got safely out of the Cotswolds. "Let's go - London . . ."

Kenny pretended not to hear. His mind was furiously working how to extricate him from this murder charge. If he could warn the rozzers that Joe Hawkins was heading into London it might just clear him of a major sentence.

Joe walked to the door after Randall. Kenny was the least of his worries. In fact Kenny was his ace in the hole. He trusted the wart-nosed rat to blabber. He prayed Kenny would try to save his hide.

*

Road blocks on every route into London accomplished nothing. Inspector Bishop spoke to four men.

"I believe Hawkins deliberately baited a trap for us! He knew Walker would contact the police so he took a different direction."

One of the men jabbed a finger at a large-scale map on a desk. "How about Birmingham, Inspector?"

Bishop shook his head. "Not very likely. Even a Hawkins would select somewhere less probable." The inspector bent over the map, traced a road and smiled suddenly. "That could be it . . . Devon or Cornwall. At this time of year where better to seek a tourist-filled haven?"

A second man grunted. "If he's down there, sir - it could be chasing our tails!"

"We have the Jag's number, remember?"

The men nodded silently. It made sense. All they wanted was the Jaguar turning up anywhere in the country. The number had been circulated - on a priority basis. That, and that alone, would pin-point

Hawkin's progress.

"We'll get full co-operation from the Devon and Cornwall lads," Bishop said. "Murder isn't their cup of tea either!"

The paper under the map gave a reason for their conference. Police Constable Norman Dawes had died in hospital as a result of a gunshot wound in the spine. A shot fired by Joe Hawkins, according to the State's witness, Kenny Walker!

*

Joe laughed as Tom Randall tried to bluff. The gun in Joe's hand made Randall's objections seem pathetically immature.

"You can't kill me," Randall said.

"I can, and will if you don't fork out the dough!"

"Look, Joe . . ."

The gun flicked and the sound of the hammer cocking filled the tranquil green with terror. Half-timbered houses slumbered into centuries' old accustomisation of violence. They had seen Roundheads and Cavaliers fighting it out on those self-same battlefields and none of the strife and mayhemious conduct had drastically changed their outlook. The green remained as a peaceful place for contemplation and cricket. The surrounding countryside stayed as it had for Doomsday recording. Only small holes in the ground and a few grave markers remained to testify to the struggles that had taken place within these precincts.

A Joe Hawkins or Tom Randall more or less would not shatter their facades . . .

"The money," Joe demanded.

Randall sighed. He was a fatalist by nature. He worked crime's fields like a farmer contending with wind and rain and bad crops. He handed over the money, conscious of the unwavering shooter pointed at his belly.

"I won't stay here, you know," Joe said.

"You'll try to make it into Wales," Randall remarked.

Joe shrugged. If that was his estimation - good luck to him.

"Do I get out now?"

"Damned right!" Joe motioned with his gun as Randall retreated to the door. Inch by reluctant inch. "You could have had the five hundred if you'd been content," Joe said as a parting shot.

"I'll have satisfaction," Randall smiled and closed the car door behind him. He stood on the green - a lonely figure lost in a country world that was not of his choosing.

Joe slipped behind the steering wheel. He was far from an expert driver. In fact, he had never held a licence. He knew just about enough to start the ignition, put the vehicle into first and steer it away.

When the car sounded like a wheezing old lady climbing Everest, he sought a new gear and rolled along with hands tight on the wheel, eyes glued to the white line separating him from oncoming traffic.

He had reached Kingswood when he decided that the effort of combatting the rush-hour was more than he dared attempt. He jerked up onto the pavement, left the Jag there and took off on foot. Public transport was much more reliable. Much safer.

CHAPTER ELEVEN

INSPECTOR Bishop had been relegated to an inferior position. The murder of Constable Dawes called for top-level consultation and the Chief Constable had requested the Yard to assume command of the enquiry. As a professional, Bishop knew the hazards of passing the buck. A County force could, within reason, keep the Yard out. But few ever did. When a criminal roamed the length and breadth of England somebody had to guarantee a certain co-operative spirit between the various police units involved in hunting down the wanted man.

Scotland Yard had the facilities, the know-how to track clues. To keep a watch on every sector of the nation. To block ports and airfields. To get nationwide coverage of all police forces in what he considered was a strictly local investigation. He knew, now, that the Jag had been traced to the Bristol area. Knew that his finger-jabbing route had not been a pipe-dream but a spark of originality and fact. Hawkins was heading for the West Country. For Devon. Or Cornwall. To mingle with the tourists and make himself an invisible target where the chances of picking him out from the merry-making crowd was next-door to impossible.

"Are you coming to bed or not?"

Bishop stirred and gazed at his pipe. The bowl was cold. The television screen was a hum, a blankness, a sign of immersion in thought - not visual fact.

Switching the TV off, Bishop lit a match and slowly got his pipe drawing again. He could hear water running into a bath. She had plans for him . . .

He stood in the doorway of their large bathroom and eyed her nudity speculatively. She had more fat round the middle than when he last performed this ritual.

"How about washing my back?"

He grinned and set his pipe on the toilet flush cover. In a minute he had divested himself of clothes and had her soaped flannel in his hand.

"Remember how you used to do this every second night?" she asked.

"I sure do!" He rubbed down her spine, around and over her shoulder blades. He went under her armpits and onto the mature mounds of her extraordinary breasts. The nipples shot into hardness after a few swipes across them.

"Want me to stand?" she asked.

He glanced down at himself and smiled. "I'm doing that," he confessed.

She looked, sighed and huddled back to the tub's curved end. "Jump in," she said.

Unashamed, he climbed in with her, his feet sliding along the porcelain bath to grasp her flanks in their grip. His desire probed above the soaped water like a clarion call to arms.

"Want me to wash you?" she asked.

"If that's the way you feel . . ." He had reservations on what had once been considered an exciting interlude. Being a policeman, and hearing what others thought of as perversity, had softened his approach to "normal" sex. Now, he saw everything in terms of crime, sadism, perverse love-making. This so-natural arousal had lost its flavour. Its special enjoyment.

Her hands moved under the water and grasped him. Her eyes pleaded. "What about me?"

He bent forward and cursed his profession. His finger touched her hairy haven and, suddenly, he was a man again. An ordinary man. Not a policeman.

She moaned and slumped back in the water. He didn't stop what he had started. He increased the pressure, the variations . . .

239

Joe climbed down the ladder and viewed the beach with a critical eye. He liked some of what was there, detested the fat old ladies with their poodles and ancient husbands and settled for a stroll along the reddish sands. The cliffs rising like impossible havens should the tide sweep in gave him the willies. They were temptresses decoying shipwrecked mariners into a trap.

Nobody seeking sanctuary could scale those Devon-red crumbling slopes!

He walked through water where small creatures scattered before his advance. He heard dogs bark and saw gulls lufting on a breeze. He paid little attention to the restless sea as it foamed and churled and crested into moderate breakers forward-marching into the land. He had the isolated rock at the next cove for his target and he kept walking . . . walking . . . walking.

The girl packed her beach-bag and dusted loose sand from her lovely limbs. She had enjoyed her plunge, the battle with an incoming tide. Now, she felt the moment had come to make the trek back to safety and her hotel.

After two weeks here she understood the local problems. Along the Esplanade there were no difficulties. The shingle's rattle soon gave warning of an encroaching sea. Not so where she was. It wasn't until the water reached danger level at this particular point that one was aware of the necessity for speed. For a dash to safety where the ladder came down to link with the concrete shelf and those council-built huts.

She started down the beach and saw the youth. He seemed oblivious of the danger.

"Go back," she called and continued walking.

Joe looked at her and the bikini she sported. He visualised what was so briefly hidden and enjoyed the mental strip.

"Tide's coming in . . ."

Joe hesitated, watching a wave roll further up the beach than its predecessor. She was right. The tide was coming in. He was caught between landfalls.

"Wait for me!"

The girl kept walking, but not so quickly now.

Joe grinned, concentrating on her figure. It was something worthwhile. All motion and promises. He particularly liked the way her arse shifted inside the bikini. The way she moved from the hips. The long thighs.

He ran across the sands.

"Thanks for the warning," he panted.

"I'd do that for a dog," she said off-hand.

"I've only been here a few days ..."

"There's a notice on the Esplanade telling about the tides," she snapped.

"I'm from London - we don't know how to read tables on tides!"

She laughed. Her pert breasts jiggled inside the bikini's scant halter. "You Londoners don't know much about anything, do you?"

Joe had a comeback, but let it slide. He wanted to ingratiate himself with this girl, and getting into a discussion on the pro's and con's of Londoners was not a way to make friends and influence a girl into his bed.

"Where are you from?" he asked.

"Warwickshire!"

He knew one town in that county. "Coventry?"

She smiled and he felt like tearing the bikini off. "Warwick, silly!"

"I'm terrible on geography," he admitted.

"So was I until I started to travel." She stepped on a pebble, yelped and hopped on one foot.

His hand touched her hip, strayed down and round and cupped her buttock as he pushed against her side. "Hurt?" he asked.

"I'm fine but isn't what you're doing being more than sympathetic?"

He squeezed a cheek and drifted his hand away as the palm slid back round the curvature of that so wonderful rump. "If it is so what? I like it!" There was a touch of the master-mistress in his tone.

"I'm not a bloody virgin but I do want respect," she snapped.

"And?" He asked the pertinent query with his eyes.

"That, too! Nothing queer, mind you."

"The normal way is fab!"

"If you're as good as the advance publicity I'm going to need encores," she quipped and leant against him.

"What's your job?" he asked suspiciously.

"I keep the accounts for a pop group." She laughed. "Pop goes some pretty teenager's knickers but never mine."

"Don't you let them know what you're after?"

"Hell, no! I'm paid to do a job - not strip every time some half-

241

witted guitar twanger comes out of an alcoholic or pot fog. Oh, they're not bad as groups go, I suppose . . ." She drifted into thoughtful silence.

Studying her, Joe couldn't understand what made girls built for screwing come to visit a town like this one. If it had been Brighton or Southend or Weston - yes. Not this. Not where the top speed was the pace of an invalid carriage or a doddering old retired Midland's industrialist with more spare cash than sense left.

"Where are you staying?" he asked.

The girl pointed lazily to a huge hotel rising from the front. A wave lapped across her feet, a dog barked and plunged into the sea after a stick.

"Expensive?"

"I get good money," she countered.

"Can I come up to your room?"

She hesitated then burst out laughing. "You've got a bloody nerve! No, you can't. I'll meet you tonight if you wish - for a few drinks."

Joe nodded. "And after that?"

"We'll see, friend. Don't push your luck."

*

From the outside the house looked dark and dismal. Inside, it was worse. The thatched roof came down too low and the small windows in each room were almost floor level. Even in brightest sunshine there was a gloom that could not be broken.

Seated on his creaking bed, Joe thrust the girl's picture from his mind. He had four hours before he would see her in the flesh. Between now and then he had this problem . . .

Every newspaper had carried the story. The copper was dead and the hunt covered every corner of the country. An identikit picture had been flashed on the telly but the worst was coming. He knew that from this morning's editions. They had a name to go with the artist's impression now. Soon, they'd start showing real pictures of him. Police photographs.

He felt no remorse for what he'd done. Only rage for Kenny Walker. The runt had brought this about. What a bleedin' fool he'd been letting the trendy bastard in on the robbery. Jeeze, how he wished that his old mob had stuck to him. They'd have pulled off the job easily - without needing shooters or getting a fuzz killed.

242

When he recalled some of the times they'd had, he wanted to lash out and damage furniture. Christ, he thought, what stupid idiots they'd all been! He blamed himself most for embracing a totally alien culture when he switched from skinhead to suedehead. He had played at being one. His frilly shirts, bowler, and umbrella, had all been trade marks manufactured by Terry types and necessary because he had a thing about making Mayfair his happy hunting ground.

His sojourn in prison had taught him how to look back and capitalise on previous mistakes. He was what he was and no amount of frills or environmental change could take away his East End-ness. Maybe he had lost some of his native patter, his "accent". That didn't give a damn. Inside where he lived he was Joe Hawkins, son of a docker, bigot de luxe. Aggro was his choice, his excitement. Putting the boot in on a bloody Paki or hippy or busting a Hell's Angel head stood for something terrific in his being. Being leader of a mob meant more than the loner he now was.

He counted his loot and felt the ecstasy of money flow in his veins. With this lot he could stay on the dodge and laugh at the rozzers when they were forced to admit defeat.

He didn't need a ouija board to tell him the next few days were of paramount importance. How he acted, how he stayed out of the spotlight could mean prison or freedom.

And that brought him back to the girl on the beach!

He wanted her - badly. He could taste her sweetness in his loins right then. But could he afford her? The luxury of getting her naked and thrashing under him was one he had to evaluate against years rotting away in some stinking prison.

This town was murder for the likes of him. It didn't click. It was staid and strictly for the old. He stood out like a sore thumb here. Add to this the way the local fuzz kept watching the front for deviants and he became a target for every do-gooding citizen.

Leaving his bag on the bed, he went out. There were garages and used car salesrooms nearby. All he wanted was a banger for a few hundred. Something legal to take him a hundred miles. After that, he'd flog it or steal a better model.

*

The man had an in-built slimness that manifested itself in a sneering smile and probing eyes. He bent over her like a father about to commit incest. His hand, when he asked in a silky voice what she wanted to drink, kept trying to touch her arm, her shoulder, her palm.

She waited as the man went to the bar and laughingly conversed with those residents he knew.

Damn that bloody bastard!

The image of her beach-walking "hero" turned sour. Who did he think he bloody was standing her up? She'd waited ten minutes - longer than she'd ever waited on another man. Then, she'd come into the bar and met the old geezer.

Christ, she yearned for a bit tonight - and not from her current boozing companion. He'd need splints to keep it erect! Her perfume annoyed her. What a waste of Arpège!

She fumed. She wouldn't forget that face - not in a million years! She'd remember him and if she could ever do him dirt, she would!

*

She closed the door and swore as she caught sight of her perspiration-filmed nudity in the wardrobe mirror. She flung herself on the rumpled bed and beat at the pillows with ineffectual fists.

Splints be damned! The old bastard had kept it good too bloody long. She hurt from his incessant demands. She had been pleasured alright - twice over the limit. And that made her furious.

She climbed off the bed, sniffed the aroma of sex and turned disgustedly to the television. At least that would still be working.

She was in time for the news round-up. She heard - through a self-recrimination fog - about the shooting of a policeman in Cheltenham. She saw, faintly, a picture flashed on the screen . . .

Then . . .

"That's him! That's the bloody bastard!"

She dashed to the telephone, all pain, all frustration ebbing like the sea from her heart. God, this was what she'd wanted . . .

CHAPTER TWELVE

CONSTABLE Derek Field had been a policeman since he left the army. Several times he had seriously considered quitting the force. Like when his teenage daughter had taken up with a yobbo and been involved in a brutal robbery. Not that the girl had known what was afoot. She had been a tool of a vicious thug and tricked into acting as a decoy. But the experience had shown Field how little his family saw of him and how he had fallen down on the job of fatherhood.

Another time he had tried to write his resignation had been when Marie - his wife - told him she was expecting again. At their age - then - an additional burden on his salary had seemed like the breaking straw.

But he had survived. And he was still a constable. A lonely symbol battling rising tides of vandalism and a youth revolution which decried any form of authority.

Since the beat constable had been replaced by Panda cars, Field had grown fat. And slow. Walking the streets of his small town day or night kept him fit. Seated in the heater-comfort of a Zodiac had let his natural inclination to put on weight gain an upper hand. Or belly roll!

Like every policeman in Britain, Field had seen Joe Hawkins picture. Scotland Yard had worked overtime to reproduce the mug shot and circulate it nationwide.

Armed with a list of stolen car numbers, Hawkins' picture and a description of a would-be rapist whose only claim to fame so far was three attempted "interludes" with desirable women and a warning to keep the cemetery under observation, Field drove along the road safe in the knowledge that his shift would terminate in two hours. His thoughts, even as he saw the car shoot out from a side turning without regard for on-coming traffic, were on Marie and the kids.

Tomorrow was Marie's birthday. The kids had - surprisingly - bought her a beautiful gift. His own present lay in the glove compartment - an expensive ring and matching earrings.

He goaded the Zodiac to top speed and set his lights working. He cut across the other car's bonnet and forced it into the side. He got from the Panda car and walked slowly towards the motorist. All the had in mind was a warning. A legal chastisement. He seldom, if ever, believed in booking a motorist at first sight. He thought that a police lecture gained more friends for the police and curbed more reckless driving habits than any appearance in magistrate's court.

*

Joe watched the fuzz approach. It wasn't a matter of being hauled in on a driving offence now. It was life or death. He got his shooter out and held it down by the door. He rolled the window down six inches - enough for whatever the gods demanded from this confrontation.

For a moment, Joe had the man in his sights - smack in front of the car. He held back. No driver could get a car into gear, roll forward and be sure of smashing an enemy before the target jumped safely to one side.

He waited . . .

"That was a bad mistake, sir," the policeman said.

Joe grinned. Maybe this yokel wouldn't do more than talk. He rolled the window down to its limit.

"Can I see your driving licence?"

Joe tensed. He had none. He had taken lessons in the coal lorry but had never held a valid licence in his life.

"Your licence sir!"

The fuzz peered into the car now, straining to see Joe's features in the murky disguising dark.

"I've left it at home," Joe said.

"Ahhh . . ." The policeman sounded different somehow.

"What did I do wrong?"

The policeman took a notebook from his tunic and flipped it open. A picture partially escaped and he pushed it back inside the paper. And stopped. And drew the picture out again.

Joe tensed.

"Would you step out of the car, sir?"

Joe brought his shooter up and pointed it at the fuzz.

"Joe Hawkins!" It was statement, not question.

Joe fired. He felt the gun buck in his hand, the explosion almost deafening him in the enclosed space of the car.

The policeman staggered back, hands now on his face, notebook dropping into the dirt.

Joe placed the shooter on the seat, calmly geared the car into motion and swung to avoid the Panda car angled across his lane.

The doctor shook his head in regret. Marie Field covered her face with splayed hands as tears rolled freely and sobs made her body heave.

"He's alive," the doctor said softly, seating himself on the couch beside the distraught woman. "Maybe, in time, he'll be able to see again . . ."

Marie cried. The small package containing Derek's present to her lay on the couch un-opened. Across the sterile hospital waiting room her children listened to a sergeant explaining the seriousness of Derek's injuries.

Placing a hand on the woman's shoulder, the doctor felt impotent. All the advances of this modern age had not been able to cure this woman's husband. The flash and the bullet which had glanced off his temple had done their deadly work. Constable Derek Field was blind. And probably would be until he died.

"Why, doctor? Why?" Marie asked.

The doctor couldn't tell her. That was for the criminal who had done this dastardly deed . . .

*

The lights of Andover burned off to one-side of the by-pass. London wasn't far away now. Basingstoke and then, *home!*

London was a trap. A gigantic underworld-infested trap. He would have to be more careful here than elsewhere in the country. But it would be worthwhile. At least he would not be an Alice lost in some lousy Wonderland full of mad hatters and crazy rabbits. He knew this warren. Knew it inside out.

His mind worked at top speed. Native cunning, the intelligensia called it. Strictly speaking, they would anticipate him getting back to London along the M3. He detoured - across Hampshire and Surrey. Through Aldershot, Farnham, Goldalming, Guildford. He came up from the South. At Godstone, he swung into the Croydon road and dumped the car near Whyteleafe.

The sight of the gasometers gave him a wild idea which he put down quickly. It had been a lovely thought, if crazy. What a bonfire it would have made - the car covered with flames shooting upwards from those bloody tanks!

He took a bus and tried to look like an IRA man bringing a bag of bombs into London. It seemed that nobody paid those murderous bastards much heed. Christ, if only they'd turn a few thousand skinheads loose on the uppety sods the troubles would be over in a week.

The East End was out! So was Soho and central London. He took another bus and got off in Hounslow. The sound of jets roaring overhead was a comfort. He studied a few boards and settled for one ad - SINGLE ROOM TO RENT. BREAKFAST INCLUDED. There was a 'phone number but no address. He found a telephone kiosk and dialled the number . . .

*

Nancy worked every day from nine till six. Inside two minutes, Joe knew she was available. Her references to morality and the permissive society and the number of Saints scattered throughout the house belied her house-coated readiness. Her eyes, too, spoke volumes.

"I'm sorry to get you out of bed at this hour," Joe said.

"Don't worry," Nancy replied and squeezed his hand. "*We* understand!"

I've got it made, Joe thought. Bed and breakfast and left-overs when the old man goes to work.

"You're not Irish," Nancy complained.

You are, bitch! Joe told himself. Her brogue could cut bacon, never mind butter.

"Isn't it awful what those Ulstermen are doing to the Catholics?"

It was an effort for Joe to control himself.

Nancy went first upstairs. She was small, dark and light on her feet. She bounced, a bundle of vivacity. "Father O'Neill says we should pray for them - and I do. Every night!" She opened a door and showed him into a sterile room with bed, dresser and a pathetically small wardrobe. "It's nice and clean," she chortled.

Joe looked at the bed. A single. He'd have a bloody job getting her worked up in such a confined space!

She closed the door. "Seven-fifty a week," she said and plucked at her housecoat so that it fell open to reveal her transparent nightdress and a cluster of hair that beckoned him like a call to arms.

He paid three weeks in advance and deliberately stared between her

248

legs. "That should get me extra service," he said.

She was breathing hard, fast. "Mike goes to work at six every morning," she mentioned.

"I like it at night," Joe said.

She closed her eyes and swayed dramatically.

He shoved her hand between her thighs and felt her up.

"Don't be naughty," she said.

"I'm bloody randy," he told her, leaning against her.

She reached down and touched him.

"How about it?" he asked.

She groaned and pulled away. "It's a sin! It's not good for your health! In the morning - okay?"

Joe grinned. He could wait a few hours. If she couldn't relieve him then no woman could!

"Mike would kill me . . ."

"Does he sleep sound?"

She touched him again and sighed. "I can't let you . . . not the *right* way!" She squeezed him, hard. "It wouldn't waken him if I did it like this . . ."

Joe stood still as she opened his zip and started helping him attain a partial relief. Nancy had it down to pat, and upright. She knew exactly how to control his climax with her self-indulgent delight. She kept kissing his ear, moaning and moving as she handed him a pleasant interlude. Then, when it was over, she lay against him and whispered: "I'll bring you tea just after six-fifteen . . ."

"Forget the tea," Joe snapped. "Bring me this . . ." He dipped into her thighs and gave it an impromptu feel.

"Oh, God!" she moaned and tore away from him. He saw the thatch and was reminded of the place he stayed at in Devon. *Nothing gloomy about this one, though*, he thought!

Nancy backed to the door, consciously leaving her housecoat gaping, her nightdress moistly clinging to her abdomen. "Afterwards," she said with more than a little emphasis, "I'll cook a good breakfast for you!"

"Have a fast wash," Joe advised with a grin. "I don't want whatshisname getting nasty on my first night here!"

She glanced down at her hand, at her nightdress and blushed. "Oh Mary - Mother of God!" she hurled and fled.

The sexy cow! Joe thought.

He opened his bag and placed the money under his mattress.

Nancy, he felt, was a curious sort. The type of landlady who would willingly clean a bloke's room just to nose into his clothes and personal papers. She was also the right type for him at present. A stupid self-indulgent Irish bitch with a mind full of priests and Holy Water and getting what she couldn't have from her husband.

He let his mind form a picture of Mike - a big, burly construction worker or street cleaner. The type to crush a man's hand in a handshake that meant less than a trial of strength. Joe knew the Irish - knew that a firm grip in that Ould Sod meant precisely nothing. They were all a nation of heavywight boxers a flyweight could knock over with one punch. All mouth and blarney and not much between the ears. All hatred and violence and mouth. Not a particle of generosity of feeling or sympathy for those recovering from incomprehensible terrorist tactics.

A people torn apart by religious fanaticism and a belief that the Pope would bless them regardless of what atrocity they committed. After all - Ireland was - or so the pundits claimed - the brightest jewel in the Pope's crown!

Joe undressed feeling satisfied with his introduction to Nancy and an Irish household. He had a bigger glow thinking about the morrow - and how an English "bastard" was going to contribute to the ruination of a "pure" Irish Catholic woman . . .

*

Nancy left the cuppa on a table and sat on Joe's bed. "Mister Royce . . ." That was the name Joe had given on the spur of the moment. "Mister Royce . . ." Nancy shook him a third time and heard him grunt.

She loved the shape of him outlined against the few blankets she provided. She shook him again, and saw his eyes open slowly.

"Your tea . . ."

Joe turned and lifted an arm from under the bedclothes. The hand fell across her lap.

"Wait until he leaves," Nancy whispered urgently.

Joe was fully awake now. He had been dreaming - seeing a huge Irishman tearing him apart, limb from limb, as Nancy stood by laughing and begging for more blood to splatter her carpet.

"He's in the house?" Joe asked.

"He wants to talk to you," Nancy said.

Joe accepted the tea sitting up. He wore his Chinese pyjamas he had bought from the proceeds of the robbery. The ones he liked to believe set him apart from the common herd.

"Shit!" Joe said.

"Please . . ." She didn't object to his language.

"Christ . . ."

"Don't take the Lord's name in vain," she said, conscious of her church up-bringing.

"Where is he?" Joe asked.

"*Mike!*" she yelled, almost deafening him.

A kindly face poked round the door within seconds and Joe was thankful he had not insisted on having a pre-tea grope.

Mike was the complete opposite of any Irishman Joe had ever seen. He stood less than five feet, looked happy and yet, if the chips were down, tough enough to take care of a man three times his size and weight.

"This is Joe Royce," Nancy said, carefully adjusting her clothing so that the parish priest himself would have difficulty proclaiming her a trollop.

"Hello, Joe. Glad you decided to take the room," Mike said and stepped inside.

Joe grinned and fell into Nancy's pattern - he pulled his bedclothes up over his Chinese pyjamas as if modesty was his forte.

"I've got to go now," Mike said and stuck out his hand. "If you like a drink there's a pub down the street which isn't bad!"

"Tonight," Joe promised.

Mike grinned and kissed Nancy on the cheek. He barely made it. She was four inches taller than him. She smiled, followed him from the room, and, as the door was left open, her voice carried back to Joe . . . "Tell Sean we'll be at the club tomorrow. I've got a present for his sister's birthday . . ."

Joe tasted the tea. It was strong, not much sugar. He jumped out of bed, opened the window and poured it out. He was back inside the sheets when Nancy returned.

"Do you want breakfast now . . . or later?" she asked.

Joe got the message and whipped the sheets back again. "Much later," he told her.

She removed her housecoat with a sly smile. "I can't be late!"

"That depends, doesn't it?"

She pulled her nightdress over her head - a different one from last

251

night. Nude, she looked exactly what she was - a married woman with a hard body and small tits. Older than Joe wanted his women but experienced enough to give him the best possible relaxation.

"Take your P.J.s off," she said.

He shrugged out of the Chinese creations and lay naked.

"Mary, Mother of God . . ." she whispered and flung herself at him.

*

Joe reclined on the bed as Nancy used an old hanky to wipe herself. She was glistening with perspiration. And no wonder. She had given him a ride he would remember to the grave. There hadn't been anything she refused to do - and if she confessed to this lot her priest would have to devise more than Hail Marys to satisfy her continued standing in the Church community.

"Do you have any beer in the house?" Joe asked.

"Lord, no! That stuff is bad for your health," she replied quickly.

"It's bloody good for my condition," he laughed and grabbed her head, forcing her to kiss his moist stomach. She moaned and tried to twist around but he thrust her away and climbed off the bed.

"Don't you want . . ."

He stared at her unashamed nakedness. "Not again." Enough was enough. The smell of sex and perspiration in the window-closed room was beginning to make him ill. Anyway, there wasn't anything he hadn't done to her, and the novelty had worn off with that last bang. She was just an older woman, a wrinkled-faced working bitch. *God yes, she is wrinkled*, he thought and hurriedly grabbed his clothes.

CHAPTER THIRTEEN

ACCORDING to the *Mirror* - Joe Hawkins was in hiding in Norfolk. The *Express* believed - Joe Hawkins has been seen in Southampton. The *Sun* came nearest - a bus conductor swore he had carried Joe Hawkins on his bus in the Hounslow area.

All the 'papers kept the story on their front pages. Some continued to exploit the national condemnation with editorials spotlighting youths' rebellion and this "horrible attachment to violence".

Joe read the 'papers eagerly. He had not dared watch television with Nancy and Mike. They didn't concentrate much on what the box showed and he had no intention of being in the same room with them when his picture flashed on the screen. Nancy had a habit of catching snatches of conversation or scenes and referring to people she had once known as "speaking like that" or "looking like that". The last thing Joe wanted was Nancy getting suspicious.

He had been living with Nancy and Mike for a week now. Every morning, except Sunday, Nancy had come begging for her daily ration. Twice, at night, he heard Mike banging her, too. For a keep-fit addict she certainly liked her physical jerks.

I'm bleedin' fed up with this, Joe thought as he sat on his bed and carefully folded the papers to inside pages. *I've got to get out of here!*

A train rattled past, a plane swooped low for its Heathrow landing and the entire house vibrated. Although the district was leagues above Plaistow he still hated the noise factor that threatened his sanity at times. It was like living perched on top of a volcano that growled and spat and shook so bad that every day was a suspense, a wondering when the lid would blow off.

Christ! He got to his feet and paced back and forth. The money under the mattress assumed galactic importance. What was the sense of knocking off a fuzz if he was doomed to spend his time shut up in a pathetically small room! He wanted to buy gear, to live high, to arrange another robbery with some dependable blokes for his mates.

Nancy was just another bug in his bed. Her passion for sex was driving him crazy. He had always been virile, always willing to sample illicit flesh. But this was ridiculous. The bitch could certainly shake it and move it and bring him shooting to fantastic heights. But did he want to be in the saddle with something her age? Frankly, he wanted 'em young and full of the juices of spring.

He had a map now and he spread it on the bed. Slowly, tracing roads with a ball-point pen, he considered every inch of the paper. Manchester! Now that appealed!

He took seven hundred quid and stuffed it into his hip pocket. He packed his bag and left a fiver for Nancy. The last thing he wanted was her getting annoyed at being cheated out of rent.

At seven-thirty the front door closed and he moved downstairs with his bag. They always went to the club on this night. So Nancy had said. She didn't enjoy the drinking and stuck to orange juice but she loved the group with their noise blaring through amplifiers. Mike just went for the beer apparently - and Joe fleetingly sympathised with him!

The house was empty. He dialled a number, but got no reply. It had been an impulse and he sweated blood in thanks that nobody had been at the taxi rank. God, cab drivers were the worst menace. They always remembered wanted men!

There was a used car lot not far distant. He walked and tried to console himself with visions of Manchester. He had heard it swung. And that the underworld there was just as important as London's. Anyway, it was Merseyside loosely. And didn't the United fans support skinheadism?

A long haired youth with leather trousers and a Brando-type shirt open to his hairy navel stood on the lot. Grease covered him and his fingernails were longer - and blacker - than those old films about Fu Manchu.

Joe ignored him, picking a car strictly on price. He liked the Sovereign but they wanted too much. He almost went overboard for a sporty, low model but, again, its price soared. He settled for UVX - he nicknamed it "Uffix" for some quirky reason. It was old, a few ironed-out dents on the wings, but, generally, not in bad nick.

Grease-ball hung back as a natty dresser came up. Joe argued with him, got the car started and tried to pretend he knew a lot about engines as he feigned an ear for its running sound. The natty gent got the car out and suggested Joe take it round the block. Throwing his bag into the back, Joe hauled out his cash.

Something about the natty dresser's attitude bothered Joe. He examined the tax disc. It still had a month to run. He listened to the engine again. It did not excite him but neither did it give cause for alarm. He looked at the tyres - all with tread. Then what?

The grease-ball had vanished from the lot and Joe spotted him in the office, speaking on a telephone.

That was it!

Joe tore the sticker from the windscreen, counted out the exact money and held it out.

"I'll have to make out a receipt," the natty dresser said.

Joe held back an urge to say "forget it" and nodded. As the man hurried across the lot, Joe jumped into the car and placed his foot on the pedal. Then, he froze. If he had no receipt the bastard could call the fuzz and accuse him of stealing the car. He slammed out of the car and followed the man into the office in time to hear . . .

"Sure we're sure its him! I tell you . . . er, yes - that's right, we buy cars, sir!"

Joe grinned. "Make it snappy, please - I've got to get to Southampton to meet a friend coming off the boats!"

Thank God for the *Express*, he thought. Grease-ball seemed confused as his party squawked into the telephone. Natty dresser looked like he wanted to put an arm-lock on Joe but, instead, scribbled an official receipt. Joe seized it.

"How do I get to Southampton from here?"

Natty dresser sent a silent message to grease-ball and took Joe's arm. steering him to the door. It was all so patently obvious Joe began to wonder if the world at large had formed the opinion he was a total wash-off, a nincompoop.

"Straight through Hounslow, lad," natty dresser said. "Follow the signs for Staines and the A30. You'll pick up Southampton markers."

Joe grinned. "Thanks. Hope the car makes it there and back."

He drove away, carefully following natty dressers instructions. For two miles. Then, with rubber burning, he took a series of back routes and finally reached Ealing. He wanted the M1 . . .

*

Charlie McVey raged. His wife stood naked at the sink and washed her hair, listening to his tirade with a patience she had matured over years spent hearing grandiose schemes for their future happiness and assorted plans for what Charlie was going to do to Joe Hawkins once his boys caught up with him.

"Those stupid bastards," Charlie said for the tenth time. "They let the little bleeder slip through their fingers. Why the hell couldn't they hold him? Why?"

Rinsing shampoo from her hair, the woman crossed the room and rubbed furiously with a towel for a few minutes then wrapped the damp material round her head in a turban. "Maybe they were afraid of his gun," she suggested.

Charlie nodded. "I've thought of that but bloody Ron was a paratrooper. He knows how to disarm a geezer like Hawkins!"

"He hasn't been in the army for years, Charlie!"

McVey grinned and slapped her bare bottom. "You'll get a soldier's farewell if you don't put something on."

255

"Chance would be fine," she quipped and flaunted her sex. Unlike most criminals, Charlie stuck to his wife. He believed in singularity in marriage. If he was desperate he gladly suffered until his arms wrapped round this one woman. He had not yet reached the stage of considering her plump, or aged. She was his missus, his choice. And when she offered he had to accept.

"You've asked for it," he laughed.

"And I hope I'm going to get it, too," she said and walked to the bedroom door . . .

CHAPTER FOURTEEN

GETTING close to Manchester, Joe began to realise that one of his prison mates had been right when he said that every county and every region of England had its own particular character and flavour. On the journey, Joe had noticed how the scenery changed, how subtle differences altered the passing villages. Now, he was very aware of the greyness, an encroaching sensation of being hemmed-in and an overall sootiness. It was as if some vital spark had been extinguished.

"Bleedin' Plaistow is bad enough," he told the fresh air blasting in from his open side-window.

He had left the motorway near Newcastle-under-Lyme. The chances of either McVey or the fuzz being able to trace his car were slim but he was determined to cut risks to an absolute minimum. He saw a new signpost: Gatley - Manchester one way, Warrington - Liverpool the other. Almost involuntarily he swung the car and headed for Warrington - Liverpool. Much as he loathed United supporters he had dreamed of being in the Kop and kicking the balls off some Scouse git. Maybe . . .

Uffix wasn't so bad. In fact, the car ran fairly well. If he worked out a deal to his advantage he could come out with fifty quid extra. That was the bleedin' trouble with being on the run. Every form of transport had to be sacrificed within set time limits. Go from point A to point B and ditch the banger! The law of the escaped. Every change of car, every new address meant an added percentage in favour of the escapee.

The shooter on the seat beside him - under a quilted jacket he had purchased for a mere three nicker - was his guarantee of reaching the next destination. Come McVey or fuzz he intended to keep rolling along!

Built-up areas filtered past his windows without reaching him emotionally. He caught sight of a poster outside a run-down newsagent's and, for the first time, began to know the meaning of fear. It said: DEMAND FOR HANGING GROWS.

Wouldn't it be just his luck if the deaths of two bleedin' coppers brought back the rope!

And he was the first to swing in ages?

The full impact of what he had done suddenly hit home! The word "murderer" seared his brain. Until that moment he had been play-acting, carrying out a role destined for him even before his old man and old woman got around to tearing off a piece in a drunken stupor. Now, the value of "free choice" hit him smack in the kisser! He had not been condemned by any given rule book. All that had been part of Joe Hawkins' make-up was strictly how Joe Hawkins had wanted it. He had enveloped the skinhead cult. He had taken it upon himself to rise above his station in life and gone queer-suedehead. He alone had taken the decision to use a shooter and kill fuzz.

If only McVey wasn't against him!

*

He found a sleazy hotel near Lime Street station. His first view of Liverpool had been one of contradiction. Slums coming into the city, magnificent buildings covered in grime clinging to some century-old glory that no longer existed huddled in the partially-reconstructed centre.

Uffix was safe - temporarily. In a huge multi-story parking complex. Lost in a dark corner with two huge concrete pillars blocking snooping fuzz eyes.

For a week now he had not shaved and his beard was beginning to show signs of prospering. His upper-lip had a definite smear. Nancy had bitterly complained about these. She had objected - but only in token - when he rubbed her thighs raw with his stubble. Not that he gave a damn about the Irish bitch now. She had fulfilled her purpose. She was past tense - kaput!

Some of the dolly birds walking around Liverpool had excited him. Would they, too, complain when he got down to the essentials?

He had bought a small metal box on the journey. From a junk shop, no less. It had a key and he deposited the money in this, placed it at the bottom of his bag and layered dirty underwear across it. Next he put the bag in a wardrobe, locked this and kept the key in his pocket.

Looking from his window into a backyard filled with empty cement bags, trestles and planks, he saw Plaistow-type delapidation all round. What looked half-way decent from the street was rotten to the brick-core out back. Supports held walls from caving in, patchwork repairs covered areas where damp and hurriedly-installed pipes had demanded urgent attention.

No wonder they're building bleedin' flats, he thought.

With thirty quid in his kick, he left the hotel, pausing in the entrance hall to glance at the telly. One of those all-knowing, all-wise bastards was holding forth about social problems and stealing a panel of experts' thunder before they could get a word in. He heard the mention of murder, policemen needing protection and the mobility of today's criminals. He smiled and stalked out of the hotel. Nothing that bleedin' idiot or his panel said would catch Joe Hawkins. Nothing they said would change circumstances. Not even public opinion . . .

*

As he came from The Wildcat Cavern with its discordant sounds shrieking at the gathering night, Walter Blair gulped air into his lungs and tried to delay his need to vomit. He felt the booze and Chinese grub swelling up into his gullet and hurried down the street to a vacant lot. He bent over a railing and spewed until he wanted to yell. The agony in his middle was something awful.

Wiping his face, Walter swung unsteadily from the railing and faced a shattering thought - he couldn't drink the way he boasted!

Admittedly, he had taken on a skinful - all day long he had been guzzling beer and shorts. The meal had been a concession to his mates. Now, he wished to blazes he had told them to get stuffed. What he blamed most, though, was that bloody place with its airlessness and the smell of pot heavy on cigarette fumes.

He hung to the railing until his eyes managed to focus. It was some change to see things as normal and not double-imaged.

"Jeeze, I feel terrible!" he said aloud.

258

"You look worse," a voice answered.

Walter turned slowly, hand on the railing in case he got the staggers again.

"Want a beer?" the voice asked.

Walter belched. "Christ - no!"

"Up the 'pool . . ."

Walter swore. "Everton, mate."

Everton? Joe stared at the swaying youth and wanted to laugh. Everton! Christ, they didn't even come into his reckoning. Maybe up here, in Scouseland, the rivalry between Liverpool and Everton was legendary but not in West Ham's fandom. Hell, hadn't Everton sold Ball to Arsenal?

"I'm for West Ham," Joe said.

"Fuckin' Hammers! Shit on them!"

Joe formed fists with his hands.

Walter belched again, swung fast and was sick for the second time. When he eventually turned he was beyond being arrogant. "Me mates made me eat Chink nosh," he said lamely.

Joe studied the other. He was lean and tallish although a few inches shorter than himself. He wore a coat with a long pointed collar, cardigan and mohair trousers with Squires. His hair was between suedehead and long and he looked like he could handle himself when sober. Or reasonably so.

"These mates of yours - are they in the market for bread?"

Walter smiled round his pallor. "You betcha."

"I've got a shooter. I'm on the run. I want a gang."

Walter felt worse. He recognised the partially-disguised features now. They'd been discussing this bastard only the other evening.

"Joe Hawkins . . ."

Walter nodded. "Yeah, mate - I know!"

"How about it?"

Walter shook his head and it hammered. "No, thanks!"

"Why not?"

"Man, who wants to get ten years?"

Joe smiled and stuck his hands in his pockets. "They've got to catch us first!"

"Like they won't?" Walter let go the railing and did a pirhouette before grabbing hold again. "Jeeze, I'm pissed still!" he complained.

"What's your name?" Joe asked.

"Walter. Walter Blair."

"Okay, Walter - get your mates. Let's leave the decision to them, eh?"

Walter shook his head and it hammered anew. He would have to watch that movement. It wasn't worth the anguish. "You're crazy, you know," he murmured. "Tellin' me could land you in clink."

"I'm fed up being on the run," Joe allowed. "I want mates. Guys who'll follow me. I've got plans."

"'pool fuzz is bad," the other complained.

"We can branch out. I've got a banger . . ."

Walter felt a trifle more sober now that his gut had been cleansed. "One of 'em could grass," he warned.

"I'll take the chance," Joe said.

"It's your life . . ."

*

Walter ventured into the club and came out with five dock-type individuals. All had that "beware I'm tough" swagger and all wore uniform - the new-look skinhead image. Their sheepskins were strictly mail order as befitted Everton fans but the rest of their gear cost plenty.

"Me mates," Walter said without enthusiasm. He still felt put on by their antics.

Joe watched them form a solid line across the pavement. He was glad he still had his shooter inside his waistband.

"Frank MacGee, Tom Carter, Doug Haskett, John Riodan and Colin Kelly," Walter said.

Bloody Irish Micks! Joe thought. *Trust me! IRA men and he was worried about them grassing! Like shit they would!*

I've told them," Walter informed him. "I agree - we want bread, man . . ."

CHAPTER FIFTEEN

ALBERT Duckham had a thing about spending half of every day at the bottom of his garden pottering around with his tomato plants and those other hard-to-cultivate items. He firmly believed that plants got to know those who tended them and could be trained to respond to loving kindness. For several years now, he had come first in the various local competitions held by the many societies catering for gardeners and allotment-holders. His marrows were, without question, the best in Lancashire. The County show had been the proof of this.

As a pensioner, Albert had no demands against his time. A day meant no more than sunshine or rain and the difference between digging and nursing and watching racing on telly. Always providing the weather was kind to him, Albert spent the day hours working diligently on his beds and peering through his trimmed edge to see how the filling station was coping with the switched-over traffic which now thundered past their village on the newly-opened stretch of motorway. It had been a surprise to find that business for the A6 had hardly dropped off.

Forking manure into a bed, Albert smiled to himself. What a stupid name for a garage! "A6"... Now, if Brian Jones had called his station the "A6 Hopley" that would have meant something sensible.

His back ached and he placed the fork against his old lean-to with its corrugated sides. He stood erect and wheezed. His chestiness was worse today than usual. He would have to visit Dr. Knight again for more tonic.

The car entering the service area looked ordinary enough. Albert watched as young Stan Barr left his kiosk and went to the pumps. Regardless of what he personally thought about Stan's long hair, he had to admit the youngster was an excellent attendant. Nobody could ever complain about service when Stan was on duty.

As Stan inserted the nozzle into the filler, two men climbed from the car. Albert froze. He was an avid watcher of every newscast. He was also an ex-policeman. Trained for observation.

"Oh, God - no!" he moaned and rushed as fast as his creaking legs could carry him into the bungalow.

Peggy, his wife, looked up from her knitting and frowned. She didn't like to see her Albert hurry. The doctor had warned them both - "Do anything you like but do it quietly".

"Blasted telephones," Albert growled as he jiggled the hooks.

"What's wrong?" Peggy called anxiously.

"That scamp Joe Hawkins just drove into Brian Jones's garage!"

Peggy stiffened. Something nagged at her - a dream, a premonition from the past when Albert had been walking a beat night after night.

"Hell!" Albert threw the 'phone at its mount and started to hurry towards the back door.

"Albert . . ."

The man hesitated.

"Please, dear - don't!"

The man shuffled self-consciously.

"Try the 'phone again!"

He swore, charging to the telephone. His nature demanded action yet - hell, he had promised! "Once I retire I'll never again mix in police affairs, Peggy," he had sworn.

"I'm sure Sally will answer soon . . ." his wife said, hopefully.

Albert rattled the hooks. His temper was gaining an upper hand. If only the blasted Post Office could see fit to make them automatic! They charged enough for services never given!

*

Joe smiled at Frank. John moved from the car now, too. Not another car in sight. Only this long-haired youth and a few more quid in the kitty!

Stan didn't count the crawling sensations up his spine. At first, when he accepted responsibility for evening and night shifts he had been overwhelmed by the feeling that every customer was a potential stick-up artist. He had got over this. In daylight, he was less susceptible to those old worries. Nobody would rob a service station in daylight! Nobody!

Removing the nozzle and replacing the filler cap, Stan set the pipeline back into the pump and wiped his hand on a cloth. "That'll be one-seventy-two, sir," he said.

Joe brushed his jacket aside and let Stan see the butt of his shooter. "Forget the price - let's have what's in the till."

Stan wanted to yell for help, and couldn't. It was actually happening! What he'd dreaded ever since taking the job . . .

"Move - or else!"

Stan hurried across the forecourt and into his kiosk. He placed his key in the cash register and turned it. The drawer sprang out.

"How much?" Frank asked.

Joe grinned. "Sixtynine quid and change."

John waited until Joe moved aside and slammed Stan over the head with a tyre-iron. The long-haired youth slumped into a corner of the kiosk.

"That'll keep him quiet," John remarked icily.

Joe held the money and raced to the car. Doug was driving.

"How much?" Walter asked as Joe climbed in.

"Sixtynine plus."

"Not bad, not good. Let's get to the next one."

Frank and John took their time. They seemed to be holding back.

"Get in!" Joe shouted.

"They should have more somewhere," Frank said.

"Forget it!" Joe bent forward, glaring at the pair. "Inside - we've got lots to do yet!"

John took more time than Frank. He still clutched the tyre-iron. His eyes had a wild look.

"Chicken feed," Frank said.

"Our bankroll," Joe explained, and tapped Doug on the shoulder. "Wheel it, man!"

*

Albert glared at his former sergeant. "Don't dare tell me I'm not seeing so good!" he barked.

"Al, I . . ."

"Albert," Peggy corrected.

"Albert," the sergeant said with a smiled nod to the woman. "Don't get me wrong but we all suffer from . . ."

"I saw, I telephoned and young Stan is in hospital. Does that seem like I was wrong?"

The sergeant dug into his pocket and produced a pipe. He glanced at Peggy, got a go-ahead and lit the briar. In this house he felt companionship. He had always seen fit to disagree with Albert but he would have been the first to admit that the old constable was probably the best man they ever had on a local beat. Even now, he wasn't questioning the man's eyesight. He just wanted stronger proof that Joe Hawkins had been in the car.

"How is Stan?" Peggy Duckham asked.

"Fair," the sergeant said. "He had seventeen stitches in his skull."

"Young thugs," Albert growled.

"Exactly," the sergeant agreed. "Thugs. Young. Hardly in Hawkins's class."

"He isn't old . . ."

"I didn't mean that Al . . . bert!" The sergeant grinned over his pipe and Peggy smiled her pleasure. She had always insisted that Albert was a nice name and not one to be abbreviated into the common Al. More than one copper had come a cropper trying to telephone "Al"!

"Put out an all points bulletin . . . as those American television programmes say, " Albert laughed.

The sergeant shrugged. He could tell there was no shifting Albert's claim that Joe Hawkins - currently the most wanted man in the U.K. - had taken part in their filling station fracas.

"Albert's always right, " Peggy said.

The sergeant took a final puff, held the pipe for it to extinguish itself and moved to the door. Albert's eyes followed him, lightly laughing.

"She knows, you know, " Albert said.

The sergeant gave them both a salute - meant sincerely. "I'll be in your boat next year, Albert," he said. "And God knows, I'll need advice on how to grow tomatoes . . ."

*

The pub lacked the brass and copper of other County inns and the clientele were less inclined to accept strangers than a down-South tavern. Somehow, there was an atmosphere of severity and recognition that men only came here to indulge their alcoholic passions than to engage in conversation between a couple of half-pints.

That's another thing about the North, Joe told himself.

"What's it to be - seven pints of wallop?" Tom Carter asked.

Walter nodded fast. Frank eyed the bottles behind the bar and snapped: "Make mine Irish whiskey." John and Doug shuddered for effect and replied: "Wallop's fine!" Colin sighed. "I'd like Irish but it doesn't like me. Wallop, Tom." Joe grinned. "Same!"

Their first day as a team had been hectic but profitable. Four filling stations knocked off and a total of £280 in the kitty. All the petrol and oil had been free and they'd even managed two spare tyres for "nowt" - as Walter remarked at the time.

"Do we stay in Preston?" John asked as Tom went to the bar.

Joe thought about it. What he'd seen of the town left him

convinced they were wasting their time sticking around it. All he'd been able to make out was "Fishergate" - and "Fishergate". No matter how many turns Doug made that bloody street name seemed to chase them.

"Where's the nearest swinging place?" Joe asked.

"Blackpool!" came the chorus.

Even Joe had heard about Blackpool. "That's going to be rough," he said.

"And fun," John laughed.

"I had a dolly under the pier once. From Wigan," Walter remarked. "Jeeze, she bloody drained my sump!"

They laughed. It fitted with the day's raids.

"I want something bigger than filling stations," Joe told them. "How about a jeweller's store? Why not?"

"'Cause the Blackpool coppers are not going to be lenient, is why!" Frank snapped.

Tom arrived with their booze. "Grab," he shouted.

Joe belted half his down and wiped his lips. "If you're afraid . . ."

Tom stopped a quarrel. "Afraid of what? Let me in on this . . ."

Walter acted as go-between. "Joe wants to climb mountains. Filling stations are out. We hit a store next."

"So why not?" Tom asked.

"You fuckin' twit," Frank shouted. "Hittin' a shop means organisation and military precision . . ."

"And you're telling me I haven't got the ability?" Joe asked.

Frank glanced at the bulge inside Joe's pocket. "Naw, I'm against this on principle! We're doing okay - let it ride!"

"No!" Joe said. "No, I won't! I'm not content to make fifteen or thirty quid a day. I want big lolly - maybe five thousand. We hit or we split. Take your choice."

Tom said: "We hit!"

Walter finished his beer and said: "Another round and I'm for Joe."

John shrugged. "The IRA can make good use of a few hundred. That'll blow up some more Orange bastards. I'm in."

Colin grinned. "Make that double. Five hundred will buy a lot of Tommy-guns."

Doug hesitated, finishing his beer. "I'm only the driver but this could be dangerous. These fuzz have experience of setting up road blocks now. I'm not happy - I vote no!"

Frank sneered. "No for me, too!"

"That's a majority in favour," Joe declared. "If you ..." speaking to Frank, "Want out with Doug?"

"A majority drags me in," Doug said.

Frank scowled, lowered his gaze and studied a wet circle where his beer glass had been. He finished the drink, shoved the glass at Walter and said: "You got us into this - you buy! I'm in - but not willingly!"

Joe was already wondering which type of store had the most money, the most pawnable loot ...

CHAPTER SIXTEEN

AFTER four days, the Blackpool "curse" permeated Joe's soul. He was bewitched, captivated, a prisoner of this Northern playground. He knew why, now, the town held such an attraction for those within a six-hour ride of its endless sands. Until this moment, Southend had been his special favourite. No longer!

From the fabulous Tower to the equally fabulous Golden Mile, Blackpool offered more deviations, more crumpet, more distractions than a thousand Southends.

Regardless of the older folk who came to relax on deckchairs and play bingo as an evening chill settled over the colourful lighting displays, Joe knew that youth could have its fling here. Promiscious bitches paraded their wares openly. From Wigan, Bolton, Blackburn, Oldham, Preston, and all points radiating in direct lines from the "mecca" of sexual delight they came to offer unvirginal pleasures under the pier, or in shelters scattered along the many miles of secluded sands.

Secluded?

Hardly! There were more horny bastards getting to grips with willing fleshpots in Blackpool than the lecher could count. Every shelter had its private peeping Tom. Every inch of beach had its sand-dip and voyeur.

No wonder, Joe thought, *that crooks could come and go and plan big robberies here!* The whole scene was open to private enterprise.

The girl worked for a local department store. She was a cashier. She knew the procedures for collecting the cash and banking what the store considered to be over and above the safe amount to carry. She had a yen for strong, silent men with lean frames and the ability to make her *coo* when she wanted to coo, to make her *pant* when she wanted to pant, to make her. End of description!

She was a redhead - Ginger to her mates - with huge tits and a wiggle that drove her boss wild. She told Joe: "The old bastard wants to stick his hand under my shirt every time I go to the safe - and that's a laugh! He doesn't believe in being safe . . . he's a Catholic with six kids."

Joe had to admire her boss. The man wasn't so stupid if he paid attention to this choice morsel. At twenty one, Ginger had had more screws than hot meals. She admitted this. The first night Joe took her along the sands. Right in the middle of him trying to feel her up. After fish and chips at a stall along the front. Before he calculated it had cost precisely 75p for thirty five minutes of sheer bliss. Oh, she knew how alright! There wasn't anything Ginger didn't know about taking them off and finding a place under the pier and doing it so that, even from a few dark feet, it appeared that they were just petting rather heavily.

"You're terrific, Joe," she said when they had climbed to their feet. "Not gentle, mind you - but damned good when it's happening!"

"How about tomorrow night, Ginger?"

"If you want to, Joe," she said.

"I want!" He grinned, and climbed the steps to the promenade. "We could meet earlier and have a few jars, eh?"

"Great. Do you like football?"

"Yeah!"

"I can get tickets for the game this Saturday."

"Seats?" he queried. He disliked sitting down at a match. There was no fun being confined to a specific seat. No chance of putting the boot in.

"If you want the terrace?"

"that's my style."

"Won't your mates object?" She seemed to be suggesting a crowd.

"Naw - they'll go along, too!"

"Fab," she breathed and pressed a tit against his arm. "I'll wear my gear!"

Their boarding house was one of those tall, fifteen steps to the

267

glass-fronted door types with carpets throughout and semi-decent furniture in every room. The landlady had not stinted on blankets, either. At the height of summer a sleeper would feel boiled under the weight of covers. The meals were satisfying considering the rock bottom prices charged. Regulations were at a minimum and the door was never locked before one o'clock in the morning.

All the houses in the street carried bed and breakfast signs, some sporting neons calling themselves exotic names like TOWER HIGH HOTEL, EL RANCHO CABANA, THE SANDS HOTEL. *A far cry from Southend's staid names*, Joe thought.

That nobody had bothered to give their place a name meant nothing in Joe's estimation. It simply had a street number, a landlady's surname and that was enough for the regulars who came back year after year to rent deckchairs and spend their holidays dashing between beach and table, bingo hall and table, boozer and late-night tea and biscuits.

Joe shared a room with Frank and Walter.

"Bloody bird wanted me to strip right there," Frank complained as he scratched his arse.

Walter smiled, and discreetly turned to remove his briefs. Joe wanted to point and cackle. He'd seen Marks and Sparks latest creations - those multi-coloured shorts for men that had no fly and looked like a bloke had borrowed his sister's knickers. He didn't go for them. Unisex may be fine for some but he still clung to his jockey shorts with the proper outlet for manly loo-ing.

Sand fell to the carpet as Frank chucked his undershirt on his bed.

"Looks like she got you down to that," Joe remarked.

"The hell she did," Frank snarled. "She was so bloody wriggling I got more sand down my clothes than she got . . ."

Walter interrupted: Frank, shut up! I want to hear what Joe has to say about this Ginger bit." He looked at Joe then. "Does she seem like she can be used?"

Frank spat: "Used? Christ, he banged her - didn't he?"

Joe sat on his bed. "Okay, Frank - enough! We all like nookie. That's agreed. Ginger puts out and good but she's not going to let me get information unless I butter her up. She wants us to go with her to a Blackpool game this Saturday."

"Blackpool?" the others wailed in disgust.

"They're playing Chelsea!"

"Ahh," said Frank maliciously.

"Shit!" Walter moaned.

Joe screwed his socks off and let them on the floor. "We could have some extra fun," he mentioned. "An aggro ..."

Frank touched his ear. "With a bird along?"

"She said she'd wear her gear," Joe informed them.

"Gear?" Walter repeated and pulled his bedclothes back. He was nude, like Frank now. All modesty had vanished in the heat of discussion. Joe had a sudden thought - *if only that randy, handy bitch Ginger was here we'd all have it.*

"She doesn't look like a skingirl," Frank remarked.

"You don't look much like a skinhead," Joe said.

"I'm bloody not," came the sharp retort. "I'm bloody Irish - and fuckin' proud of that!" Frank's jaw stuck out as if daring them to comment.

"Murderers," Joe said calmly. "Bleedin' bomb-throwing bastards!"

Frank got his hands into fists. "You're asking for it, mate," he growled.

"For Christsake," Walter groaned from under the covers. "Forget the Irish, Frank. You was born in Liverpool."

"The capital of Ireland," Joe said nastily.

"Bloody right, you London git!"

"Are we going to the match or not?" Walter shouted.

Joe glared at Frank and, for a moment, it was one of those pregnant interludes when neither party wanted to back down yet circumstances dictated the wise course was to suspend hatreds.

"Hell, I'm cutting out!"

Joe turned on Walter. "Why?"

Frank slumped onto his bed. "I'll bury the hatchet in the bastard's head after we do the job!"

Walter sighed. "Satisfied?" he asked Joe.

*

Waiting for Saturday and the match meant an extra delay in their plans. Joe was aware of mounting pressures in their camp. It was one thing to have mates and go places together for a day, or an overnight stay. It was a horse of an entirely different hue to share a room, or rooms as the case was, and expect blokes of vastly varying beliefs to get along on a friendly basis. Joe knew the root cause of their problem. They were all individualists to a large extent. They were all of a violent nature. Without exception. Some did not show this trait in speech, or in isolated deed. But, under the surface of their criminality, they exuded violence like a hot spring spewed forth a torrent of searing sprays.

Regardless of what Frank said about not being a skinhead he was the most ferocious of them all. Life, for Frank, revolved around viciousness for Protestant members of the Irish community. No outrage, no indiscriminate bombing was beyond his comprehension. Death to the Prods was his war cry. It didn't matter that some of his own people suffered the loss of a limb or eye or both. Providing one Protestant cunt got his that justified the ends.

Irish politics left Joe cold. He enjoyed a boot-up, an aggro. He lived for a punch-up between rival factions. But he did not believe in the type of massacre Frank advocated.

Colin and John, in their quieter way, deplored Frank's outspoken desire to rid Ireland of all Protestant bastards. They had their nationalist feelings. Granted. But they did not condone the Aldershot affair or the Abercorn slaughter.

As Colin said at breakfast: "I've got Cork friends who support Manchester United. They don't want George Best murdered. If it doesn't matter in sport why the blazes should it count when women are having a meal?"

Joe, as always, jumped in. He could see Frank's simmering reply forming on his lips. "Forget Ireland. It bleedin' isn't worth fighting over - not here! For God's sake, Frank - we're out for money. Not blood!"

Frank turned a cold eye on Joe. "You should talk, *killer*!"

CHAPTER SEVENTEEN

COMMANDER Henry Hawthorne hated police work. There had been a time when he sincerely believed in the old adage that "a policeman's lot was a happy one". No longer. Since the war he had grown to loathe his job, and only stuck it out because he would collect a reasonably decent pension when he eventually retired. He could recall days when mixing with villains in his manor had been an enjoyable dalliance. Not now. The old-style villain had given way to a virulent brand of hoodlum moulded on American lines. A breed who thought nothing of using a gun, a knife, or simply booting a victim to death.

The days of chatting up a crook and knowing that sound advice was heeded, had long since evaporated into myth. The boys who carried out robberies today were beyond chatting. Beyond comprehension.

Looking across his paper-scattered desk at Sgt. Patterson, Hawthorne asked a vital question: "How do we reach this Hawkins?"

"We don't, sir," came the immediate reply.

"That seems too pat, sergeant. There has got to be a meeting point. A time and place and mental moment when it is possible to communicate."

"According to Criminal Records, sir . . ." and Patterson consulted his notebook, "this Joe Hawkins is unpredictable. He is not a common thief or criminal. He is just a kid gone wrong!"

"What the hell have we got in records these days? Bloody do-gooders? Don't hand me that nonsense about kids going wrong," Hawthorne yelled. "Kids in my day didn't go wrong. They went straight or they went bent. One or the other!"

Patterson smiled and placed his notebook in his pocket. At thirty-three he could still remember how it was to come from an area where fifty percent of the inhabitants respected the coppers and the other half tried their damndest to get around legalities. If only to eke out a living.

"Kids in your day, Commander, didn't have to combat trends."

"You're saying skinheads and the like?"

"Those, and others," the sergeant said. "Skinheads aren't the worst of the bunch. Take the protestors, sir - the professionals like Maoists and Black Power sympathisers. They're a thousand times worse than all skinheads. Those boys play for keeps. Bombs, guns, you-name-it and they're for anything to bring this country to its knees. Anarchists, the lot! Hell, sir - begging the language, skinheads don't ask for more than an aggro and the occasional pop concert punch-up."

"And that's good?" Hawthorne asked scathingly.

"No, sir, it's not! But it isn't the worst crime. I count child molestors as the lowest of the low."

Commander Hawthorne had the decency to admit his faults. "All right, sergeant - you've won that point. Now, tell me if you want to protect Joe Hawkins?"

"No, sir - I don't."

"Why?"

"He killed a policeman - two policemen!"

Hawthorne rose from behind his desk. He had grown fat in the past few years and his belly stuck out like a seedy heavyweight's. His jowls hung and his face had a permanent flush that spoke of beer in huge quantities combined with an over-rich diet. "If skinheads aren't our prime concern why is it that the most wanted man in England today is counted as nothing more than a skinhead gone wrong?" he asked smugly.

"If we brought in a Paki and found him guilty of smuggling other Pakistanis into the country would you condemn every coloured person in the manor, sir?" Patterson countered.

Hawthorne smiled and slumped back into his chair. "I've underestimated you, sergeant. You should have been upped in rank ages ago."

"I agree, sir," the sergeant smiled coldly.

"I'll put in a notification to that effect," Hawthorne said, ignoring the sarcasm. He knew - as did Patterson - who had been directly responsible for non-promotion . . . himself! It was not too late to undo past injustices.

"Anything else, sir?"

"Yes!" Hawthorne rifled through his papers and brought out a sheet. He read it slowly, summarising for the sergeant: "Hawkins must be apprehended before he is tempted to use his gun a third time. All stops are out, sergeant. This is nationwide. We suspect he is on our manor. We'll nab him . . . right?"

Patterson shrugged. "We're stretched thin, sir. We have those two child murders and the Thornton rapes."

Hawthorne considered the current cases and reached a decision. "I've a feeling, sergeant - a hunch, if you want! Circulate Hawkins's picture to the off-duty boys for the match . . ."

Sgt. Patterson smiled. For once he inclined to agree with the commander's hunch. In seventeen years he had only known five hunches to pay off against a possible thousand. This one he liked!

*

I don't like the ground, I don't like the crowd, and I don't like the way those coppers keep staring at faces!

From the middle of the terrace, Joe Hawkins kept a watchful eye on the fuzz working round the ground. It was a difficult process to separate face from face gazing up at the packed stands, he knew. But - there was always the off-chance! That was the one he hated.

Blackpool didn't have a prayer against Chelsea. In form, the home team were capable of holding any side in the league to a draw. But their form, at present, was bad. And Chelsea were cock-a-hoop after their astonishing win over Leeds. That made the difference. Even an own goal victory had its merits.

That money Joe had not shown to his new-found friends had bought his gear - Squires, mohair trousers and colourful braces. He wore a Ben Sherman with rounded collar and a sheepskin coat. He felt right in the old groove standing beside Ginger in her check skirt down to her knees, her suede jacket with zip, her flat-heeled shoes with the crepe soles.

"You going to do a Blackpool supporter?" Ginger asked.

"Why not?" Joe grinned.

"Christ, pick a Chelsea yobbo."

"Show me one," Joe said pointedly.

"Over there . . ." She pointed and Joe tensed. It was like the old days when his mob ran rampant through every park in the league.

A long banner hung partially limp between a group with the slogan: CHELSEA FOR THE CUP just barely visible.

"What bleedin' cup?" Joe asked.

"Maybe it's for being the best targets," Ginger suggested.

Joe got the immediate impression the girl was begging for an aggro. And, if he wasn't jumping his guns, that she was more than willing to throw in her lot with a man who could satisfy her craving for violence.

"You want a boot-in?"

Ginger sighed. "God, I could be better than ever for that!"

Joe's elbow nudged Walter. "She's wet for it if we screw those Chelsea skins."

"So what's holding us back?" Walter laughed as he started to shove aside fans.

*

The kid was almost alone, shouting his foolish head off for Chelsea and Peter Osgood. He was carried away with the train journey to

273

Blackpool and what he'd seen of the birds here. He wasn't one of the mob - he honestly believed that Chelsea were worth supporting and that the match was more important than any partisan bash-up.

A few old men stood near him, grinning as the kid yelled his lungs out every time Ossie stroked the ball or made an important contribution to the play.

Nobody bothered much about lone voices in the wilderness of Blackpool football. Middle-of-the-table would have satisfied the most hardened, most fervent 'pool supporter!

Joe got in behind the kid. Ginger to his right. Walter on his left. Somewhere behind the others followed - reluctant and filled with a no-contest detachment.

"Show me, Joe - show me," Ginger yelped.

Joe puffed out with pride. He squeezed in directly behind the kid. "Come on - blast 'em!"

Joe tapped the kid's shoulder. "Fuck Chelsea - and you!"

The kid screwed round in his confined space.

Joe smiled, brought his leg back and planted a solid kick where it most hurt. As the kid paled and doubled, Joe smashed him in the face.

Two spectators away, another dedicated Chelsea fan saw what was happening and shouted: "Aggro!"

In seconds, the Blackpool supporters were swept aside and Joe - with Ginger squealing delightedly at his side - was fighting for his life. He wished he had a tool . . .

The shooter!

He hesitated in the middle of countering a kick and felt the boot graze his balls. He slammed a fist into the Shed boy's mouth and drew his revolver. The metal barrel slashed across another face, the muzzle rammed into a set of ivories . . .

*

Every third Saturday, Commander Hawthorne spent at home. Depending on what was showing on *Grandstand* or *World Of Sport* he either stayed indoors watching telly or spent it in the seclusion of his small garden attending to the many chores which growing things demanded. He did not like seeing the nags run nor wrestlers go through sham performances to win by holds which were physically impossible or worked out in a dressing room prior to screening. He enjoyed those extra-special afternoon contests - ice-hockey from America, rugger from Down Under or a top motor-racing event broadcast live from some God-forsaken spot on the map.

This Saturday, he was in the garden. Up to his wrists in fertilizer. Sweating from turning over soil for yet another bed of his wife's favourite flowers.

The telephone jangled a discordant noise on the tranquil air. His wife came from the sunporch. It was for him . . .

"Hawthorne," he said when he finally took the receiver.

"Hawkins has been positively identified as being at the match," Patterson's voice told him.

Hawthorne felt a wave of satisfaction wash over him. "And?" he asked.

"Afraid he got away, sir - there was an awful eruption in the crowd!"

Hawthorne swore - loud and long. He had another hunch - that lapse could cost them all!

CHAPTER EIGHTEEN

GINGER rolled onto her back and opened her thighs. She was naked, her clothes lying on the sand near them. Joe had his clothes round his knees, poised above her.

"Yes, Joe, yes . . ."

He witheld his pleasure.

"God, don't make me wait!"

Joe came an inch closer, and felt her respond to the temporary touch of flesh on flesh.

"What do you want from me?" she wailed, struggling to join them together.

Joe whispered, keeping his buttocks arched to prevent her from gaining the final gratification. He kept whispering and making hurried explanations until she was writhing with demented frustration.

"Yes, Joe, yes - I'll do it! Just go into me . . ."

He slammed hard against her, hearing the whoosh of air from her lungs as she seized him in passion-steel legs. She was beyond anything but the most basic four-letter talk. She surged and gave, straining to match her companion's violence of that afternoon. She had been eagerly wanting this moment ever since she saw her hero in action. Now, the accumulated desires burst forth and devoured him . . .

*

"He's an old nanny," Ginger said as she pulled her skirt back on. "I could convince him to let the loot build up if I thought it was worth my effort!"

Joe stopped her in the middle of a wriggle. His fingers moved over her abdomen. "For me?"

"God, yes . . ." She yielded to his grope.

"What's the best day?"

Ginger moaned and flung herself supine on the sand. "Night, Joe . . . night!"

He stopped fondling her. "Pull yourself together," he ordered.

"Christ, you're terrific!"

"The best day?" he reminded.

"Monday's hopeless," she panted. "Usually the weekend. Friday morning or Saturday late afternoon."

"How much on a Tuesday?"

"A few thousand . . ."

"That's all?"

"Well . . ." She squirmed and grabbed hold of him again. "Joe, please?"

"After this . . ." He stuck his hand up her clothes. He knew she was loving it and trying hard to concentrate on what was most essential to him. "Well, what?"

"He carries a float of about two thousand but that's always locked in the safe . . ."

"You could make him open it, eh?" He fingered her.

"Christ - that's beautiful!" She wormed closer to him. "Yes, I could . . . Oh, Joe - I'm ready!"

He stopped asking questions and concentrated on bringing her those joys she found most exciting. It wasn't hard to provide her with additional thrills - she was jelly waiting to be devoured . . .

CHAPTER NINETEEN

DOUG had insisted on having a different car for their escape. According to him, Uffix had guts but no stamina. In a chase stamina was vital. Against police-mechanic tested vehicles, the criterion was an ability to keep going at top speed for an unlimited number of miles.

Uffix failed in a relatively simple test. Along a stretch of the M6 between Garstang and Lancaster. It failed to keep up with, or pass, a Hillman. That, in Doug's book, left it wanting.

Armed with his unblotted licence, Uffix for trade in and another hundred quid of Joe's money, Doug went searching the car lots for a bargain capable of holding police cars at bay.

"Do you know the side roads?" Joe asked.

"I should!" Doug sat like a martyr and munched on his roll with cheese. "When you bastards have been busy screwing I've been driving round every back alley in Blackpool! I can get out of this town in ten minutes - and that doesn't count police blocks, either!"

Joe smiled. "You deserve an extra one percent."

Frank scowled. "Why? He's only driving the car!"

"Can you get us out?" Joe asked.

"No - but . . ."

"You fuckin' Irish bastard!" Joe exploded. "All mouth and nothing between the ears!"

"I'll take an equal share if all goes according to plan," Doug said hurriedly.

"That's up to the Mick," Tom Carter said.

Colin stepped in with a broad Paddy smile and a lot of Liverpudlian common-sense to boot. "He's not a Mick! He's Dublin-Protestant of all things! But shit on that - we're not fighting Ireland's war. We're fighting for a prize worth a few thousand . . . and I, for one, would like a slice of that!"

Joe stood facing his "mates". "Is everybody agreed?"

"I'm for Ireland but meself first," John Riordan laughed.

"Money, not bloody politics," Doug snarled.

"Same here," Walter agreed.

Tom Carter stepped forward and glared at Frank. "You bastard! You no good bastard! The trouble with you is you're scared to make a real stand! You're always shootin' off your mouth but what have you ever done? Nothing. That's what. You're so scared of being clobbered you hide behind anybody - even Shiela! For once, meet it like a man - say yes or no and don't shit me with what fuckin' Ireland needs or hasn't got!"

"It hasn't got anything," said Colin softly.

Frank eyed his companions, meeting nothing but hostile stares. He twitched, knuckled his fingers in his lap and dropped his gaze . . .

"So?" Colin asked firmly.

"I didn't hide behind Shiela," Frank finally said.

"No?" Colin shot upright and stood within inches of Frank. "How come she cried her bloody eyes out to me when you left the United game without getting an aggro?"

"I didn't meet up with a bloody United supporter."

"The hell you didn't!" Colin paced back and forth between the beds in the room. "You were smack in the middle of the cunts!"

"Who says . . ."

"Shiela!"

Frank melted slightly. "She was mistaken! I heard a few of 'em shouting but . . ."

"You didn't have a bomber or a bunch of the bhoys, eh?" Joe chortled.

Frank dissolved into pathetic nothingness.

"I'll give you five quid and that's all," Joe said. "As from now . . . fuck off!"

Frank looked at his mates.

"He's right," Walter said. Colin, Doug, Tom and John nodded.

"You'll be sorry," Frank muttered.

"I wouldn't grass," Joe said.

"I certainly wouldn't," Colin agreed.

Frank directed his venom at Joe. "We'll meet again, one day!"

"If we do - don't bother to say hello," Joe retorted.

Frank silently got his belongings together - including the fiver Joe threw on the bed. When he had packed he went to the door.

"If you grass you'll be worse off than an IRA squealer," Joe said.

Frank tossed his head in the air and left . . .

CHAPTER TWENTY

IN the North, Blackpool's reputation stood for many things but, chiefly, for its ability to cater for every member of a family without fear or favour. Elsewhere, the image of Blackpool conjured up dreams of dolly birds putting it out on sand or shelter, and con men ut-shouting each other in an effort to entice the unwary into gimmicky exhibits.

Television had not treated Blackpool with kid gloves. Those who had, at some time or another, considered the Golden Mile as an expanse of shimmering sand and little else had been rudely awakened from the dream state by the portrayal of a fairground come-on artist. as nothing less than a trickster.

Another programme had shown the Northland's playground as a haven for randy rugger players and mill girls willing to go into a tackle together.

Factually, Blackpool was a little of both with a generous helping of middle-aged deckchairism for a catalyst. Unlike Margate, Southend and Brighton in the South-East, Blackpool's popularity with the near-retired had not been dented by hooliganism. There was room enough for all - miles of glorious sand, a pleasure beach capable of supporting any teenage invasion, and a town that continued to grow annually. Probably what saved the resort from becoming a ghost town was the availability of a copper. At the height of the trouble-making season, it seemed there was a blue uniform every few hundred yards - a solid figure keeping out of the mainstream yet there, ready to pounce and prevent disturbances reaching gigantic proportions.

Joe was far from happy by the number of fuzz dotted round the town. As they drove slowly down streets he got the impression that every corner was a hangout for one of the officious bastards. He counted fifteen coppers before they reached the department store. "Is it always like this?" he asked Walter.

The Liverpudlian shook his head in wonderment. "I don't know! I've never seen this many!"

"I wonder if that bloody Frank ..." Doug started to say.

"He wouldn't dare," Colin snapped.

Joe was not quite so sure. Frank had struck him as a vindictive person. If Frank had grassed ... He felt panic but brushed it aside when Doug parked near the store.

"I'll go in first. When Ginger sees me she'll get the manager worked up!"

Colin laughed. "That bitch could make a brass monkey get hot balls!"

Joe smiled. It was a matter of pride. Ginger had not even glanced at his mates with anything but the barest of interest. She belonged to him. And the others were bleedin' jealous!

"What happens to her?" John asked.

"She goes with me!" Joe sat back and waited for the anticipated yells. He had arranged this with Ginger - after all, she was a good screw and she could finger them all if she was left high and dry. Unknown to his mates, Joe's future plans did not include them after today. Once Doug had them safely out of Lancaster, Joe and Ginger were splitting.

"I thought you'd tell us that," John said softly.

"I'm not in favour but I'm not going against it, either," Walter said.

Doug grinned. "She'll be our ace in the hole. The fuzz wouldn't dare try anything dangerous with a girl in the car!"

Joe waited as Colin digested the words. He could see that Tom was playing a waiting game, too. Wanting the last say.

"If we're all in this together then Ginger belongs to us, right?"

Tom chuckled. "Randy bastard!"

Colin nodded. "She's some piece."

"That's your price?" Joe asked quietly, trying hard to stop his hand closing on the shooter.

"My only price?" Colin said.

"All right. She's communal property," Joe announced.

The others stared at him. Joe felt mighty important. He had proven beyond any shadow of doubt that he could handle situations without displaying his innermost feelings. If words could integrate them then words would get the show on the road. What he said and what he meant did not correspond. Mentally, he swore and wanted to kick each of them where it hurt most. And he would - after they pulled off the job! After they cleared the police network!

Tom got out of the car and stood on the pavement. "Come on, let's collect our bang!" he said with a guffaw.

Ginger spotted Joe immediately he entered. She suppressed a

tremble and gave her full attention to a couple she was serving. She felt no surge of adrenalin. Only emotion. Joe's brand of loving had captivated her. No other man had ever made her react so hysterically, so irrationally.

When the couple departed, Ginger closed her till, removed the cash and went straight to the manager's office.

This was the difficult part. Her vamp role had to be spontaneous and she hoped to convince the man that she had finally fallen for his furtive handling of forbidden fruit. It would be a supreme test of her womanly wiles. One she had thought about all the sleepness night.

It wasn't even as if she had time to perfect her act. Joe had been adamant. Ten minutes flat - no more, no less.

In her estimation, Horace Black was a mother's boy with a demanding wife. As a man, he rated less than half a star in her book. His six kids did not count, either. They were the result of a church demand for more converts and a fruitful mate.

Her flesh crawled as she entered the office with its disorganised sheets littering two desks, till rolls scattered across a third and glorious piles of money already banded for the bank . . . Joe's bank! . . . on Black's safe.

"Why, Ginger - what are you doing here?"

The girl smiled - weakly. "I don't feel so good, Mister Black. I thought you wouldn't mind if I had a break!"

Black simpered, his eyes automatically racing over her lush figure. The girl always set him off. There was that sensual something about her that started his hormones working at disastrous top speed. She reminded him of the woman he should have married. The woman his mother had accused of being a non-Catholic slut.

At forty seven he should have known better than to become enamoured with one of his shop girls. He knew the risks attached to liasons of this kind. He also realised that his occasional uncontrolled handling of Ginger's person left him wide-open to a criminal charge. Yet, he didn't care. She was an obsession. A desperate need!

"Sit down, Ginger!" He jumped to his feet, hurried round the cluttered desks and placed his hands on her sides. The touch of her was excitement. Heady stuff. He helped her into a chair, hands trailing upwards to lightly brush against her swelling breasts.

"Mister Black!" Ginger expressed surprise - and a coy liking for what had happened.

Something snapped. This was the first time she had ever permitted him an encouragement. Previously, she had flushed and stormed out of the office . . .

"Ginger . . . oh, Ginger . . ." His hands cupped her marvellous breasts and he bent forward, his lips planting kisses on her throat.

Christ, he's as stiff as a poker! Ginger thought as she watched him progress to madness.

He was struggling with her bra through her clothes, gutteral sounds coming from his chest.

"Oh, God!" Ginger moaned, touching him.

He went crazy. He got on his knees, pushed her clothes up, began kissing her soft warm thighs as his hands probed higher . . . higher.

Bloody bastard! The filthy swine!

Ginger pushed his head away, his hands, too! She forced herself to look composed - if a trifle emotionally disturbed. "Not now, Mister Black . . . let's be sensible. Put my takings in the safe . . ." Her eyes darted at the locked box.

"Yes, Ginger . . . yes!" He stood, not at all embarrassed by the thrusting evidence of his lust.

Her watch said nine minutes since she had entered the office. She got off her chair, let him feel her nearness as he fumbled with the combination lock. "Hurry, Mister Black - I'm all . . ." She leant against his shoulder, breathing heavily in his ear. "I'm all wet . . ."

His fingers were thumbs but he managed to flip open the safe. Perspiration rolled down his face. It was an effort to refrain from raping her.

"Give it to me," he panted.

He was completely unaware of the office door opening, of Joe Hawkins coming across the room.

"You're a darling, Mister Black," Ginger whispered and quickly jumped aside.

Joe's shooter descended and crunched on Black's skull. The manager slumped, hand clawing down the safe door as he faded into unconsciousness.

Joe laughed, a brittle echo for the departed. "How much?" he asked as Ginger started to empty the safe.

"About four thousand - we had a good morning . . ."

Doug geared down for a sharp bend, and sent the car screaming into a series of twists as the road wound through a built-up area with school-crossings and crossroads galore.

"Four thousand, eight hundred and forty nine quid," Joe counted from the back seat.

"Bloody hell!" Colin exploded.

"Oh, Joe . . ." Ginger inched closer and kissed Joe's cheek. He could feel her increased warmth - a result of what she had undergone and the natural reaction to having this much wealth within reach.

From the front of the car, Tom's laughter sounded hysterical. "Jeeze, ain't it sweet!"

Walter in the back looked glum. "Let's divvy, Joe."

"Now?"

"Bloody right! Ginger's hot . . ." said John, and Colin echoed this with: "That's no lie!"

"Fuck you bastards!" Walter snapped. "I'm not thinking of a screw."

"Sorry - go ahead," Colin graciously consented.

Ginger giggled and placed her hand on Joe's upper thigh. Any reference to her "ability" gave the girl a thrill.

"Joe," Walter continued with a finger indicating Ginger's non-mercenary interest. "I'm not against birds having a right share in the spoils but when they can only think of sex then I'm scared stiff! She's crazy for it, man. And that could be trouble. I want out. Now! With my cash!"

Joe had to admit that Walter's tirade was a saving grace. If only he could convince the others of the necessity of bailing out then all his problems were solved at a stroke. Like Ted Heath, he had opportunity on his side but unlike the Prime Minister, he had freedom of action to settle his disputes single-handedly. He didn't have powerful unions resisting his decrees. He didn't have class warfare to contend with. He had mates - erstwhile, admittedly - and Ginger . . . a real redheaded angel in disguise.

"Okay," Joe said. "I'll split the haul. We all agree to split, eh?"

Doug sent the car into a tight turn and straightened out with difficulty. "Knock the cost of this off my share and I'll be content."

Joe counted the money into equal amounts. There was a little over. He pushed that to Ginger. "Spending money for clothes," he said and handed each their divvy.

Walter looked foolish as he accepted his share of the money. "Sorry, Joe, but . . ." He stared at Doug. "Let me out at the next bus-stop!"

Tom and John sighed, placing their wads in their pockets. "Me too," said John. "And me," said Tom.

Colin eyed Ginger speculatively and shrugged. "Shit!"he said. "I'll get out as well!"

"How about you Doug?" Joe asked.

"Did I cop the car?"

"Yeah - but I want to be driven to a place where I can get another," Joe said.

"How about Accrington?"

"They used to have a football team," Joe laughed. "That's okay with me ..."

Ginger sat with skirt pulled up around her knickers and chewed gum. Every so often she reached across the seat and stroked Joe's arm. She was not aware of the countryside flashing past the windows. She only had her thoughts and the scent of her man not far distant from her.

"Is London really swinging?"

Joe kept the speedometer needle holding the eighty mark. Nothing had managed to pass them for the last fifty miles. He enjoyed the thrill of speeding by lumbering lorries and cautious legal-speed-limit passenger cars. He was a bloke in a hurry. A bloke with somewhere to go, something to do.

"The greatest, Ginger," he said and placed his hand on her sleek thigh. The world was treating him like a prince. He had this, and lolly. Nothing could stop him now. Not the fuzz, not McVey. He had all the bastards beaten. He would keep them on the hop. Joe Hawkins was smarter than all their specialists and all their underworld informants. God, how he loved the almighty feeling permeating his being!

CHAPTER TWENTY ONE

FOR fifteen years, David Newbery had been in and out of prison with a regularity that astounded probation officers ordered to present evidence in court. Regardless of his convictions, David had somehow wangled the minimum sentence for each charge brought against him. That he was a plausible bastard did not lessen the astonishment of those who interviewed him. Even the beaks sometimes expressed wonderment at their own leniency when confronted with his record in the privacy of their chambers.

Of course, David had one thing going for him. He was a nark. He could no more go straight than a corkscrew could extract a cork without its twists. But he had a reputation for supplying the fuzz with information leading to arrests and convictions they could not normally have achieved. For that, and that alone, he got treated with a certain degree of leniency!

He had just pulled off a successful robbery but his trademarks pointed conclusively to him. In an effort to gain sympathy, he grassed . . .

"I was conned into it, sir" he told Detective-Sergeant Knowles. "There was this bleeder called Hawkins . . ."

Knowles felt a tremor of satisfaction race down his spine. Hardly a copper in Britain dared hope that a nark would come up with such a juicy piece of data.

"'E forced me to open the bleedin' safe, sir!" Newbery added.

A wave of triumph passed through Knowles's frame. "Did he say where he was staying?"

Newbery paused, sweating blood. "Do I get orff?"

"That depends, David."

"The bleeder's important, eh?"

"We want him - yes!"

"Drop the charges?"

"Not entirely - but we'll make them no more than three months!"

"Christ!" Newbery exploded. "That's bleedin' robbery!"

"Suspended?"

Newbery laughed. "Six months?"

"Agreed!"

"And you let me have two days freedom?"

Knowles considered the request. "Okay - where do we find Hawkins?"

"I've got to check, guv'nor!" David said.

"Two days and the high jump if you don't come up with Hawkins," Knowles said.

"I'll find the bleeder," Newbery stressed . . .

Playing both ends against the middle was nothing new to David Newbery, and being accused of double-dealing did not deter him from his life of crime. As a "peterman" he was unique. There wasn't a safe he couldn't crack in less time than a fuzz had a coffee at the canteen. He had an affinity for mechanical trickery where safes were concerned. No matter how many precautions the manufacturers put into their products, David had the answer in advance. He knew, instinctively, that changes had been made and how to circumvent them.

The underworld, in general, knew that David grassed to protect himself. That was why so many of the people behind David's capers refused to identify themselves. Masks and various other methods of camouflage were always the *modus operandi*.

Except in the case of Joe Hawkins!

Joe wasn't a member of the clan. He had heard how good David was with a peter and he farmed-out the job accordingly. It was another Ginger getting the boss hot for her! Another soft touch!

Way back before pot and pornography on the newsstands, the club had catered for a clientele verging on the elite - writers, television personalities and showbiz generally. No more. Since the very young took over Soho and made the scene one of youthful enterprise, the club's management had sold out and the customers had dwindled until, now, only those searching for near-virginal applicants for perversion sessions bothered to come.

People like Newbery were accepted because they could be used. People like Joe and Ginger because they were young and notorious. The youth rebellion liked their martyrs!

"S'truth, mate - it's a died-in-the-wool cert!"

Joe listened with half-an-ear. He was only conscious of Ginger pressing her sizzling loins against a randy bastard with fuzzy, long hair and tight jeans which showed where he was heading.

"Christ, Joe - ain't you interested?"

Joe got to his feet, face tense. He shoved through the gyrating crowd, and stood in front of Ginger and her partner. "Back to the bench," he told Ginger.

The fuzzy-wuzzy glared at him, and deliberately rubbed himself on Ginger.

Joe growled and tore the girl from her dancing partner. "You bleedin' asked for this, mate," he snarled and lashed out with his foot. He felt the blow jar his thigh. Felt satisfaction travel along his leg.

The fuzzy-wuzzy doubled, clutching his groin.

Nobody stopped to pass comment. Nobody bothered.

"Back to your seat," Joe commanded.

Ginger walked back to where Newbery sat in a state of near-paralysis.

"You was saying?" Joe asked as he sat opposite the peterman.

"Jeeze . . ."

Joe grinned. "That's only friendly stuff. Imagine what he'd got if he'd double-crossed me!"

David Newbery suddenly reached a conclusion. This was outside his league. He was an amateur playing in a strange, unfathomable combination featuring unrealistic creatures. His type had gone by the boards of progress. The old-style professional creed no longer counted. The new was uppermost, and unless he got to recognise the changes he could easily be the late David Newbery!

"The coppers asked me to finger you," David blurted.

Joe smiled, content with this advance information.

"They suggested the set-up!"

Joe felt Ginger's thigh. "And?" he asked.

"They want you, mate! Want you bad!"

"How bad?"

"Enough to let me get off with the last job!" This, to Newbery, was tantamount to a carte blanche approval of all his activities.

"We'll do it," Joe announced.

"Fuck me!" David said.

"And me," echoed Ginger . . .

CHAPTER TWENTY TWO

INSPECTOR Bishop and Commander Hawthorne got the news simultaneously. Each man wished he, personally, was on the squad keeping watch as Joe Hawkins pulled yet another job. Neither of them had much confidence in the Metropolitan officers handling the "arrest". They had adequate proff of Hawkin's durabilty, his ability to evade traps.

Outside the warehousing area, Joseph English, distributors to the magazine trade and owners of a string of shops dealing in near-pornography, fifteen officers attached to South London division waited.

From information received via Newbery channels, the hit was

tonight. Not tomorrow as originally scheduled.

It was a cold night. The warehouse looked like a huge concrete block standing against the moon in white angularity. It was windowless except for one small four-squared section above the printing plant. And this did not warrant observation.

Not in police eyes . . .

Above the single opening, Joe dangled on a rope held by David and Ginger. He had rigged a pulley but it still required the expertise of two companions.

"Down . . ." he called softly.

The rope stretched and he jerked down . . . down . . .

"Hold it!"

He tumbled with the loose catch, using a celluloid strip supplied by David. The catch opened. He levered it upwards, held it against the ratchet and called: "Next!"

He was almost totally inside the building when David descended the rope.

Joe smiled to himself. The bleedin' fuzz would be wild when they discovered that their grass had betrayed them for geld . . .

Sergeant O'Malley watched Joe Hawkins climb down the rope into the warehouse area. All the reports he had received showed Hawkins as a bad lad! Especially as he was also wanted by Charlie McVey. O'Malley had his own sources of information. Most of them were strictly contrary to Home Office edicts. It was enough, though, that O'Malley and his parish priest hated the current goings-on in Northern Ireland and had formed a pact to filter information regarding this religious campaign down through channels.

A priest in Liverpool had passed along data. A priest in Birmingham had passed it further. O'Malley had the full data . . .

O'Malley waited patiently. He was directly beneath Joe as the "bhoy" reached six feet above the concrete floor of the warehouse.

There was no going back! No possibility of reaching for the shooter that had brought about two deaths already.

O'Malley held his arms out - huge Irish arms with a power of restraint in their embrace . . .

"Don't struggle bhoyo," O'Malley said.

The accent brought a lump into Joe's throat. Of all the bloody people to arrest him . . .

THE END

288